LORI FOSTER

"Count on Lori Foster for edgy, sexy romance."
—*New York Times* bestselling author Jayne Ann Krentz on *No Limits*

"Emotionally spellbinding and wicked hot."
—*New York Times* bestselling author Lora Leigh on *No Limits*

"Storytelling at its best! Lori Foster should be on everyone's auto-buy list."
—#1 *New York Times* bestselling author Sherrilyn Kenyon on *No Limits*

"Foster's writing satisfies all appetites with plenty of searing sexual tension and page-turning action in this steamy, edgy, and surprisingly tender novel."
—*Publishers Weekly* on *Getting Rowdy*

"Foster hits every note (or power chord) of the true alpha male hero."
—*Publishers Weekly* on *Bare It All*

"A sexy, believable roller coaster of action and romance."
—*Kirkus Reviews* on *Run the Risk*

"Foster rounds out her searing trilogy with a story that tilts toward the sizzling and sexy side of the genre."
—*RT Book Reviews* on *Savor the Danger*

"Steamy, edgy, and taut."
—*Library Journal* on *When You Dare*

LORI FOSTER

heartbreakers

HQN™

Recycling programs
for this product may
not exist in your area.

ISBN-13: 978-0-373-77998-7

Heartbreakers

Copyright © 2015 by Harlequin Books S.A.

The publisher acknowledges the copyright holder of the individual works as follows:

Treat Her Right
Copyright © 2001 by Lori Foster

Mr. November
Copyright © 2001 by Lori Foster

This edition published by arrangement with Harlequin Books S.A.

For questions and comments about the quality of this book, please contact us
at CustomerService@Harlequin.com.

® and TM are trademarks of Harlequin Enterprises Limited or its corporate affiliates.
Trademarks indicated with ® are registered in the United States Patent and
Trademark Office, the Canadian Intellectual Property Office and in other countries.

www.HQNBooks.com

Printed in U.S.A.

CONTENTS

TREAT HER RIGHT   7

MR. NOVEMBER   195

Dear Reader,

I very much hope you enjoy this 2-in-1 reissue of two of my favorite books, *Treat Her Right* and *Mr. November*. They originally came out in 2001 as part of my Men to the Rescue series, and I hope you'll have fun revisiting these everyday heroes, or discovering them for the first time.

You can see all my books with their new and original covers, and a brief description, on my website at lorifoster.com/bookshelf.

All my best,

Lori Foster

LoriFoster.com

treat her right

ONE

"DAMN YOU, CONAN! That's it!"

Zack Grange jerked upright in his bed, heart pounding, muscles coiled. His sleep-fogged brain felt in a jumble. He'd been dreaming, a very hot dream about a sexy lady—faceless, but with a gorgeous body—and then he'd heard the loud female shout. Caught between drugging sleep and abrupt wakefulness, confusion swamped him.

He looked around his shadowed bedroom and found it as empty as ever. No one lurked in the corners, certainly not the lady he'd been dreaming of, yet the voice had seemed to be right upon him. Heart still tripping, he strained to hear, and caught male laughter floating in through his open window. He frowned.

A glance at the clock showed it to be only seven-thirty. He'd barely been in bed at all, not long enough to recoup from the strenuous night. Certainly not long enough to finish that tempting, now elusive dream.

The deep female voice came again.

"It's not funny, you moron, and you know it," the woman groused, showing no consideration for those people still trying sleep. "I can't believe you did this to me."

"Better you than me, sweetheart." Then, "Ouch! Now that hurt."

Zack threw off his sheet. Wearing only his boxers, he went to the window to look out. He shivered as the morning air washed over his mostly bare body. The mid-September nights were getting cool, but he preferred the fresh air for sleeping. He stretched out aching muscles, still cramped from all the lifting he'd done just a few hours ago, scratched his chest, then slid aside a thin drape and peered down into the yard behind his house.

His was a larger, more private corner lot, and the street behind him ran perpendicular to his own. His bedroom window, at the back of his house, faced the side lot, so that he could see both the front and backyard of the home behind him.

New neighbors, he thought with disgust, noticing the For Sale sign now lying flat, and cardboard boxes piled everywhere around the yard. Squinting against the blinding red haze of a half-risen sun, his tired eyes gritty, he searched for the source of the screeching.

When his gaze finally landed on her, he stared in stunned disbelief.

Extremely curly brown hair was only halfheartedly contained in a sloppy ponytail. He couldn't see the details of her upper body beneath an overlarge, misshapen sweatshirt, but her shorts showed off mile-long, athletic legs and dirty white tennis shoes. Zack surveyed her top to bottom, and because a lot of distance stretched between those two points, it took a good minute.

As a basic male, he immediately considered those long

strong legs. With the erotic dream still dancing around the corners of his mind, he pictured them twined around him, or perhaps even over his shoulders, and speculated on how tightly they might hold a man when he was between them, buried deep inside her.

As a discriminating man, he wondered why her hair looked such a wreck and what her upper body might present once out of that awful sweatshirt.

And lastly, as a neighbor, he wanted to groan at the lack of consideration that kept her squawking and carping in a voice too deep and too loud to be called even remotely feminine. The future didn't bode well, not with her living behind him.

"Daddy?"

Zack turned with a smile, but he felt ready to commit murder. Evidently, the noise had awakened his daughter, which meant there would be no going back to bed for him. Exhaustion wrought a groan in protest, but he held out a hand, smiling gently. "Come here, sweetheart. It looks like our new neighbors are moving in."

Rubbing her eyes with a small fist, Dani padded toward him, dragging her favorite fuzzy yellow blanket behind her. Her wee bare feet peeked out from the hem of her nightgown. Standing out around her head, her typically mussed blond hair formed a halo, and one round cheek was creased from her pillow. She reached him and held up her skinny arms. "Let me see," she demanded in her adorable childish voice.

Obligingly, Zack lifted her. His daughter was such a tiny person, even though she was now four. Petite, as her mother had been, he thought, and hugged her close to his naked chest. He breathed in her little girl smell, rubbed his rough cheek against her downy soft hair, kissed her ear.

She liked to be held, and he loved holding her.

As usual, Dani immediately gave him a wet good-morning kiss on his whiskered cheek. She wrapped her arms around his throat, her legs around his waist, and looked out the window. Her blanket caught between them.

Zack waited for her reaction. Dani never failed to amuse him. For a four-year-old, she was very astute, honest to a fault, and he loved her more than life itself.

Most of the kids her age asked constant questions, but not Dani. She made statements instead. Other than two days a week at a preschool, she was always in the company of his friends. Zack assumed her exposure to adults accounted for her speech habits.

"I see her butt," she said with an exaggerated frown.

Startled, Zack lowered his head to peer out the window again, and sure enough, the woman bent at the waist, her legs straight and braced apart for leverage as she tugged on a large box. Her shorts were riding rather high and he could just see the twin moons of her bottom cheeks.

Nice ass, he thought appreciatively, lifting one brow and looking a little harder. Dani poked him, and he shook his head, remembering that this woman had just awakened him from a much-needed sleep and a pleasantly carnal dream. "Wait until she stands up, Dani."

The woman tugged and pulled and when the box broke apart, she fell backward, landing on that nice behind. From somewhere on her porch, a man hooted with loud laughter and called out, "Want some help?"

Zack fancied he could see some of her curly brown hair standing on end. She all but vibrated with temper, then snarled in a voice reminiscent of an enraged cat, "*Go away,* Conan!"

"But I thought you wanted my help?" came the innocent, taunting reply.

"You," she said back, standing up and dusting herself off with enough force to leave bruises on a less hearty woman, "have done enough."

Zack tried to see the mysterious Conan, but couldn't. Her husband? A boyfriend? What kind of name was Conan anyway?

As the woman gained her feet, Dani said in awe, "She's a giant!"

Chuckling, Zack squeezed her. "She looks as tall as me, doesn't she, honey?"

His daughter nodded, watching the woman unload the box with jerky, angry movements, rather than try to move it again. Dani laid her head on Zack's chest, quietly thinking in that way she sometimes did. Zack rubbed her back, waiting to see what she'd say next.

She shocked him speechless by suddenly leaning forward—leaving it up to him to balance her off-balance weight—and cupping her hand to her mouth, she shouted out the window, "Hello!"

The woman turned, looked up with a hand shading her eyes, searching. She spotted them and her frown was replaced by a bright toothy smile. She waved with as much enthusiasm as she'd used to dust her bottom. "Hello there!"

In his underwear, Zack quickly ducked behind the curtain. "*Dani*," he said, ready to muzzle his daughter. "What are you doing?"

She wrinkled her little nose at him. "Jus' being neighborly, like you said I should."

"That was to the old neighbors. We don't even know these people yet."

She wiggled to get down, and when he set her on her feet, she said, "We'll go meet 'em now."

Zack caught her by the back of her cotton nightgown as she started to barrel out of the room. "Hold on, little lady. We have breakfast and chores and washing up to do first, right?"

Again, she wrinkled her nose. "Later."

He almost grinned at her small, sweet hopeful voice—a voice she only used when trying to wrap him around her itty-bitty finger. "Now."

Disgruntled and grumbling under her breath, she trod back to the window and yelled, "I'll be out later!"

The woman laughed. It was a nice rich husky sound, much better than her screaming. "I'll surely still be here."

Zack looked out, feeling as if he'd landed in the twilight zone. Now that his daughter had drawn attention to them—and the neighbors knew they'd been watched—he couldn't very well ignore them.

The man from the porch sauntered into the yard, smiling. Zack blinked with yet another surprise. *Massive* was the only word for him. Built like a large bulldog, he stood a few inches shorter than the woman, but was twice as thick and all muscle. He lifted an arm as stout as a tree trunk and waved.

"I'm Conan Lane," he called out, "and this squawking shrew is Wynonna."

To Zack's amazement and Dani's delight, the woman elbowed Conan hard, making him bend double and wheeze, then she corrected sweetly, "Call me Wynn."

Seeing no hope for it, Zack shouted back, "Zack Grange, and my daughter, Dani."

"Nice to meet you both!" And then to further exasperate him, Wynn said, "Since we're all awake and it's such a beautiful morning, I'll bring over some coffee so we can get acquainted."

Zack stammered, unsure how to deny that audacious imposition, but she'd already turned and hurried into her house, the enormous Conan following her. He frowned down at Dani, who shrugged, grinned, and said, "We better get dressed." And off she dashed, her blanket dragging behind her.

Zack dropped to the side of his bed and scrubbed his hands over his face. He was badly in need of a shave and a long shower. At the moment he had no doubt his eyes were more red than blue. He'd worked twelve grueling hours last night, tended two especially trying emergencies, and he was starved as well as fatigued.

Luckily, this was his day off, which he'd intended to spend shopping with Dani. Because his daughter liked to play hard, and paid no mind at all to the knees of her jeans or the elbows of her shirts, she was desperately in need of new fall clothes.

He did not want to be bothered with outrageous neighbors.

Especially not neighbors who'd awakened him too early and were too damn large. And loud.

Shoving himself off the bed, he determined to get through the next few minutes with as much politeness and forbearance as he could muster.

The doorbell rang not three minutes later. He'd barely had time to pull on jeans and a sweatshirt. He picked up his running shoes, carrying them loosely in his hand. On his way to the door, he peeked in at Dani. She stood there in a T-shirt and blue-flowered panties, surveying her closet with a studious frown.

Zack leaned on her doorframe. "Dress warm, honey."

She nodded, frowned some more, and looked through her clothes. Zack bit back a grin and asked, "Hard decision?"

She was so intent on her choice, she didn't answer.

Because jeans were a given, he said, "How about a sweater?" preferring that over what she might have chosen otherwise—

a ratty sweatshirt. He posed it as a suggestion, rather than an instruction, because he knew she liked to make her own decisions—about everything—any time he gave her that option.

She nodded agreement. "Okay. What sweater?"

He walked into the room, reached into her closet and pulled out a soft red sweater with multicolored buttons. "This one is nice," he suggested, trying his best to sound serious and sincere.

She studied the sweater, considering, until the doorbell rang again. Snatching it out of his hand, she pushed at him and said, "Go! Go get the door, Dad!"

Zack laughed as he walked away. His daughter, the social butterfly. Most times, Dani didn't give two cents for how she dressed. She'd pull on the same clothes from the night before if Zack didn't get them out of her room and into the hamper fast enough. But let them have company and she agonized. Not that she wanted to wear dresses. Heaven forbid! And anything other than sneakers or boots repulsed her four-year-old sensibilities.

But she did like color. Lots and lots of color. Often if left to her own devices, she'd clash so horribly it'd make his eyes glaze.

Still sporting a grin, Zack bounded down the stairs and went to the front door. He turned the locks and opened it, wishing he didn't have to do this today. He'd wanted nothing more than to sleep in, then take a long leisurely soak in the hot tub, eat an enormous breakfast, and spend the day with his daughter.

Now he had to be neighborly.

The second the door opened, the woman looked at him and her smile faded. "Oh dear," she said. "We woke you up, didn't we?"

Zack went mute and stared.

Up close, she seemed even taller, and she did indeed look him in the eye. At six feet tall, that didn't happen to him often. His two best friends, Mick and Josh, were both taller, Mick especially, who stood six foot three. But then they were both guys. They were *not* female.

A light breeze ruffled her flyaway hair, which seemed to have been permanently crimped. The color was nice, a soft honey-brown, lighter around her face where the sun had kissed it. Curls sprung out here and there and everywhere, like miniature springs. He doubted such unruly hair could ever be fully contained.

A soft flush colored her skin—high across her cheekbones, over the bridge of her narrow nose and the tip of her chin— either by the warmth of the day, her exertions, or the bright sunshine. Zack suspected the latter.

Sporting a crooked smile, she stared right back at him with the most unusual hazel eyes he'd ever seen. So light they were almost the color of topaz, they were fringed by thick, impossibly dark lashes, especially given the color of her hair. After a silent moment, her arched brows lifted and her smile stretched into a full-fledged grin.

Zack caught himself. Good God, he'd been staring at her as if he'd never seen a woman before. He'd been staring at her…*with interest*. He shook his head. "What gave me away?"

"What's that?" She now appeared confused.

"How could you tell that you woke me?"

"Ah. The hair standing on end? The all-night whiskers? Or it could be the bloodshot eyes." She made a tsking sound. "Have you slept at all?"

He ran a hand through his hair and mumbled, "I worked pretty late last night," and left it at that. He wasn't with it enough yet to start rehashing the past evening's events. He pushed the screen door open and stepped aside. "Come on in."

She looked behind her. "Conan will be right along. He's getting some muffins out of the oven. He's a terrific cook."

Conan-the-massive cooked?

The woman held up a carafe. "Fresh coffee. French vanilla. I hope that's okay?"

He hated flavored coffees. "It's fine," he lied, "but totally unnecessary."

"It's the very least I can do now that I know I got you out of bed."

If she hadn't, he thought, perhaps he'd have finished that sexy dream and not been so edgy now. But as it was, he couldn't quite seem to get himself together.

She hesitated at the door. "I really am so sorry. This is my first house and I'm equally stressed and excited and when I get that way, I unfortunately get—" She shrugged in apology. "—loud."

Her honesty was both unexpected and appealing. Zack forced a smile. "I understand."

Yet, she still held back. "I don't mean to barge in. If you have some cups, we could sit here on your porch. We'll share one cup of coffee, chat a little, and that's all, I promise. It's a beautiful morning and we are all awake now, right?"

Great. If he kept her and her husband outside, he could probably get rid of them quicker. "Good idea. Have a seat and I'll go get some cups."

Just then, Dani came dashing down the steps. Zack turned, saw her small feet flying, and said softly but sternly, "Slow down."

She skidded to a halt on the second to the bottom step, gave him a quick, offhand, "Sorry," and looked up at the woman as she finished approaching. "Hi."

Wynn's face lit up with her smile, making those golden eyes glow and the color in her cheeks intensify. "Hello there!" Kneeling down in the doorway, she said, "It's so good to meet you." She held out a hand that Dani took with formality. Zack watched in awe. "I hadn't realized I'd have another female for a neighbor. The Realtor only told me that a single man lived here."

"I'm Dani. My mom died," Dani said, "so it's jus' me and Dad."

Given half a chance, Dani would voice anything that came into her mind. Normally he didn't mind, but this time it rankled.

Her sweater was hiked up in the back and the left leg of her jeans had caught on a cotton sock. Zack smoothed the sweater, tugged the jeans into place, and frowned at her hair. His daughter, bless her heart, had the most impossible baby-fine, flyaway blond hair.

Then he glanced at Wynn again and revised his opinion. Dani had difficult hair, but definitely not the worst.

Softly, probably because she realized Dani had touched on a private topic, Wynn said, "Well, I'm very glad to have you for a neighbor, Dani." She glanced up at Zack warily. "And your dad, too, of course."

Zack took his daughter's hand, not about to leave her alone with a virtual stranger, and said, "Wynn, if you'd like to make yourself comfortable, we'll get the mugs and be right out."

Wynn stood again, stretching out that long tall body. Zack's gaze automatically dropped to her legs, but he quickly pulled it back to her face even as a wave of heat snaked through him.

She was married, he thought guiltily, and he had no intention of ogling a neighbor anyway.

Rather than looking put out by his quick, intimate perusal, Wynn smiled. "Sounds good," she murmured, her eyes warm. She turned back to the porch, giving Zack a back view of those strong shapely legs and tight bottom, and the screen door fell shut behind her.

Dani stared up at him, but he shook his head, indicating she should be quiet for a moment. When they reached the kitchen, he plunked her onto a chair opposite him and took a moment to pull on his shoes. That accomplished, he looked at his daughter. "Juice?"

"Apple." Dani swung her feet, then tilted her head. "She's not taller than you."

"No, not quite," Zack said, locating a tray beneath the sink and loading it with three mugs, a glass of apple juice and a bowl of cereal for Dani. "It's close, though. She looked me right in the eye, but she had on thick-soled shoes and I was still barefoot."

Dani squirmed. "I want my hair in a ponytail like hers."

He smiled. Maybe a female neighbor, even a very big one with corkscrew hair, wouldn't be a bad thing. Eloise, Dani's sitter during Zack's working hours, was a very kind, gentle and attentive woman. But she was old enough to be Zack's grandmother, with bluish hair and support hose—not a woman to inspire a young girl.

Zack's company was mostly limited to Mick and Josh, and though Josh knew everything there was to know about legal-aged females, he knew next to nothing about four-year-olds. Since Mick had married, Dani got to visit with Delilah now and then, and the two of them had really hit it off, which proved to Zack that Dani needed a woman around more often.

For Dani's sake, he'd decided he needed a wife. But finding someone appropriate was proving to be more difficult than he'd thought, mostly because he had so little time to look.

When he did have time, he didn't run across any suitable women. A wife would need to be domestic, neat, lovable, and she'd have to understand that his daughter came first. Period.

"A ponytail it is," Zack said, forcing his mind away from that problem. He stroked his big rough fingers through Dani's fine hair. "Why don't you go get your brush and a band, and then come out to the porch?"

"Okay." She slid off the chair and ran from the room again. His daughter never walked when she could run. She was never quiet when she could talk or laugh, and she always fought naps right up until she ran out of gas and all but collapsed. She exuded constant energy, and she had an imagination that often left him floored.

She was his life.

Wynn and Conan were arguing again when Zack opened the screen door. He stalled, uncertain what to do as Wynn poked the bulky bruiser in the chest and threatened his life.

Ignoring most of her diatribe, Conan said, "Ha!" then flicked her earlobe, hard.

Zack's mouth fell open, seeing the physical byplay.

Before he could say anything, Wynn lit up like a live wire, clutching at her ear. "That *hurt!*"

"Well so does your pointy little finger trying to bore holes in my chest."

"Bull." She leaned in to him, nose to nose, and deliberately gave him another, harder prod. "You can't feel anything through that layer of rock and you know it."

Conan rubbed his chest, opened his mouth to say God-only-knew-what, then noticed Zack. He scowled. "You're making a spectacle of yourself in front of your neighbors, Wynonna."

Frozen half in, half out of the door, Zack just stared. Domestic troubles? God, he didn't want to be involved in this.

Wynn rushed forward and took the tray from him. "Just ignore Conan," she said, "he's a bully."

Conan ran both hands through his blond hair, which Zack noticed wasn't the least bit frizzy, and growled. His eyes turned red and his face blue. "Wynonna, I swear I'm gonna—"

He reached for her and Zack, without really thinking, stepped between them. The tray in Wynn's arms wobbled, but she maintained her grip.

"Look," Zack said, not sure if the woman would need any help or not, "this is none of my business, but—"

Wynn rudely pushed her way around him. "You're gonna what?" she taunted Conan. "What else can you do?"

Conan reached for her again, and Zack grabbed him. *"That's enough,"* he roared.

Zack hadn't had enough sleep, he was still disturbed by the calls he'd made the night before, and he had no tolerance for petty bickering.

And he absolutely, positively, would not put up with a man hurting a woman, not even a pesky too-big neighbor woman he barely knew and who looked like she could damn well defend herself.

Silence fell. Conan, with one brow raised, stared at Zack's hand wrapped around his thick wrist. Zack had big hands, but still, his fingers barely touched.

Conan's gaze shifted to Wynn, and he made a wry face. "A gallant in the making?"

Wynn set the tray down and rushed to put herself between the two men, facing Zack. Her fingers spread wide on his chest, pressing, restraining although he could have easily moved her aside and they both knew it. Wedged between the two of them, she was so close to Zack he felt her breath and the heat of her body. He twitched.

Wynn stared into his face with an expression bordering on wonder, patted him, and then said with quiet sincerity, "Thank you, but Conan would never hurt me, Zack. I promise. He just likes to needle."

Conan, still caught in Zack's unrelenting grasp, snorted at that. But he replied easily, "She's right, you know. I might want to swat her every now and again, but I wouldn't hurt her."

Swat her? Zack peered into Wynn's large golden eyes and imagined all kinds of kinky sexual play between the two of them.

He wasn't sure if he was disgusted or intrigued, and his indecision on the matter was unacceptable. He frowned, feeling very put upon.

Then Conan continued lazily. "Wynn, however, has never shown any such consideration. She's been kicking my ass since we were both in diapers."

Wynn gave Zack an apologetic nod. "It's true. Conan is such a big lug, he's always let me practice up on him."

Conan tugged on his hand, and Zack, feeling numb and rather foolish, and for some damn reason, relieved, released him.

Brother and sister?

"She's so big," Conan continued, "she's always looked older than her age. When she was in ninth grade, college guys were hitting on her! She needed to know how to fight off the cretins. So I've been her personal punching bag for longer than I care to remember."

Still with her hands pressed to Zack's chest, Wynn glanced

over her shoulder and smiled. "Not that he feels it," she said to her brother, "regardless of how he carries on." Facing Zack again, she explained, "A steamroller could go over Conan and he's so thick with muscle he wouldn't notice."

Zack inhaled and breathed in the scents of vanilla coffee, fresh blueberry muffins, early morning dew on green grass— and Wynn. She smelled...different. Not sweet. Not exactly spicy. It was more a fresh scent, like a cool fall breeze or the forerunner to a storm. His muscles twitched again.

Damn, but this day was not going at all as planned.

And he could only blame one very big, and somehow very appealing, woman. A woman who was not only his neighbor, but still touching him, still looking at him with a mixture of tenderness, humor, and...hunger.

He'd known tall women, hell, Mick's wife Delilah was tall. But he'd never known such a...*sturdy* woman. Her open hands on his chest were nearly as large as his own. Her shoulders were broad, her bones long. Unlike Delilah, Wynn wasn't delicate.

But she was sexy.

He needed some sleep to be able to deal with the likes of her. And he needed more time.

And most of all, he needed sex, because he knew when he started getting turned on by a loud, pushy amazon, it had been far, far too long.

TWO

GATHERING HIS SCATTERED wits, Zack looked at both Wynn and Conan, then stepped out of Wynn's reach. "I see," he said, for lack of anything better. His brain was all but empty of responses. This had not been a memorable morning.

Wynn fought off a smile, at his expense. "I do appreciate your consideration for my welfare, though."

The way she said it made him feel ten times more foolish. He could see why Conan thought she needed a good swat. At the moment, he wasn't totally averse to the idea himself.

Conan saved the awkward moment by pouring the coffee. The rich aroma of vanilla intensified, but Zack could still smell *her*. She'd been working and her skin was hot, dewy with her exertions.

He growled low in his throat, hating his basic response to her.

Thankfully unaware of the source of his disgruntlement, Conan said, "Sit down, Zack. You look like we've wrung you out already. And I have to tell you, it's only going to get worse."

How in the hell can it get worse? Zack accepted the coffee and seated himself in a padded chair. Conan sat across from him, Wynn on the settee. Mustering a tone of bland inquiry, Zack asked, "How so?" while eyeing the golden brown muffin, bursting with ripe blueberries, which Conan passed his way.

Nodding to his sister, who had reverted back to frowning, Conan explained, "Mom and Dad are moving. They needed somewhere to stay for two weeks and since Wynn just got this place, I convinced them she was a better choice than me." He flashed a wide, unapologetic grin.

Wynn huffed. "Not that I don't love my parents, but when you meet them you'll understand why I'm considering wringing Conan's neck."

Zack didn't want to meet her parents. He hadn't even wanted to meet her. With any luck, from here on out he'd successfully avoid the Lane clan altogether.

"But hey," Conan said, and punched Zack in the shoulder, nearly making him spill the distasteful coffee. "I like it that you wanted to protect her. Knowing she'll have a neighbor looking out for her makes me feel better about her living alone."

Conan had fists like sledgehammers, and not enough sense to temper his blows. The muscle in Zack's shoulder leaped in pain. He refused to show any weakness by rubbing it.

And he refused to become Wynn's protector, though God knew with a smart and loud mouth like hers, she'd likely need a battalion to shield her from retaliation. But before he could find words to express his thoughts, Dani appeared. She hesitated, showing unaccustomed shyness, her soft-bristled brush clutched in one hand, the other on the screen door.

Setting aside his coffee, Zack held out his hand and she

skipped to him. He put her on his knee and began brushing her silky hair. "Dani, Conan is Wynn's brother."

Dani leaned close to his ear and whispered loudly enough for the birds in the trees to hear, "What do I call 'em?"

Wynn answered for him. "Well, neighbors can't very well stand on formality, now can they? So, if you don't mind us calling you Dani, you can just call us Wynn and Conan. Deal?"

Dani twisted, stuck out her hand, and said, "Deal."

Conan laughed and enfolded the diminutive fingers with his massive paw. Muscles flexed and rolled along his arm, yet Zack couldn't help but notice that he was very gentle.

After Wynn shook Dani's hand, too, Dani stated, "Your hair looks funny."

"Dani." Her habit of speaking her mind was often humorous, but this wasn't one of those times.

She blinked at her father uncertainly. "It doesn't?"

It did, so what could he say? He settled on, "You know better than to be rude."

Far from insulted, Wynn laughed out loud and shook her head so more corkscrew curls sprang wild. "It feels funny, too. Wanna see?"

Dani looked at Zack for permission, and he could only shrug. Never in his life had he known a woman who behaved as she did, so how was he supposed to know how to deal with her?

Dani reached out, nearly falling off Zack's knee, and put her fingertips to the bouncing curls. She gave a tentative stroke, and then another. Her brow furrowed in concentration. "It's soft." And then to Zack, "Feel it, Daddy."

Zack nearly choked. "Uh, no, Dani…"

Conan must have had a wicked streak, because he taunted, "Ah, go ahead, Zack. Wynonna won't mind."

"Wynonna will loosen your jaw if you don't stop calling me *Wynonna!*"

Dani laughed. Zack was a little bemused to realize his daughter recognized the lack of threat in their repartee while he'd been alarmed by it.

"My name's Daniella, but no one calls me that. 'Cept Dad sometimes when he's mad."

Wynn gave a theatrical gasp. "Your father gets mad at you?" she teased, holding one hand to her chest. "Whatever for? Why, you're such a little angel."

Dani shrugged. "Not all the time. Sometimes I get into mis…mis…"

"Mischief," Zack supplied, "and don't make me sound like an ogre to our new neighbors."

She beamed at him. "He's the best dad in the whole world."

"Much better." Zack smiled and kissed her soft plump cheek. "She has her moments, and if angels can be rowdy and rambunctious, then the description does fit."

Conan laughed, but Wynn gave him another of those tender, intent looks. He frowned and turned away.

"You don't really fight with Conan," Dani told Wynn, as if Wynn might not be aware of that fact herself.

"I would never take a chance on hurting him," Wynn boasted. Then, pretending to share a confidence, she added, "Besides, he's my brother and I love him."

Dani sat back against her father's chest and crossed her arms. "I want a brother."

Zack choked.

Conan handed him a napkin, again staving off the awkward moment. "If you want to hear the real joke about Wynn's hair," Conan said, "then you should know that our father is a coiffeur."

"What's that?" Dani asked.

"A coiffeur," Wynn explained, "is just another word for a hairdresser."

Again and again, they took him by surprise, Zack thought. "That's…interesting," he remarked, and gulped down more of the awful vanilla coffee.

Wynn chuckled. "The fact that I won't let him touch my hair makes him crazy. Which is why I won't let him touch it, of course. Every time he sees me, he wails like he's in pain."

"And when she says wails, she means wails." Conan sipped his own coffee before setting the cup aside. "My dad is likely to be the only flaming heterosexual you'll ever meet."

Zack stared. *Flaming heterosexual?* Did these two know any normal or mundane conversational tidbits? Couldn't they go on about the weather or something? Together, they were the strangest people he'd ever met so he had no doubt the parents had to be beyond odd as well. He kept silent.

His daughter did not.

"Does that mean hairdresser, too?" Dani asked.

Wynn quickly swallowed her bite of muffin. "No, Dani, that means he likes to dress in silk and lots of gold chains and he has this enormous diamond earring."

Oh Lord, Zack thought, and wished he could escape.

"Our mother, on the other hand, is the original hippie. She's into all things natural and doesn't wear any jewelry at all except for a plain wedding band."

"But," Conan interjected, casting a sly look at Wynn, "she loves my father enough to let him keep her hair trimmed."

"Daddy would have a heart attack if I asked him to do my

hair now. You know that. Besides, he likes to have something to gripe at me about."

"Does your mom's hair look like yours?" Zack heard himself ask, curious despite himself.

"Heavens no! I got my hair from some long-deceased ancestor."

Conan leaned forward in a conspiratorial manner. "And believe me, we're all beyond grateful that he is long deceased."

Wynn shoved at him. "My father's hair is brown and sleek, and my mother's hair is blond like Conan's, but longer—all the way to her waist."

Dreading the answer, Zack asked, "When are they supposed to join you?"

"Next week," she mumbled, sounding despondent and resigned. "And I was so looking forward to living on my own."

"You lived at home until now?" As Zack asked that, he finished brushing the tangles from Dani's hair, smoothed it back and expertly wrapped the covered band around it, securing it in place. She bobbed her head a bit, making the ponytail bounce, then smiled and kissed him again. Zack gave her an affectionate squeeze—and noticed the silly smiles on his neighbors' faces.

He now felt conspicuous, all because he'd fixed his daughter's hair. It was no big deal, nothing elaborate, just a ponytail. And it wasn't like there was someone else to do it. Anything his daughter needed, he supplied. Except female company, but he was working on that.

"No," Wynn said, still looking too soft and female and approving, which for her was a gross contradiction. The contrast...intrigued him.

No, it did not!

"At twenty-eight," she continued, oblivious to his inner

turmoil on her femaleness, "I've been out of the house for a while. But I had two roommates, and they were both awful slobs. I'm sort of what you'd call…"

"Fanatical," Conan supplied, toasting her with his coffee cup. "She likes to keep an immaculate, organized house. Drives me crazy."

"Dad's fatical, too," Dani told them. "Mick and Josh tell him he'll make a good husband for some lucky woman some day."

"Is that right?" Amused, Conan eyed Zack.

Wynn drank more coffee, cleared her throat as if embarrassed, and finally put her cup aside. "Well, I can't stand having things thrown just anywhere. Busy people need to be organized."

Since Zack felt the same way, he could empathize with her. Other than Dani's toys, which he left scattered around so Dani wouldn't feel stifled, he liked to have a place for everything and everything in its place. He kept the house clean and once a month a service came to do a more thorough job, getting the baseboards and the ceiling and the air ducts—all the places he seldom had time to tend to.

The idea that they might have something in common was a little alarming, so he didn't belabor the point.

Dani slid off his lap to sit beside Wynn. She situated herself in the exact same pose as the neighbor, shoulders back, spine straight, head tilted just so. Except that Dani's legs hanging over the edge of the padded settee didn't even come close to touching the ground, while Wynn's not only touched, they folded so sharply her knees were practically in her face. Zack shook his head. He'd never seen legs so long. Or so nicely shaped.

Dani gave Wynn a toothy grin, then picked up her bowl of cereal and dug in.

"Conan falls into the slob category." Wynn handed Dani a napkin almost without thought. Zack wondered if she was around children often, then decided it didn't matter to him one iota. "Which is probably why my folks decided to spend their two weeks with me. It's far too easy to get lost in his cluttered apartment. He keeps newspapers around for weeks, and there's always something rotting in his refrigerator."

Zack couldn't stop his shudder of revulsion. Watching him, Wynn nodded in perfect accord. "It's disgusting," she confirmed.

To change the subject, Conan asked, "What do you do for a living, Zack?"

Both he and his sister stared at Zack with expectant expressions.

Dani answered for him, saying around a mouthful of cereal and milk, "He saves peoples. He's a hero."

Settling back in her seat, Wynn slowly nodded. "Mmmm. I can see that." She eyed Zack up and down…and up again, letting her gaze linger here and there. He felt that interested gaze like a lick of fire and wanted to groan.

"Your dad," she said, "has all the right makings of a hero. Big, muscular, handsome and kind." And then with an impish, very intimate and inviting smile, "I'm glad he's my neighbor."

It was the most curious sensation, Wynn thought, as if her heart had started to boil the second she'd seen him. Then, when he'd held his daughter on his knee and patiently brushed her hair, her heart outright melted. She'd never felt anything like it. She'd never seen anyone like him.

And she was all but bowled over with a mixed jumble of emotions.

Dani herself caused part of the effect; Wynn couldn't imagine a more adorable little girl than the one sitting primly beside her, milk on her upper lip and her riotous hair neatly contained in a bouncy ponytail. The child had an impish demeanor that proved she was both smart and precocious.

Most of the effect, though, came from Zack Grange. *Wowza*. She hadn't believed one man could carry such a sizzling emotional and physical wallop, but Zack did. He stood the smallest bit taller than she, maybe an inch at most. Which meant he must stand a flat six feet. Her height, however, apparently didn't distress him.

No, before he'd recalled himself, Zack had looked at her with male appreciation, and she liked it. A lot.

She wished she hadn't worn the bulky sweatshirt with the stretched out neckline and the hem that hung midway down her shorts. Her upper body was as toned as the rest of her, and she wondered how he'd look at her there.

When she'd first dressed, the early morning air had carried a nip, but she was nowhere near cool now. In fact, she felt a little overheated. Maybe downright hot.

She guessed Zack to be around thirty, given the age of his daughter and his overall physique. It was his physique that had her doing more than her fair share of ogling. The man was put together just fine.

He wasn't a muscle-bound behemoth like her brother, but lean and toned, with an obvious strength that was partly innate male, partly specialized training. His chest was wide, his shoulders wider. He had narrow hips, long straight legs and large, lean hands and feet. There was no fat on his middle, no slouch in his stance.

Light brown hair, bone straight and disheveled from being roused out of bed, complemented gentle, intense blue eyes. His brows and beard stubble were darker, his jaw hard and stubborn.

But it was when he looked at his daughter that his gorgeous blue eyes held the most impact.

Only seconds after seeing Zack, she'd wanted him. The man exuded raw sexuality tempered with gentleness and caring. A highly potent combination.

Being around him felt...comfortable, in a dozen different ways.

With an acquaintance not quite an hour long, she knew enough to respect him. She'd already learned that he loved his daughter, was a natural defender of women, and showed politeness even when rude neighbors pulled him from a much-needed sleep.

She sighed, earning a strange look from both men and Dani.

"Sorry," she mumbled, wishing she could crawl over onto his lap now that Dani was no longer in it. But a big hulking girl like herself didn't sit in laps. In fact, she couldn't remember the last time a man had held her. "So what title applies to your heroic deeds, Zack?"

He rubbed his hands over his tired eyes while explaining. "I'm an EMT paramedic. Dani thinks Mick, Josh and I are all heroes. Actually I believe she has Mick's wife, Delilah, in that category now, too."

"They're heroes," Dani insisted with a child's love and devotion.

And Zack responded, "Don't talk with your mouth full, sweetheart."

"So you drive an ambulance, huh?" Conan leaned forward with interest. "Who do you work for?"

"The fire department. Josh is a fireman there. We've known each other forever."

Wynn tipped her head, recalling the other name he had mentioned. "And Mick? What does he do?"

"Mick is a cop. His wife, Delilah Piper-slash-Dawson is a—"

"Novelist!" Conan finished for him, surging to the edge of his seat with excitement. "Are you kidding me? You know Delilah Piper?"

"Don't forget the 'slash-Dawson' part or Mick will have your head." Zack grinned, showing even white teeth and a dimple in his left cheek. *A dimple!* Wynn's melting heart thumped so hard, she nearly missed the rest of Zack's explanation. "Since she and Mick married, he's been understanding about her name already being well known. He's proud of her career, but insistent that those of us who are familiar remember she's a married woman now."

"Possessive, is he?" Wynn asked.

And Conan said, "Are you nuts? She's *Delilah Piper*." He snorted. "I'd be possessive, too."

"You always are," Wynn said with a shake of her head. Her brother drove his present girlfriend crazy with his possessive, overbearing ways.

"I take it you're a fan?" Zack asked.

"I just finished her newest. That scene at the river was incredible."

"I can get your books signed for you if you want."

Wynn watched in disgust as her muscle-bound brother looked ready to get up and dance a jig. She glanced at Dani, and they shared a woman-to-woman smile. Dani even shook her head and rolled her big blue eyes, causing Wynn to chuckle.

While the men continued to work out the details of the

books, Wynn turned to Dani. "So you're close to Josh and Mick and Delilah?"

"She wants to be called Del, only Mick won't. I think it's jus' to tease her."

"And Mick and Josh?"

"They're fun. Josh has lots of ladies, but he says none of 'em are prettier than me so he can't marry 'em."

"Smart man."

"Yeah." She nodded with a look of pity for the poor unwed Josh and the not-pretty-enough women. "Dad wants to get married, too, but he's gotta find a wife first." Dani scrunched up her face, studying Wynn.

Wynn squirmed under such close scrutiny. *From a child!* Luckily, Dani whispered to her father that she had to go in to the potty. After she went in, Zack returned to his conversation about Del Piper, keeping Conan enthralled.

Wynn looked at Zack. So, he wanted a wife, huh? Or was that something Dani had misconstrued?

How in the world was it that he hadn't already remarried? A man like Zack probably had women by the dozens. But then…she rethought that and shook her head at herself. Zack was very dedicated to his daughter, and she knew EMTs worked long shifts, sometimes up to sixty hours a week. That wouldn't leave him much time for dating, much less cultivating a lasting relationship.

He must have felt her gaze, for he glanced at her while Conan waxed poetic about Ms. Piper's remarkable talent. Their gazes met and held and Zack frowned. He glanced away, then back again. Wynn blinked at him, feeling soft and hot and excited.

She stared, knew she stared, and couldn't seem to help herself. Zack shifted, glaring at her then crossing one ankle over a knee.

He had thick ankles. And wrists. And long fingers and... one thought led to another and she couldn't keep herself from peeking at his lap. His jeans were old and faded and appeared very soft. They cupped him lovingly, outlining a bulge that proved most noticeable, even without him being aroused.

Her heart dropped into her stomach and began jumping erratically. Her palms tingled, craving to touch him, to weigh him in her hands—

"Stop that!"

She blinked hard and looked up at him. Conan went silent, confused. A red flush crept up Zack's neck. He cleared his throat and stood.

"The coffee and muffins were great. Thanks."

As dismissals went, it wasn't the least bit subtle, but Conan didn't seem to find anything amiss. He shook Zack's hand, saying, "I'll bring the books to you soon, if you're sure she won't mind signing them."

"Delilah's great. She won't mind." Zack didn't look at Wynn at all, and she had the feeling his avoidance was deliberate. But then, he'd caught her staring at his crotch, all but salivating.

She blushed. She'd known the man one hour, and already she'd behaved like a shameless hussy. Or worse, like a desperate spinster.

Oh God! Maybe that was how he saw her. After all, she was twenty-eight and single. The only male helping her move in was her brother; no fiancé, not even a boyfriend. He couldn't know that it was by choice, because she hadn't yet met a guy who...made her blood sing, not like he did.

Damn, damn, damn.

Not being of a shy or withdrawn nature, she stuck out her hand, daring him to continue ignoring her. She wouldn't allow it.

His jaw locked. With a false smile pinned to his tired face, he took her hand. His touch, his look, was beyond impersonal, and she hated it. "Welcome to the neighborhood, Wynn."

"Thanks." He tried to take his hand back, but she held on. "I'm sure we'll be seeing each other again."

After she said it, she winced. It sounded like a threat! Then she realized he was trying to tug his hand free and here she was, doing the macho "grip" thing. Good God, she was making things worse by the second.

She turned him loose and put her hands in her pockets so she wouldn't be tempted to get hold of him again. Conan gathered up the carafe and the muffin plate.

Feeling like an idiot, she said, "Well, thanks again. And really, I am sorry we woke you."

Dani bounded back outside, then skidded to a disappointed halt. "You can't leave."

Zack put his hand on the top of her silky head. "I'm sure Wynn wants to finish unpacking, sweetheart. And you and I are going shopping."

Dani groaned, wilted, all in all acting like a child being sent to the woodshed.

Barely hiding a smile, Zack said, "None of that. We'll have lunch out and it'll be fine. You'll see."

Conan gave a crooked grin. "I gather she doesn't like shopping?"

"Not for clothes, no. But she's about worn out everything warm she has."

"Sounds like Wynn. She hates shopping, too."

Dani's eyes widened. "You do?"

Wynn shrugged. "I know it's supposed to be a girl thing, but I've never understood it. Thank goodness I don't need a lot of clothes."

Conan leaned forward. "She used to outgrow her wardrobe daily, but we're hoping she's done growing by now."

Wynn elbowed him, caught Zack's look of disapproval, and wanted to throttle her brother. Zack didn't approve of their physical sparring, and she'd meant to cease it in front of him. But Conan had a way of egging her on. "I quit growing ten years ago. And with my job, casual clothes are perfect."

"What do you do?" Zack asked, then looked like he wanted to bite his tongue off.

"I'm a physical therapist. I work two days a week at the high school, two days a week at the college." She nodded toward her brother. "Conan owns a gym and I sometimes help out there, too, when the bodybuilders overdo it."

Zack looked dubious, but nodded. He said to Conan, again ignoring her, "A gym, huh?"

"Small, but it's all mine and I'm a good trainer. I do a lot of private stuff." He winked. "The clientele is as much female as male."

Bristling at Zack's disregard and her brother's caveman attitude, Wynn said, "Rachael will get you if she hears that particular leer in your tone."

Conan shrugged, unconcerned with the warning. "Rachael is my current girlfriend, not my wife. And speaking of Rachael, I should get going." He gave one last wave and headed off.

Wynn gazed after him, watching him go down the steps and then around the porch toward her new house. She sighed. "Me, too. I've got a lot of unpacking to do yet." She turned to Zack, who appeared anxious to finish the goodbyes. "Being as we're neighbors," she thought to say, "feel free to borrow if you ever need to. You know, the proverbial cup of sugar or whatever."

"Thanks." Zack's tone was dry. "I'll keep that in mind. And thanks for the coffee and muffins. They were...great."

With nothing left to say, Wynn stepped off the porch with a lagging step. "Okay, well...bye."

"Goodbye, Wynn."

She glanced over her shoulder to see Zack escaping into his house. He closed the door behind him, and she heard the lock click. Well, hell. His goodbye had sounded entirely too final.

That just wouldn't do. She wanted him. One way or another.

THREE

"LOOK, DAD!"

Zack pulled the car into the driveway and put it in Park. He didn't want to look. Because of the direction Dani pointed, he already knew what—or rather who—he'd see. And he wanted to keep her out of his mind, not dwell on her further. He'd done enough dwelling.

All day long, his mind had wandered to her, and he didn't like it. Even while buying miniature jeans with butterflies sewn on the pockets, and lace-up brown boots meant for a boy that had his daughter begging for them, he'd thought of Wynn. While hauling armloads of shopping bags filled with pastel sweatshirts and soft sweaters and long-sleeved T-shirts, he'd remembered the way Wynn had stared at him—*where she'd stared at him*—and he'd been distracted.

Not just distracted, but edgy with a sort of vague arousal. Well, not really vague, either. More like...acute.

Damn, damn, damn.

He'd been forced to fight himself all day. And all that did

was add to his exhaustion and detract from the pleasure he usually enjoyed while spending special time with Dani.

He'd pictured Wynn in his mind as they ate lunch in the food court, and he'd missed most of the matinee movie because his brain not only conjured what had already transpired, but what might yet come if he were to be friendlier to her.

And that wouldn't do! She was a neighbor living right behind him, so anything casual, *like hot, gritty, satisfying sex,* was out of the question. And anything less casual, like friendship, would only make him want the sex more.

Wynn came nowhere near meeting his requirements for involvement, so it'd be best if he stayed clear of her altogether.

"Dad, *look.*"

Dani, with her insistent, squeaky voice, gave him little choice. Zack glanced up to where she pointed, even as he said, "We need to get all these clothes put away…" His words died as he took in the sight of Wynn, now wearing a soft beige halter top, struggling with a long flat box. His driveway was at the side of his house, leading to an attached garage, which gave him a clear view of her house. Her yard was now empty of the packing boxes; it was the huge department store box that held her attention. Zack couldn't see the picture on the box to determine what she'd bought, but then, he wasn't exactly focused on the box.

Beneath the hot early-evening sun, Wynn's broad, toned shoulders looked dewy with perspiration and flexed with feminine muscles. Her belly… He swallowed hard. Her belly was flat, taut with her straining efforts, her waist lean and supple, dipping and curving. She looked sexy and healthy and strong and so utterly female his muscles cramped.

The effect of those long legs had nearly been his undoing that morning. Now seeing her upper parts more bare than covered was enough to make him sweat along with her. He just adored female bellies, and hers was especially enticing.

He felt Dani's hand on his arm and managed to wipe away the gleam of lust before looking down at her.

"You should help her," Dani declared.

Oh, no. Zack had no intention of getting anywhere near Wynn. He shook his head and finished undoing Dani's car seat. By age, Dani was old enough to forego the special seat, but by size… His daughter was so petite it'd probably be another year before he felt comfortable with only a seat belt for her protection. "We've got our own work to do, Dani."

But no sooner did he have his daughter free from the seat than she opened the car door and slithered out. "Hello, Wynn!" She waved both arms, drawing the neighbor's attention.

Wynn stopped struggling with the box and looked up. She wiped a forearm across her brow, squinted in their direction, then broke out in a smile. Even from the distance, Zack could see the open welcome in that smile.

He cursed, but silently.

Cutting across the yards, Wynn headed toward them. He wanted to groan. He wanted to ignore her and go inside.

He wanted sex, damn it. With her.

No.

"Heym you two!" She stopped by Dani's side of the car, hands on her hips, legs braced apart. "How'd the shopping go?"

Dani tipped her head way back to grin up at Wynn. "We bought lots of stuff. And we saw a movie, too."

Wynn automatically went to her knees. Zack remembered her doing that earlier, too, when she'd spoken with Dani. Was it an allowance she made for her height? A man wouldn't be expected to do that, but a woman?

Or did she just like kids enough that she wanted to greet them on an eye level?

"A whole new wardrobe, huh? Terrific." She glanced up at Zack. Her hazel eyes looked warm and welcoming, even intimate, at least to his overeager imagination. "Got it all taken care of?" she asked.

He cleared his throat. His brain was already in sexual overdrive, his body too long deprived, and now Wynn got on her knees in front of him. Her face, her beautiful mouth, were level with... No. It was too much.

Zack turned away and began yanking bags out of the car. "She should be all set for fall."

"I went shopping, too," Wynn told him, her voice now sounding confused by his dismissal. "I bought a hammock for the backyard."

Zack froze with his arms loaded down. Slowly he turned to face her. "A hammock?" Surely she didn't expect to lounge around in a hammock. Not where he could see her? "Where do you intend to put it?"

She pointed. "Those are the only two trees big enough and close enough together to work. I always wanted a hammock, almost as much as I wanted my own house. After I finished unloading boxes, I couldn't resist. This weather is perfect for lying around outside and reading or napping."

A thousand questions went winging through his mind, but he heard himself ask, "You went shopping in *that?*" The way he was staring at her halter, which looked far too enticing molded over soft, heavy breasts that were in perfect proportion to the rest of her big body, he knew she knew just what he meant.

Then when he realized what had come out of his unruly mouth, and how incredibly possessive he'd sounded, he quickly added, "You're talking about in *my* trees?" Both yards had an abundance of shade, but the trees she'd pointed at were the ones edging his property.

She'd be right there, visible to him, flaunting herself to him, wearing on his determination. He couldn't handle it. He'd never had a problem with temptation before, but he'd never met Wynn before, either.

She blinked those awesome hazel eyes at him, and even that seemed provocative, deliberate. Hell, her breathing seemed designed to drive him nuts.

Her expression intent, watchful, she came to her feet. He didn't mean to, but his gaze switched to her legs, then quickly lifted back to her belly. She wasn't overly muscular there, not in the least mannish, just very smooth and lithe and softly rounded just as a woman should be.

His heart punched into his ribs.

Hands on her naked waist, one hip cocked out enticingly, she waited for his gaze to finally rise up to hers. It took him far too long to get there, but then, she had a lot of skin showing.

When their eyes met, Wynn smiled, but there was nothing friendly in the tilt of her lips or the narrowing of her eyes. "I changed when I got home," she informed him, "before getting the box out of the car. And the trees are actually mine. I specifically asked before buying the house. The Realtor checked the property line just to be sure."

Zack wanted to howl. He wanted to tell her that he didn't give a damn about the trees or whom they belonged to. He wanted to put his daughter down for a nap, then drag his neighbor off to bed—or to the floor or the ground or against one of those stupid trees...

He managed his own strained smile. "I see."

Dani, not understanding the sudden tension between the adults, reached up to tug on the hem of Wynn's shorts. "We got pizza for dinner."

Wynn's smile was genuine when she looked at his daughter. "Sounds like you've had a wonderful day." She ruffled Dani's hair, then saluted Zack. "I better get back to work. I want to get the hammock set up."

"You can eat with us!"

Zack cursed softly at his daughter's invitation, but not softly enough. Wynn heard.

Even though her chin lifted and her eyes were direct, she looked hurt. And that hurt *him*. Damn it, he didn't want to insult her, but neither did he want to be further forced into her company.

"Thanks, sweetie," Wynn said to Dani though she continued to look at Zack, "but I've got too much to do."

"Don't you like pizza?" Dani asked, stubborn to the core and always determined to get her own way.

"I do, but it's been a busy day, and I'm not done yet. Maybe another time, okay?"

Wynn turned away and almost stumbled. For the first time, Zack noticed the weariness in her long limbs, the slight droop to those surprisingly wide, proud shoulders.

Suspicion bloomed, with it annoyance. Using the same tone that always worked for his daughter, Zack uttered, "Wynn."

She paused, turned to face him with one brow raised.

He stared at her face and noticed the exhaustion. Damn it. "When did you eat last?"

"What?" She couldn't have looked more confused by his inquiry. Beside him, Dani all but jiggled with excitement. She knew her father too well and knew he'd just made up his mind.

"Did you have lunch?" Zack demanded, and got a blank expression. He sighed. "Have you eaten anything since the muffins and coffee this morning?"

Rather than answer him, Wynn replied, "I appreciate your concern, Zack, but I'm sure you've got more important things to do than keep track of my meals." Again, she turned away.

He should just let her go, Zack thought, watching her leave and doing his best to keep his gaze off her ample and well-shaped rear end. But his daughter watched him with a look she'd probably picked up from him, one that showed extreme disappointment in his behavior. Dani no doubt expected him to rectify his bad manners, and he knew he should. Even with the womanly sway to her hips, Wynn looked ready to drop, her feet dragging.

She'd been neighborly and friendly and he'd been a surly jerk. All because he hadn't had a woman in too long and she appealed to him on some insane yet basic level. That couldn't be blamed on her.

Zack bent low and said to Dani, "Start carrying the bags up to the porch and I'll be right back."

With a severe look, Dani ordered, "Talk her into eatin' with us."

He sighed. "I'll try."

Dani pushed against him. "Go! Before she's all the way home."

Wynn had nearly made it before Zack reached her. She had to have heard his approach, but she ignored him. He caught her arm and turned her around to face him. "Wait a minute."

Seeing he was alone, she barked, *"What now?"*

He couldn't help it. He smiled, then actually laughed. "Without Dani listening, I get the full brunt of your temper? Is that it?"

"Don't kid yourself." She looked furious and still hurt. Pushing her wild hair out of her face, she sneered, "If you had my full temper, you'd be flat on your back right now."

Her threat brought with it an image of him on his back, her over him, riding him slow and deep. Her legs were so long and so strong he had no doubt her endurance would be endless, mind-blowing. He glanced down at her breasts, thinly covered by the soft material of the halter. Without his mind's permission, he imagined them naked, her nipples puckered, begging for his fingers, his mouth. Her chest glistened from the heat, her skin was radiant and so very soft looking.

No words came, no reply, but she must have read his mind because she drew back and her anger melted away. "I didn't mean that," she whispered in a shaky voice.

He couldn't stop himself from asking, "Mean what?"

She hesitated, their gazes locked, then she shrugged with a blatant challenge. "Sex. That's what you were thinking. Though I suppose you'll deny it now."

Zack rubbed his face. "No, I won't deny it." His neck and shoulders were still sore from the night before, when he'd dealt with two very unusual crises, and now his body throbbed with sexual tension. "Look, Wynn…"

"Hey, I understand. Dani is a sweetheart, but kids have a way of speaking out of turn. No harm done, and I really do have plenty more work to do."

He dismissed what she said to ask, "You've been working all day, haven't you? I bet you haven't eaten at all except for that muffin at dawn."

"It wasn't exactly dawn—"

"Close enough."

"—and my eating habits aren't your concern."

Why did he have to have the most frustrating woman in

creation move in behind him? Why did he have to find her so appealing that even his teeth were aroused? He was tired, achy, sexually frustrated, and now he had to deal with this.

Knowing Dani would only show so much patience before she decided to come help him out, he admitted, "I want you. That's why I was rude."

Those golden eyes opened so wide, she looked comical. He heard her swallow. Her mouth opened, but nothing came out.

Zack looked toward the trees where she planned to hang her hammock. "Between Dani and work, I don't get a lot of chances to date and it's been a long time—too damn long— since I've been with a woman. I didn't get enough sleep last night or I'd probably show better restraint today, but I'm running on four hours tops, and all my understanding and restraint is saved up for my daughter."

She said, "Oh."

"I don't want you to worry that I'm going to come on to you—"

"I'm not worried," she rushed to assure him.

"—because I have no intention of doing that."

She said, "Oh," again. This time with regret, if his tired ears didn't deceive him.

"Yeah, oh." He shook his head. "Come and eat with us, then I'll help you get that box to the backyard and from there we can be sociable, but not overly friendly. Okay?"

"Not overly friendly," she repeated, "because you don't want to want me?"

"That's right." Talking about it wasn't helping. He felt like an ass, more so with every word that left his mouth. "It wouldn't be a good idea what with us being neighbors and everything."

"I see."

She looked perplexed. Zack sighed again and looked around to see his daughter watching intently, arms crossed and foot tapping. He turned back to Wynn. "You understand, surely. Being neighbors is one thing. But it could get awkward if we took it any further than that."

She nodded. "Awkward."

His eyes narrowed at her patronizing tone. "That's right. Relationships have a way of complicating things, especially if they don't work out, and since I'm not looking to get involved—"

"It couldn't work out?" She smiled. "Well, you got me there."

What in the world did she have to smile about? *He* wasn't amused. In fact, he was getting close to annoyed. "We'd still be living next door to each other."

"I'm sure not planning on moving!"

"And then we'd both—"

"Feel awkward." She gave a sage nod. "I see your point."

Zack ground his teeth. "Will you join us for pizza or not?"

She licked her lips and tilted her head. "Can I clarify something first?"

"Make it quick. Dani will be on us any minute now."

"I'm standing here all sweaty and hot and my hair looks worse than usual and yet...you say I'm turning you on?"

Zack wanted to throttle her. Not wanting to hurt her feelings, he'd tried being honest with her, and now she felt free to provoke him.

She did look hot and sweaty—like she'd just been making love most vigorously. He stiffened his resolve. "Let's not belabor the point, okay?"

"Okay." She searched his face. "I just wanted to be sure."

Together they started back toward Dani. Zack could feel the

heat of Wynn at his side, could smell the intensified scent of sun-kissed feminine skin, of shampoo and lotion and woman.

"How long's it been?" she asked with unparalleled nonchalance, as if that wasn't the most personal topic around.

Of course, he'd brought it up. He didn't look at her. "Long enough."

"For me, too." She smiled toward Dani and waved. "Although I don't think that's why you turn me on." She glanced at him, her long lashes at half-mast, her lips slightly curled. She leaned closer and breathed into his ear, "I think it's your gorgeous bod that's doing the trick."

Zack stumbled over his own feet, which left him standing behind Wynn. She walked over to his yard, took Dani's hand, and together they marched around front to the porch. He heard Dani say, "I can show you my new clothes!"

And Wynn replied happily, "Right after we eat. I'm starved."

Wynn finished off her fourth slice of pizza and sighed. She hadn't realized she was so hungry until she'd taken the first bite. Then she'd had to be careful not to make a glutton of herself. "That was heavenly. Thank you."

Zack just grunted, but Dani said, "You ate as much as Dad."

"Not true! He had one piece more than me." Then, eyeing Zack, she added, "But he has a lot more muscle so he naturally needs more to eat."

Zack choked on the drink of cola he'd just taken, and slanted her an evil look. It was all she could do not to laugh. *He wanted her.*

He didn't want to want her, but he did. That was a good start. She could work with that.

On her end, she was crazy-nuts about him already. Not only

was the man handsome and well built, but he had a soft streak for his daughter, an outrageous honesty, and his house was spotless. She'd never known a bachelor who enjoyed cleanliness as much as she did.

"Your house is set up different from mine." She looked around, admiring the orderliness of it.

Zack lounged back in his seat. "It's basically the same, I just had a few walls taken out to open things up."

She'd have done the same if she could afford it, but for now, having her own home more than satisfied her. "It's bigger, too."

He shrugged. "Not by that much. I added on to the dining room when I got the hot tub, and had the patio doors put in."

Wynn had noticed the large hot tub right away. It sat outside his dining room, to the left of his kitchen at the edge of the patio, and was partially shielded by a privacy fence.

The sliding doors really made the dining room bigger and brighter. Her house only had the one kitchen door that opened to the side yard. Wynn had noticed that from Zack's kitchen or his patio doors, he could look at the entire side view of her house, and see into her front and backyard. The only thing that would obstruct his view were the trees.

This topic didn't have him grinding his teeth, so she pursued it. "The landscaping in the back is gorgeous." He had as many mature trees as she had, with one especially large tree close to the house. Long branches reached over the roof and shaded the kitchen from the afternoon sun. Zack had hung a swing from one of those sturdy branches for Dani.

Around the patio, he had a lot of lush ground cover and shade-loving flowers bright with color. It took a remarkable man to plant flowers, but then she'd already made that assessment about him.

"Thank you. I needed the covered deck so we could get to the tub in the winter without plodding through the snow."

"You use it when it's cold?" Imagining Zack mostly naked and wet made her tongue stick to the roof of her mouth. It'd be great if he offered to share, but she wouldn't hold her breath.

He shrugged. "Off and on all year."

Wynn cleared her throat and steered her mind to safer imaginings. "I like the way you've decorated. It's nice and casual and comfortable." Everything was done in mellow pine with shades of cream and greens. There were a few plants, lots of pictures of Dani, and a couple of photos she assumed to be of his deceased wife. The woman was pretty, fair like Dani, but with longer hair. She looked very young, and Wynn made a point of not looking at the photos too long, despite her curiosity; she didn't want to dredge up bad memories for Zack. When she asked him about his wife, it would be without Dani listening.

"Can Wynn and me be excused now?"

Zack said, "May Wynn and I. And yes, you may. Wash your hands first, though."

Dani ran to the sink, used the three-step stool in front of it, and turned on the water. Over her shoulder, she said to Wynn, "My stuff's in my room."

Wynn watched Zack push back his chair. He didn't quite look at her. "I'll go carry that box to the backyard for you while Dani shows you her new clothes." He paused beside Dani, bent and kissed the top of her head. "I'll be right back, okay?"

She nodded. "Okay."

He went out the kitchen door and was gone before Wynn could agree or disagree.

When Dani dragged Wynn upstairs, she got a peek at the

rest of his house. There wasn't a speck of dust anywhere. Not that she was looking for dust, but the complete and total lack of it was evident, and impressive.

Everything was neat and orderly, except for Dani's toys scattered here and there. She noticed two pine chests in the family room, one opened to reveal an assortment of dolls and games inside. The top of a desk was littered with crayons and construction paper and safety scissors.

She passed Zack's bedroom at the top of the stairs and, hoping Dani wouldn't notice, she peered in. More polished, heavy pine furniture filled the moderate size room. The bed was made up with a rich, dark-brown down comforter. A slight breeze wafted in through the open window, through which Wynn could just see Zack, in the corner of her yard, the large box hefted onto his shoulder.

They were of a similar height, but the difference in their strength was notable, and arousing. The box had been heavy and cumbersome to her, yet Zack handled it as if it weighed no more than a sack of flour.

She watched him for a long moment before it dawned on her that if she could see him now, he could see her...anytime she was in the yard.

She asked Dani, "Is this where you and your dad were when we first said hello, today?"

"Yeah, 'cept Dad was still in his underwear then 'cuz he'd just woke up."

"I see." Boy, did she see. Not wanting to give away her interest by lingering, she allowed Dani to hustle her along to her room. This time the furniture was white, with a pale yellow spread and yellow-striped wallpaper on the bottom half of the wall, topped by a white chair rail. An enormous corkboard hung behind the bed, filled to overflowing with pictures Dani had drawn.

With Dani's bedroom on the same side of the house as Zack's, Wynn was tempted to peek out the window again. Instead, she concentrated on the multitude of bags tossed onto Dani's bed.

When Dani began pulling out the clothes, Wynn couldn't help but laugh. Other than small detailing here and there, the clothes could have been for a boy. No frills for Dani, evidently. Wynn approved.

She and Dani spent a good fifteen minutes looking at everything, paying special attention to a tiny pair of rugged lace-up brown boots that would look adorable on Dani's small feet.

Wynn commented on Dani's obvious artistic talent, after which Dani determined to draw Wynn a picture. Since she didn't want Wynn to watch, Wynn headed back downstairs. She found Zack in the kitchen, cleaning up the remains of their dinner. She picked up two glasses and carried them to the dishwasher. "I was going to help you with this."

"No need." He moved around her to the table and spent an inordinate amount of time crushing the pizza box.

It amused Wynn that he wouldn't look at her. She leaned back against the sink, her hands propped on the counter at either side of her hips. "It's the least I could do after imposing on you. Twice."

Again, he moved around her to the garage door. He put the garbage in a can, secured the lid, and came back in. "You were invited."

"Grudgingly."

Zack paused, rubbed the back of his neck, flexed as if trying to rid himself of tension. When he looked at her, his eyes were a very dark blue. "I explained that, Wynn."

"Indeed you did." She crossed her ankles and watched his gaze flicker toward her legs and back again. How odd for him to be attracted to her while she was such a wreck. Odd, but exciting. "About the hammock…"

"What about it?"

"If you don't want it in the trees, I can return it. We're neighbors and the last thing I want to do is cause any hard feelings. I realize the trees are almost smack-dab on the borderline."

He shook his head. "It's not a problem."

"That's not the impression I got when I mentioned it."

Head dropped forward, hands on his hips, he stopped. He stared at his feet for a long moment, then lifted his gaze to her face. "Look—"

The ringing of the phone made him pause. He took two almost angry strides to the phone on the wall and picked it up. "Hello?"

Wynn tried to look like she wasn't listening, but it was apparent he was speaking with a friend. The infamous husband to a famous novelist? The lady-killer Josh?

A lady-friend of his own?

She didn't like that idea at all, and went about wiping off the table, closing up the dishwasher. Zack watched her as he spoke casually, saying, "Sure, I could use the company. That'll work. All right, fifteen minutes." He hung up.

Dani bounded into the room, a colorful picture held in one hand. "Who was it?"

Zack scooped her up and held her to his chest. "Mick and Josh are coming over. If you want to get your bath a little early, you'll have time to visit before bed."

Mick and Josh must be very special to Dani, Wynn assumed, given the way her sweet face lit up.

She leaned around Zack to see the picture. "Is that for me?"

Suddenly looking shy, Dani said, "Yeah," and held it out. Zack looked at it first and chuckled. Then Wynn had it and she held it out, studying it.

Dani had drawn the two trees in the backyard, Wynn and her hammock. Wynn grinned when she saw that she and the trees were the same lofty height, and her hair was accurately portrayed as a tornado. "It's beautiful, Dani." She held the picture to her chest, curiously touched, and smiled. "I love it."

Dani laid her head on Zack's chest. "Really?"

With a strange lump in her throat, she nodded. "Really." Wynn wished she could hold the little girl, too, that she could be the recipient of that adoring hug. She'd never thought much about kids before, but now she did, and an insidious yearning filled her. "May I keep it?" she asked, feeling overly emotional. "I'd like to put it on my refrigerator so everyone who visits me can see it, too."

This pleased Dani a lot. "Okay." And with a distinct lack of subtlety, the little girl added, "I could even visit you and see it sometime."

One look at Zack told Wynn that he didn't consider it a good idea. Tough, she thought. There was no way she'd hurt Dani's feelings just because Zack had some strange hang-up about getting friendly with her.

Feeling defiant, she said, "I'd like that a lot."

And on impulse, she leaned over and kissed Dani's cheek. Zack reared back, well out of reach, but Wynn still felt the sizzle of being so close to him.

She told Dani goodbye, winked at Zack, and let herself out through the kitchen door.

The sun had almost completely set, leaving long shadows

over the lawns. If she hoped to get her hammock up in time to enjoy it tonight, she'd have to get a move on. She went in her house first to retie her hair. It was forever in her face, making her nuts. She found her small box of tools and headed back out.

Fifteen minutes later, when she'd almost finished, she heard the car pull into Zack's driveway. Curiosity got the better of her, and she peered toward the house. A floodlight mounted over Zack's garage door lit the area. Wynn saw two men get out, both of them tall and handsome. One had dark coloring, like a fallen angel, and the other was a golden Adonis. Mick and Josh, she decided, and it was easy to figure out which was which.

Sheesh. Living next door to Zack-the-hunk would be hard enough without him having other impressive hunks over to distract her. She should have been immune to gorgeous men, considering she helped out at Conan's gym and saw well-built muscular guys every day, often in nothing more than skimpy shorts and athletic shoes. But these three…what a visual variety!

The golden one looked up just as she started to turn away, and he kept looking. *Busted!* He knew she'd been eyeing him and no doubt knew why. His type—tall, sexy, well-built and handsome to boot—expected female adoration.

His companion turned, too, then propped his hands on his hips and did his own share of staring. Good Lord, her first day in her own house and she kept making a spectacle of herself.

Seeing no hope for it, Wynn summoned up a friendly and hopefully casual wave, which both men returned. The dark one looked merely polite and curious, but the other watched her with interest.

A second later Zack's door opened and both men got yanked inside.

FOUR

"GET AWAY FROM the damn window," Zack growled.

Josh, still holding aside the café drape on the small window over the kitchen sink, peered over his shoulder at Zack. "Who is she?"

"Nobody. Just a neighbor."

"She's Wynn." Dani, perched in royal splendor on Mick's thigh, showed none of her father's reservation. "She's our new neighbor."

Josh lifted a brow. "Is that right?"

"She had breakfast with us." Dani smiled after that statement.

Mick shared a look with Josh. "Breakfast, huh?"

Zack threw ice into three glasses. "Quit jumping to conclusions. She woke me up this morning, that's all."

Josh dropped the curtain and turned. "Long, tall and sexy got you out of bed, and you say that's *all?*"

Mick choked on a laugh.

Zack, after casting a quick glance at his daughter, scowled.

Luckily Dani was busy singing and drawing Mick a picture, which Mick pretended to attend to when actually Zack knew he was soaking up every word. "It's not like that!" He caught himself, shocked at his own vehemence, and explained more calmly, "She and her brother were making a racket moving in. When she realized she'd awakened us, she brought over coffee and some muffins."

"Nice neighbor," Josh muttered, and turned back to the window.

"She had pizza with us, too, and I drawed her a picture."

"Drew her a picture," Zack automatically corrected, and realized his daughter had been all ears after all. When she looked up at him, he thought to add, "A beautiful picture, honey."

She held up her newest endeavor. "This one is, too."

Mick leaned back to see it, pretending to dump Dani, which made her squeal. "It's incredibly beautiful," he confirmed. He hugged her close and kissed her cheek.

Zack shook his head. His daughter had more than her fair share of male role models. Now she needed a female role model—preferably one who wasn't loud and pushy and too damn big.

Josh said, "Damn, does she never stop working?"

"Not that I've noticed." Unable to keep himself from it, Zack went to the window and peeked out. "What's she doing?"

"Hanging a clothesline. Hell, the moon is out. She's working from the porch light."

Dani said quite seriously, "You cuss too much. Hell and damn are bad words."

Wincing, Josh muttered, "Sorry."

Zack had long ago explained to Dani that while grown men might say certain words now and then, she was still a little girl and was strictly forbidden to do the same. He forgot his daughter's bossiness as he watched Wynn go about her business. "What in the world is she hanging up?"

Josh narrowed his eyes. "Looks like her laundry. Like—" he smiled "—her underwear."

Mick came out of his chair in a rush and crowded into the window. Being that he still held Dani, it was a tight fit. He snorted. "You're both lechers. You should give the woman some privacy."

None of them moved.

Dani said, "We saw her butt today."

Both Josh and Mick turned to stare at him. Zack frowned, ready to explain, then he saw Wynn toss a nightgown over the line and clip it into place with a clothespin. It wasn't a sexy nightgown, but rather what appeared to be yards and yards of material. 'Course, for a woman her size, it'd take a lot of cloth to cover her.

For some stupid reason that thought made him smile.

Moonlight played over her flyaway hair and the slant of the porch light made exaggerated shadows on her body. Why was she hanging her laundry at night? For that matter, why hadn't she worn down yet? She'd been working all day, nonstop, and it was too damn distracting. The woman must have inexhaustible energy, and that thought did more than make him smile. It made him wonder how she might put all that energy to use.

Through the open window, they all heard her begin to whistle.

"This is pathetic," Mick groused. "You've got me here playing peeping Tom when I'd really rather be playing cards."

Josh explained, "That's because you're blissfully married and therefore immune to fantasies."

Zack glared at him. "Don't tell me you're interested in her?"

And before Josh could answer, Dani braced herself between Mick and Josh, leaned forward toward the screen, and yelled through the window, "Hello, Wynn! We's peeping Toms!"

They all three ducked so fast, their heads smacked together.

Mick, on the floor with his back against the sink cabinet, flipped Dani upside down while laughing and said, "I ought to hang you by your toes for that!" He tickled her belly and they both laughed.

Josh looked at Zack and said, "Do you think she heard?"

"That one? She hears everything." Then to his daughter, "Sweetheart, you don't tell people when you're looking at them."

"Why not?"

Josh crept up the edge of the sink and peeked out. With a resigned expression he completely straightened and called out, "It's a little late to be doing laundry."

Realizing Wynn must have been looking toward the window, Zack stood, too. He heard her soft laugh, then, "My new washer and dryer won't arrive for a few more days. I needed clean stuff for tomorrow."

To Zack's disgruntlement, Josh smiled, walked to the kitchen door, and continued right on outside and around to Wynn's house. He should put up a damn privacy fence.

Dani pulled away from Mick and followed. Mick shrugged at Zack, hauled himself to his feet, and followed suit.

Groaning, forced into the situation he'd wanted most to avoid, Zack went along.

When Wynn saw them all approaching, she dropped an item of clothing back into her basket and walked to meet them halfway. Though the night had grown considerably cooler, she was still in the halter and shorts and Zack wanted to strip off his shirt and cover her with it. But it was too late. Josh had already seen her, and was already in charm mode.

Wynn held out her hand when he reached her. "Hello. Wynn Lane."

Josh took her hand, but not in a handshake. He held her fingers carefully, as if she were fragile. "Josh Marshall," he murmured, and his tone alone gave away his thoughts on seduction. "Nice to meet you."

Zack wanted to kick him.

Wynn tried to tug her hand free, but Josh wasn't being reasonable about it. She snuck a glance at Zack and then back to Josh. "You're the fireman, right?"

He looked briefly surprised, and Zack explained, "Dani told her all about both of you."

To Mick she said, "My brother is a big fan of your wife's work."

Mick reached out, took Josh's wrist and pried their hands apart, then indulged his own handshake. At least his was entirely casual and quick. "Mick Dawson. Nice to meet you, Wynn."

She looked at Zack. "I hope I wasn't disturbing you again?"

"We were peekin' at you," Dani informed her.

Wynn just laughed and petted her hand over Dani's hair in a show of affection that Zack felt clean down to his gut. "Well," she said with a wide smile, "I imagine anyone doing laundry by moonlight is sure to draw attention." And to Zack, "The thing is, I'm still too keyed up from moving in to relax, and I actually brought laundry with me from my apartment, so I figured I might as well get it done. Stuff dried on the line always smells so good, don't you think?"

Zack thought *she* smelled good. Working all day had intensified her natural scent, making it more potent, more intoxicating.

He snorted at his own ridiculous fancy and told her, "There's a Laundromat a couple of miles away, next door to the grocery."

"You could use our washer and dryer," Dani offered.

Feeling his smile freeze, Zack said, "Or you could use our washer and dryer."

Wynn was already shaking her head. "No, I don't mind using the line."

Josh stepped in front of Zack. "I'm not that far away. Feel free to use mine until yours arrive."

Zack considered strangling him. It wasn't that he cared personally, because he *didn't,* but it'd be almost as awkward for Josh to get involved with her as it would be for Zack. Josh wasn't ready to settle down, and in fact, since Mick's wedding, he'd been overindulging in a big way. Zack did *not* want him overindulging with his neighbor.

Mick said, "If you're about done, we were just getting some drinks. You could join us."

She took a step back. "Oh no, but thanks anyway."

"Join us, join us!" Dani sang, bouncing up and down in renewed energy.

"You," Zack told his daughter, "are about to go to bed."

Before Dani could summon up a temper about that, Wynn said, "Actually, so am I."

All three men stared at her.

She cleared her throat. "That is, I need to get showered and…" She looked from one fascinated male gaze to the other and coughed. "I'm a mess. I've been working all day."

In a feminine gesture that took him by surprise, considering he hadn't seen much in the way of femininity from her, Wynn attempted to smooth her hair.

Josh tipped his head. "You look fine."

His voice was low and appreciative and again Zack wanted to strangle him.

"Her hair is soft," Dani informed Josh in a loud whisper, then poked him in the thigh.

"Is that right?" Showing none of the reserve Zack had exhibited, Josh reached out and fingered a bouncing curl at her temple before gently tucking it behind her ear. "You're right, Dani. It's very soft."

Wynn twittered and took another step away. "I've got to finish up here. But it was nice meeting you both. Dani, sweet dreams!"

Josh murmured low and suggestively, "You, too."

She gave another ridiculous, girlish twitter and turned to hurry away. Josh stood there, hands on his hips, watching her go with his gaze southerly enough to singe her backside, until Zack elbowed him. Hard.

They all trooped back into the kitchen, Josh rubbing his ribs as if he'd been mortally wounded. Dani now had her head on Mick's shoulder and she yawned. They were all three aware of how quickly Dani would collapse into a sound slumber, and they shared smiles.

Zack scooped his daughter into his arms. "Time for you to hit the sack, sweetie." Once Dani started fading, she went fast. She'd run right up until she ran out of gas.

She blinked sleepy eyes at Josh and Mick. "G'night."

Josh bent and kissed her nose. "Night, princess."

Mick tickled her toes. "Good night, honey."

As Zack turned to leave the kitchen, he saw Mick sit at the table, and Josh go back to the open window. He grumbled under his breath as he hauled his small bundle upstairs. He was just lowering Dani to her mattress when she said in a low, drowsy voice, "Josh likes her."

Pausing, Zack said, "You think so?"

Dani nodded. "I like her, too. Don't you?"

"She's fine." Zack pulled the sheet up to Dani's chin, smoothed her hair and kissed her forehead. That didn't suffice, so he kissed her again, then cuddled her close, squeezing her until she gave a protesting squeak. "I love you, baby."

"I love you, too, Daddy."

"Do you need to potty?"

"Nope." She rolled to her side, cushioned her cheek on one tiny fist, and let out a long deep breath.

With a last peck to her brow, Zack stood. Dani was already snoring softly. For a long minute, he just looked down at her. She was by far the most precious thing in the world to him. It seemed every time he looked at her it struck him anew how much he loved her. That she was his, a part of him, was beyond remarkable.

Josh was still at the damn window when Zack reentered the kitchen. "You look like a lovesick pup."

Mick choked on a laugh. "As compared to you, who's playing the part of the snarling junkyard dog?"

At Mick's taunting words, Zack paused, but only for a second. He knew his friends, and if they had half an inkling of how Wynn affected him, he'd never hear the end of it. Casually, a man without a care, he took his own peek out the window. Wynn was nowhere to be seen, thank God. Out of sight, out of mind.

He grunted, then dropped into his seat, sprawling out and rubbing the back of his neck.

"No comment, huh?" Mick asked.

"I don't know what you're talking about." Ignorance was a lame defense, but he was too tired to think of much else at the moment.

Mick leaned forward over the table and whispered, "Possessiveness."

Josh turned. "She went in just a few seconds ago." He took his own seat. "Did you see the legs on that woman?"

"Since they're a mile long," Mick said, "they'd be a little hard to miss."

Josh lifted a brow. "She's put together right, I'll say that for her."

"You didn't have to put up with her first thing this morning." Wishing he could bite off his tongue, Zack took a long cooling drink of his cola.

Saluting him with his glass, Josh said, "She can get me up anytime."

"Ha ha." Mick shook his head at the double entendre, but amusement shone clear on his face as he looked between the two of them. "You have a one-track mind, Josh."

"And it's definitely on track right now."

Zack growled before he caught himself. "I hate to curtail whatever fantasy you're indulging, but she's off limits."

Josh hesitated with his drink almost to his mouth. "Says who?"

"Says me. I have to live by her. I'll be damned if you're going to date her, dump her, then leave her to me to deal with." Zack shook his head in adamant finality. "No way, so forget it."

Mick nudged Josh with his foot. "Besides, he's got his own plans."

Zack did bite his tongue this time. The more he said, the more they'd read into it, so denials would do him no good.

Eyeing Zack, Josh asked, "Is that right?"

"No, it is not right." He hoped like hell he sounded more definite than he felt. "Now can we talk about something else?"

"Because I can back off if you're making a personal claim."

Through his teeth, Zack said, "I'm *not* making a personal claim, but you *will* back off."

Josh stared at him a moment, then chuckled and switched his gaze to Mick. "I think you're right."

"Are we going to play cards or sit here mooning over women?" Zack barked.

"All right, all right," Josh soothed. "Don't get all fired up. We don't have to moon."

"Speak for yourself," Mick grumbled. "I'm mooning. I'd much rather be home with Delilah right now."

Josh shook his head in pity. Even Zack managed a credible chuckle. "You're still a newlywed, so you're allowed."

"And," Josh added, "Delilah is enough to make anyone moon."

Predictably, Mick bristled. Why in hell Josh continued to make those types of comments, Zack couldn't figure out. He knew there was a time when Josh had fancied himself taken with Delilah, too, but since she'd married Mick—an event Josh had supported wholeheartedly—Josh had roamed from woman to woman with a near insatiable appetite.

Mick half came out of his chair. "I wish you wouldn't speak so intimately about my wife."

Josh looked supremely unaffected by Mick's ire. "I was only agreeing with you."

"*You—*"

"Sheesh, men in love are so touchy," Josh complained. "First Zack breathing fire on me, and now you. A single man can't make a legitimate observation anymore."

"Zack isn't married, *I am*."

"Zack wants to be married," Josh pointed out. "It's almost the same thing." Then he redirected his comments to Zack. "Is that it with Wynn? You considering her suitable wifely material?"

"No."

"Did you really see her backside?"

"No."

Josh grinned. "I'll take that first 'no' at face value. No way in hell am I accepting the second without some kind of explanation."

If he knew it wouldn't wake Dani, Zack would consider knocking Josh off his chair. Resigned, he gave up with a sigh. "She was bent over…" He faltered, unsure how to explain.

Josh protested his hesitation by saying, "I'm all ears."

"Actually," Mick admitted, "so am I."

"She had on short shorts—"

"I noticed that."

"So did I."

"Do you two *want* to hear this or not?" Zack glared at them both, waiting, but they now held themselves silent. "She was bent way over trying to drag a box into the backyard and her shorts rode up. That's all there is to it. I didn't see her whole behind." But he'd seen enough to know her backside was as delectable as her legs.

"A half moon, huh?" Josh made a tsking sound. "And here I missed it."

Zack gave up and explained in full the extent of his association with Ms. Wynn Lane. He told them about her family who'd soon be moving in, her brother who was built like a chimney, and her penchant for being outspoken and brazen and pushy.

"She is not," Zack reiterated, "wife material."

Josh had listened quietly, but now he waved away Zack's disclaimer. "Why do you want to get married anyway? I mean, just because Mick here found the perfect woman—"

Mick growled.

"—and *he's* blissfully happy, doesn't mean we all need to stick our necks into the noose. I know a lot more divorced couples than I do happily married ones."

Now that the cannon had been redirected, Zack relaxed and began shuffling the cards. "Dani asked me about feminine napkins the other day."

Both Mick and Josh froze, then gave near identical groans of emotional pain. "Commercials?" Josh asked.

"Yeah. She was watching cartoons when *bam,* there was a commercial for napkins. Can you believe it? She wanted to know what they were for and why women who used them got to go horseback riding and climbing and stuff."

Chuckling, Mick shook his head. "I can just imagine this conversation."

"Whatd'cha tell her?" Josh asked with interest.

"I fumbled my way through it." Actually, he'd made a total mess of things, but Zack wasn't about to admit that. "She wasn't ready to hear about the whole reproductive cycle thing—"

"Neither am I," Josh joked.

"—so I just told her women used them like they used perfume and makeup and panty hose."

Mick snickered. "Let me guess. She wants some."

"Yup. So you see, this is why I need a wife. I foresee stuff like this coming up all the damn time. I mean, what the hell will I know about fashion trends for teenage girls, or buying training bras?"

Josh considered that a moment, then said, "I could handle it if you want help. I wouldn't mind."

"Oh God, that's all I need! I can see the headlines now, Womanizer Extraordinaire Attempts Parenting 101."

"A female is a female is a female."

Mick tapped his fingers on the table. "Delilah would have something to say about that sentiment."

Josh grinned. "I know. She loves to give me hell."

"Girls start this puberty stuff earlier than guys, as early as eleven or twelve," Zack pointed out. He was amused despite himself, at the picture of Josh sorting through adolescent underwear. It was a far cry from lingerie, which admittedly, Josh knew a lot about. He bought enough of it for his girlfriends.

"I could handle it." Josh looked thoughtful, then grinned. "Hell, it might even be fun. I do enjoy shopping you know."

Zack did know. Every Christmas and every birthday, Josh took Dani shopping. They'd make a whole day of it, and Josh would spoil her with gifts and a movie and the amusement park. It was surprising, given Josh presented the world with only his preference for bachelorhood, yet Zack trusted him completely with his daughter.

In many ways, both Josh and Mick were pseudo-daddies, picking up the slack whenever Zack ran short on time. And they did a great job. They'd helped him get through the loss of his wife, and helped even more in the transition from grief to thankfulness, because despite losing his wife, he still had Dani, and that was a lot, more than he'd ever asked of life.

Zack had inadvertently wandered down a maudlin path, so he changed the subject while dealing out the cards. "Mick, did Josh tell you his station is making a charity calendar?"

"What's this?" Mick asked.

Josh picked up his hand, rearranged the cards a few times,

then said, "Some pushy promotions broad is organizing the whole thing. She wants a bunch of the men to pose in some cheesy way to go on the calendar, then they'll sell it and the proceeds will benefit the burn center."

"Pushy promotions broad," Mick repeated slowly, as if savoring the words. "Does this mean she had the audacity to exclude you from modeling?"

"I never gave her the chance. Anyone who was interested was supposed to call her to set up an appointment." He peered over his cards at Mick and Zack. "To get ogled, no doubt. Can you believe that?"

Frowning, Zack asked, "Have you met her?"

"I don't need to. I heard all about her from a friend at a different station. She's a rich daddy's girl who plays at this charity stuff out of boredom."

Mick and Zack shared a look. Mick laid his cards facedown and crossed his arms on the table. "Since when do you care about a woman's character?"

"Yeah," Zack said. "I thought it was the size of her bra cups that attracted you."

Josh suddenly looked harassed and annoyed, not that Zack minded after what he'd just been through. About time someone else took a turn on the hot seat.

"She's supposedly really beautiful, okay? And I've had it with women like that. I want someone more like Delilah."

Mick choked and his face turned red.

"Oh for God's sake." Josh quickly got out of Mick's reach and explained, "I wasn't—not for a second—saying Delilah's not beautiful! She is. Flat-out gorgeous."

Mick stood, looking far from placated.

"But she doesn't go in for all the props. When was the last time Del painted her nails or colored her hair? Never, right?

She's genuine. Well, that's the type of woman I want." He waved a hand toward the window. "Wynn what's-her-name would do, too. I want a natural woman, not a glamour doll who thinks she can crook her little finger and a guy will come running."

Mick subsided, but he looked far from appeased.

Zack shook his head. "Mick, you're going to have to get a handle on these jealous tendencies of yours. You know Josh won't poach."

"As if it'd do him any good to try!"

Zack sighed, but it turned into a laugh. "I wasn't suggesting it would. And seeing as you know that, why do you let his every comment rile you? You know he doesn't mean anything by it. It's just how he is."

Mick grumbled, "That wasn't your sentiment when he was trying to seduce Wynn."

It was Josh's turn to choke. "I wasn't trying to seduce the woman! Hell, all I did was hold her hand."

"You're both nuts," Zack concluded out loud. "Let's forget Wynn and the calendar and women in general. Mick, you can go on pining for your wife since I know you can't help it." He grinned. "Now, let's play cards."

Three hours later Zack was ready to call it a night. His neck was still stiff and his mind refused to pay attention to his hand, so he'd lost more than he'd won. Mick, too, was yawning, and mumbling that Delilah had likely finished writing for the night. Josh, the only one to look fresh, decided to call a woman from Zack's house and made plans to visit her that night.

Mick and Zack both shook their heads.

The night was cool and crisp and black as pitch when Zack waved goodbye from the doorway. He stood there until the headlights had disappeared out of the driveway, then he locked the door and tidied the kitchen.

On his way through the house, he picked up toys and drawings and a lone frilly sock peeking out from beneath a chair. He checked all the locks and headed upstairs.

Dani slept peacefully, her small body barely visible beneath the sheet. Zack smiled and pulled her door closed.

On his way to his own room he stripped off his shirt and stretched his aching arm and shoulder muscles. He kicked his shoes into the closet, then sat on the edge of the bed to remove his socks. After he turned out the light, he went to the window, breathing in the night air as he unzipped his slacks.

And from there, in a shaft of moonlight, reclining in the damn hammock like a sexual offering, he saw Wynn. For a single heartbeat lust raged through him, making his blood churn and his imagination grind.

Then a clearer picture formed; she looked to be sound asleep, which nearly made his mind explode with incredulity. She was a single woman, alone, in a new neighborhood, and she was stupid enough to pass out asleep outside, unprotected.

Jaw locked, Zack left his room with a stomping stride and iron determination. He'd known the moment he saw her that she was going to be nothing but trouble, both to his sanity and his libido.

FIVE

THE WELL-TRIMMED GRASS was wet and slippery beneath his bare feet, and a gentle evening breeze stirred his hair. His temper remained hot; it rose in degrees as he closed in on her.

Wynn didn't so much as move an eyelash when he stood directly over her lush, limp body. She had one arm above her head, palm up, her fingers slightly curled. The other drooped over the side of the hammock, almost touching the ground. Those mile-long legs of hers were crossed at the ankle, her feet bare.

She'd changed clothes.

Zack surveyed her, at his leisure. Without those piercing hazel eyes watching him or her sharp tongue challenging him, he felt steady, more in control, free to look his fill.

The halter and shorts were gone, replaced by a long, loose white nightshirt that almost reached her knees. Or at least he thought it was a nightshirt—until he read the front. Lane's

Gym—Workout For A Better Body. Obviously an advertisement for her brother's gym.

Clouds drifted across the moon, darkening the sky so that only the faint light from her porch illuminated her. Her lashes looked feathery in the dark shadows, her mouth very, very soft.

The scent of shampoo and lotion rose from her warm body to mingle with the damp night scents.

Zack felt himself reacting to the sight of her, and it angered him. "Wynn."

She didn't move.

He didn't want to touch her. "Damn it, Wynn, wake up."

Her lashes stirred and a soft sound escaped her slightly parted lips, causing his abdomen to clench, his pulse to race. Then she resettled herself with a husky groan.

Zack's eyes flared. His stomach knotted with carnal awareness. He reached down and caught her shoulder for a brisk shake. "Damn it to hell, Wynn, will you get your ass awake before I—oompf!"

One moment he'd been indulging his temper and the next he found himself flat on his back in the dew-covered grass, the wind knocked out of him and Wynn's knee in his chest. Her fist was drawn back, ready to clout him.

Zack reacted as suddenly as she had, grabbing her legs and holding on as he flipped them both, putting her flat out beneath him. "What the hell is *wrong* with you?"

Both her knees came up to shove in his ribs and he groaned. Taking advantage, she pushed him facedown to the side and crowded in close to his back. Her elbow locked around his throat. He could hear her frantic breaths directly in his ear. "Just *what* did you think you were—"

Swallowing down a roar of anger, Zack reached back, caught her by the head, and flipped her over his shoulder.

Her grunt was much louder than his and she wheezed, trying to catch her breath. She held still, not moving, just staring up as if to see if she'd broken anything.

Zack took immediate advantage, and this time when he covered her he did so completely. He held her wrists high over her head and pinned her legs with his, not about to risk his poor body again. Her knees had caught him so hard it felt like she'd broken his ribs. He'd always known her legs would be strong, but...

When she started to wiggle he squeezed her so tight she gasped. "What," he asked through his teeth, "the hell is the matter with you?"

He hadn't meant to yell, but never in his life had a woman attacked him physically. And absolutely *never* had he thought to attack a woman! Thank God there weren't many women like her.

When Wynn didn't answer, he leaned closer to try to see her face, now afraid that he'd hurt her.

She spoke barely above a whisper. "I didn't know it was you."

Zack grunted. So she'd thought she was defending herself? He was far from appeased. If she hadn't fallen asleep outside, it wouldn't have been an issue.

"Do you realize," she continued, "that I'm letting you do this?"

Disbelieving her gall, Zack reared back. "*Letting* me?"

Her head moved in a slight nod. "I could have bitten your face just seconds ago. Even your jugular."

"Of all the—"

"Even now," she taunted, "if I wasn't afraid of hurting you, I could toss you."

In that instant Zack became aware of her long lean body

beneath him, the cushion of her plump breasts, the giving dip of her wide pelvis, the strong, sleek thighs... He had hold of her wrists—not delicate wrists, but large-boned for a woman—and he lifted them above her head, keeping her in a submissive position.

So he could control her.

Oh yeah, his body liked that a lot. Too damn much. He had no doubt she'd already noticed his hard-on, being as it was pressed rigidly into her soft abdomen. Well too bad. Zack leaned closer again so he could see her face. He looked at her lush mouth, open now as she struggled for breath, and then to her incredible hazel eyes. Damn she had sexy eyes. In nothing more than scant moonlight, they were the eyes of a wolf, and they stirred him. "Try it," he offered, and waited with his own breath held.

"Oh, no." She stared at his mouth, and he felt her attention like a hot lick. "I don't want to hurt you—now that I know it's you."

Without meaning to, Zack pressed into her. Only the thin cotton of her nightshirt and his slacks separated them from entry. He closed his eyes, tipped his head back and moved against her rhythmically.

The alignment of their bodies was perfect, chest to breasts, groin to groin. He could kiss her and ride her at the same time, and never miss a single deep stroke. That realization made his muscles ripple.

Her nipples had puckered and he felt them rasping against his bare chest. She shifted her thighs, maybe trying to accommodate him, but he refused to take any chances. Her arms hung limp in his grip, in no way fighting his hold. Still he secured her, stretching her out a bit more, aware of her strength, and her yielding.

He felt on fire. *"Wynn…"*

She lifted her head, as brazen as ever, and that was all it took. Zack had never been a man controlled by lust, never been a man to experience all that much lust.

But this…what else could it be called? Mere lust didn't seem adequate for the bombardment of sensations on his senses. He felt her everywhere, on his body, in his lungs, in his head and his heart.

She licked his mouth, making a sound of excitement and acceptance and hunger. He caught her tongue and drew it deep, then gave her his own. Their heavy breathing broke the quiet of the night, mingling with the faint sounds of crickets and rustling leaves. He switched both her wrists into one of his and brought his hand down to wedge between their bodies, cuddling her breast.

In reaction to his touch, her hips lifted so strongly she supported his weight off the ground for a suspended moment of time. It took one rough thrust for Zack to crush her down again.

He kissed his way to her throat and heard her ragged whisper. "Zack… Let me go."

"No." He thumbed her nipple, stroking, teasing.

A raw groan and a burst of movement later, Wynn had him on his back again. The woman was forever taking him by surprise. Zack almost wanted to laugh.

Until her thighs straddled his and she became the aggressor. Her hands opened wide over his bare chest, she stroked him and moaned with the pleasure of it. She nuzzled at his throat, then bit before licking and sucking and making him crazed.

The open vee of her thighs cradled his erection, and made him strain for more. He caught her behind in his hands, relishing the resilient feel of her, her softness in contrast with her feminine strength. He explored her, sliding his fingers over the silken material of her panties, pressing inward to touch her from behind. He found her panties damp, her body incredibly hot.

Cradling her hips, Zack urged her into a rough, slow roll that simulated sex and brought him dangerously close to the edge.

He was ready to take her, more than ready to get the ridiculous man's shirt off her body and touch her everywhere, kiss her everywhere.

Only he didn't have protection with him. And...

Reality dropped on his head like a ton of bricks. He actually groaned aloud with his disappointment, with the awareness of his responsibilities.

They were acquaintances of only a day, and not even a full day at that.

They were outdoors, in the open, and if he'd seen her through his bedroom window, his daughter could see them both if she should wake up and look out. Granted, that wasn't likely to happen, not the way Dani slept, but he didn't take chances with his daughter, not ever.

They were on the wet ground, mindlessly entwined and it was so unlike him, so unlike what he wanted for himself as a responsible father and server of the community, he felt appalled and embarrassed and rightfully angry.

At Wynn.

He caught her wrists again and held her hands still to enable him to gain control of himself. "Wynn."

His tone of voice had no effect on her. She wiggled free and attacked his mouth, kissing him so thoroughly he almost forgot his resolve. He turned his head aside. "No."

"Yes," she insisted. She grabbed his ears and held him still. Then, "God, you're incredible. So hard and sexy and sweet."

Sweet? Zack rolled to the side, literally dumping her off him, but the second she was flat, he stood. His chest worked like a bellows and his brain cramped at the effort it took to resist her. When he turned to look at her, his damn knees almost gave out. Her shirt had hiked up and he could see her panties, could even see her navel.

He stared—until she held out her arms to him and the sight of her offering herself, wanting him, looked so good, so right, he couldn't stand it.

Jerking around, Zack said, "Get up."

He didn't watch to see if she did as he asked. He couldn't. Finally he heard a slight creak and turned to see her perched sideways on the hammock, her feet on the ground, her hands beside her hips, her gaze direct and waiting and unapologetic.

Zack drew a deep breath. "I'm sorry."

After a heavy beat of silence, she said, "Yeah, me, too." She smirked and shook her head.

That drew him up. "Sorry for what?"

Wynn pushed to her feet and faced him eye to eye. "At the moment, I'm pretty sorry for everything." She turned away. "Good night, Zack."

He was so stunned by the dim sight of her wet back, the cotton shirt clinging to her behind and upper thighs, that he almost let her get away. He shook himself. "Wait a minute!"

"No point in waiting. Believe me, I understand."

Zack caught her arm and whirled her around. In the next instant she was on tiptoes and huffing in his face.

"Don't think for a single second that you bested me, buddy!" She poked him in the chest, making him stagger back a step. "The second I realized it was you, I went half-go. Besides that, you caught me asleep and sluggish. Now I'm wide awake and you're done kissing and you're acting all nasty and hateful again, so do *not* try manhandling me."

Zack had at least a dozen questions for her, but what came out of his mouth was, "You actually think you could best me in strength?" He was so incredulous he barely knew what he said.

Wynn snorted. "I've trained all my life. I know exactly what I'm doing."

And she thought…what? That he was a marshmallow? She'd called him *sweet*. What the hell had she meant by that? Through his teeth, Zack heard himself say, "No way, lady. Not on your best day." Then he wanted to smack his own head for challenging a woman! *What was he thinking?*

With a look of utter disdain, she said, "You keep living that dream if it makes you happy, big boy." And again she turned to walk away.

"Wynn." Even to his own ears, her name sounded like a warning. But then it had been strained through his clenched teeth.

Arms spread, she whipped around to face him and demanded, *"What?"*

He was a reasonable sort, Zack reminded himself. He was logical and calm and a pacifist. He absolutely, under no circumstances, wrestled with women, not even big bold pushy ones.

One slow deep breath helped a little. The second breath pushed the red haze out of his vision so he could see her clearly, or as clearly as the night-dark sky allowed. "Why," he asked, sounding more like a sane man, "were you sleeping on the hammock?"

She looked at the hammock as if to verify which one he

meant. Then she shrugged. "I'd worked all day, I was hot and sweaty and after my shower I just wanted to rest my tired bones and get some fresh air. Only I nodded off. I didn't mean to fall asleep."

Zack clasped his hands behind his back to keep from reaching for her. Brows raised in inquiry, he said, "Do you, by any chance, know how risky that can be for a woman?"

"You mean with crazy neighbors lurking about ready to throw me on the ground and kiss me silly and paw me until I'm all excited and ready and then stop with no warning?" She gave him a smug, distinctly mean smile. "Yeah, I do now."

"I meant," he said, inching toward her, but watching her closely at the same time, "because of strangers who would do things to you without a second's hesitation. Men who would rape or murder or…"

"Rape and murder about covers it. No reason to go overboard."

"This is not a joke, damn it!"

She crossed her arms under her breasts and cocked one hip. It shouldn't have been a seductive pose, but damn, it made him sweat.

"Did I just say it was an accident, that I didn't mean to fall asleep? I thought I did, but given your attitude, I can't be sure."

Tension mounting, Zack flexed his shoulders and rolled his head on his neck. "It was irresponsible."

"Well, thank you, Mother, for your concern."

"Wynn, I know you're excited about your new house—"

"And my new neighbor? My new neighbor who likes to tease and lead women on, then pull away and act as if his finer sensibilities have been lacerated by my coarse and carnal behavior?"

Zack was again caught between wanting to shout with

anger, and the urge to laugh. From the moment he'd met her, Wynn Lane had been too outspoken and honest for her, or his, own good. He rubbed his neck and concentrated on not smiling. "I didn't mean to tease."

"Oh? You call what you did—given the fact you pulled up short—fulfillment?" She shook her head. "You poor, poor man. You're missing the best part."

"Look, Wynn, it was a mistake for us to do—" he gestured at the ground "—this. I don't know about you, but I'm not in the habit of indulging in one-night flings."

She didn't confirm or deny what her habits were, which only made him edgier. Little by little his neck and shoulder muscles tightened into a painful cramp. He'd strained something at work the night before, and arguing with Wynn only exacerbated things.

Her eyes narrowed and she strode toward him. "What's the matter with you? Did I hurt you?"

His hand fell away from his neck. "Of course not."

"Ha! You're in pain, I can tell."

He started to say *she* was the pain, but held it in. It was past time he listened to himself. They were neighbors, no refuting that fact. They needed to get along in some civil but distant and detached way.

With that decision made, he waited until she stopped directly in front of him, then explained, "I dealt with two pretty nasty emergencies last night. The first was a case of domestic violence." His tone sounded raw even to his own ears, but the emotional devastation of the night still lingered. "I took a woman in with two broken ribs and multiple contusions. The bastard who'd worked her over had gone to a bar. Luckily the cops caught up to him there."

Zack had to be grateful that the man had been gone when

he got there. He wasn't at all certain he could have contained himself otherwise.

Wynn, evidently sensing his turbulent emotions, reached out and smoothed her hand over his arm. It was a soothing touch, and it helped him to recall himself.

He shook off his lingering anger and reminded himself that the woman had pressed charges. That wasn't always the case, but luckily this particular woman had had enough. He'd left her in the hands of the social services.

"Then there was a car wreck. We had to cut the door away to get to the woman inside. She was in shock, covered in blood from a head wound, and getting her out wasn't easy, especially since she wasn't exactly a small woman."

"She was big like me?"

Zack's temper jumped a notch. "I could handle you easily without straining a thing."

She smirked.

"No, this woman was obese." Wynn remained quiet and waiting so he continued. "The reach was awkward, and I strained something in my neck and shoulders when I lifted her out."

"Hmmm. Sounds like you strained a trap. That happens a lot in clumsy lifts. Turn around."

He stalled. "What?"

"Trapezius muscle," she explained.

And Zack said, "I know what it is. I just didn't..."

Grabbing his upper arm, she forcibly turned him—something he allowed—and then began pressing her fingers into his neck, his shoulders, his spine. Zack groaned. Her touch had an electrifying effect that both soothed and excited.

"Right there?" she asked, her thumbs now working some hidden muscle that reacted by going limp.

"Yeah." And then, "You're good at this."

"I'm good at a lot of things."

His eyes shot open.

"Have you been using any moist heat?"

God, everything she said sounded sexual to his beleaguered brain. *Moist. Heat.* He was such a goner. "No," he croaked. "I haven't had a chance."

"Bull. You're a paramedic, you know better than to ignore injuries. If need be, you make time. Maybe instead of hanging out with your friends you should have soaked in your hot tub."

His brain took a leap from her suggestion, to a vivid fantasy of them both in the hot tub, steam rising and flesh wet… "I will later."

"When is later?"

Her persistence annoyed him. "Maybe after work tomorrow."

Her hands continued to massage and work his aching muscles. He felt like butter—like *aroused* butter.

"What hours do you work?"

That, at least, was a safe enough topic. "We're all on a rotating schedule. Ten-hour days, four days a week. My hours are usually eight to six. The three days off vary and are almost never grouped together, but at least that way everyone gets a weekend now and then. And there's always overtime, so my hours end up fifty or over more often than not."

Leaning around to see his face, Wynn asked, "Who watches Dani while you work?"

"There's a lady two blocks down, Eloise. She's a real sweetheart, in her early seventies, on a fixed income. Dani adores her, and vice versa. Dani thinks of it as her second home."

"Any friends her own age?"

He shrugged. "She goes to preschool two days a week, but Dani tells me most of the kids there are 'babies.'"

Wynn chuckled. "Yeah, I can see her thinking that. She's used to adult company, isn't she?"

"Too much so. I thought the preschool would help, and she does enjoy it. One of her classmates lives in the neighborhood and she's had Dani over for birthday parties and special outings and things like that."

"Mmm. Sounds like fun for her." Hands splayed wide, Wynn worked her way down Zack's back, over his lats, then his obliques. It was all he could do to remain standing.

Zack didn't mean to, but he felt so relaxed, so boneless from her massage, he heard himself confiding before he could censor himself. "She has a hard time fitting in with other girls."

"Oh?"

Zack closed his eyes, but now he had no choice except to explain. "She's...not into the same things as other little girls her age. The whole idea of playing dress-up revolts her, and she's outraged by the idea of frilly dresses and tights." He grinned, remembering the last time Dani had worn a dress. It had been for Mick and Del's wedding, and she'd only agreed because Del had helped her pick it out, and Del wasn't into lace and frills, either.

"I was the same when I was a little girl," Wynn said.

Zack teased, "You mean you were little once?"

Her thumbs pressed deep enough to make him jerk in pain. "Hey, ouch! All right, I was just teasing."

"I wasn't born an oaf, you know."

For the briefest moment Zack wondered if he'd hurt her feelings, then decided the massage must have softened his brain as well as his muscles. Wynn wasn't the type of woman who indulged fragile feelings.

On the tail of that realization came another, more startling one. Good God, was there a chance his daughter would grow up to be like Wynn? Wrestling in her yard, argumentative and loud and far too bold? The very idea made him shudder. He *had* to find a wife, a nice delicate feminine wife who adored Dani and could, with patience and a calm quiet demeanor, guide her into being a young lady.

"If you work fifty hours," Wynn said, breaking into his thoughts, "I imagine some of those nights it's pretty late when you get home."

"True."

"Do you bring Dani home?"

"Of course." He started to look at her, but she stilled him by working a particularly achy knot in his right deltoid. Damn, but she had wonderful fingers. "I was blessed with a real slughead for a daughter," he told her around a heartfelt groan. "It takes a lot to wake her before she's ready to wake. I just bundle her up and bring her home and tuck her into her own bed."

"If Eloise is in her seventies, how much longer do you think she can continue to baby-sit?"

"I've considered that," he murmured, his reserve now as limp as his muscles. "I'm thinking of leaving fieldwork."

"Yeah? To do what?" Her fingers found just the right amount of pressure, and he groaned low before he could work up the energy to answer. "Maybe be a supervisor," he said, "or an operations manager. Or maybe I'll instruct. I think I'd like that."

Wynn made a sound of interest, and her hands moved lower, over his gluteus medius, then his gluteus maximus…

Damn, but her fingers were magic…marvelous…*intimate!*

Zack jerked around to face her. "You're seducing me!"

She tried for an innocent expression and failed. "Naw, just copping a feel of your nice tight buns."

He sputtered, both outraged and stupidly complimented, and, if he was honest, vaguely turned on. Okay, more than vaguely. He felt mellow and ready. Primed even.

She had the gall to laugh in his face, then pat his chest. "Relax, Zack, your virtue is safe with me. And you do feel better now, right?"

He flexed, rolled his shoulders in experimentation; she was right, damn her. He gave a reluctant nod.

"Good." She patted him again, this time ending with a caress of his pecs. "If you tighten up again, come see me."

He was tight already, just not where she meant.

"It probably wouldn't hurt to use a little ultrasound on the affected muscles, and I can do that at the gym."

"I'll be fine," he croaked.

She rolled her eyes. "You're a regular superhero, aren't you? Impervious to the needs of your body, both sexual and physical?"

Being pushy probably came naturally to her. She'd likely been born making demands and causing conflicts. "I'm trying to do what's right for both of us and you know it. We're neighbors. Anything beyond a friendly association would be too difficult."

She gave a heavy sigh, saying, "Whatever," and turned to leave.

"I hope you understand," Zack called out, watching her as she walked into the light from her back porch. His body felt relaxed but zinging with life, too. An odd mix. A *carnal* mix.

She sent him an airy wave without looking back. A second later she went through the door and it closed with a click that echoed around the empty yards.

Damn irritating woman.

He'd made the right decision, despite his still raging hard-on. But then why did he feel so pissed off with himself? Why did he hate the right decision?

An upstairs light came on in her house, and through an open window Zack heard her begin to whistle again. She was a woman without a care, while he still stood there in the yard churning with a riot of emotions and physical needs. He stared at her window hard, willing her to move into view, but then the light went out and he knew she had gone to bed.

From now on, he'd just have to be very careful to avoid her. Given his hours, that shouldn't be too hard to do.

Wynn watched through her dark bedroom window as Zack tipped back his head and stared up at the moon. He looked so rigid, every line of his body denoting frustration, that she half expected him to howl, but all he did was turn on his heel and head back to his own house.

Her massage had been a waste, she could see that now; the man was determined to be tense. She sighed.

What a twist of fate, she thought, her heart sinking a little at the sight of his retreating back. Her hands were still tingling from touching him, from feeling all those smooth hard muscles and hot skin and vibrating tension. She huffed. The first man who really pushed her buttons, who made her feel like gelatin on the inside and made her breathe too fast just being near, and he was a blasted prude.

Her thought process crashed there and she was forced to face the possibility that he wasn't a prude at all. A man as big and sexy and intelligent and responsible as Zack was more likely suffering disinterest than moral restrictions.

Why would he be interested in *her*?

She'd done nothing but make a fool of herself since meeting him, and her naturally forceful personality had been in rare, suffocating form. But he brought out the extremes in her, and half the time she didn't even know what she was going to do until she did it.

She closed her eyes on a wave of remorse and embarrassment. God, she'd accosted him at every turn, provoked him and even rolled on the grass with him. She'd called him names and insulted him, and here she was, wishing he'd want her just a little?

Wynn shook her head. She was a complete and utter dolt.

She left the window and moved blindly toward the hall. She needed another shower—this one preferably ice-cold to chase away the lingering hunger. She knew she wouldn't sleep tonight, not after feeling him atop her, not after inhaling his aroused scent.

She had to get herself together, and she had to give the man some space. Rushing him was not the best tactic. No, Zack was a subtle man, when he wasn't challenging her. He was a father, and his sensitivity toward his daughter only made him more attractive. He was the hero Dani had described him as being, and by far the most appealing male Wynn had ever met.

Zack needed time to get used to her, to get to know her.

She'd *ease* her way in, she'd be charming and sweet and polite…because knocking down his defenses sure didn't seem to be working.

SIX

ZACK SAW HER every damn day. He woke up in the morning and she was outside working in the yard or cleaning her driveway or chatting with the other neighbors.

He got home from work and she'd just be coming in or going out.

He ran into her at the grocery store and once while they were both taking out their garbage. Dani chatted her up every time, like she was a long-lost and valuable friend. And Wynn was forever sweet and attentive—to Dani.

It irked him, especially since she lounged in that hammock every damn night. Before bed, he'd find himself standing at his window, watching for her like a lost soul. And sure enough, she'd come traipsing out, her long legs bare and her stride sure to the point of being almost mannish. Not that anyone would ever mistake Wynn Lane for a man. She was too curvy, too soft and…she smelled too good to be male.

His whole body would go taut watching her as she relaxed

back in that hammock and stretched out the length of her sexy body. Damn if he didn't get aroused every time.

Sometimes she read until the sun went down. Sometimes she just swayed, music feeding into her ears through a set of headphones. She sometimes dozed and she sometimes whistled, but not once had she fallen into a sound sleep again.

He almost wished she would, so he'd have a legitimate excuse to seek her out, to touch her.

She no longer intruded. In fact, she seemed to have lost interest in him. Always she'd be cordial, give a wave or a friendly hello, and then she'd move on. She treated him the same as she did the other neighbors, and he didn't like it.

He'd never known himself to be such a fickle bastard before. But he missed her. He barely knew her and already he'd grown accustomed to her.

As had Dani.

Even now his daughter sat on the kitchen door stoop, wistfully staring at Wynn's house, waiting for her to appear. Dani missed her. She wasn't at all appeased by the short friendly chats or casual waves, and that wasn't something Zack had counted on.

It tore his heart out.

"Dani," he called, "come on in and eat your sandwich."

Two seconds later Dani peered in the door. "I'm gonna eat it out here."

Normally Zack would have been fine with that, but he didn't want his daughter turning melancholy. "Dani..."

"Wynn'll need a sandwich, too."

Zack went still and a strange emotion, one he refused to study too closely, swirled through him. "Is she out there?"

"She's with a bunch of big men."

Before his brain and feet could make a connection, Zack

found himself at the door looking out. Sure enough, there was Wynn, surrounded by bodybuilders—three of them. All massive, all handsome.

All fawning over her.

He scowled, thinking to duck back inside before she or her cursed boyfriends spotted him.

His traitorous daughter did him in once again.

Dani took two bounding steps down the stoop to the lawn and waved her arms like a windmill. *"Hey, Wynn!"*

Wynn looked up and her seven-watt smile shone brightly. She patted one of the guys on the chest, swatted at another's immense back and started in Dani's direction. Zack couldn't deny the pounding of his heart. It had been a week since he'd really talked to her, really been close to her. Deny it all he liked, he'd missed her. Maybe even more than his daughter had.

Dani shocked him by rushing to Wynn for a hug.

Wynn didn't shock him a bit when she bent down and scooped Dani high, tossing her in the air and then hugging her close. "What have you been up to, munchkin?"

"You can eat peanut butter and jelly with me!"

Wynn glanced at Zack, saw the paper plate with the neatly sliced sandwich that he held in his hand, and said, "I *love* peanut butter and jelly. You don't mind sharing?"

"Nope."

When Wynn sat Dani down, she took her hand and stood staring at Zack. He cleared his throat. "How've you been, Wynn?"

"Busy. My folks are moving in tomorrow. I had to get everything put away and organized so they'd have a place to store their stuff. This moving on top of my moving is exhausting."

She snagged the sandwich, handed half to Dani and took a big bite of the other half. "Mmmm. Delicious."

Zack ignored that to ask, "Who are your guests?"

She gave a negligent shrug. "Guys from the gym. They wanted to see my new house and visit. They're also going to help me set up my patio furniture. I bought a picnic table with an umbrella and a glider and chairs and tables. I've got some plants, too. I can't wait to see it all together. The delivery truck should be here soon."

"It takes three giants to set up lawn furniture?"

Her eyes sparkled at the acrimony in his tone. Hell, he'd sounded almost…jealous.

Enunciating each word carefully she said, "They wanted to see my new house, too." Then she added, "You do have a problem listening to me, don't you? Or rather, you only hear certain selective parts."

Dani said, "I'll help, too."

"I dunno." Wynn pretended to study her. "I need strong laborers. Let's see your muscle."

Dani immediately flexed her skinny arm. She tucked in her chin and puffed out her cheeks and ground her teeth, with no visible effect.

Still, Wynn made approving sounds and squeezed the non-existent muscle. "Wow. All right, I think you're strong enough." She glanced at Zack. "That is, if your dad doesn't mind."

"He don't mind."

"Dani." She had jelly on her upper lip and a pleading look in her big blue eyes. He meant to reprimand her further, but she looked so cute…

"Please," Dani begged in her most hopeful tone.

Wynn chuckled at her theatrics, then leaned toward Zack,

her hands clasped together now that she'd finished her half of the sandwich. Mimicking his daughter to a tee, she pleaded. "Pretty please, Zack. C'mon. We'll be careful. And I promise to watch her real close."

Zack eyed Wynn. She wore a baggy gray T-shirt today with denim cutoffs. She was barefoot, her frizzy flyaway hair in a ponytail on the very top of her head resembling a frazzled water fountain.

In a different way, a funny way, she was the most appealing woman he'd ever seen.

He gave up without a grumble and denied, even to himself, that he was using his daughter's wishes as an excuse. Dani wanted to be with her, so he'd allow it. But as her father it was necessary that he be there. That sounded plenty logical to him. "All right. But I'll help, too."

Wynn drew back. "You don't have to do that."

"I go where my daughter goes," he told her, letting her assume he didn't entirely trust her or her friends. She scowled in reaction, narrowing her beautiful eyes until they glittered golden with ire. He just grinned at her. Provoking her was way too easy.

"Fine." Then she said, "But you have to pass the muscle test, too."

"Don't be ridiculous."

"Hey, you're the one insisting. And fair's fair. Dani took the test."

Dani bounced. "Show her your muscles, Dad!"

"Yeah, show me, Dad," Wynn prodded, and Zack had the horrible suspicion that his neck had turned red.

Through his teeth, he said, "I promise, I'm strong enough."

Wynn shook her head. "Not good enough. I can see the muscles on my friends, and Dani proved herself." Her eyebrows lifted and her smile turned smug. "Now show me your stuff."

Zack knew he was in good shape. He had to attend daily workouts as part of his regimen for the station. He ate healthy food and his job was demanding, both mentally and physically.

But he wasn't in the habit of flaunting himself.

Wynn shoved his short sleeve up over his shoulder and said softly, "I promise this won't hurt a bit." She caught his wrist, locked her eyes with his, bent his arm at the elbow, and said, "Now *flex*."

Tightening his jaw in annoyance, Zack dutifully flexed. His biceps bulged. His arms weren't enormous like the body builders', but still plenty defined and impressive if he did say so himself.

Wynn's gaze softened and her eyes darkened. The hand holding his trembled. "Nice," she murmured in a voice that was far too intimate. "You just might do."

Dani went on tiptoe to point at Zack's upper arm. "There's where Dad got shot."

"Shot?"

Wynn started to look more closely, but Zack pulled away and jerked down his sleeve.

In that instant the delivery truck arrived and began backing into Wynn's driveway. After a long look at Zack, which promised the topic was far from finished, she turned to face the men who were milling around her yard. They appeared to be checking out every blade of grass and especially the hammock. To Zack, they looked like concrete blocks with legs.

"The truck is here," Wynn called out to them. "The payment is in on my hall table. Will one of you go grab it and sign for the stuff? I'll be there in just a minute."

Almost as an entity, they nodded agreement and began a

pilgrimage to the front of the house. Wynn turned back to Zack. "Is there a swallow of milk to go with the sandwich? I swear that peanut butter is hung up right about here." She pointed between her breasts, well hidden beneath the gray cotton shirt, but Zack still went mute.

Luckily, his daughter played the perfect hostess. "We always have milk. Come on." She took Wynn's hand and led her into the kitchen. Zack was forced to follow.

"You need to regulate your eating habits better," he grumbled.

She slanted him a look as he took a tall glass from the cabinet. "Do I look malnourished? Vitamin deficient?"

Since she was tall and strong and healthy, Zack ignored that question. He filled the glass to the top and handed it to her. "And I can't believe you're letting those men sign for your belongings. Or go through your house unchaperoned."

She'd already guzzled down half the milk when his words registered. With the glass tilted to her mouth, her gaze captured his and she blinked. Very slowly she lowered the empty glass and set it aside. She licked her lips. Two seconds passed before she said, "Marc and Clint and Bo are good friends. And they can be trusted."

Dani hovered near the door, watching the men. "They sure are big."

With an evil smile, Zack said, "Wynn evidently likes them that way."

Her smile was no less taunting as she leaned close and breathed into his ear, "But I wasn't in my backyard, on the ground, making out with any of *them*. Ever." Then she straightened and asked, "How'd you get shot?"

"By bein' a hero," Dani said, still with her head out the door.

Wynn turned to Zack. "Gunfire?"

How she managed to pack so much horror into one small word was beyond him. She acted as though the idea was ludicrous, as if he wasn't man enough… Deciding to nip that thought, and this conversation in the bud, Zack grabbed her arm and put his hand on his daughter's narrow back, urging them both forward. "If we're going to help we better get to it. No more time for gabbing."

Dani skipped ahead. "What should I do?"

"I have some new baby plants that need extra special care until I get them in the ground," Wynn told her. "You can move them from the back porch under the overhang to the yard so the men can set up the furniture without trampling them. I trust you more than I do all these big lugs."

Dani took off like a shot and Zack yelled, "Be very careful, Dani, and don't get in anyone's way."

Dani was no sooner out of hearing when Wynn asked again, "How'd you get shot?"

"It's nothing."

"Ohhh," she cooed in a dramatic voice, "I just love a humble martyr." She batted her eyes at him, laughed, then said, "No really. What happened?"

"You are such a pushy woman."

She stopped, which caused him to stop since he still had hold of her arm. Realizing that, he let her go and propped his fists on his hips.

"What?" he asked, when she continued to look at him.

For the first time that he could remember, she actually looked sheepish. "I didn't mean to be pushy," she muttered, and her face heated. She didn't blush well, Zack decided, seeing her entire face, neck and even her ears turn pink.

"It's a…well, a bad habit I guess. Sorry." She started to say more, shook her head, and stepped around him. Zack caught her arm again.

"Wynn."

She stopped, but rather than face him she looked down at her feet.

Zack stared at the back of her head where frazzled strands stood out on end, having escaped the band she'd used to contain her hair. The curls resting against her nape actually looked kind of cute, maybe even a little sexy. She had an elegant neck and broad, sexy shoulders...

Suddenly Zack felt a searing scrutiny.

He looked up and caught all three of the hulks watching him. One man had a large wrought-iron chair held aloft in his arms, which he continued to hold with seemingly no effort though the thing looked awkward and heavy.

The other two had a cumbersome settee between them, with yet another chair balanced in the middle of it. They, too, seemed more than comfortable with their burden.

Zack tugged on Wynn's arm. "That's some massive furniture you bought."

She shrugged, still staring at her feet. "I'm a big girl. I need big furniture to be comfortable."

"True. Those are also big, apparently protective guys you've got hauling it."

Wynn caught his meaning and looked up. Whatever dejection she'd been feeling fell away to be replaced by her natural arrogance. "Oh, for goodness' sake. Are you three going to stand there all day?"

One of the men, an artificially tanned behemoth, smirked. "Only until we see that you're all right."

Sounding incredibly surprised, Wynn asked, "You're worried about *Zack*?" And to compound that insult, she hitched her thumb over her shoulder toward him, then chortled. "Don't be silly."

One of the men holding the settee bared his teeth in what might have been loosely termed a smile. "Only Wynn would call us silly," he said to Zack, then added, "I'm Bo. A…friend."

The other two grinned at that, which made Wynn bristle, and Zack scowl. Just what the hell did Bo mean? Was it an inside joke? Did Wynn and Bo have some sort of understanding? Were they involved?

The guy on the other end of the settee said, "Bo, Wynn is going to get you for that," and then to Zack, "I'm Clint and that over there is Marc."

Zack nodded. "I'm her neighbor, Zack Grange."

"Yeah right." They all chortled again, looking between Wynn and Zack. "Just a neighbor."

Zack clenched his teeth. "The little one running around is my daughter, Dani."

Bo winked. "She's a sweetheart. And hey, Wynn just loves kids."

Wynn cast a quick look at Zack, then under her breath said, "You guys are in for it."

They pretended great fear, gasping and sharing worried glances—ludicrous considering their impressive sizes. Growling, Wynn took a threatening step forward and they quickly dispersed, rushing to the patio to put the furniture down.

Zack pulled her around to face him. She looked braced for his anger, until he asked, "Is Bo a boyfriend?"

Her eyes widened and she choked on a laugh before saying, "No! Of course not."

"Then what was all that inside snickering and shared looks?"

She waved that away. "Bo flirts with all women, sort of like your friend Josh. He's got about a dozen girlfriends and yes, he pretends to want to add me to the list, but it's all just in fun. I'm not an idiot and he knows it."

That brought up another issue that nettled, and Zack said, "You acted plenty interested with Josh."

"Ha! He's gorgeous and he took me by surprise. I'm used to Bo being outrageous, but not other guys. That's all." She looked Zack over and asked, "What about you? Any steady girlfriends?"

"No." But not for lack of trying on his part. He just hadn't met a woman yet who was right for him and Dani, and he saw no reason to get involved in a *wrong* relationship.

Except that with Wynn…he was tempted.

She looked skeptical, but said only, "You don't have to worry about those three. They're just a little overprotective, but now that I've assured them you're harmless, they'll let it go."

"Harmless?" He stepped closer to her, until they almost bumped noses. "One of these days I'm going to make you eat all these insults."

Her eyes brightened and filled with fascination. "Is that right? How?"

"A number of ideas are zinging through my head."

In the vein of being helpful, she suggested, "We could wrestle again. Next time you *might* win."

Damned irritating, irrational… He let her go and stalked away. He heard her satisfied snicker before she suddenly went quiet, groaned, and then began tromping after him.

And here he'd actually thought he'd missed her. Ha! He couldn't be that stupid.

But he *was* smiling.

The patio began to look just as Wynn had pictured it. She'd had the furniture rearranged three times, despite all the guys grumbling, but now everything worked. Including the beautiful new gas grill, which Zack had suggested she move away from the window, to keep smoke from coming into the house.

About half an hour ago at the hottest part of the afternoon, Zack had removed his shirt. His back and shoulders glistened with sweat, as did the straight, light-brown hair clinging to his nape and temples. His blue eyes looked even bluer in the bright sunshine, and the flex of his lean, athletic muscles made Wynn more aware of him than she'd ever been of any man.

She saw Zack lift his head and look around for Dani. He was good at doing that, at always being aware of his daughter and what she was up to. Wynn couldn't imagine a more attentive or caring parent.

Zack shaded his eyes until he located Dani sitting in the grass beneath a large tree. She was hunting for four-leaf clovers with Clint, who appeared suitably impressed with her skills while he drank an ice-cold cola.

Zack smiled, his face lit with so much love and pride, Wynn thought her heart might burst.

She needed to be with him again.

A week had gone by where she'd done her best to give him time and space, but she didn't think she could take it anymore.

Bo walked up and thwacked her on the behind. "I need sustenance after all my toils. You got any lunch meat?"

A quick peek at Zack showed his attention had shifted and he now had that scowling, disapproving look on his handsome face again. Resisting the urge to rub her stinging behind, Wynn huffed. It wasn't exactly her fault that her brother's friends were all too familiar. "I thought I'd order a pizza."

"No need, darlin'," Marc told her. "We can't stay that long. But a sandwich would hit the spot."

She flapped her hand toward the kitchen. "There's all kinds of lunch meat and fixings in the fridge. Go help yourself."

Bo thwacked her again, almost knocking her off her feet with the sharp swat. She was just irascible enough to give him a reciprocal punch to the shoulder, which he most likely didn't even feel despite his cringing facade of pain.

Clint called out, "Fix me one, too!" and Marc nodded as he went inside with Bo.

Wynn walked to the other end of the patio and dropped down into her settee. The forest-green and cream striped cushions were soft and plush and she smoothed her hand over them with deep satisfaction. This was hers, all of it, the house, the tree-shaded yard, the hammock and…her neighbor. All hers.

She caught Zack watching her and she smiled. "It looks good, doesn't it?"

Zack appeared to be so annoyed she wasn't at all sure he'd answer. Then he sat down beside her. "It's very nice. You have good taste."

As he spoke, he stared out at the yard toward his daughter, giving Wynn his profile. She sighed, knowing his thoughts when he hadn't shared them. "Bo is just…Bo. I've known him almost as long as I've known Conan. They went through school together and stuff. He really doesn't—"

"Show any hesitation at touching your behind? Yeah, I noticed. I also noticed that you don't seem to mind."

Her lips tightened as her temper rose. "He treats me like a kid sister most of the time."

"Uh-huh." Zack turned to face her, his expression set. "I don't know why I'm even surprised, considering…" He made a disgusted sound and turned away again.

Her heart thumped hard and her stomach roiled. "Considering what?" When he didn't answer, she said, "Zack, don't you dare be a hypocrite. I wasn't the only one out there that night. We both got carried away."

He ran a hand through his hair. "I've never in my life done anything like that, so it had to be because of you."

He said that so casually, casting the blame without hesitation, that she wanted to throttle him. "*You* snuck up on *me* that night!"

"I did not sneak," he grumbled.

"Ha! I was asleep."

"Yeah, and what woman does *that?*" He jerked around to face her, looking angry and befuddled and very much like an attentive male. "What woman sleeps out in her backyard at night, exposed?"

"I wasn't *exposed,* you ass. You make it sound like I was naked or something." She shook her head, realized she'd just insulted him again, and wanted to bite off her tongue. She drew a breath and tried to sound reasonable. "Zack, I was just—"

He didn't let her finish. "I don't get carried away like that. Ever."

To Wynn, he still looked accusing, and all she could think to say was, "You did that night."

His eyes narrowed, then his gaze flicked over her. "Yeah. Bad judgement on my part."

Wynn sucked in a breath. *Damn, that hurt.* She wasn't sure if she wanted to punch him or cry. She wasn't much of a crier and seldom indulged, but now she felt dangerously close to giving in to tears. Her bottom lip even quivered before she caught it between her teeth.

For a brief moment, Zack looked guilty. "Look, Wynn, it's really none of my business what you do."

"I want it to be your business," she admitted softly.

His spine stiffened—and Bo shoved a sandwich into his face. "I figured you had to be hungry, too."

Zack studied Wynn a second longer, then warily looked up at Bo. "Thanks."

"No problem. 'A friend of Wynn's,' and all that." Bo pursed his lips and continued to glare down at Zack. "You *are* a friend, right?"

Wynn quickly stood and placed herself between the two men. "Back off, Bo. I mean it."

In the next instant, she yelped as she found herself yanked back down onto the soft settee. Zack had grabbed the waistband of her shorts and literally jerked her off her feet. She sat gawking at him while he stood and met Bo eye to eye. Zack wasn't as bulky as the bodybuilders, but he was all lean hard muscle.

"Actually," Zack said, "I'm more of an acquaintance at this stage."

"A friendly acquaintance?"

"You got reason to think otherwise?"

The male posturing had Wynn on edge. She would definitely strangle Bo later, and what in the world was wrong with Zack? She thought him to be a sweet, considerate, passive man. Not one to indulge in games of male one-upmanship. Yet he'd brought on as much attitude as Bo, and that was saying a lot.

A new voice intruded, full of good humor and mocking concern. "Making yourself the center of attention again, Zack?"

Wynn twisted in her seat, and found herself almost face-to-belt buckle with Josh, who stood just at the end of the patio, right behind the settee. He wore tight faded jeans and a white T-shirt that read: Firefighters Take The Heat.

Zack, too, turned to face him. "What are you doing here?"

Josh smiled and leaned down, bracing his arms on the settee back, looming over Wynn. She wanted to scoot away, especially with the dark frowns Zack sent her way, but she was a bit too surprised to move.

"I came to let you know that lunch is cancelled for today," Josh said. "Mick insists on escorting Del to a coroner's for some research she's doing." He nodded at the sandwich still squeezed into Zack's hand. "But I see you'd forgotten all about our lunch."

Wynn lurched to her feet, feeling dreadful. "Ohmigosh. I interrupted your plans?" She looked between Josh who was smiling and Zack who was scowling. She ignored Bo.

Josh skirted the settee and again placed himself close to her. He even slipped his arm around her waist. She wasn't sure what to do. "Don't worry about it, Wynn. We meet nearly every week for lunch, so missing one now and then isn't a big deal."

Zack handed the sandwich to Wynn, who accepted it without thinking. Then he crossed his arms over his chest in a confident pose and said, "Josh, meet Wynn's erstwhile protectors. Bo and Marc and out there in the grass with Dani is Clint."

Bo and Marc nodded, but Clint was unaware of the additional guest. He was a grade school teacher with three daughters of his own and loved children in general. Wynn thought of him as a gentle giant, and smiled when she saw he was making Dani a flower garland out of clover buds.

Josh reached out to shake hands. He had his engaging grin in place, but his dark green eyes were alight with mischief. "Josh Marshall. How're you all doing?"

"They were just about to leave," Wynn said, trying for a not-so-subtle hint.

Bo just rolled his eyes. "Quit worrying, doll. We're not going to manhandle your neighbor."

Josh sputtered on a laugh. "Manhandle Zack? Of course not. You know he's a paramedic, right?"

Blank faces stared at Josh.

"Well, he is, and paramedics have to stay in great shape. So, don't let him fool ya. I've seen Zack lift three-hundred-pound men and carry them like they were infants. I've seen him work tirelessly through frozen snow for hours when cars piled up on the highway, and I've seen him go twenty-four hours without a single sign of exhaustion. He's got more dexterity and physical coordination than you can imagine, and he—"

Zack interrupted to say, "Can leap tall buildings in a single bound? Is faster than a speeding bullet?" His tone was dry, his expression chagrined.

Josh laughed. "I don't know about jumping buildings, but I've seen the bullet wound on your arm, so no, you're not all *that* fast."

Wynn jumped on that verbal opportunity. "I've seen it, too. How did it happen, do you know?"

"Sure I know. I was there."

"Josh," Zack warned, but now that everyone had redirected their attention from animosity to curiosity—all but Zack who still looked plenty defensive—Wynn wasn't about to back down.

And neither was Josh. "We were called to the scene of a riot. Buildings burning, glass everywhere, people down in the street."

"Dear God," Wynn muttered, easily able to picture the chaos. She'd never thought of Zack being involved in something so violent, and now that she did, fear swamped her.

Josh nodded. "Innocent people were cowering in alleys, afraid to move, *unable* to move. A woman had caught a stray bullet in the chest and she was just lying on the ground right in the middle of the worst of it, literally bleeding to death. Police were everywhere, SWAT teams were on the way. But we were afraid she'd die before we could get to her."

Wynn already knew what Josh would tell her, and in that moment she felt herself tumbling head over heels in love. To hell with logic or time or background. Her heart knew all it needed to know; she sank down onto the settee with her very first case of weak knees.

Zack shook his head. "It wasn't nearly so dramatic. Plenty of officers provided cover for me."

"Not well enough," Josh pointed out. "You took that slug to the upper arm. Actually," Josh continued, "he got shot when he covered the woman with his own body, trying to protect her from getting hurt worse. No doubt her body couldn't have sustained another serious injury."

"It was all fine in the end," Zack grumbled, and he started looking around for his shirt.

"Yeah." Josh grinned. "As I recall she was so grateful to Zack after that. Really grateful, if you get my meaning."

Marc and Bo chuckled in male understanding. Wynn rolled her eyes.

Zack said, "Shut up, Josh."

"My lips are sealed."

Zack finally found his shirt and pulled it on. Wynn mourned the loss of seeing his sexy naked chest, and she really wanted to examine that scar from the bullet more closely. "Dani said you were a hero."

He grunted. "Dani is four years old and adores me, which is only right since I'm her father. Truth is I just do my job, the same as anybody else."

Josh, still pretending to have zipped his lips, hummed a reply to that.

"Oh, knock it off," Zack snapped. He took his sandwich back from Wynn and took a healthy bite.

Wynn shook herself. "Since I interrupted your lunch, Josh, can I make you a sandwich, too?"

Bo clutched his heart. "You're going to make him a sandwich? Hell, we're the ones who worked for you all afternoon and you didn't offer to serve us."

Wynn elbowed him hard. "All of you behave," she said, and she encompassed Zack in that order, before heading toward the patio door. She caught Josh's arm as she went and dragged him along with her. "We'll be right back."

SEVEN

WYNN GOT JOSH inside the door, pulled him around the corner and flattened him against the wall. "I'm so glad you dropped in."

Josh, looking startled, said, "Uh," and clasped her upper arms to keep her from getting any closer. "Yeah, see, I sorta thought...well..." He looked around and to Wynn, he appeared hunted.

It took her a second to figure out what bothered him, and then she laughed. Men could be such big frauds!

"Look, Wynn..." He inched her a little farther away from him, while keeping his own body plastered to the wall. "Do you think it's safe to leave them all alone out there? I sensed some hostilities going on when I arrived."

"That's why you started defending Zack?"

"Hey, he's a friend. Besides, it's true. He can take care of himself. You know that, right?"

She shrugged, then daringly pressed closer, just to watch him squirm.

"The thing is," he blurted, looking all around again as if he expected someone to jump him at any second, "I thought you had a thing for Zack."

Wynn smoothed her hand over his very solid, very large shoulder and whispered, "I do."

"Because I'm not at all sure—" He did a double take. "You do?"

"Mmm-hmm." She looked him in the eyes, licked her lips, and continued, "That's why I dragged you in here." She patted his cheek and added, "To find out more about Zack."

"Oh. *Oh!*" Josh laughed and his confidence returned in his quirky smile and the way his shoulders relaxed. "Good. That's real good. Just what I wanted to hear."

"But Zack doesn't like me much."

"I think he likes you *too* much. That's the problem, at least as far as he's concerned." She stepped back and together they headed toward the kitchen. "Personally, I think you're perfect for him."

Wynn had never in her life been described as perfect. Her father harped on and on about her imperfect hair, and her mother harped about her lack of femininity and her brother drove her crazy telling her she was too aggressive while constantly challenging her. It was a rather nice compliment to hear. "No kidding?"

"Hell yeah." He pulled out a chair for her. "Look at you! You're attractive and healthy—being a paramedic, and having lost his first wife, Zack is big on health."

Wynn blinked at that sentiment.

"You're also fun and funny and you seem to like Dani." He frowned. "That's a must you know, that you like his daughter. And you can't fake that because plenty of women have tried and he's always seen through them."

Wynn fell speechless at such a wealth of verbal outpour-
ings. She hadn't had to ask a single question!

He looked a little worried at her continued silence. "You
do like Dani, don't you?"

Unwilling to lose this golden opportunity, she gathered her
wits. "Of course. She's adorable. Smart, precocious, bold." She
shrugged. "Beautiful like her dad."

Josh grinned. "Zack is beautiful, huh? What a hoot."

Wynn realized exactly what she'd said and blushed. "Don't
you dare say anything to him."

"Oh, no, no, of course not."

Wynn didn't believe him for a second. "Josh…"

"Do you really have something to eat?"

One thing about men, you could always count on them
wanting food—especially the big ones. Josh obviously spent
his fair share of time in the gym pumping iron. His physique
and looks were so impressive, he could have posed for a cen-
terfold. "Sure. Help yourself."

He laughed at that. "So your muscle-bound friends were
right, huh? You don't cater to men?"

Actually, she'd been so preoccupied formulating all her
questions, she'd forgotten all about her manners. "Sorry." She
stood. "I've had a lot on my mind."

Josh immediately pressed her back into her seat and then
patted her shoulder. "Hey, you've been working all day and
I'm a big boy, I can feed myself. It was just an observation."

Propping her head on both hands, she groaned. "This is
awful. It's been so long since I dated, or since I tried to attract
a guy, I'm going about it all wrong."

She heard the cabinets open. "You trying to attract Zack?"

"Without much success."

"Not true." The refrigerator opened and Wynn watched

through her fingers as Josh poured out a glass of juice and hauled out sandwich fixings. She'd have to remember to stock up on more lunch meat now that she had her own home and had such big men living nearby and visiting.

Taking his own seat, Josh said, "Zack has noticed you big time. He's just in denial."

"You think?"

"I know." He piled enough meat on his sandwich to make a meal. "Zack hasn't acted this upside down about a woman since his wife."

Wynn wondered how to broach that subject, then decided against trying to dredge up tact she didn't have. It was pointless. She said simply, "Will you tell me about her?"

Josh popped a whole slice of bologna into his mouth and nodded. "Young, beautiful. Very sweet and very petite." He eyed Wynn. "Nothing like you, expect maybe the beautiful part."

Heat rushed into her face. Josh was such an outrageous flatterer! She decided the best thing to do was ignore it. "I'm only twenty-eight. Not exactly old myself."

"Ancient compared to Rebecca."

So, Zack was attracted to young, petite women? Just what she didn't want to hear. "That was her name? Rebecca?"

"Yep. She would have turned twenty-one a month after having Dani if she hadn't died."

Very young. Though Wynn didn't know the woman, it hurt her to think of it. Dani and Zack had lost so much. She rubbed her forehead. "How long had they been married?"

"Only about seven months. The pregnancy was a surprise, and the reason for the marriage. Once Zack found out, he insisted, and Rebecca gave in. I'm not sure it's what either of them really wanted at the time."

Wynn did some math in her head and decided Zack was around twenty-five or so when he'd married, not much older than that when he became a father. Wynn swallowed hard. "How did she die?"

Josh laid the food aside and leaned back in his chair. He looked past Wynn, and he appeared more somber than she'd thought possible. "Rebecca had a hard time with the pregnancy. She was so small that it put a hell of a strain on her body. Her ankles swelled, her back hurt, her...well, you get the idea."

"Yes."

"She wasn't at all happy about the physical changes, so her emotional state of mind wasn't the best, either. She wanted Dani, no doubt about that, but she was pretty damn miserable those last few months. Physically and emotionally."

"I think that's pretty common, isn't it?"

Josh shrugged. "I suppose, what with hormone changes and all that." Then he shook his head. "Zack and I were both at a huge warehouse fire when she went into labor five weeks early. She called the station, and they immediately went to work on getting someone to replace Zack, but the destruction was huge and they were running short on manpower. Damn near everyone had already been called into service. Zack was working his ass off, dealing with a dozen different traumas, worried and anxious and madder than hell because he couldn't just leave. Leaving would have been a firing offense, though, which might not have stopped him except that he would never deliberately walk away from seriously injured people. And that's what he would have had to do. He thought Rebecca was okay, that she'd made it to the hospital and they were taking care of her..."

"But?"

Josh got up from the table. Like Zack's house, she had a window right over her sink, and that's where he went. He shoved his hands into his back pockets and stared out at the yard. "The contractions came too fast and she couldn't drive. She lost control of the car and it went off the road, flipping into a ditch. She took two other cars with her, but no one else was seriously hurt. By the time she was airlifted to the hospital, she'd died. They managed to save Dani."

Wynn nearly strangled on her own emotion. Her throat felt tight, her stomach ached and her heart beat painfully. She could only imagine what Zack had gone through.

"He's usually a rock," Josh said quietly. "Nothing rattles him. He's always calm and polite and reasonable. Always."

She looked up. *Zack* was calm and reasonable? Well, yes, he could be, she supposed. But he could also be forceful and outrageous and around her, he was seldom calm.

"That was the closest I've ever seen him come to losing it." Josh turned to face her. "That bullet wound he's got? Well, he knew he'd get shot when he went after that woman. I don't mean that he thought the odds would be good, I mean that he knew some of the rioters were firing *at* her, determined not to let her be saved, just to prove some fanatical point. Zack put himself between her and those bullets. He willingly risked his life for a person he didn't know from Adam. That's just how he is. He can't bear to see anyone hurt."

He drew a breath, then finished. "You can imagine what it did to him that he wasn't there for Rebecca."

"He blamed himself?"

"Yeah, he did. For a while. Then Dani got to him. For almost two weeks she was a perfect baby. Cooing when she was hungry, sleeping sound, and then bam, right out of the blue she became a tiny demon." Josh laughed. "Man, she put

Zack through hell. He'd come in off a long shift and the sitter would say that Dani had slept and had been happy. Then she'd hear Zack and start making demands. When he was around, she wanted him to hold her. She wouldn't let him give her only half his attention."

Wynn considered all that. "You're saying he ignored her at first?"

"Hell, no. He made sure she was taken care of and he kissed her goodbye and hugged her hello, but he wasn't yet attached to her. He felt a responsibility for her, but he had so much grief, so much remorse, there wasn't much room for anything else, much less love. Till Dani took over."

"He's a good father."

"He's a *great* father. The absolute best. And he'd make a helluva husband, too."

Wynn was just digesting that not so subtle hint when Zack growled from the doorway, "I appreciate the accolades, Josh, but you're *way out of line.*"

Josh said, "Uh, you didn't leave any dead bodies outside, did you?"

"Knock it off." He walked farther into the room. "You know I'm a pacifist."

"Right. Whatever you say." He skirted around Zack with theatrical fanfare, and said, "I think I'll talk to your friends, Wynn. They seem like very nice fellows."

The screen door fell shut a second later. Wynn slowly came to her feet to face Zack. "Nice fellows," he mimicked. "They seemed like possessive, jealous fellows to me."

"Protective, not possessive. I told you I haven't dated any of them."

"Did you? I don't seem to recall that conversation."

She cleared her throat. "Everything okay outside?"

He advanced on her, his gaze locked on hers. "If you mean has everyone played nice, yes. But your bully boys gave me the third degree."

"They didn't!" Dismay filled her. How could she make a good impression on a man like Zack if Bo kept behaving like an ass?

"They did."

As he reached her, she stepped behind her chair. She wasn't afraid of Zack, but she didn't understand his mood either. He seemed on edge, yet also sort of...accepting. But accepting of what? Something was definitely different, of that she was certain. "I'm sorry."

"They seem to think you have your 'sights set on me,' as they put it."

Oh God, oh God, oh God... She just knew her face was flaming. She only had one brother, and he was enough to contend with without his friends trying to take over the role, too. Hoping to excuse their bizarre behavior, she said, "I, ah, don't show a lot of interest in the opposite sex."

Zack cocked a brow. "What are you telling me? *Males* don't interest you?"

"No! That is, I meant that I don't show a lot of interest in *any* sex."

One side of Zack's mouth curled in an amused, mocking smile.

She bit her tongue, then took two long breaths. "I *mean,*" she stated, "that I don't usually chase a guy. I've got friends, and that's it." And so she didn't sound pathetic, she added, "That's as much as I want."

His voice was oddly gentle when he quipped, "Glad to hear it."

He was now so close she felt his breath when he spoke. Just

two inches and she could be kissing him again. She considered it, but held back because she didn't know if he'd be receptive to the idea. So far he'd acted really put out over their mutual attraction—even to the point of denying it was mutual.

Which, she realized, meant he was so close because he wanted to intimidate her. She frowned. "That was before meeting you, Zack. I want you. I haven't made a secret of that. But you should understand that what happened in the yard the other day was an aberration for me, too. I don't regret it, but no way has it ever happened before."

His mouth twisted, and she got the awful suspicion he didn't believe her.

Wynn lost her temper. "Just because I have big male friends—"

He rolled his eyes.

"—and I got carried away with you—"

"We *both* got carried away."

She completely missed his confession in the middle of her tirade. "—doesn't give you the right to assume I'm free with all men."

"It also doesn't give you the right to go snooping around in my private business. If you wanted to know about my wife, you should have asked me."

Her chin lifted so she could look down her nose at him. "Would you have told me anything?"

"No." Before she could finish her full-fledged huff, he added, "Because it's none of your business."

Wynn threw up her hands. "There, you see? Talking to you is pointless!" She realized she wasn't helping her case any, but really, what could she do? She couldn't change herself; she wouldn't even know where to begin. She let out a sigh and dropped her head. "Actually," she muttered, "I guess all of this is pointless, huh?"

Zack drew himself up. "What does that mean?"

"It means I'm beginning to accept that you're one hundred percent not interested." She lifted her shoulder in a half-hearted shrug. "I did hear all about your wife, and I know now that you're more attracted to petite women." She even snorted at herself in self-disgust. "God, I'm so far from petite it's laughable."

"Wynn." He said her name like a scold.

She held out her arms. "I'm a great big lummox of a girl and I know it. I'm not cute or petite or any of those nice things. You like little weak women who you can protect, and I don't need protection. I'm not even weaker than you."

His expression bemused, he rumbled, "Uh, actually you are. A lot weaker, damn it."

But she barely listened to him now. She was too upset with the realization that Zack would likely never want to be involved with her. "I'm all wrong for you."

She paced around her kitchen, for the first time unmindful of the fine cherry cabinets and her new stainless steel sink and her side-by-side refrigerator, which just yesterday she'd kept touching because she loved it so much. Even the pleasure of getting her patio set up was now ruined.

Dejected, she turned to face him and said, "I'm sorry. I guess I've been a total pain in the butt."

"Yeah."

Though he said it gently, her shoulders slumped.

Then Zack stepped closer and he cupped her face carefully in his two hands and he said almost against her lips, "You are a pain in the neck, Wynn, and a pain in the ass and everywhere else. But you know why." And with a small laugh, "What bullshit, to say I'm not attracted to you."

She blinked at him, so startled she almost toppled over.

He shook his head. "You're not blind and you sure as hell aren't stupid. You *know* I want you."

"You do?"

"I do."

He briefly kissed her, but it was enough to make her breathless. "Even now," she questioned, "with us standing here in my kitchen and everyone else right outside? Even though I haven't just jumped you and dragged you to the ground?"

"Is that what you thought?" A sexy smile played with his mouth, making her heart punch. "That just because you took me by surprise and actually got me flat on my back was the only reason I acted as I did last week?"

Ignoring the part about taking him by surprise, Wynn nodded. The how and why of their interlude last week wasn't important. Not when right now, all she really, *really* wanted was for him to kiss her again. But he just kept staring at her mouth while his big rough thumbs stroked her cheeks and that was so nice, too, she held still and didn't dare complain or ask for more.

"Wynn, you did just take me by surprise, you know that don't you? You're strong, honey, but there's no way in hell you'd best me in a physical confrontation."

"Okay."

He laughed, a low husky sound, and shook his head. "You're placating me." And he kissed her again. "You're something else, you know that? I've never met a woman who wanted a man, yet continued to insult his manhood with every other breath."

"Your, ah, manhood?" Her gaze skipped down his body to

his lap. He lifted her chin, keeping her from that erotic perusal while making a "tsking" sound.

"My machismo," he explained, "my masculinity." He tipped her face up and kissed her throat, the soft spot beneath her ear.

Wynn's toes curled inside her gym shoes.

"One of these days," he added while licking her ear and driving her insane, "I'm going to prove it to you."

"Yes." She had no idea what he wanted to prove, but whatever it might be, she was all for it.

His laugh was a little more robust this time. He looked at her, studied her dazed eyes and nodded. "All right. So, the challenge is made. What am I to do? I'm just a man after all, and I can only take so much without caving in."

He said all that with a wicked smile.

She said, "What?"

"Will you be at your hammock tonight?"

That caught her attention. Hope and excitement flared inside her. "Yes. Sure, of course."

"So anxious." He grinned and kissed her bottom lip. "I know this is wrong, I swear I do. But damn I want you. You're making me nuts, woman."

His machismo sounded just fine to her attuned ears. She smiled dreamily. "You're making me nuts, too. I tried to leave you alone, to let you get used to the idea of me…"

"Ha!" Shaking his head, smiling, Zack said, "That'd take a lifetime."

She liked the sound of that. A lifetime with Zack. With each day, with every damn minute, she was more attracted to him, in a million different ways.

Seeing her expression, his hands gentled and he waggled her head. "Wynn, I'm not making any promises about anything. If we meet tonight, it's strictly for sex."

Her hopes plummeted, but the excitement was still there. She bit her lip, undecided what to do. On the one hand, she'd never been one for casual sex.

But on the other, she'd never wanted a man like she wanted Zack.

And then suddenly there was a shrill yell from the yard and Zack moved with a blur of speed. He was outside before Wynn could catch her breath. Recognizing Dani's squeaky little voice, now filled with sobs, she quickly followed.

They found Dani held in Josh's arm, screaming her heart out. Josh, a study of frantic concern, blurted, "She got stung by a bee!"

Bo and Marc and Clint stood in a circle around Josh, wringing their hands and fretting like old women. The sight would have been laughable if it hadn't been for the fat tears streaming down Dani's cheeks.

Zack took Dani and cradled her close to his chest. "Shh, honey, it's okay."

Josh lifted her foot and peered at it. "The stinger is out," he said, and his voice shook.

It amused Wynn that five large overgrown men would quake at a child's cry. Good grief, their panic would feed her own and the whole yard would soon be bawling.

"Is she allergic to stings?" Wynn asked, and both Zack and Josh said, "No."

She walked up to Dani and touched her tiny foot. In soft, soothing tones, she said, "If you think you're hurt, just think how the poor bee feels." She began steering Zack toward the patio. He hugged Dani so close she could barely get her head off his shoulder.

"I don't care about the dumb bee," Dani said, and hiccuped over her tears.

"That's good," Wynn told her, "because he's a goner now. Once they sting someone, that's all she wrote."

Dani looked mollified by that notion. "Really?"

"Yep. They can't grow a stinger back, and what good is a bee without a stinger? Zack, sit down here with her and I'll turn on the hose. The cold water will make it feel better." And to Dani, "You feel like soaking those little pink toes?"

Dani smiled and nodded, but her bottom lip still quivered.

Zack sat, rocking his daughter in his arms.

Wynn shook her head and fetched the hose. After about half a minute of freezing cold water running over her tiny foot, Dani struggled to sit up. She took one look at Zack, and patted his chest. "I'm 'kay."

He hugged her close, half-laughing, but still shaken. He also kissed her foot, then had to move so Josh could kiss it, too. Dani accepted the healing kisses as her due.

Zack kissed her one more time, then asked, "Dani, why did you have your shoes off?"

Evidently, this was something forbidden, for Dani summoned a pathetic, apologetic look, and then pointed at Bo. "I was tryin' on his shoes."

Bo took an appalled step back and his entire face darkened with guilt. "My shoes!"

"They're so big," Dani explained, looking down at her lap and giving another little sob. "Even bigger than Daddy's."

Everyone looked at Zack's feet. He muttered, "Size twelve."

Bo, still flushed with guilt, shrugged. "Thirteens," he admitted. "She's right, they are bigger."

Wynn had been stationed by the hose, watching the byplay, the way everyone looked from Zack's feet to Bo's and then to Dani's, doing some sort of bizarre comparison.

Her emotions had been on a roller-coaster ride since meeting Zack, keeping her on edge. Now the idea of a bunch of gargantuan men comparing foot sizes with a child who was so petite she barely reached any of their knees, just struck Wynn funny. She burst out laughing and couldn't stop. When everyone stared toward her, she laughed even harder.

On the edge of embarrassment, no doubt afraid he was the object of hilarity, Bo chuckled, too. Of course, that made Clint and Marc laugh. Dani finally started to giggle, drawn to the sound of the hilarity, though likely her humor wasn't for the same reasons. And with laughter being so contagious, within minutes everyone roared. Dani bounced on Zack's lap, her sting totally forgotten.

Watching Zack laugh was a special delight. Wynn had the feeling he didn't often give in to great displays of any kind of outward emotion. He wasn't, according to Josh, a man who lost his temper or his control.

Yet, with her he'd gone from one extreme to another. Surely, that counted for something. What, she didn't know, but perhaps she'd find out tonight.

Now that she'd made up her mind, she could hardly wait.

EIGHT

ZACK CHECKED ON Dani one last time. Her tiny foot stuck out from under the sheet, and from the glow of the hall light he could just make out the rainbow print bandage she'd insisted on putting over her bee sting. He bent and kissed her toes, then tucked the foot away.

Dani stirred and stretched. "Daddy?"

A lump in his throat nearly strangled him. She only called him "daddy" when she was very tired, or hurt. He sat on the edge of the bed and smoothed her cheek. "Yeah, sweetie. It's me."

She yawned hugely, then reached for his hand. "We had a swell time today."

Smiling at the way she consistently phrased everything as a statement, Zack said, "Yes, we did."

"I really like Wynn."

"Do you?"

She nodded against her pillow. "You do, too."

Zack hesitated. His daughter had never played matchmaker

in her life, so this particular statement totally took him by surprise. He said finally, "I like her fine."

"I like her more than fine. She's the funnest."

"Brat," Zack teased, and asked, "More fun than me?"

"The funnest *woman*," she clarified, and yawned yet again. "I'm gonna keep her."

Her voice had been faint, on the edge of sleep, but still he heard. "Dani? What do you mean you're going to keep her?"

"I want her to be mine," his half-awake daughter announced.

This was something totally new, like the feminine napkin discussion and Zack just knew he was going to start running into more of these torturous episodes. Heart pounding, he asked, "Yours, like as a friend?"

"Uh-huh. And a rela…retal…"

"Relative?"

"Yeah. That."

"She's not our relative, Dani. Remember, I explained relatives to you."

"I know. But she could be a wife and a mommy."

Zack stared at his daughter, and if he hadn't been sitting, he'd have fallen down. Dani's eyes were closed, her cheek nestled into her pillow.

Her sweet little mouth curled into a pleased smile when she said, "And we could have a brother." She peeked one eye open. "I want a brother."

"Honey…"

"A brother like Conan."

God forbid!

"I'd help with diapers and stuff."

"I know you would, sweetheart. But things like brothers take a lot of time."

She closed her eyes again and sighed. "Josh likes Wynn, too."

Zack froze, and found himself asking, "You think so?"

"Maybe he wants a brother." Her brow puckered. "I mean a son."

Zack had tried to talk to Josh about his interest in Wynn, but he hadn't had the chance. By the time Wynn's friends had left, which would have afforded some privacy, Josh had been ready to go, too.

He sat there thinking, recalling what Bo had told him. Wynn didn't date, and she very seldom showed sexual interest in men. Her reaction to Zack, according to those who knew her best, was extreme. Zack had been a little disconcerted to realize they all knew of Wynn's pursuit, but they said it was because she acted so differently with him. In the normal course of things, she pretended to be one of the guys.

Marc had warned him that Wynn was an uncommon woman, who looked at the world in an uncommon way.

As if he'd needed the warning! He'd already figured that out firsthand. Her flirting skills were nonexistent. She said what she wanted, and left Zack to deal with the shock.

Clint had added that she was a good sport, but still hated to lose. At anything. If she wanted Zack, then it'd be difficult to dissuade her.

And they all agreed, she wanted Zack.

He smiled. Wynn's approach was bold, but also refreshing. And now that he believed the reaction was as unique for her as it was for him, his resistance had disappeared.

Zack sat quietly, contemplating all he'd learned today, along with his daughter's sentiments until he heard her breathing even into a light snore. He kissed her forehead and stood.

Her bedroom window was open, letting in a cool breeze and plenty of fresh air.

Zack went to the window and looked out. As she'd promised, Wynn sat in the hammock, waiting. At the sight of her, he felt the rush of his blood and the swelling of muscles.

There was a lot to consider, especially his daughter's growing attachment to a woman totally unsuitable for any type of permanency. But for now, none of that seemed to matter.

For now, he had to have her.

He left his daughter's room in a silent rush, closing the door softly behind him. He'd already removed his shoes so his bare feet made no sound as he moved through the house and out the back door. The grass felt soft and cool as he crossed through the darkness to Wynn. As he went, he unbuttoned his shirt, letting the evening breeze drift over his heated flesh.

What he planned, what *they* planned, felt wicked and enticing and so sexual he was already hard.

She stood with her back to him, her arms wrapped tight around her middle when he finally reached her. "Wynn."

Whirling so fast she almost lost her balance, she gasped, "I didn't hear you!" and in the next breath, with relief, "I was afraid you'd changed your mind."

Her lack of self-protection shook him; she put her heart on the line without reserve, and he felt her trust like a deep responsibility—a responsibility he didn't want. "I had to get Dani settled down."

Her eyes a faint glow in the light of the moon, Wynn looked toward his house. "Will she be all right in there alone?"

"Dani sleeps like a bear hibernating. But if she should wake up, she'll look in the hot tub for me. We'd see the patio light."

With her arms still squeezed around herself, she nodded. "That's good."

"Are you nervous?"

"A little." She shifted her feet, moving a tiny bit closer to him. "I've never had a sexual assignation before."

Zack smiled. "Me, either."

"No?"

"I don't bring women to the house because of Dani. This is her home and I would never do that. My work schedule is crazy enough that when I get time to be with her, I don't generally like to waste it with women."

"Waste it with women," she repeated slowly, as if figuring out the meaning to his words. "You haven't dated much since your wife died?"

"More recently than ever before." He'd been bride hunting, so it had been necessary. "Not that more means very much."

"I know you haven't been celibate."

He laughed at her incredulity. "What is it about you, Wynn, that you can amuse me at the most awkward times?"

She frowned. "I didn't mean to amuse you. And what's awkward about now?"

Zack touched her cheek, let his fingers trail down to her throat and her bare shoulder. She wore a dark sleeveless cotton dress—like a long shirt—and she felt warm and very soft. "This is awkward because I'm so turned-on I can barely breathe."

"Zack." She rushed against him, clinging to him, her hands strong on his shoulders, her body pressed full length against his own. "How...how are we going to manage this? Not only haven't I had any assignations, but I've never made love in a hammock before either." She lifted her head and he felt her gentle breath on his jaw. "Have you?"

"No, but it doesn't matter." He kissed her, a light kiss to her temple, the bridge of her nose, the corner of her mouth. "Are you one hundred percent certain of this, Wynn?"

She offered a slight hesitation that just about made his heart stop, then nodded. "Very certain."

"Thank God." He kissed her, tasting her excitement and her urgency, which almost mirrored his own. Her lips were soft, and they parted for his tongue. Kissing Wynn was...well, it was definitely exciting. But it was more than that. Kissing her affected him everywhere, making his head spin and his abdomen cramp and his thighs ache.

He slid one hand down her back to her lush behind and pulled her in close, then groaned when she rubbed herself against his erection.

They both panted.

Wynn went to work on getting his shirt pushed off his shoulders. He shrugged it off, letting it land in the grass. With a sound of approval her fingers spread wide over his chest, tangling in his body hair, caressing his muscles, teasing over his nipples.

He backed her into the tree and briefly pinned her there with his hips, grinding himself into her. He filled his hands with her breasts and their mouths meshed hotly, licking and sucking. Zack felt her pointed nipples, felt the lurch of her body as he gently rolled one sensitive tip. It wasn't enough. He caught the narrow shoulder straps and pulled them down to her elbows. She slipped her arms free and the dress bunched at her waist.

Moonlight made her breasts opalescent, made her nipples look dark and ripe. Shuddering with lust, he bent his head and drew her right nipple deeply into the heat of his mouth.

"Zack!"

"Shhh...." He licked and tasted and plucked with his lips.

The husky sounds she made, hungry and real and encouraging, fired his lust. He lifted her dress.

She wasn't wearing panties.

"*Damn.*" Zack stared at her wide eyes while his hands moved over the silky skin of her bottom. He closed his eyes, exploring her, relishing the feel of her, the carnality of the moment. "Damn, Wynn," he said again.

Her voice was a breathless, uncertain murmur. "I...I thought underwear might just be in the way, and I didn't know if..."

Zack went to his knees and pushed the dress higher.

Startled, Wynn tried to step away, but the tree was at her back and Zack held her securely. "*What* are you *doing?*" She sounded frantic as she pulled at his shoulders.

"It's dark." Zack glanced up, saw her embarrassment even in the night shadows and asked gently, "No man's ever kissed you here?"

She smacked at his shoulder. "*Zack,*" she hissed, and to his amazement, she looked around.

He couldn't help but laugh. "It's a little late to be worrying about voyeurs, Wynn."

"But..." She held his shoulders securely, as if she could keep him away. "You can't do that out here!"

"We can have intercourse, but not oral sex?"

She gasped, thoroughly scandalized by his words, and quickly looked around the deserted yard again. Zack loved it. For once he had the upper hand and no way in hell would he give it up. Especially since he was dying to taste her, to hear her moan out a climax.

He taunted her, saying, "You'll like this, Wynn. And so will I."

"I don't know..."

Knotting the dress in a fist, he anchored it high at the small of her back. He cursed the clouds that made the moon insufficient light. He wanted to see all of her, not just hints of her, curves and hollows exaggerated by the shadows. He wanted to see each soft pink inch of her sex, the dent of her navel, the dimples in her knees.

He groaned; what he could see was spectacular. Her thighs were beautiful, sleek and firm and now pressed tightly together as he stroked them each in turn. He looked up at her breasts, as large as the rest of her, full and white.

He couldn't tell the color of the hair on her mound, but he guessed it to be the same as her eyebrows, slightly darker than the honey brown hair on her head. He sifted his fingers through her curls and heard her indistinct whimper of excitement. Leaning close, he pressed his cheek to her belly as he touched her.

Her belly…well he'd always loved female bellies. To Zack, they epitomized femininity, soft and slightly rounded and smooth. Wynn's belly was extremely sexy. He felt her quiver and turned his face, kissing her, licking her navel; all the while his fingers continued to pet her. Nothing more, just petting, but it made him so damn hot he felt burned.

Night sounds closed in around them, the hum of insects, the rustle of a soft breeze through the treetops. Clouds crossed the moon repeatedly, first softening the light, then obliterating it. The air felt thick, charged, damp.

"Zack, I don't know if I like this…"

"You'll like it," he assured her in a rough whisper. He trailed his fingers lower, cupping her, then working his fingertips between her clenched thighs. Her buttocks pressed back against his fist holding her dress. Zack urged her forward again.

He felt her. Her lips were swollen, warm and slick. He touched her gently, sliding back and forth until she grew even wetter, then he pushed one finger deep inside.

Her knees locked and she made a long, raw sound of surprised pleasure. "This," she rasped, "isn't at all what I expected."

Had she expected him to be *sweet?* Zack wondered. Had she thought to be the aggressor? The idea tormented him. Her misconceptions about him could be alternately amusing and enraging.

"Open your legs, Wynn."

Her head tipped back against the tree and she said, "The way you say that..." She looked down at him. "It really turns me on."

Zack stared up at her, his finger still pressed deep into the heat of her body, clenched by her muscles, and she wanted to talk? "Open them, Wynn."

After a long look and a shuddered breath, she obliged him. Zack damn near came watching her long legs shift apart— for him.

"What will you do?" she asked, and she sounded almost as excited as he felt.

"This," he told her, sliding his finger deeper, then slowly pulling it out. Her muscles gripped him, held on tight. He worked a second finger into her. "You're tight, Wynn."

She reached above her head and clasped a branch for support, then moved her legs wider apart. "You expected something else from a big girl like me?"

"I never know what to expect from you." That was certainly the truth. Tired of talking, Zack kissed her thigh, her hipbone. "You smell incredible."

She groaned a protest when he pulled his fingers from her,

until he began petting her again, spreading her wetness upward, over her clitoris.

She cried out, and her whole body jerked. He continued to touch her, circling and plucking and stroking. Her hips thrust toward him, her whole body straining. He could smell her, the fresh, pungent scent of aroused woman.

It had been so long, too damned long. He leaned forward, opened her further with his fingers, and drew her into his mouth, savoring her with a raw sound of hunger and satisfaction. The contact was so startling, so intense, she tried to lurch away, but he gripped her hips in his hands and held her pinned to the tree while he got his fill.

She gave up and with his support, her thighs fell open further, giving him better access, which he quickly accepted, licking and sucking at her hot sweet flesh. Her hands tangled hard in his hair, pulling him closer still.

Zack's heart punched hard in his chest and his cock strained in his jeans. He couldn't wait another second. He stood and turned her. "Hold onto the tree."

Panting, rigid, she looked at him over her shoulder and said, "What...?"

Zack had his jeans opened and the condom out in a heartbeat. He rolled it on, moaning at the sensation of the rubber on his erection, his teeth gritted with the effort of holding back. He stepped up to her, slipped his fingers under her to open her for his entry, and took a soft love bite of her shoulder while he pressed in.

Wynn flattened her hands on the rough bark, bracing herself, groaning with him. He wanted to touch her everywhere, and did. He felt her breasts, rolled her nipples, stroked her belly and below, fingering her until she cried and relaxed and he could sink deep into her.

"Oh yeah," he rumbled, finally where he'd wanted to be almost from the first second he saw her. He had to catch his breath and his control before he could start the rhythm they both needed. "Tilt your hips. Push back against me, Wynn. That's it, sweetheart."

He gripped her hips and helped her. When she caught the frenzied rhythm, he returned to pleasuring her, one hand on her breasts, one between her legs.

Sweat dampened his back though the night was cool. He squeezed his eyes shut and concentrated on not coming, on not giving in to the raging need to let go. He wanted her with him, wanted to know that she'd climaxed, that he'd satisfied her. He pressed his face into her shoulder while his every muscle grew taut and rippled and suddenly she went still, holding her breath.

"Yes, Wynn," he urged her, knowing he was a goner, that he'd last maybe two seconds more and that was it. Her head dropped forward between her stiffened arms and her breath came out in a long, low earthy moan that obliterated any last thread of his control. She didn't scream, but at the end she said his name on a seductive, satisfied whisper of sound that licked along his spine.

He shuddered as he came, holding her tight and pounding into her, not the least bit worried about hurting her, not when she continued to roll her hips sinuously against him, continued to make soft sounds of completion and satisfaction.

A big woman was nice, better than nice.

He slumped into her, which made her slump into the tree. They both struggled for breath.

A few seconds later, she groaned and shifted the tiniest bit. "Zack?"

"Hmmm." Their skin felt melded together, her back to his

chest, her sweet backside to his groin, the front of his hairy thighs to the smooth backs of hers. He didn't want to move, not ever.

"The tree isn't all that comfortable," she complained. "Do you think we can totter over there to the hammock?"

His legs were still jerking in small spasms. His heart hadn't completely slowed its mad gallop yet. There was a low ringing still in his ears.

He felt stripped bare down to his soul. His lungs burned. "Yeah, sure. No problem."

Determined not to crumble, he straightened slowly. He felt like an old man with arthritis, very unsure of his ability to stay on his feet. He removed the condom, dropped it into the grass with the mental reminder to dispose of it later, then tugged his jeans back up.

All that took more effort than he could spare and he nearly collapsed again. Wynn didn't help, not when she turned and leaned into him. She was a woman, but she was no lightweight. He remembered lifting his petite wife after sex and holding her in his arms. Ha!

Zack eyed the hammock that wasn't too far away considering they were against the tree supporting it at one end. He slung an arm around Wynn and fell into the canvas. She laughed as the hammock swung wildly, almost tossing them both, but when they stayed more in it than on the ground she snuggled around until she was mostly on top of him.

"Will the ropes hold both of us, do you think?"

"If not, I'll buy you a new one."

"You will not." She leaned up and looked at his mouth, then touched him with a gentle fingertip. In the most sweetly feminine voice he'd ever heard from her, Wynn said, "I really liked what you did."

Zack closed his eyes and grinned. She'd damn near yanked him bald with her enthusiasm, so he'd assumed as much.

He said, "I told you so."

"It seemed sort of…kinky."

Still grinning, he said, "It only seems kinky the first time. Trust me."

"Did you like it?"

He opened one eye. She looked uncertain. "My only complaint is that once again you pushed me over the edge."

"I didn't!"

"I wanted to spend more time tasting you. More time hearing you make all those sweet little squeaking womanly noises."

He was dead to the world, barely able to drum up a little teasing, and she had the energy to slug him in the shoulder. Luckily he was still numb so it didn't hurt.

"I do *not* squeak!"

He smoothed his hand down her back, discovered her dress was still hiked up, and patted her bare bottom. It was a nice big bottom, filling his large hand. "You squeak and you moan and I like it."

"You did your own share of moaning."

"Men don't moan," he informed her, "they groan. There's a definite difference."

"Whatever you say."

He smiled. "I like how you taste, too."

She ducked her head and rubbed herself against him.

Because he was too comfortable, too replete, he admitted, "At least I should finally sleep tonight."

"Are you saying you haven't slept well lately?"

He used both hands to hold on to her backside and anchor her close. "No. I've been as restless as a horny teenager."

That had her laughing, but she quickly sobered. "My parents are moving in tomorrow."

Zack yawned. "Yeah, I remember."

Turning shy on him, she curled her finger in and around his chest hair and said, "I was hoping we could maybe do this again."

Her meaning sank in and Zack stilled. Ah hell, he couldn't possibly be expected to get his fill of her in one lousy night! He'd been too primed and ended it too quickly. He hadn't luxuriated in her, hadn't explored her as he'd meant to, as he'd thought about doing.

A week, maybe two weeks, would take the edge off. But not one damn night.

"May I assume by your frown that you want to do this again?" Wynn asked.

Zack lifted his head enough to feast on her mouth in a long, slow, wet, eating kiss. When he released her, they were both panting again. "Yeah," he said, "you can assume that."

Wynn tucked her head into his shoulder. She had one leg bent across his abdomen, the other stretched out to the bottom of the hammock. Zack had one leg on the outside of hers, the other over the side with his foot firmly planted on the ground so he could keep them swaying.

He mulled over a few possibilities and then asked, "Are your parents the protective sort?"

She snorted. "No."

He didn't like how quickly she answered that. Parents should be protective, especially of a daughter living alone. But since he had his own plans, he didn't say so. "I've got stuff planned tomorrow and Tuesday. But Wednesday I should get home from work around eight. By nine-thirty I can have Dani tucked away." His mind conjured all sorts of erotic possibilities and he growled, "Is it possible you could come visit me, say to use the hot tub, and they wouldn't check up on you?"

Though Wynn didn't move, the rushing of her heartbeat gave away her excitement. "They wouldn't think a thing of it. They're used to me being pals with guys."

That made Zack chuckle. Damn, she tickled him with her strange replies and stranger relationships. "It'll be dark by then. I'll watch for you."

"Let's make it ten o'clock. My parents will be in bed by then."

Her position left her soft sex open and vulnerable to him. Zack trailed his fingertips over her bottom cheeks until he could feel the heat of her. He pressed. "Have you ever made love in a hot tub?"

"No." She reared up to glower at him, and the heat in her eyes was a combination of suspicion and arousal. Because of where and how he touched her, her voice shook when she demanded, "Have you?"

Zack thought she might be jealous, and oddly enough, he liked that. "No." He could see her face clearly now, the incredible hazel eyes, the long lashes and the very kissable mouth. "I've never made love against a tree before either. Or in a hammock."

He touched her tender lips, still swollen and wet from their lovemaking, then pushed his middle finger into her.

She panted. "Me, neither."

With her practically straddling his abdomen, Zack kicked the hammock again, making it rock. She grabbed his shoulders for support. He looked at her naked breasts bobbing and swaying before him and immediately grew hard. "I just might prove successful at all three."

Wynn made a low sound of agreement. "Based on what I've seen so far, I wouldn't be at all surprised."

"I have another condom in my pocket."

"A man who comes prepared. Incredible."

Zack started to laugh at that, but then she came down over him, her breasts pressing into his chest, and she kissed him and all he could think about was making love to her again. Wednesday seemed a long way off, so he'd have to make this last. And to do that, he'd have to slow her down.

"Wynn?"

"Hmm?" She continued to kiss his mouth, his chin, his jaw.

"Scoot up."

She stilled, lifted her head to stare at him. "Why?"

"Because I want to kiss your breasts. And then your belly— you have an adorable belly by the way. And then maybe I'll even nibble on this sweet rear end of yours."

Her eyes almost crossed; she swallowed hard. "Are you going to…do what you did to me again?"

He nodded slowly. "Oh yeah. You can bet I am."

Wynn froze, caught her breath, and with barely contained excitement, she attacked him. For Zack, it was the strangest sensation to laugh and lust at the same time. Strange, but also addictive.

It was well past midnight before he finally dragged his spent, satisfied body into his own house. And as he suspected, he no sooner collapsed onto the bed than he was sound asleep, with a very stupid smile on his face.

NINE

"DARLING!"

Wynn jerked so hard at the sound of that loud, wailing voice, she lost her footing on the ladder. It shifted against the gutter, making her yelp and attempt to grab for the roof, but it was too late. Her hands snatched at nothingness.

As if in slow motion, the ladder pulled farther away from the house and Wynn found herself pedaling the air for several suspended seconds before she landed in the rough evergreen bushes with a hard thud. The wooden ladder crashed down on top of her.

"Ohmigod! Wynn! Wynn!"

A flash of red satin blurred in front of her eyes as her father knelt in front of her. The sunlight caught his diamond earring and nearly blinded her. "My baby! Are you okay?"

Her head was ringing and her side hurt like hell. She had a mouthful of leaves and something sharp poked at her hip. Her father began picking debris from her hair, tsking and fussing until her mother showed up and shoved him aside.

"Dear God, you nearly killed her, Artemus!"

Wearing faded cutoffs and a colorful tie-dye smock, Wynn's mother leaned over her. "It's a good thing we're here, Wynonna. You look hurt."

Wynn could only stare. A good thing? She wouldn't be hurt if her father hadn't startled her so. She hadn't even heard their car arrive. Of course, her thoughts had been on Zack, on that mind-blowing episode the night before, not on her parents' extended visit. She'd slept little last night, too busy going over and over all the wonderful things Zack had done to her and with her.

Her mother sat back on her heels. "Artemus, will you look at her? I think she hit her head."

Artemus leaned down and waved his hand in front of her face. "Yoo-hoo, princess? Baby, can you hear us?"

Suddenly Artemus was shoved aside again, but not by her mother. Zack, wearing only jeans that weren't properly fastened and a very rugged shadowing of beard stubble, crouched down in front of her. "Wynn?" Unlike her parents, his voice was gentle and concerned. He touched her cheek, which she realized had been scraped raw by a bush. "No, don't move, sweetheart. Just hold still and let me make certain you're okay."

Sweetheart? She glanced at her parents and saw them both staring with speculation. Oh dear. Wynn blinked at Zack. "Um…what are you doing here?" It was very early still, not quite seven, and Zack should have been home getting ready for work.

"I was making my coffee when I saw you climb the damn ladder. Before I could get dressed and tell you how stupid you were being, you fell."

Her mother asked, "You were making coffee naked?"

Without looking at her, Zack said, "No, in my underwear."

A wave of heat washed over Wynn. Her parents began staring even harder.

Wynn cleared her throat. "My father startled me."

"Well!" Artemus took immediate exception to that accusation. "If your hair wasn't in your eyes, maybe you would have seen me coming and you wouldn't have *been* startled!"

Zack turned to him to say something, and went mute. Her father was in top form today. He wore a red silk shirt, open at the collar to show a profuse amount of curly chest hair. He had two rings on his fingers, a gold chain around his neck and the big diamond earring he almost never removed. His pressed dark-blue designer jeans were so tight they fit like his skin, and his low boots were polished to a shine. His golden brown hair, so unlike Wynn's, was parted in the middle and hung nearly to his shoulders.

At Zack's scrutiny, he tossed his head and huffed.

Zack snapped his mouth shut and turned back to Wynn without uttering a word. "Where are you hurt?"

"Nowhere. I'm okay." But when she started to sit up, she winced and Zack caught her shoulders.

"No, let me check you."

"Daddy?"

Dani stood there, still in her nightgown and holding a fuzzy yellow blanket. Wynn smiled at her. "I'm okay, munchkin."

"You're in the bushes."

"Luckily they broke my fall."

Dani smiled. "I saw you on the roof. I wanna get on the roof, too."

Zack turned so quickly everyone jumped. "Dani, if I catch you even thinking such a thing you'll be grounded in your room for a month!"

"Wynn did it."

Zack ground his teeth together. When he turned to Wynn, his expression was no longer so concerned. Now he looked furious. "Wynn will tell you what a dumb stunt that was, won't you, Wynn?"

Everyone stared at her. Her parents looked particularly interested in seeing her response, and she knew it was because they expected her to chew Zack up and spit him out in little bits. Never, ever, did she let anyone speak to her as he did.

But there was Dani, watching and waiting, and the thought of the child trying to get on a roof made her skin crawl. "I should have waited until there was someone to hold the ladder steady for me, Dani. Sometimes I do things without really thinking about them. It's a bad habit."

Her mother gasped and her father pretended to stagger. After a long second, Zack gave her a thankful nod.

Relieved, Wynn said, "Mom, Dad, this is my neighbor Zack Grange and his daughter Dani. Zack is a paramedic."

"Well, that explains everything," her father said with facetious humor.

Wynn winced again as Zack pressed his fingertips over her side. She said quickly, "Zack, my mother Chastity and my father Artemus."

Dani said, "I like Wynn lots."

"We're rather fond of her, too," Artemus said, and he patted Dani's head, then frowned at her hair.

Zack paid no attention to the introductions. "Let me get your shirt up and see what you've done."

Chastity laughed.

"No, Zack, really I'm fine, I just... Zack, stop it..."

Chastity said, "Oh be still, Wynonna. Let the man have a look."

Zack looked.

A long bloody scratch ran up and over her ribs almost to her breast. Zack looked furious. "This needs to be cleaned."

"I'll take care of it as soon as you *let-me-out-of-the-bushes!*"

He began checking her arms, her legs. Wynn, peeved at being the center of attention, scrambled out of his reach, gaining more scratches in the bargain. Using the side of the house for support, she stood.

Her efforts ended in a gasp and she almost dropped again. Zack caught her under the arms. "What is it? Your leg?"

"No." She squeezed her eyes shut and whimpered. Damn damn damn. There was no help for it. Drooping, she said, "It's my toe."

"Your toe?" her father repeated.

"My baby toe." She was balanced on her left leg, so Zack rightfully assumed she'd injured her right toe.

"I'm going to lift you," he told her. "Tell me if I hurt you."

"Zack!" The whole situation was going from bad to worse. "You can't lift me."

"She weighs more than I do," her father said.

Wynn gasped. "I do not!" She tried to slap him, but he ducked aside.

In the next instant she found herself securely held against Zack's bare chest. His arms didn't shake and his legs were steady. He didn't appear the least bit strained.

Awareness mushroomed inside her.

She couldn't remember the last time anyone had lifted her up. Even Conan didn't do it anymore, claiming she was too big, and he could easily bench-press four-fifty.

It felt kinda nice. Dumb but nice.

She wrapped her arms around his neck, but said, "You can put me down, Zack."

He stepped out of the bushes. "Dani, come with me into Wynn's house. We'll get you dressed in just a minute."

"We'll be late," Dani predicted with an adult sigh, and skipped after him.

Wynn looked over Zack's shoulder and saw her parents watching the display with fascination. She groaned. "This is awful."

"Wynn?"

"What?"

"You'll notice I'm not even breathing hard."

She looked at him, his hair mussed and his eyes still heavy from sleep. His sleek, hard shoulders were warm and his chest was solid. He smelled delicious. "I did notice that."

"And I'm not straining, either."

Despite her humiliation at having fallen off a ladder, shocking her parents and making Zack run late, she smiled. "Superhero."

He grinned. "C'mon, Dani. You can open the door for me. I think Wynn's parents are a little confused by all this."

"They're confused," Wynn responded, "by the sight of a male neighbor feeling me up in the bushes and toting me around with a lot more familiarity than has ever been exhibited in the past."

"I wasn't *feeling you up*. I was checking you over. There's an enormous difference."

"Yeah, well, I could tell by my parents' expressions, they considered it one and the same."

Zack paused to look down at her. His breath smelled of toothpaste and was warm. "I was watching you through that window, cursing you if you want the truth, and when I saw you fall, my heart almost stopped."

At the husky tone of his voice, something inside Wynn

turned to mush—probably her brains. But it sounded as if he cared about her, at least enough to not want her to break her neck.

Wynn drew a breath. "I'm sorry," she answered, her voice just as husky. "I didn't hear them drive up."

"Mmmm." Zack stared at her mouth. "Had your mind on other things did you?"

"She was daydreamin'," Dani said and pulled the door open with exaggerated impatience.

"Is that right?" Zack stepped into the kitchen and went through to the family room. "Were you daydreaming, Wynn? About what, I wonder."

She muttered close to his ear, "As if you didn't know," and saw his small satisfied smile.

He lowered her carefully to the couch. "Let me get your shoe and sock off."

"I can do it."

Of course he ignored her wishes and untied her laces. "Zack, my feet are probably sweaty by now. I've been up and working since about five."

"Do you ever not work?" Pushing aside her fretful hands, he eased her sneaker off. "Sweaty," he confirmed as he peeled her sock away and began examining her toe.

Wynn stretched up to see. Dani stood beside her and patted her shoulder.

Her poor little baby toe was already black and blue and the bruising had climbed halfway up her foot. It was swollen and looked awful. Seeing it made it hurt worse, but she forced a laugh and said, "Big and sweaty. Betcha wish now you'd left my sock on."

"Damn, Wynn," Zack muttered, touching her foot with a

heart-wrenching gentleness. "It's definitely broken. You need to ice it, then get it taped. Can your doctor see you today?"

"For a baby toe?" She snorted. "Don't be ridiculous." Wynn seriously doubted she could hobble her way to the doctor right now, the way her foot felt. How one small toe could cause so much pain was a mystery.

The kitchen door opened and closed and her parents joined them at the couch. Her father went straight for her head and began trying to groom her hair. Her mother asked, "Do you have any herbal tea? That always helps."

Zack looked pained, then resigned. "I need to be getting to work. But she has a broken toe, maybe even a broken foot, so it should be X-rayed. She's also got a lot of cuts and scratches that'll need to be cleaned."

Her father said, "Wynn, Wynn, Wynn."

She swatted his hands away from her hair. "I'm fine, Dad."

Chastity looked Zack over from head to toe and back again. "Well." She smiled. "You run along, young man. We're here now and we'll take good care of her."

"You're a hippie," Dani said with awe.

Zack said, "Dani!"

But Chastity laughed. "Did my daughter tell you that?"

Dani nodded. "And you gots rings on your toes."

"Just two rings, but they're made of a special metal that has healing powers. Perhaps I'll put one on Wynn and it'll make her toe heal quicker."

"No!" Zack caught himself and stood. He looked frazzled and harassed and undecided. "No rings." Then, stressing the point by speaking slowly, he said, "She needs an X-ray."

"Zack," Wynn said, "I'm a big girl."

"Indeed." Her father moved from her hair to Dani's and

Dani appeared to love the attention. She even gave Artemus a huge grin.

"I can take care of myself. I'm not an idiot!"

"No, just an intelligent woman who climbs a rickety ladder to the roof before the sun is even all the way up."

"If Dad hadn't snuck up on me…"

"Now don't go blaming me again, darling! Your young man is right. You had no business being on that ladder in the first place." He said all that without looking up, too busy working on Dani's hair.

Zack opened his mouth, then closed it. He shook his head. "Wynn, promise me you'll go get an X-ray."

"But…"

"It's likely just a broken toe and they'll tape it, but it's better to be safe than sorry. Being a physical therapist, you should know this."

She did know it. "Oh, all right."

As if making a decision, Zack said, "I'll check on you tonight. In the meantime, Mrs. Lane, why don't you get her some ice to soak her foot for the swelling? And, Mr. Lane, you could maybe get her a phone so she can make the call to the doctor?"

Her parents looked pleased with the direction. Artemus quickly finished fooling with Dani's hair and rushed off. Chastity followed him.

The second they were out of the room, Zack bent over Wynn. "I wish I had more time, but if I don't get going now, I'll be late."

"I understand. Really, I'm fine."

"When I get home I expect to find you taking it easy."

"Me and my large feet will make a leisurely day of it."

He touched her cheek. "Large feet for a large, beautiful woman."

Now her brain and her bones were mush. She managed a lopsided silly smile.

Zack straightened. "I'll see you tonight."

"I thought you had plans."

"I do." He didn't explain beyond that.

Wynn wanted to ask him what his plans were, but she was afraid he'd be out with another woman. And because she had no exclusive rights to him, she couldn't complain, so she was better off not knowing.

Dani kissed her cheek. "I'll see ya tonight, too. I'll even draw you a picture."

It was then that Wynn noticed Dani's fine, fair hair had been plaited into an intricate braid and tied with a tiny yellow ribbon. She shook her head in wonder. Did her father carry ribbons in his pockets?

She wouldn't be at all surprised.

Zack noticed his daughter's hair, too. He did a quick double take, then said, "Well I'll be."

Dani smiled and kept reaching back to feel it. She looked very pleased with the results. "It's pretty."

Wynn said, "Very pretty!" and meant it.

Chastity hustled back in with a big bowl filled with ice and several dishcloths over her arm. She dropped onto the foot of the couch, making Wynn groan. To Dani, she asked, "You're the artist who created that masterpiece on the refrigerator?"

Wynn managed a smile to help cover the discomfort of her mother's rough movements. "That's right. Isn't she talented?"

"Very much so." As Chastity wrapped ice in a towel, she said, "You'd love finger paints. Have you ever tried them?"

Both Wynn and Zack winced. "Mom, they're awfully messy."

"So?" She flapped a dismissive hand at Wynn. "You and your cleanliness quirks. She's a child! You can't stifle her creative spirit just because she might get a little paint under her nails." Chastity was gentle as she applied the ice to Wynn's foot.

Watching Zack, Wynn thought he might have jumped her mother if she hadn't shown what he considered adequate care. "I brought my paints with me, Dani. It'll be lovely, you'll see."

Beaming, Dani said, "Thank you!"

Artemus waltzed in with the phone. "Found it!" He handed it to Wynn, along with her small phone book, then turned to Dani. He patted her hair with pride. "Lovely." Then to his daughter, "Wynn," he said, "wouldn't you like for me to do something with your hair while you make your call?"

Wynn said, "No," and her father's face fell with comical precision.

Zack scooped Dani and her blanket into his arms. "We have to run. Wynn, remember what I said."

"Me and my big feet will follow doctor's orders."

There was a general round of farewells, and five seconds later, Zack was gone. Wynn fell back against the couch. Her foot throbbed and ached, her ribs pulled, she itched from all the shrub scratches and now her parents were standing there staring at her with tell-all expectation.

The day had started out being so promising, but now...

She doubted it had dawned on Zack yet, but after all they'd just witnessed, no way would her parents believe a simple visit to the hot tub. Nope, they were eccentric, but they were not dumb.

And they knew sexual chemistry when they witnessed it.

Her mother, pretending a great interest in Wynn's bruised and swollen toes, said, "My, my, my. What a hottie." She slanted Wynn a look and an I'm-onto-you grin.

"Quite virile," her father agreed, while tugging distractedly on his earring and eyeing his wife's legs. Despite years of marriage and the fact that he was more colorful, Artemus remained highly attracted to her mother. He made no effort to hide his sexual willingness, which pretty much started from the time Chastity woke in the morning and ran until she fell asleep at night. It was almost comical.

He visibly pulled himself back to the subject at hand. "I, ah, take it he's single?"

Wynn sank further into the cushions. "Yes."

Silence reigned for only a few seconds, and then her father clasped his hands together and sighed. "Well, the little girl has *fabulous* hair! Or at least she will when I finish with it. All in all, I say they'll be a wonderful addition to the family. What do you think, dear?"

Chastity smiled. "I think we got here just in time to watch the fireworks."

Zack heard the noise from Wynn's house the second he stepped out of his car. Blaring music competed with laughter and the din of loud conversation.

It was six-thirty and he was tired, hungry, worried and rushed. It seemed he'd been running late from the moment he woke that morning, and there'd been no let-up since.

He'd started the day by oversleeping. After the excesses of lovemaking the night before, he'd slept like the dead and hadn't even heard his alarm until it had been ringing for almost half an hour. When he got over that disquieting phenomenon, he'd washed his face and brushed his teeth in two minutes flat, then gone for coffee before attempting to put a razor to his throat.

He never had gotten around to shaving, he realized, and now he felt scruffy and unkempt. He rubbed his rough jaw, remembering the trials of the day.

It was as he'd measured coffee that he glanced out the kitchen window and spied Wynn precariously balanced on an old wooden ladder, attempting to clean her gutters. His hair had been on end, his eyes still gritty, his feet bare on the cold linoleum floor, and he lost his temper.

He ran upstairs to awaken Dani, hastily pulled on pants, then ran back downstairs and outside to confront Wynn before she fell and killed herself.

He'd been too late.

It still made him tremble when he remembered opening the door just in time to see her wildly flailing the air as she plummeted to the ground. His stomach cramped anew.

Damned irritating, irrational, provoking female! She was lucky she'd only broken a toe!

He thought about her parents and cringed. "Flaming heterosexual," she'd called her father, and now he knew the description was apt. He'd never met a more flamboyant, dramatic man; his every word and gesture had been exaggerated.

But he'd done a wonderful job with Dani's hair. She'd looked so cute…

Zack shook his head.

Wynn's mother was, as she'd claimed, a hippie. Her long blond hair had streaks of gray, but her figure was still youthful. Wynn had likely gotten her beautiful legs from her mother. Chastity's legs weren't nearly as long, and the rings on her toes were a distraction, but all in all, she was an attractive woman. Loony, but attractive.

After Zack secured Wynn's promise to see a doctor, he'd rushed back home to prepare for work. He left the house right on time. Unfortunately, when he reached Eloise's house to drop off Dani, he'd found the elderly woman ill.

With Dani hovering nearby, Zack did a medical check on Eloise. She was feverish and pale, her pulse too weak. Eloise claimed it was no more than the flu and she warned Dani to beware of her germs. She said she'd been sick off and on all night, so she'd called Zack that morning. But it must have been while he was at Wynn's house, and he hadn't thought to check his answering machine in his hurry to get out the door.

He called his supervisor and explained why he'd be late so one of the men from the shift before could stay over, then he'd bundled Eloise up for a trip to the emergency room. He wasn't willing to take any chances with a woman her age, especially when she looked so weak. While he gathered a few things for her, he'd called Josh, who was off that day.

A woman had answered.

Zack thought about hanging up and calling Del or Mick instead, but Josh retrieved the phone, discovered the dilemma and made plans to pick up Dani at the hospital.

En route to the hospital, Zack got hold of Eloise's granddaughter, who also agreed to meet them there in case Eloise needed to be admitted.

By the time he finally got to work, he was almost two hours late. The women he worked with teased him about his unshaven appearance and harried demeanor.

And throughout it all, he'd thought of Wynn.

She plagued him, making his brain ache and his body hot. He alternately worried about her and her broken toe, and contemplated making love to her again.

He glanced to the front of her house now where the driveway, just visible from his side yard, could be seen overflowing with a variety of vehicles.

A party.

She'd promised him she'd take it easy, that she'd prop her large feet up and rest. Instead, she was having a party.

Zack locked his jaw tight and stomped up to his kitchen stoop. Fine. Whatever. He'd simply ignore her and her irresponsible ways. It wasn't as if he wanted to worry about her, or even think about her.

No, he just wanted to take her again and again, in about a hundred different ways. He wanted to kiss her body all over, starting on her toes and working his way up those sexy shapely legs until he reached her...

"Oh hell." Zack jerked his door open, called out, "I'm home," and was greeted by silence. He suddenly realized there had been no extra cars in *his* driveway, which meant Josh wasn't here with Dani as he said he'd be.

But just to make certain, Zack went through the house. It was empty.

He was so tired he ached, and now he stopped in the middle of the living room and looked around, trying to decide what to do next. Where would Josh be?

He'd left the kitchen door open and now he heard a robust laugh carry across the yards. His mind cramped as he considered the possibilities. With deliberate intent, feeling ill-tempered and irked, he went to the kitchen to look out the window.

There in Wynn's yard were close to a dozen people, including Josh and Dani. A boom box blared from the patio and a badminton net had been set up. A woman he didn't recognize partnered Conan against Marc and Clint, while Bo leaned against a tree and shouted encouragement. It appeared to be a highly competitive game, given the viciousness of the play.

On the patio, he could see Chastity singing as she wielded a long-handled fork on the grill. Artemus, now dressed all in black except for a large silver buckle on his belt that glinted in the late-day sun, danced with Dani. His daughter appeared to be wearing one of Chastity's tie-dyed shirts. It hung down to her feet.

Zack looked around without conscious thought and finally located Wynn. She sat on the settee with Josh, her foot in his lap.

Zack felt as though the top of his head had just blown off.

Before he'd even made the decision to move, he was halfway across the lawn, his gaze set on Wynn who was, as yet, unaware of his approach.

Today she was dressed in a pale-peach camisole that almost exactly matched her naked hide, and a pair of loose white drawstring shorts that showed every sexy inch of her long legs and put on display a tiny strip of her delectable belly.

Zack's lungs constricted. When he reached her, he'd—

Conan stepped in front of him. "Whoa, where ya going there, Zack?"

Zack heard a few snickers from behind Conan and knew he'd gained the players' attention.

Conan leaned closer. "The thing is," he whispered, "you look mad as hell and my sister's already been upset all day."

"Yeah," Zack said, still watching Wynn while she smiled and laughed with Josh. "She looks real upset."

Conan blinked, then laughed. "Jealousy is a bitch, ain't it?"

Zack snapped a look at Conan and the man backed up two steps. "Okay, okay," he said, swallowing down a laugh and holding up his hands as if to ward Zack off, "I take it back. You're not jealous."

Zack narrowed his eyes. "What reason would I have to be jealous?"

"None! No reason at all. I mean, believe it or not, Wynn's in pain and... Hey, wait a minute!"

Zack allowed Conan to pull him back around. Wynn was in pain? He couldn't stand it.

Conan laughed. "I'm sorry. Really, I am." Zack vaguely heard the other men laughing and offering comments, but he paid them no mind.

Over his shoulder, Conan shouted, "Shut up, Bo!" To Zack he said, "Ignore Bo. He's been giving Wynn hell all day for being *smitten*. I was about ready to flatten him myself when he finally realized she wasn't taking it well."

Zack drew a deep breath and attempted to ease his temper. Most times, he didn't have a temper, and he blamed the emergence of one solely on Wynn Lane. She brought out the worst in him.

She also turned him on more than any woman he'd ever known. "Why not?" he asked, hoping he sounded merely calm, not concerned. "What's going on?"

"Whew, finally you sound like a reasonable man." Conan clapped him on the shoulder hard enough to make Zack lose his balance. "At first you were looking like a charging bull. Nostrils flared, eyes red, steam coming out your ears. Bo told me, but I didn't really believe him. I mean, when I met you, you seemed so..."

"Conan."

"Sorry. The folks threw this surprise housewarming party for Wynn, but she's obviously not really up to it. I mean, her damn toe is broken in two places. Two! Can you believe that?

Her feet are bigger than most, that's true, but it's still just a baby toe."

Zack closed his eyes and counted to ten, but he still heard the smile in Conan's voice when he continued.

"Your buddy has been fending everyone off, including my parents. He pulled Wynn's foot into his lap after the third person accidentally bumped her and made her yelp. Not a pretty thing to see Wynn yelping."

"Damn."

Conan rubbed his neck, looked up at the fading sun, then back at his teammates who were now clustered together and waiting. He faced Zack again. "The folks mean well. It's just that Wynn never complains much, and she never admits to being hurt, so they don't realize..."

"Dad!" His daughter ran hell-bent toward him, cutting off Conan's explanations. Not that he'd needed to continue; Zack already understood the situation and more than anything he wanted to shake Wynn for putting up such a ridiculous macho show. That was something a man would do, but it wasn't expected of a woman. And despite being hardy and strong, she *was* still a woman.

And damn it, he wanted to protect her.

Dani threw herself at Zack, and he noticed his daughter now wore sandals rather than sneakers. And she had a silver ring on her big toe.

He scooped her up and hugged her to him. "Look at you, Dani," he teased. "Wearing a dress."

She laughed, cupped his face and gave him a loud smooch. "It's not a dress. It's Chastity's. She let me wear it while I finger painted. Ain't it pretty?"

Zack didn't bother correcting her speech, not this time,

not while she was so excited and happy. "Yes it is, especially on you."

"Conan said I was a flower child."

"But prettier," Conan clarified.

Zack hugged her again and started toward Wynn. He stopped, turned back to Conan and said, "Thanks."

Conan pretended great relief. "Yeah, anytime. I mean, she's a pain in the ass, but I still love my sister." His voice lowered to something of a warning. "And I wouldn't want anyone to upset her. Or hurt her." He stared at Zack, making sure Zack caught his meaning.

Zack nodded, which was the best reply he could offer, for the time being.

"So," Zack said to his daughter, staring at that silver ring on her toe, "you've had fun today?"

"I've had the bestest time! Artemus is teaching me how to dance and look what he did to my hair!" She primped, turning her head one way and then the other.

Her hair had been braided and then twisted into a coronet with tiny multi-colored crystal beads shaped like flowers pinned into place. Two curling ringlets hung in front of her ears.

Zack felt a lump the size of a grapefruit lodge in his throat at the sight of his daughter's proud smile. Artemus met him at the edge of the patio.

"I need your permission to give her a trim," he said before Zack could greet him. "She has *fabulous* hair, just fabulous. But God only knows how long it's been since it was shaped. It *begs* to be shaped."

Zack looked at Dani, who watched him hopefully. "Do you want your hair shaped?" *Whatever the hell that means.*

She nodded.

"You have my permission."

Artemus clapped his hands in bliss.

Chastity turned to Zack. "Hamburger or hot dog, Zack?"

He eyed this remarkable woman who had managed to birth Wynn. "Do hippies eat meat?"

"Honey, when they're my age, they do any damn thing they want to."

Artemus leaned close to nip her ear. "And there's a lot they want to do, too." He winked at Zack. "Hippies are a delightfully creative lot."

"Ah." Zack grinned, amused by the obvious affection between them. "In that case, I'll take a hamburger. Thank you, ma'am."

"Be ready in a moment."

Josh eased Wynn's foot out of his lap and stood to greet Zack. "How's Eloise?"

"I called the hospital before I left work today. She has bronchitis. With the medicine they gave her, she's feeling a lot more comfortable."

"Has she got anyone to take care of her?"

Zack nodded, not quite looking at Wynn yet. If he looked at her, he'd want to pick her up and pet her and coddle her. *Insane.* As she'd said, it was only a broken toe. "She's going to stay with her granddaughter for a week until she's had time to recuperate."

Dani and Artemus danced past them, moving to the tune of the Beach Boys. "A week, huh? What about the rat? Who's going to watch her?"

Zack glanced at his daughter as she threw back her head and laughed. "I finagled an early vacation week. It wasn't easy, but I got Richards to trade with me."

Josh looked pleased. "So you'll be around the house—" he glanced at Wynn "—day and night, for a week, huh?"

"That's what I just said." Done with that conversational gambit, he knelt down in front of Wynn. "How're you feeling?"

"Fine."

Zack could tell she lied. Her face looked pinched, her mouth tight. He gave her a frown that let her know he knew, and then took Josh's seat. He lifted her foot into his lap to examine her toe.

She wore no shoes and where the bandage didn't cover, he could see the dark, colorful bruises. Her foot still looked swollen and for some dumb reason, he wanted to kiss it. It's what he would have done for Dani, and now he wanted to do it for Wynn, too.

He manfully resisted the urge and met her gaze. "Have you taken anything for pain?"

"Aspirin."

Josh leaned on the armrest next to Wynn and peered down at them both. In a carrying voice, he said, "I'm sure you both know that ice for swelling is good, but soaking it in hot water is best for relieving the pain."

Zack rolled his eyes; Josh knew nil about subtlety, or medical matters.

Wynn just stared at him.

"I was thinking of your hot tub, Zack." Josh cleared his throat and forged on. "A good neighbor would offer to let her use it."

Without turning their way, Chastity said, "Oh, I'm sure he'd have thought of it sooner or later."

Artemus chortled at his wife's wry humor, and then swung Dani in a wide circle, ending their dance with a flourish.

Dani came over and, natural as you please, climbed into Wynn's lap.

Wynn positioned her comfortably, as if she'd been holding Dani since the day she was born.

Zack almost choked on another lump of emotion. Damn it, men didn't get lumps of emotion, and certainly not over something so simple as seeing a neighbor hold his daughter. But Dani was smiling and looking secure and confident in her welcome.

He silently cursed again.

Wynn was *not* the right woman for him. Whenever he'd envisioned the right woman, he'd pictured a woman who was discreet and circumspect and responsible. A woman who'd be a good influence on his daughter and the perfect domestic partner for raising a child.

Wynn was rash and outspoken and irresponsible. She didn't protect herself or think things out before doing them. She knew too many men who knew her too well... No, that wasn't exactly right and he felt guilty for even thinking it. But he found he was the jealous sort when he'd never been before. And that irked him, too.

Wynn dressed provocatively, didn't eat right, and her family was beyond strange.

She was big and beautiful and so sexy he couldn't stop thinking about her.

What the hell was he supposed to do?

"Eat," Chastity said as if she'd read his mind. She shoved a paper plate with a loaded hamburger, chips and pickles into his hand. She handed the same to Wynn, and gave Dani a hot dog.

Everyone came in from the badminton game and Conan introduced Zack to his girlfriend, Rachael. She was a pretty, slender woman of medium height. *She* was dressed reasonably in long tan walking shorts and a loose blue polo shirt. And none of the men swatted *her* behind.

However, the second Wynn said she needed to go inside a minute, the guys lined up to carry her. They jokingly compared muscles, trying to decide who was strong enough to bear her weight.

Not giving them a chance to get so much as a pinkie finger on her, Zack lifted Wynn into his lap and then stood. There was a general round of oohing and aahing and muttered respect for his strength.

"What do you bench?" Conan asked, and Zack rolled his eyes.

Wynn dropped her head to his shoulder. "This is totally dumb, Zack. I'm more than capable of walking, you know."

"I know. But no one else seems to." He turned to Dani. "Stay right here with Josh, sweetheart."

"I will!"

Zack headed for the back door. Truth was, she felt good in his arms, a nice soft solid weight. Warm and very feminine. He liked holding her. And no way in hell was he going to let any of her "friends" pick her up so they'd experience the same sensations.

"They're just nettling you," Wynn said, "and you're letting them." She reached down to open the kitchen door when Zack stopped in front of it.

"Where to?" he asked.

She sighed, then finally said, "The bathroom."

Zack grinned. The door closed behind them, shutting out some of the party noise. Now that they were in private, he nuzzled Wynn's ear, carefully because of his rough beard, and then asked, "Are you coming over tonight to…soak your foot?"

She looked up at him, surprised. "I thought you had plans?"

"I'll be free by eleven. It's been a total bitch of a day and I can't imagine a better way to end it than with a repeat of last night." He touched his mouth to hers and added, "That is, if you're up to it."

She said, "Ha! I sure wouldn't let a little broken toe keep me from it!"

Zack kissed her chin, feeling all his tension and aggravation melt away just from being near her. Leaving her behind this morning, knowing she was hurt, hadn't sat right with him. "And you called me a superhero," he teased gently.

Wynn hesitated, then made a face. "Okay, I give up. Just what are you doing tonight?"

They stood in the hallway outside the bathroom door. Wynn didn't ask to be put down, and Zack was in no hurry to release her. He looked at her mouth and wanted to groan. He could feel himself getting hard and ruthlessly brought himself under control.

"Del and Mick are coming over. They, Josh and I, are going to watch an interview Del did for her upcoming book. It's going to be on channel—"

They heard a thump and looked up to see Conan collapsed against the wall, a large fist pressed to his massive chest.

Zack was briefly alarmed before Conan wheezed, "Delilah Piper is going to be here? Right next door? Oh my God."

"Delilah Piper-slash-Dawson. Remember, I told you Mick's funny about that. And yeah, she is."

Conan's eyes rolled back and he wheezed some more. "A celebrity in our midst! Wait until I tell everyone else."

"Conan," Wynn said suspiciously, "what are you doing in here?"

Briefly taken off guard, Conan stammered, then looked

much struck. "I brought Ms. Piper's books over to be signed and I was going to give them to Zack!"

Wynn said, "Uh-huh."

"But now I can just give them to her myself." He rubbed his hands together. "I can't wait."

Whatever Conan had really wanted—and Zack assumed it was to check up on his sister—was forgotten as he rushed back outside to share the news.

Zack looked down at Wynn, then readjusted her weight so he could kiss her throat.

She sighed. "I'm sorry, Zack, but I have a feeling your intimate little night with friends has just been ruined."

He kissed her throat again. "Conan is more than welcome. It'll tickle Del and it'll keep Mick on his toes. He gets rattled any time a guy looks at her with admiration—even if it's admiration for her work."

"Zack?"

"Hmmm?"

"You can set me down now."

"I'm not sure I want to."

Wynn hugged him, but said, "If you don't, Conan won't be the only one visiting us. My parents will come trooping through, too, and then the guys…"

Being especially careful of her injury, Zack slid her down his body. She kept her hands on his shoulders and her gaze on his mouth. "I like you in your uniform. It's sexy."

Zack grinned. "Is that right?"

She trailed her fingers over his jaw. "And this looks interesting, too."

"I didn't have time to shave this morning." He nuzzled her, letting her feel his whiskers. Then added in a gruff whisper,

"But I'll shave before you come over tonight." He gazed down at her breasts and said, "I wouldn't want to give you a burn."

"Zack…"

The way she sighed his name was such a temptation. Zack turned her toward the bathroom. "Go, before I decide I can't wait until tonight."

She gave him a vacuous smile and hobbled in, favoring her injured foot while trying to strut like a man, just to prove she wasn't hurt. Zack shook his head and a warm feeling expanded inside him, making him hot and hard and filling him with tenderness.

Her ridiculous false bravado shouldn't have done that to him. *She* shouldn't have done that to him. But she did, and he knew he was in deep.

Problem was, for some strange reason, he just couldn't work up the energy to fight it.

TEN

IT WAS ELEVEN o'clock and her parents had retired to their room half an hour ago. Wynn could still hear them talking and laughing, though. Because her parents remained frisky even after all these years, she made a mental note to run her ceiling fan at night for background noise, and slipped out of her room.

Unfortunately, she was almost to Zack's house when she realized the additional cars were still in his driveway; his company hadn't yet left. She was about to turn around when a female voice called out, "You must be Wynn."

Wynn froze. Zack had his porch light on and so did she, so she knew the woman could see her, but still she considered hiding.

The woman laughed. "I'm Del. Come on over and chat."

Wynn hadn't joined her brother and the others earlier when they'd gone to worship at the writer's feet. She wasn't much of a mystery reader, and beyond that, she hadn't liked the idea of forcing herself into Zack's company any more than she already had.

Her foot hurt and she was self-conscious in her robe, but she crept forward and even pasted on a smile. "Hello. Yes, I'm Wynn. A neighbor."

Delilah Piper-Dawson stood leaning against a tree admiring the sky. When Wynn got close, Del offered her hand. "I've heard a lot about you."

"Oh?" Who had talked about her? she wondered. Zack? What had he said? She stepped closer.

Though Delilah was tall for a woman, Wynn towered over her. Del had the type of slender willowy build that made Wynn feel like a lumberjack.

Delilah looked her over and asked, "You're ready for bed?"

"Oh, no." She fidgeted with the belt to her terry cloth robe and explained, "I have my bathing suit on. Zack invited me to use his hot tub. I, uh, I broke my toe today."

"That's right! I heard about that, too."

Wynn studied the smaller woman. "What exactly has Zack told you?"

"Well, not much. Zack, as I'm sure you know, is very close-mouthed and private."

Wynn didn't know any such thing.

"He's also very calm and controlled."

"Oh?"

Delilah laughed. "Yes, but Josh and Mick have both told me that around you, he's just the opposite. Always losing his temper and grumbling and growling. I love it. It was so funny when he first started talking about getting a wife. He had all these absurd notions of what qualities he'd want." Delilah shook her head and her beautiful, very shiny and sleek inky-black hair caught the moonlight, making it look almost liquid. Wynn reached up to smooth her own hair, which she'd ruthlessly contained in a tight knot on top of her head.

When she realized she was primping and why, Wynn dropped her hand and said again, "Oh?"

Delilah nodded. "Let me warn you though, if you do marry Zack, they'll all expect you to get dressed up for the wedding."

She said that as if it were the worst fate possible. Wynn despised dressing up, too, so she understood.

Del made a face. "But it's not that bad, considering the end results."

Wynn looked around, wondering what the hell she was supposed to say to that. When Delilah just waited, she blurted, "We won't be getting married. Zack isn't all that serious about me. He just wants to…well, he just *wants* me." And to be completely clear, she added, "But not for marriage."

Delilah stared at her, then took her arm. "Come on. Let's sit down. Here you are with a broken toe and I've got you standing in the yard sharing confidences." She turned, holding on to Wynn as if she, with her measly delicate strength, could offer substantial support. "Let's be really quiet though. The guys are yakking and I escaped out here to get some fresh air. I don't want them to join us yet."

They stopped at the hot tub and Delilah sat on the edge, crossing her ankles. "The patio curtains are closed," she pointed out, "so they won't notice us. You can go ahead and get in if you want."

Wynn shook her head.

"Okay, but let's get back to this sex business."

"I didn't exactly mean to say that." Wynn had no idea why she'd confessed such a thing to a complete stranger. Delilah had just asked and she'd answered.

"That's okay. People are always confiding in me. I'm a writer, you know."

Wynn had no idea what that had to do with anything.

"Your brother told me a lot about you, too. He says you've never been this serious about a guy before."

"I'll kill him."

Delilah laughed. "Don't worry. No one overheard him. But you should know, it's the same for Zack. I thought Mick was a recluse when it came to women, but Zack is even worse. It's amazing considering they're both friends with Josh, and that man knows no moderation where females are concerned."

Wynn started to say, "Oh?" but caught herself in time. "I gather Josh is something of a lady's man."

"He likes to think so. Unfortunately, most of the ladies agree with him." Then she said, "Now back to you and Zack. I want to tell you, whatever you do, don't give up. I almost gave up on Mick, but luckily his family talked me out of it. Since we're like Zack's family now, I feel honor bound to do the same for you."

Wynn gave up without a whimper. She flopped down beside Delilah on the edge of the tub and hung her head. "It's no wonder Zack isn't interested in getting serious with me. Every time I'm around him, I end up doing something dumb. Like wrestling him to the ground—"

"No kidding?" Delilah looked very curious about that.

"And insulting him and then I fell and broke my stupid toe…"

"Why do you insult him?"

Wynn shrugged. "I've always been treated like one of the guys. It's all I really know. I speak my mind, tease and harass."

Delilah nodded. "Yeah, Mick and Josh and Zack do that all the time."

"So does my brother and the guys from the gym."

"Hmmm." Delilah got up to pace. She wore a tiny T-shirt with a smiley face on the front, baggy jeans, and strappy sandals, and still she looked utterly feminine. If the woman wasn't being so nice, Wynn might not have liked her. She sat again and took Wynn's hand. "I think you should tell Zack how you feel."

"Really?" Wynn winced even considering it. "Is that what you did with Mick?"

She laughed. "Too much so. Poor Mick didn't know what to think of me. But I'm not used to hiding my feelings, especially feelings that strong. I knew almost from the moment I noticed him that I wanted him for my own."

Wynn nodded in understanding. She'd felt the same about Zack. Almost from the first, she'd known what a wonderful person he was.

"Okay." Delilah stood. "Off with the robe and into the hot tub. I'll get Mick and Josh to leave and I'll send Zack out. What's your bathing suit look like?" Her eyes widened and she asked with scandalized delight, "Or are you wearing one?"

"Of course I'm wearing one!" Wynn almost sputtered at the idea of traipsing across two yards in nothing but a thin robe. "I wouldn't leave my house naked."

Delilah looked let down. "Okay, let me see the suit."

"It's…um, kinda skimpy."

"Because you wanted to entice Zack? Good idea, not quite as good as being naked, but still… Not that he needs any enticement, you know. He's been antsy and pacing and impatient all night. We all knew he wanted us gone so he could visit with you, so of course that made Mick and Josh more determined to hang around, just to watch Zack fret." Delilah shook her head. "They're all nuts, but I love them."

Once she finished talking, Delilah just waited. Then she cleared her throat. "Can I see the suit?"

Wynn hadn't had any really close female friends before. She hung more with the guys, and that had always suited her just fine. But Delilah, well, she was easy to talk to, friendly and open. Wynn liked her on the spot.

"Okay, but don't laugh."

"Why would I laugh?"

Wynn squeezed her eyes shut, gripped the lapels of the robe, and held it open. She wasn't naked, but the string bikini was as close as she could get.

Delilah whistled. "Wow. Zack'll be lucky if he lasts half an hour. You look great. Like a model."

Wynn snatched the robe shut. "The only time Zack and I made love it was pitch dark and he couldn't really see me."

"Well, that suit'll make up for it! I almost wish I could hang around for his reaction. Will you call me tomorrow and let me know how it goes?"

Dumbstruck, Wynn stammered, "Uh, well, yeah. Sure."

"Wait! Better still, let's have lunch. I just finished a book so I've got some free time. I need to let my brain recoup before I start plotting again. Where do you work? I could meet you there."

Overwhelmed by Delilah's enthusiasm, Wynn heard herself giving the address for her brother's gym. "Conan will wet his pants if you actually come and say hi."

"Your brother is a real sweetheart. It always makes my day to meet up with a reader. In fact, don't tell him yet, but I'm thinking of setting a book around a gym. Can you imagine? With all that weight equipment and the pool and the sauna, why, all kinds of stuff could go on there. Like maybe…" Delilah caught herself and laughed. "There I go, plotting again. Ignore me."

Wynn was charmed. "I think it's interesting. And I'm sure Conan would be thrilled to help out by showing you around and answering questions." Her brother would owe her big time for this one, Wynn thought, and smiled.

"That'd be great. So what time is lunch?"

Delilah Piper-Dawson had a quick mind and Wynn could barely keep up. "Eleven-thirty?"

"Perfect. I'll be there. Now into the tub and I'll send Zack out."

"It was nice meeting you, Delilah."

Over her shoulder, Delilah said, "Same here. And call me Del."

Wynn stared after Delilah, feeling like she'd gotten seized in a whirlwind. Then she caught herself and realized Zack could be out any second. She didn't want to have to disrobe in front of him! She dropped the terry robe over a chair and slid into the warm water. The jets weren't turned on yet, but the hot water felt heavenly—and it covered her mostly bare body.

She only hoped Zack appreciated her immodesty.

Zack stared at Josh and Mick, who stared back, and wondered how in hell he could get rid of them. The show featuring Delilah's interview was long since over, but still they hung around, drinking more coffee and chatting as if no one had anywhere to go. Delilah had tired of it and gone outside to stretch her legs, or so she said.

No sooner did Zack think of her than she reappeared. She walked to her husband, took his hands and pulled him from the couch. "Let's go."

"Go where?" Mick asked, teasing her.

"Home. Zack has company and we've overstayed ourselves."

All three men turned to stare toward the kitchen where Del had entered. Zack asked, "Wynn is here?"

"No, her dad."

"What?"

Del laughed. "Just teasing. Yeah, it's Wynn. And what a nice woman! I really like her, Zack."

Zack's eyes narrowed. "Just how long has she been out there, Del?"

"About ten minutes, that's all." She winked. "We were chatting and getting to know each other."

Mick shook his head. "Honey, why didn't you bring her inside?"

"She didn't want to come in."

"Why not?"

"She's in this teeny tiny little string bikini."

With arrested looks on their faces, the men all turned toward the kitchen.

Del caught Mick around the neck. "Oh, no you don't. If you want to see a mostly naked woman, you can just take me on home."

Mick grinned and his dark eyes heated. "That's a hell of an idea."

Josh took two steps forward and Zack stepped in front of him. He crossed his arms. "I don't think so."

Trying for an innocent look, Josh said, "But it wouldn't be neighborly of me to leave without saying hello first."

"I'll give her your regrets and tell her you said 'hi.'"

Josh almost laughed. "Ah, c'mon, Zack. You can at least appease an old friend's curiosity."

"Get out. And you can leave by the front door."

Josh sauntered over to Del and slung an arm around her

shoulder. "Del, honey, I guess you'll just have to tell me all about it."

Del smiled. "She's gorgeous, Josh. I can see why Zack is hooked." Then she turned to Zack. "But she's also very nice."

Josh nodded. "Agreed."

Zack hastily bent to kiss Del's cheek as she stepped out front. "Do me a favor, will you, hon? Make sure neither of them sneaks around back."

As soon as he got Del's laughing promise, Zack closed and locked his front door then raced for the patio. Dani was long since asleep, his company was finally gone, and Wynn was already in the tub. Finally, the day was beginning to improve.

He pushed the patio curtains aside and stared at Wynn for several seconds before opening the doors and stepping out. She looked beautiful, though he could only see her from the shoulders up. The rest of her was hidden beneath the water.

She had her impossible hair piled on top of her head, but the steam from the hot water had still affected it. Tiny curls at her temples sprang free, giving her the appearance of a newly hatched baby bird.

Zack smiled and he had to admit, it wasn't just lust making his stomach tight. "Hey."

Wynn lifted her head from the back of the tub and stared at him. "Hi."

Watching her, he began unbuttoning his shirt. "I didn't realize you were here or I'd have come out sooner."

"That's okay. I didn't mean to interrupt your visit with your friends."

"Did you and Del have a nice chat?" More than anything, he wondered what they had talked about. With Del, there was no telling.

"She's really nice, isn't she?"

"Del's a sweetheart." He dropped his shirt and sat in a lawn chair to remove his shoes and socks. "Mick's crazy about her."

He set his shoes aside and stood to unfasten his slacks. He heard Wynn squeak, and looked up. "I'm not going to bother with trunks. You don't mind do you?"

She stared at his abdomen and shook her head. Zack was already so hard there was no way she could miss his erection. He wanted her, even more now that he'd had her and knew how incredible it was.

They were behind the privacy fence, so no one could see them. Still he reached inside and flipped off the lights, casting the hot tub into shadows.

Wynn muttered a complaint, which made him laugh. "Your eyes will adjust, but I don't want to take the chance of your parents wandering over."

"They're in bed," she said. "Nothing short of a natural disaster would get them out of there now."

Zack removed his wallet from his pocket. He took out two condoms and put them close at hand, then pulled his slacks and his boxers off and put them over the back of a chair. He stepped into the tub. "Do you want the jets, or is this good enough?"

Wynn swallowed. He stood in front of her and he could feel her stare like a hot touch moving over his groin. He braced his legs apart and waited.

"Zack?"

"Yeah?"

"My eyes have adjusted."

He grinned and started to sit down, but she caught his hips. "No, wait just a minute. Let me...look. I didn't touch you much the other night. I kept thinking about that, you know, that I should have and wishing I had. Now I can."

Her hands slid down to his thighs then back up again. Zack watched her watching him, and it was so damned erotic he almost couldn't bear it. "I didn't give you much of a chance to touch me."

"You were remarkable." Without warning she leaned closer and cupped his testicles. Her hands were hot from being in the water, wet and gentle. His heart pounded.

She used her free hand to touch him everywhere, except where he most wanted her touch. His cock pulsed and flexed, but she ignored it as her wet palm moved over his lower back, his abdomen, his butt, with a gentle and exciting curiosity.

When she leaned forward and kissed his hipbone he groaned. "Wynn, you're a tease."

"No, I just want you so much. All of you."

Because she was always so open, so bold, he knew she meant it, every word.

He couldn't take it. He reached down, caught her wandering hand. "Right here, Wynn," he said, and curled her fingers around him.

Looking up at him, her beautiful eyes bright, she said, "Like this?"

A woman with large hands was a blessed thing, he decided. Her fingers circled him, firm but cautious, strong but soft. The contradictions made him wild. A sound of pleasure escaped his throat and he said, *"Yeah."*

Without releasing him, Wynn shifted to kneel in the tub. Zack caught sight of her barely contained breasts in the skimpy bikini top at the same time she indulged him with a long, slow, heated stroke.

Steam rose around him, expanded within him. He said, "That's enough," and reached for her hands.

"But…"

He hauled her up and held her in front of him. "Easy," he said, looking her over with hunger. "Don't hurt your foot."

She gave him a lopsided grin. "What foot?"

He smiled too, and reached out to cup her breast. "Christ, you're beautiful."

"I'm big," she said.

"And sexy."

"I've never worn a suit like this before."

"Thank God for small favors."

"My mother bought it for me when she was trying to get me married off."

His head snapped up. *"What?"*

Shrugging, Wynn explained, "I told you I don't date much. That bothers my folks. They hooked up young and they've always been happy and they want me happy."

Zack eased her closer, trying to quell the sick feeling in his stomach. "You need marriage to be happy?"

She looked away. "I'm in no hurry."

He wasn't at all sure he liked that answer anymore. "Why not?"

"Like you, I guess I'm looking for something special. That must be why I've never been that attracted to too many guys, right? And I did just get my own house. I want to have fun with it for a while before I start changing things again."

"I see." But he didn't, not really.

"Can we stop talking now?"

"You want to get on with it, do you?"

She moved her hands over his chest, and then lower. "Yes, I do."

Zack eased down into the water on the bench. "Come here, Wynn."

She stepped close and he reached around her to unhook her

bikini bra. He draped it over the side of the tub. "One of these days," he said, "I'm going to get you laid out in the sunshine so I can see all of you." Before she could respond to that, he leaned forward and suckled her right nipple.

She clasped his head. "Zack!"

"Shh, sweetheart, keep it quiet. We don't want to wake anyone up."

He switched to her other breast, flicking her with his tongue, and she moaned low. "I'm ready now, Zack," she whispered urgently.

"Impossible," he said. "We're just getting started."

"But I've been thinking about it all day, even during that stupid party." She lifted his face to hers. "Please, Zack."

He stared at her while he slipped his fingers beneath the leg of her suit. Hot water swirled around her, but she was hotter still, wet and slick, her flesh swollen and soft. He removed his fingers and hastily pulled her bottoms off. Raising himself to the edge of the hot tub, he donned a condom, then eased back into the water to sit on the very edge of the bench seat.

"Straddle my hips, Wynn."

As she did so, her breasts moved over his chest, their skin wet and slippery and hot. He helped position her, taking care not to jostle her bruised foot.

"Brace your hands on my shoulders."

She did, and he eased up into her, hearing her soft moan, feeling the stretch of her inner muscles as she gripped him. He pressed his face into her throat, filled with so much emotion, so much pleasure, it was almost pain. He held her carefully and rather than thrust, he rocked them both, constantly kissing her and whispering to her; there was so much he wanted to say, but he didn't understand himself anymore. He only knew he wanted her, and now he had her.

When he felt Wynn tightening around him, he pressed his hand between their bodies and helped her along. She bit his shoulder as she came, and licked his mouth when he came seconds later.

Resting against him, she murmured, "Will we ever make love in a bed do you think?"

Zack wanted to say yes, that he wanted her in his bed right now. The more he saw her, the more he wanted to be with her. He didn't want to say good-night and send her back to her own home. He wanted to hold her all night, wake up with her in the morning, share breakfast with her and Dani, even argue with her.

But nothing was decided. All the issues still remained. He didn't have only himself to think about; he had to think of his daughter, too.

He said only, "I'm off for a week now. Dani has preschool two afternoons so the house will be free. If you can get away then…"

She kissed his chin. "I'll get away. But, Zack?"

"Hmmm?" He'd just finished loving her, and already he was thinking of when he'd have her again. He felt obsessed.

"Are you seeing anyone else right now?"

"No, why?" He tried to see her face, but she kept it tucked close to his chest.

"You said you were looking for a wife. You said you had plans tomorrow night, too. I just wondered."

He smiled. "Tomorrow I planned to do my cleaning. That's all."

"Oh." She lifted up to look at him, winced when she bumped her toe, and finally got comfortable. "If you should decide to see anyone else, I want you to tell me."

Zack cupped her cheek, so smooth and sweet. "Why?"

"Because then I wouldn't see you anymore."

Just hearing her say it made him want to shout, made him want to drag her inside and keep her there. His chest felt tight, but he nodded. "All right." He smoothed his thumb over her bottom lip. "Same goes for me."

Wynn stared at him, then resettled herself on his chest. "All right."

ELEVEN

"DO YOU TWO realize we haven't been to Marco's in a month?"

Zack, sitting restlessly at his kitchen table, glanced up at Josh. Used to be he and Mick and Josh ate lunch at Marco's at least once a week. Now Mick was married and Zack…well, for the past three weeks he'd enjoyed spending his spare time with Wynn. She'd taken over his brain and his libido and probably even his heart.

That thought shook him and he stood to pace.

Mick chuckled. "There he goes again."

"Wynn has him on the run." Josh laughed. "Not that it'll do him any good. You were as bad once."

Mick just shrugged. "It's scary falling in love."

Feeling haunted, Zack turned to scowl at them. Love? *Love.* He hadn't known her long enough, only a little over a month, but he did know she wasn't what he'd always wanted in a female. She obviously had what he enjoyed, but that kind of enjoyment wasn't appropriate for the father of a little girl.

He said very quietly, "Shit."

"Oh give it up, Zack." Josh threw a potato chip at him and it bounced off his chest. "You walk around looking like a dying man, and there's no reason for it. Just bite the bullet. Tell her how you feel."

Even now, Dani was next door with Wynn. They were sitting in the grass, a giant roll of paper between them, finger painting. It had become Dani's favorite new pastime, thanks to Chastity. She and Artemus, with all their outrageous, oddball, delightful ways, had become surrogate grandparents and his daughter loved them. They hadn't yet found a place of their own, but Zack knew when they did move, Dani would miss them.

It was nearing Halloween and the fall air had cooled, breezing in through the open kitchen window and the screen door. But still Zack felt too hot, too contained. He dropped back into his chair and said, "I don't know."

Mick sipped his coffee. "Don't know what?"

"Anything. I don't know what to do, what I feel."

Josh offered, "She's a pretty special woman."

Zack propped his head on his open palms and tunneled his fingers through his hair. "She's not what I was looking for."

"I wasn't looking for anyone when I found Delilah. It doesn't make any difference."

"I can't just think about myself."

Josh tipped his head. "What the hell does that mean?"

"It means I'm a father. I have to consider Dani."

"Dani adores her, and vice versa."

Zack clenched his hair. "I wanted someone domestic, someone calm and reasonable."

Josh laughed out loud. "Domestic you got. Calm and reasonable? And you wanted her to be female right? Good luck."

"Having women troubles, Josh?" Zack asked suspiciously.

Mick grinned. "Woman—singular. Amanda Barker, the lady putting together the charity calendar? Well, they've already started shooting and Josh here still hasn't agreed. She's getting…insistent. Seems she won't take no for an answer."

"She's a pain in the ass." Josh shrugged. "Everywhere I turn, there she is. But I just ignore her."

Zack dropped his hands and shook his head. "Yeah, right. Like you'd ignore any woman."

Josh sat back and crossed his arms behind his head, a man at his leisure. "She's not like Del and Wynn."

Both Mick and Zack straightened. "What are you talking about?"

"They're real women, straightforward, funny, down to earth. They don't whine and cry and complain just to get their way, and they don't continually fuss with their nails and their hair. I doubt you'd catch either of them getting a facial. I like all that earthiness." He nudged Mick with his elbow and said, "They're both everything a guy could want—and more."

Mick glanced at Zack. "Do you want to kill him or should I?"

Zack shook his head. Everything Josh claimed was true. Wynn worked hard, played and laughed hard, and she never seemed concerned with the typical things women considered. Not in a million years could he imagine her whining. "I think your Amanda sounds responsible."

"She's not *my* Amanda, and yeah, so? Wynn is responsible."

Zack stood again. "Ha! Wynn is outrageous. She speaks before she thinks, acts before she's considered the consequences. She pretends to be one of the guys and dresses so damn sexy it makes me nuts."

Mick and Josh looked at each other. "She wears sloppy clothes."

"Sloppy sexy clothes that fit her body and show glimpses of skin and… How the hell would I live with someone like that?"

Mick stared down at his coffee mug. Very quietly, he asked, "How would you live without her?"

Zack drew back. Feeling desperate, he said, "Dani has all of us to teach her to do guy things. I wanted a woman who would be a good influence on her, someone who did all those female things you just mentioned, Josh. Someone to be a role model, ya know?"

"You're an ass, Zack." Josh shook his head in pity. "Wynn is terrific. She's independent and intelligent and honest. Yeah she's outspoken, but so what? You never have to guess at what she's thinking. And I like the way she dresses."

Zack's eyes nearly crossed. Josh had totally missed the point. He opened his mouth to explode with frustration, and noticed Wynn standing frozen just outside the open kitchen door. "Oh, hell."

Without a word, Wynn jerked around and hurried away. Zack took off after her, slamming the screen door open in his haste. Before it could slam closed again, Josh and Mick were on his heels.

"Wynn!"

"Go to hell!" she shouted over her shoulder. She all but ran—*from him*—on her not yet healed foot and Zack worried. The blasted woman hadn't even given him a chance to explain!

He stomped after her, cursing her impetuous reaction, worrying about her foot because he knew *she* wouldn't worry about it. Her legs were long and strong, but his were as long, and whether she wanted to believe it or not, stronger. He closed the distance between them.

From Wynn's yard, he saw his daughter and Chastity look up. On the patio, Artemus and Conan, along with Marc and Clint and Bo, all lifted their heads. He could hear Mick and Josh just behind him.

His jaw clenched. When he got hold of Wynn, he thought he might strangle her.

He reached out, caught her arm—and she whipped around on him in a fury, letting out a war cry that rattled his ears and totally took him by surprise. She jerked his arm, stuck her foot out and sent him sprawling.

For three seconds Zack lay flat on his back, staring up at the blue sky, hearing snickers and whispers and feeling his temper rise.

Wynn leaned over him, her eyes red and her mouth pinched. "Don't ever touch me again. You want rid of me, well, you're rid of me!"

In a flash, he grabbed her elbow and tossed her to her back beside him.

She yelled, "My foot!" and Zack froze at the thought of hurting her.

At the same moment he heard Conan call out, "It's a trick!" but it was too late.

Wynn landed on top of him, her knees on his shoulders, her hands pinning his wrists to the ground, her big behind on his diaphragm. He could barely breathe. "For the record, you miserable jerk, I never asked to be your wife. As to that, I wouldn't be your wife now if you went down on your knees."

It was hard, but Zack managed not to laugh. The fact that he couldn't draw a deep breath with her bouncing astride him helped. "You were eavesdropping!"

"Another of my less than sterling qualities," she sneered. "But don't worry." She leaned in, almost smothering him with her breasts—not that he was complaining. "I won't force my-self on you anymore. You're free to go find your little paragon of domesticity! I wish you luck."

She started to rise, still a little awkwardly since her toe hadn't entirely healed, and Zack caught her with his legs. "Oh, no you don't!" He flipped her again and sprawled his entire weight on top of her. He heard her loud grunt, but paid no mind. "You don't get to just barge in in a huff after listening to a private conversation, just to give me hell and then leave."

Wynn bowed and jerked and, realizing she couldn't throw him off, she subsided. "I get to do whatever I please! It's none of your damn business." She looked him over with disdain, but Zack saw her bottom lip tremble. "Not anymore."

His heart hurt. Emotion swelled inside him. "Wynn."

She jerked again, but couldn't free herself. "I don't even know why I bothered with you," she muttered.

He wanted to kiss her, but figured if he loosened his grip at all, she'd run from him again. "Because I'm sweet?"

"Ha!"

"You're the one who said it, Wynn, not me."

He heard low voices and looked up to see everyone gath-ered around them wearing expressions of curiosity and ex-pectation and anticipation. They blocked the sun.

He turned back to Wynn. "You're not walking out on me."

"I don't think she was walking," Bo pointed out. "Looked more like running."

"Did to me, too," Josh agreed. "Not that I blame her."

To hell with it, Zack thought, and he leaned down to kiss her. She almost bit him, but he laughed and pulled away. She looked ready to spit on him, and he said, "I love you, Wynn."

Her gorgeous golden eyes widened, and then they both

oofed when Dani leaped onto Zack's back and began hopping up and down. "We're keeping her, we're keeping her!"

Laughing, Zack said, "Not yet, honey. She has to tell me she loves me, too."

Dani flattened herself on Zack's back and leaned over his shoulder into Wynn's frozen face. She put her tiny hand on Wynn's cheek and said, "I want you for my mommy."

Wynn drew a broken, shuddering breath and said, "Ohhh," and her face crumbled. She blinked hard, but big tears welled up.

Zack turned his head to kiss his daughter's cheek. "Move, Dani."

"'Kay, Dad." She scampered off and stood there fretting until Mick picked her up and whispered something in her ear. Then she smiled and nodded.

Zack nudged Wynn with his nose. "We need privacy, sweetheart. Don't fight me, okay?"

She nodded, attempting to duck her face against him. Knowing Wynn as well as he did, Zack imagined that to her, a spate of tears equaled the gravest humiliation. She would laugh heartily, yell like a fishmonger, and she loved him with enough intensity to leave him insensate. But she wanted to hide her upset.

He'd allow her to hide her tears from the others, but he didn't want her hiding anything from him.

Zack stood, hauled Wynn over his shoulder and turned away from everyone to head back into the privacy of his house.

Conan yelled, "For once in your life, Wynonna, be reasonable! Don't blow it."

Bo and Clint and Marc all laughed, offering suggestions to Zack on how to best her. They said, "Watch her legs!" and

"She fights dirty, so protect yourself," and "If she gets the upper hand, just remember that she's ticklish!"

Zack waved his free hand in an absent "thank you."

Artemus called out, "Darling, I *will* do something with your hair for the wedding, so get used to the idea right now!"

At that dire threat, Wynn started to push up, but Zack put his hand on her bottom to hold her still. Grinning like a fool, he realized he felt better than good. He felt...incredible.

He went through the kitchen and the living room, took the stairs two at a time, went into his room and dumped Wynn on his bed. He rubbed his back and groaned dramatically. "Damn, you're heavy."

She held her arms out to him.

Amazing, Zack thought, loving the sight of her in his bed and knowing he wanted to see her there every day for the rest of his life. He lowered himself onto her. "I love you," he said again.

She squeezed him tight. "I love you, too."

His heart expanded until it nearly choked him. "Enough to marry me and be Dani's mommy?"

She pushed him away. "I won't change for you, Zack." Her eyes glistened with tears, but she still looked ferocious. "I am who I am, and I like me."

"I like you, too." He kissed the end of her nose and smiled. "You scare me to death, sometimes infuriate me and drive me to unheard of depths of jealousy, but I wouldn't want you to change, sweetheart. Well, except that I'm going to have to insist all other males keep their hands off you. Other than that..."

She laughed and swatted him, but her humor ended with a quiver. "I so badly wanted to be Dani's mommy. I love her so much." More tears gathered in her eyes and she groaned. "Oh God, this is awful." She used his shoulder to wipe her eyes.

Zack smiled. She so seldom said the expected. "How would you feel about giving Dani a brother? She mentioned that, too."

"She did?"

"Yes. Back when she first explained to me that she was going to keep you."

Wynn drew a shaky breath. "I'm twenty-eight. I'd like to have a baby before I'm thirty."

"In other words, you want me to get right on it?" He nudged her again. "I'm ready, willing and able. And I love you."

She choked back a sob and then viciously shook her head. "Josh would be appalled if he saw me snuffling like an idiot."

Zack kissed her wet cheeks and then the corner of her mouth. "Who cares what Josh thinks?"

"I care what Josh thinks. After all, he's the one who changed your mind about me."

Zack laughed. "I already knew I loved you and you can believe Josh didn't have a damn thing to do with it."

"Right. So what was all that in the kitchen about?"

He shrugged. "I was just mouthing off, fighting the inevitable, posturing like any respectable man would do." He eyed her and said, "*You* ought to understand that."

She made a face. "I heard you, Zack. I'm not at all who you wanted."

"But you're who I love. You're who I need." He cupped her face and kissed her. "Ever since meeting you, I've been thinking about leaving the field, becoming an instructor. I even took steps in that direction."

"You have?"

"And I've thought about moving Dani's room farther down the hall to the guest room—something she's mentioned before because that room's bigger, but I always wanted her close and until you, I never considered having a woman in the house with Dani. Then I started thinking about privacy."

Her brows lowered in thought. "You do get rather loud when you're excited," she remarked with grave seriousness. "You groan and if I touch you right here, you shout and—"

Zack drew away her teasing hand and quieted her with a mushy, laughing kiss. "Wynn, I know you won't be easy to control—"

"Control!" She reached for him again and he pinned her down.

"—but the upside to that is we'll get to spend lots of time wrestling." He bobbed his eyebrows. "And now that I've made up my mind, you should know I'm not at all sweet. I'm actually ruthless when there's something—or someone—I want."

Wynn quit struggling and gave him a coy look. "And you want me?" He pushed against her, letting her feel his erection. She grinned. "Well, since we love each other, then I suppose we should get married."

Zack collapsed on her. "Thank God. You do know how to drag out the suspense, don't you?"

"There's something you should know, though."

He opened one eye.

"My parents have already told me that if we marry, they want my house." Zack made a strangled sound, but she quickly continued. "I think they suspected this might happen, which is why they let you carry me off and why they've only been halfheartedly looking for another place to stay." She pressed back so she could see his face, and with a crooked impish grin, added, "But I know how you feel about awkwardness with neighbors…"

He pinched her for that bit of impertinence, then grunted when she pinched him back.

Zack rolled so that she was atop him. "I like your folks and so does Dani. As long as you live with me, the rest doesn't matter." They kissed and it was long minutes later before Zack again lifted his head and looked down the long length of his future wife. "We're going to need a bigger bed."

Wynn immediately asked, "Do you think Dani would like to be a flower girl?"

Zack laughed. "At least it'd get her into a dress."

★ ★ ★ ★ ★

mr. november

ONE

WITH GREAT INTEREST, Amanda Barker peeked into the locker room. She'd been at the fire station—*hounding him*—many times, but she'd never ventured into this private area.

There was a partitioned-off shower area adjacent to the room, and steam from recent use still crept around the ceiling, leaving the air damp and thick. A few of the lockers stood open and empty. Discarded white towels littered the floor, the benches and an array of varnished wooden chairs. Amanda wrinkled her nose. The room smelled of men and smoke, soap and sweat.

Except for the smoke, it wasn't an unpleasant odor.

On the far wall, opposite the door she'd entered, a framed copy of the *Firefighter's Prayer* hung slightly askew, droplets of water beading on the glass cover. Next to that, a plaque reading Always Loved, Never Forgotten, listed local firefighters who had died in community service.

Amanda drew a shaky breath and crept inside. The prayer

drew her and she found herself standing in front of it, reading words she already knew by heart.

*Enable me to be alert, and hear the weakest shout, and quickly
and efficiently to put the fire out.* She touched the glass covering those incredible words, wiping away the moisture. She
dropped her hand and turned away, troubled as always whenever she remembered.

With self-taught discipline, she shook off the familiar feelings and surveyed her surroundings.

The locker room and connecting showers appeared empty,
but she knew he was in there. The watchman had told her
so—had even given her permission to go in, smiling all the
while, ready to conspire with her to get their most infamous
lieutenant to finally cooperate.

Behind her in the main rooms, she heard firefighters talking, laughing as the new shift arrived and the others headed
home. They were a flirtatious lot, sometimes crude, always
macho and fun loving to counteract the heavy responsibilities of their jobs. They were also in prime condition, lean and
hard, thanks to rigorous physical training.

They all looked good, and they all knew it. With only one
exception, they were willing—even eager—to help her out
with the charity calendar by posing for various months. The
money they made selling the calendar would benefit the local
burn institute.

Amanda hoped none of the men came in behind her; it
was past time she and Josh Marshall got things settled. Since
the start of the project he'd refused to take part and avoided
her whenever she tried to convince him. He even failed to
return her calls.

The man was bullheaded and selfish and she intended to tell

him so, but she didn't want an audience. Confrontations were not her thing. In fact, she avoided them whenever possible.

He wouldn't let her avoid this one.

Much as she hated to admit it, she needed Josh Marshall. She needed him to understand the importance of what she hoped to do, and then she needed his agreement to take part in her newest charity effort. While it was true all the men looked good, Josh Marshall looked better than good. He looked great. Sexy. Hot. He'd make the perfect Mr. November and the perfect model for the cover. They'd use him in advertising in local papers, bookstores and on the Web.

One way or another, Amanda intended to get his agreement today.

A muted sound, like the padding of bare feet on wet concrete, reached her ears. She turned and there he stood, all six-feet-plus of him. Casual as you please, a man without a care, he leaned in the doorframe. His blond hair was wet, his muscles were wet and the skimpy towel barely hooked around his lean hips was wet.

Slow rivulets of water dripped over his chest and through his body hair, slinking down his ridged abdomen and into the towel. He had his arms and ankles crossed. The towel parted, and one bare hairy thigh was exposed all the way to the lighter skin of his hip, up to the insubstantial knot in the towel. It wouldn't take much more than a very tiny tug to remove that towel.

She'd seen him in his lieutenant's uniform, she'd seen him hot and sweaty fresh from a fire, and she'd seen him relaxed, sitting around the station, on duty but not occupied.

She'd never seen him mostly naked and it was definitely... an eye-opener.

Amanda stood a little straighter and met his gaze. She had

to tip her head back because he stood so much taller than she did. At only five feet four inches, she was used to that and refused to let it bother her now, just because the man was mostly naked and *trying* to bother her. She said, "Lieutenant Marshall."

His dark green eyes, so often remote in her presence, now looked her over, starting at her dress pumps and advancing to her soft pink suit and up to the small pearl studs in her ears. He gave a crooked smile and sauntered three steps to a locker. "Ms. Barker." He opened the locker and pulled out a bottle of cologne, splashing a bit in his hands, then patting his face and throat.

His scent overrode that of the smoke, and Amanda breathed him in, all warm damp skin, clean soap and that dark, earthy scent he'd just added. She recognized it from previous contact, but now was different. Now his big body was mostly bare.

Her nostrils quivered and she took an involuntary step back, bumping into the wall.

Of course, he noticed; his smile told her so, the glitter in his dark green eyes told her so. She held her breath, waiting to see what he'd say, how he'd mock her, and instead he reached for a comb. He turned to face her fully while tidying his hair. "How'd you get in here, anyway?"

Never in her life had she watched a man groom himself. Josh Marshall…well, it was unexpected. The heavy muscles in his raised arms flexed and bulged as he dragged the black comb straight back through his wet hair. She could see his underarms and the soft, darker hair there. Her heart bumped into her ribs with startling force. Somehow, that part of Josh seemed more intimate than his exposed thighs and abdomen.

"Cat got your tongue?" He reached for a T-shirt, which he pulled on over his head with casual disregard for the hair he'd just combed. The front of the shirt read: Firefighters Find 'em Hot—and Leave 'em Wet.

Her pulse raced and she had to clear her throat before she could speak coherently. "The watchman let me in so we could talk."

"You're a persistent little thing, aren't you?"

She ignored the sexist comment even as she acknowledged it for truth; she was persistent, and she was most certainly little. "You haven't returned any of my calls."

"No, I haven't, have I?" His deep voice held only mild interest in her visit. "Ever wonder why?"

As he asked that, he lifted out a pair of black cotton boxers and she just barely had time to avert her face before he pulled the towel away.

Cheeks scalding, Amanda gave him her back. "You're being stubborn."

"Actually, I was trying to be direct. I don't want to do the calendar, so there's no point in wasting my time or yours."

"But I need you."

Amanda felt the pause, his utter stillness in response to her words, and wanted to bite off her own tongue. Instead, she asked impatiently, "Are you decent?"

He gave a short laugh. "Never."

"I meant…" She wanted to groan, she wanted to ask him why he had to taunt her and be so impossible. But that wouldn't win him over so she drew a breath and asked instead, "Have you got your pants on?"

"Yeah."

She turned, and saw he'd only been half-truthful. He wore his boxers and the T-shirt, but that was all. Even sitting on the bench, his jeans next to him, he looked more manly than any man she knew. His large hands were braced on the bleached wood of the bench at either side of his hips, his powerful thighs casually sprawled, his gaze direct.

Amanda could see the bulge of his sex in his underwear and found herself staring. It was a contrast, the sight of that soft, cuddled weight when the rest of him was so hard and lean.

"Should I take them back off?"

She jerked her gaze to his face and asked stupidly, "What?"

"The underwear." His voice was silky, the words and meaning hot. "I can skin them off if you wanna get a better look."

She started to laugh to cover her embarrassment over being caught, except that he looked serious. Was he enough of a reprobate to do as he suggested? One look into those intense green eyes and she knew the answer was an unequivocal *yes*.

In fact, he looked…anxious to do so.

She'd allowed things to get way out of hand. "Lieutenant—"

"Why don't you call me Josh? Being as you just stroked me with those pretty brown eyes, I feel we're on more personal terms now."

"No." Amanda shook her head. "I apologize for the staring. It was dreadful of me, I admit it, and I promise you it won't happen again. But I prefer to keep things professional."

"Oh, but that won't do." Josh stood and that damn crooked smile warned her that she wouldn't like what was about to come next.

She edged to the side, ready to escape him, and banged into an open locker. Her high heels threw her off balance and she nearly fell before catching herself. Josh didn't give her time to be embarrassed over her lack of grace. He stalked her, his gaze locked onto hers as he closed in, refusing to let her look away.

He came right up to her and crowded her back until the only air she could breathe was heated and scented by his big body, until the only thing she could see was his broad hard chest in that dark T-shirt.

Flattening his hands on the locker at either side of her head, he caged her in. His thick wrists, incredibly hot, touched her temples.

"Lieutenant…" Amanda seldom panicked anymore; the feelings had been tempered by seven years of distance. But at the moment, panic seemed her wisest choice.

"Uh-uh," he murmured, "none of that." Very slowly, suggestively, he leaned down, making her think he might kiss her and bringing her very close to a scream.

She froze, her heartbeat skipping, her pulse racing. One second, two… The kiss never came and a riot of emotions bombarded her, none of them easily distinguishable except relief and a faint feeling of disappointment. He made a small sound of surprise, as if she'd somehow taken him off guard, and her damn knees went weak.

His nose touched her neck and he inhaled deeply.

Amanda quivered. *"What* are you doing?"

"I've decided how I'm going to handle you, Amanda." His hot breath brushed her ear, sending gooseflesh up and down her spine. She was aware of the cool contrast of his damp hair grazing her cheek.

Handle her? She couldn't move a single inch without touching him somewhere. She held very still. "What are you talking about?"

He tilted his head away to smile into her shocked face. Watching her with heavy eyes and a load of expectation, he said, "I want you in my bed."

Her mouth fell open.

No, surely he hadn't just said… But he had! He'd actually suggested… Amanda laughed. Such a ridiculous, ludicrous…

Shaking her head, she managed to say, "No, you really don't."

He looked a little confounded by her reaction. He tilted his head and narrowed his eyes to study her. "Now there's where you're wrong, sweetheart. You've been pursuing me—"

"For a charity event!"

"—for over a month now. I decided it was time I did the pursuing. And once I thought of it, I couldn't think of anything else." His gaze wandered over her face, and landed on her mouth. He leaned in again. "Damn, you smell good."

Of all the bizarre things that could have happened, Amanda hadn't expected this one. Josh Marshall coming on to her? A man who wouldn't normally look at her without frowning, a man who only told her "no," when he bothered to tell her anything at all?

Her reserve melted away, replaced by the unshakable facade of apathy she'd built years ago. Josh Marshall didn't matter to her, so he couldn't hurt her. No one could.

Her heart now safely concealed, her mind clear, she put both hands on Josh's chest to lever him back.

He allowed her the small distance.

Hoping she sounded reasonable, she said, "Lieutenant, you can trust me on this one, okay? You don't want me. You're not in the least interested in me."

"I didn't think so at first, either." His hands covered hers, keeping them snug against his chest. Under the circumstances, she barely registered the firm muscles, the heat of his skin through the soft cotton and the relaxed thumping of his heart. "But as I said, I've changed my mind."

Gently, because she hoped to nip his outlandish plan in the bud without causing any hard feelings between them, she said, "Then unchange it, Lieutenant. Really."

He looked a little baffled by her response to his come-on. She nearly smirked. No doubt most women would have been simpering, eager to get to know him better, excited by the prospect of sharing his bed.

Amanda shuddered. She didn't waste her time on impossible dreams, and she definitely didn't waste it on men. Not in that way.

The reasons behind her behavior didn't matter. What mattered was that Josh Marshall not pursue her. That scenario would only agitate them both.

He lifted a hand to her cheek and gently stroked with his fingertips. His gaze appeared troubled, concerned and sympathetic. In a voice barely above a whisper, he asked, "What are you so afraid of?"

Amanda almost fell over. Her throat closed and her knees stiffened. No! He couldn't possibly see her fear. She kept it well hidden and buried so deep, no one, not even her family, ever saw it. Men accused her of being frigid, gay, a total bitch…but none of them ever noticed the gnawing fear she lived with.

"Shh. It's all right. I just didn't know." Josh continued to touch her, and then he stepped away. Not far, but at least she could breathe. He stared into her widened eyes and said with a mix of gentleness and determination, "Whatever it is, Amanda, we'll go slow. I promise."

"We won't go at all!" Her heart thumped so hard it hurt and her stomach felt queasy. She pressed a fist to her belly and sought lost composure. "I'm not in the least interested, Josh… Lieutenant Marshall."

He smiled. "Oh, you're interested. I wager you've even considered things between us a time or two. Maybe a hot fantasy late at night?"

"You'd be pathetically wrong." The bite in her words was unavoidable; she did not, ever, delude herself with fantasies.

Taken aback by her vehemence, Josh whistled low. "An abusive ex? Poor home life?"

"No and no."

Rubbing his chin, he said, "You might as well tell me. I'll get it out of you sooner or later."

The man was impossible! "Why do you even want to?"

He shrugged. "It's obvious there's a problem, and we can't get on to the lovemaking until it's solved."

Her mouth fell open again. "My God, your conceit is incredible."

"Confidence, not conceit." He lifted one massive shoulder. "I know women, inside and out. You're hiding something, something that scares the hell out of you, and now I'm doubly intrigued. All in all, I'm beginning to think this is going to be fun. Not at all the chore I'd first envisioned."

His every word, every action, threw her. She caught herself barking a very unladylike laugh. "A chore? *A chore.* You expect to ingratiate yourself with me using comments like that?"

He winked as he pulled on his jeans and sat on the bench again to don socks and lace up black boots. "I don't want to win you over, sweetheart. I just want you in my bed."

Tension prickled her nerve endings, started the low thrum of a headache. Amanda rubbed her temples, trying to think. "We've gotten off course here somehow." She drew a steadying breath and dredged up a vague smile. "All I want is for you to agree to have your picture taken. An hour of your time…"

Josh stood and began threading a thick black leather belt through his belt loops. "Have dinner with me."

An audible click sounded when her teeth snapped together. "No. Thank you."

He buckled the belt and pulled out a black leather jacket, slinging it over his shoulder and hooking it with his thumb. He looked her over, the epitome of male arrogance and savage resolve. "I thought we'd discuss the calendar."

Indecision warred with hope. Would he relent and allow her to get the photographs she needed? Was he just leading her on to get his way?

The biggest question was whether or not she could handle him—and she had serious doubts on that issue. In a thousand different ways, she knew Josh Marshall was unlike any other man she'd encountered. He was persuasive, a lady's man in every sense of the word, walking testosterone with an abundance of charm. To top it off, he had a killer body that got double takes from females of all ages.

They *wouldn't* end up in bed, of course, so that wasn't a real worry for Amanda. His confidence and past successes were irrelevant. The worry was how much hell he'd put her through before he accepted defeat. Somehow, she didn't think he took defeat very well.

In her case, he'd have to learn.

But if he would agree to the calendar, did it really matter if she had to put up with his seduction tactics first? She would resist because she had to, and in the end, she'd get what *she* wanted.

With a sense of dread, in spite of the pep talk that she'd just given herself, Amanda nodded. "All right."

Josh's expression softened. "I promise it won't be near the degradation you're imagining."

"Not at all." She needed his agreement, and antagonizing him would gain her nothing but his continued refusal. "The dinner will be fine, I'm sure."

Without her permission, he walked up to her and put his

large muscled arm around her back. She felt the heat of his hand as it opened on her waist. Before she could react, he urged her forward.

"I have a few rules we can discuss on the way out."

"Rules?" She felt vague and uncertain with him touching her so much.

"That's right. And rule number one is that you have to call me Josh. No more 'Lieutenant' formality."

She could live with that. "If you insist."

"Rule two—no discussions of any actual fires. I like to leave my job behind when I'm off duty."

"Agreed." Amanda realized she'd answered a tad too quickly when Josh stopped and looked down at her. The last thing she wanted to discuss, now or ever, was a real fire. "I…I understand," she stammered, trying to keep him from looking inside her again.

For a long moment, he just stood there, considering her, and then he nodded. "Let's go."

As they walked through the station, firemen looked up. A few laughed, a few called out suggestions and Josh, without slowing, made a crude gesture in their general direction and kept going. But when Amanda peeked up at his face, she saw his satisfied…maybe smug, smile.

Ha! Let him be smug, she didn't care. All she cared about was her project.

And that meant she had to care about him. But just for a little while.

Josh watched Amanda as they stepped outside into the cool October night. He was just coming off a twelve-hour shift, and after two emergency calls that day, he should have been tired. He *had* been tired, clear down to the bone. He'd thought

only of getting home and falling into bed. But now he was...
expectant. And a little horny.

For Amanda Barker. He grinned.

There'd been a recent drizzle and the station's lights, as well
as a bright moon, glistened across the wet pavement. The cool
air was brisk, stirred by an uneasy breeze.

It matched his mood.

With his hand on Amanda's back, he could feel the nervousness she tried so hard to hide. It wasn't a reaction he was used
to from women. But then Amanda wasn't what he was used to.

She also wasn't what he wanted, not even close.

Not that it seemed to matter tonight.

Once he'd made up his mind to turn the tables on her, he'd
found himself thinking about her a lot. About getting her out
of her perfect little feminine suits and letting down her perfectly coiffed hair.

He wanted to see if Amanda Barker could stop being so
sweet and refined and classy. He wanted to see her wild, un-
reserved.

He wanted to hear her screaming out a climax, to feel her
perfectly painted pink nails digging into his back as she bucked
beneath him.

Josh stopped and drew a deep breath. He put his hands on
his hips and dropped his head forward with a laugh. Damn,
he'd let his lust get out of hand.

He hadn't expected her here tonight, had in fact been too
wiped out from the emergency calls to do much thinking
at all. Yet, she'd surprised him by hanging out in the locker
room, waiting for *him*.

A pleasant surprise and a very nice distraction.

He'd made his decision a week ago and had been thinking about it ever since. At least a dozen different ways, he'd

imagined their encounter, how he'd approach her and what he'd say, how she'd react to his come-on.

Not once had he imagined seeing fear on her face.

"Lieutenant Marshall?"

He whipped his head up and snared her gaze, making her brown eyes widen in startled reaction. "Josh, remember?"

"Sorry." She licked her bottom lip, apparently undecided, then that iron determination of hers came to the fore and she stiffened like a sail caught in the wind. "Josh, is something wrong? Because I want you to know if you've changed your mind—about dinner I mean—that's fine with me. We can just set up a time for the shoot and part ways here."

She really, truly, wanted nothing to do with him.

Josh hated being forced to face his own ego, but...he was stunned. Oh, he'd known women who hadn't wanted to be involved with him. He was twenty-seven years old and he'd had his fair share of rejections. Women who were already involved or those who didn't like the risks associated with his work. Women who'd been looking for marriage and those who'd just gotten divorced and needed time to regroup.

Most recently, he'd been rebuffed by two incredible women who'd chosen his best friends instead. He smiled at that, thinking how happy Mick and Zack were.

Oh, Wynn and Delilah liked him, they even doted on him occasionally, but only as a friend.

Other than Amanda, he'd never suffered complete and total disinterest.

Why she was so disinterested was something he intended to find out.

"I haven't changed my mind." Josh saw her delicate jaw tighten and felt just perverse enough to add, "I was imagining how you might be in bed. If you'd be so prissy and ladylike then, or if you'd really let go. Maybe do a little screaming or something."

A variety of expressions crossed her face in rapid succession—mortification, incredulity and finally, fury. She turned away from him, her arms crossed under her breasts.

The first words she spoke took him by surprise. "I'm *not* prissy."

A slow grin started and spread until he almost laughed out loud. Had he managed to prick her vanity? "No?" He drawled the question, just to infuriate her more. "Seem prissy to me. I can't know for sure, but I'm willing to bet even your toenails are painted, aren't they?"

"So?"

He'd love to see her feet. They were small and narrow and forever arched in sexy high heels. She had great calves, but the skirts she wore were too long to see her thighs, more's the pity.

"It's cold." She stared up at the glowing moon, rubbed her arms briskly and shivered. "Do you mean to stand here and insult me all night?"

Amanda had pulled on a soft, cream-colored cashmere coat with matching leather gloves. The outerwear was fashionable, but probably not very warm.

He could warm her, but she didn't look receptive to that idea. "I didn't consider it an insult. More like an observation."

"Then I'd hate to hear your idea of an insult."

Even miffed, she looked picture-perfect…and about as approachable as a china doll.

The woman stymied him. But then, he was up for a challenge.

Holding out his hand to her, Josh said, "My car's this way."

She slanted a suspicious, sideways glance at him. "Just tell me where we're going and I'll meet you there."

Hell, no. Now that he had her, he wouldn't take any chances on her changing her mind. For some reason, being with her tonight mattered more with each passing second. "Nope. We ride together."

Her face fell. "But I have my car with me." She gestured toward the street to a powder-blue Volkswagen Beetle. Not the new spiffy version, but an older model.

Josh did a double take. That car most definitely did not fit her image of refined ladylike grace. The car looked...playful.

Amanda Barker was chock full of secrets. First, that disbelieving laugh when he'd propositioned her. Then her indignation at the suggestion she might be prissy, which was a bona fide fact as far as Josh was concerned. And now that fun car. He shook his head.

He could discuss the car with her later, Josh decided. "So? I'll bring you back here for it after dinner." She looked ready to refuse, and he added, "We can discuss the calendar along the way."

That easily, she gave in. "Very well." She stepped closer, but stayed just out of reach of his extended hand.

Challenged, Josh snagged her arm and held on to it. She didn't pull away, but her nose did go into the air.

She had a beautiful profile, especially with her features softened by the shadows of the night and the opalescent sheen of the moon. Her neck was even graceful, and looked very kissable with tiny tendrils of tawny hair teasing her nape.

"Do you always wear your hair up?" He tried to imagine it loose, to guess how long or thick it might be.

In a voice snooty enough for a queen, she said, "My hair has nothing to do with dinner or the calendar."

"It has to do with my fantasies though." He tightened his hold when he felt her preparing to slip away. He lowered his voice and said, "I close my eyes at night and imagine your hair hanging free. Sometimes I can almost feel it on my stomach, or my thighs."

She stopped so abruptly he nearly pulled her off her high heels. Gathering her poise and clutching her purse in front of her like a blockade, she said, "This is sexual harassment!"

Actually, it had turned into a wet dream a few nights ago, but Josh thought it might not be a good time to share that with her. "I see you're out of practice."

Indecision and frustration tightened her features. "What do you mean?"

Leaning close, Josh touched the end of her reddening nose and said, "Seduction, sweetheart. Not harassment."

"I don't *want* to be seduced!"

A couple of passersby stared, then laughed before hurrying away.

Josh took her arm and started her on her way again. "Take deep breaths, Amanda. It'll be okay."

One gloved hand covered her mouth. "Oh God, this is just awful."

He didn't want to say it, but he couldn't let her start thinking of his pursuit as harassment. "You don't have to be here, you know. You don't work for me, I have no hold over you—"

"I need you for the calendar!"

"No," he said, giving her arm a gentle squeeze, "you *want* me for the calendar."

Miffed, she grouched, "I don't know why. You're absolutely—"

"Sticks and stones may break my bones…"

She looked like she wanted to scream again, but instead she stopped and straightened her shoulders, her spine. She pasted on a serene expression and even managed a smile.

Poor little thing, he thought. She worked so hard at maintaining all that elegant dignity when what she really wanted to do, what her nature demanded she do, was turn loose her temper and wallop him. He waited, anxious to hear what she'd say.

With shaking fingers she tidied her already tidy hair and smoothed her coat. "Where will we be eating?"

Josh waggled a finger at her. "That was way too restrained. I had myself all prepared and then, nothing but fizzle. I'd say I'm disappointed, but I think that's what you're after." He leaned down to his car, unlocked and opened the door. "In you go."

"This is yours?"

"Yep. Like it?"

She admired the shiny black Firebird convertible. "It's very nice. Very…macho." She settled herself inside, placing her feet just so, her hands in her lap. Amused, Josh reached around her to hook her seat belt.

"Oh!" She pressed herself back in the seat, avoiding any contact with him. "I can do that."

"I've got it." He liked buckling her in, taking care of her. He smoothed the belt into place, and in the process, skimmed her stomach with the backs of his fingers. Even through her clothes and a winter coat, the simple touch aroused him.

Pathetic.

He'd have laughed at himself, but he was too busy inhaling her perfume. He'd first caught the soft, seductive scent in the locker room, and it had been all he could do not to kiss her. With his nearness, her shiny pink-painted lips had trembled, enticing him.

But the panicked look in her deep brown eyes—a look she didn't want him to see—had struck him deep.

Someone had hurt her, and he didn't like it.

Josh walked around to the driver's side, using the moment

to come to grips with himself. Amanda wasn't a woman he should involve himself with. She appealed to him sexually, but she wasn't his normal type, wasn't the type of woman he'd come to appreciate.

She wasn't at all like Delilah or Wynonna. They were casual women, up front and honest and outspoken. He'd learned to appreciate those qualities.

Amanda, on the other hand, was so buttoned up she might as well have been wearing armor. And secrets! He was beginning to think everything about her was a mystery.

He'd meant to tease her, maybe teach her a lesson by turning the tables on her. He'd definitely meant to make love to her. Probably more than once.

But he hadn't meant to start delving into her past, discovering her ghosts, involving himself in her life.

Yet, he knew it was too late. Like it or not, he was already involved. And it hadn't taken any work on her part to get him there. No, she wanted nothing to do with him beyond using him for her damned calendar.

Josh intended to change all that.

But first there was something he had to know. As soon as he pulled into traffic, he girded himself, took a deep breath, and asked as casually as he could manage, "Are you afraid of me, Amanda?"

TWO

"WHAT?" AMANDA'S CONFUSED frown was genuine, relieving Josh on that score.

He shrugged. "We both know you're afraid of something. I just wanted to make sure it wasn't me."

She went rigid with indignation. "You do not frighten me, Lieutenant."

"Ah, ah," Josh chastised. He reached over and tickled her chin before she jerked away. "There you go again with that Lieutenant stuff. It's Josh. We have an agreement."

Silence fell heavily in the car, then she sighed. "Where are we going for dinner?"

He wasn't about to tell her, not yet. "Someplace nice and quiet, so we can talk. But nothing fancy."

"I'm not dressed for fancy anyway."

He glanced at her. Other than the lights of passing vehicles and streetlamps occasionally flickering by they were held in a cocoon of darkness. Her nose was narrow and straight and aristocratic. With her wide eyes, that stubborn chin and the most luscious mouth he'd ever fantasized over, she was a beauty.

But that wasn't what drew him. That wasn't what had him suddenly hot with need. He'd known plenty of women, beautiful and otherwise. No, it was something else, something he couldn't put his finger on yet.

"Amanda, you could go anywhere, anytime, and be suitably dressed." As far as compliments went, it was subtle, not in the least aggressive, nothing for her to shy away from.

But she didn't respond, so he added, "You always look great."

She ducked her head, then bit her bottom lip. "Thank you." She quickly added, "Now, about the calendar. I'd like to discuss something special for your photo."

"Special?" He wasn't at all sure he liked the sound of that. In fact, the very idea of the calendar bugged him. Firefighters should, in his mind, be respected for the hard work they did, not just for their bodies. The whole beefcake approach didn't sit well with him.

"That's right. I want to put you on the cover and use you for the promotions."

If he hadn't been driving, he'd have closed his eyes with disgust. The cover. Damn.

With the new topic, Amanda had turned all businesslike on him, twisting in her seat to face him, her expression more animated, open. Because Josh liked the change and enjoyed seeing her less reserved, he didn't immediately disregard her offer.

"Why?"

She blinked at him. "Why what?"

"Why do you want to use me for the cover?"

Confusion showed on her beautiful face, then chagrin. She gestured at him, her small, gloved hand flapping the air.

"Well…look at you, for heaven's sake. Out of all the firemen who agreed to take part, you're by far the most handsome, and you have a fabulous physique."

"You noticed, huh?"

Amanda rolled her eyes. "Because those assets will certainly help sell calendars—which is the whole point—yes I noticed. You're the obvious choice."

Josh drove in silence for a moment, his hands relaxed on the wheel, his thoughts hidden. Only the hissing of tires on wet pavement intruded. That, and her scent.

Her scent was making him nuts.

"I've got a question for you." He pulled into the parking lot of a take-out chicken joint. It didn't look like much, but he knew firsthand how good the food was.

Amanda looked around in consternation. "We're eating here?"

Josh ignored her question to ask one of his own. "If you think I look so good, why in hell do you refuse to get involved with me?" He pulled in to the line for the drive-thru. There were two cars ahead of him, so he braked and turned to face her.

She had her purse clutched tightly in her lap and that panicked look on her face again. "What are you doing?"

Because he knew she'd already figured it out, he said gently, "I'm buying some food."

Her chest rose and fell with agitated breaths. "For what?" She looked ready to leap from his car.

Josh reached across the seat and touched her cheek. His heart squeezed tight when she leaned away from him and that awesome fear widened her eyes and drained the color from her face.

His plan had gone horribly awry, he thought. He didn't want to tease her, didn't want to taunt her.

He just wanted her—sexually, and otherwise.

"For us to eat," he admitted, watching her closely, trying to better read her. "At my place—where as I said, it's nice and quiet and we can talk."

It was the last that got her. She jerked around, blindly, wildly reaching for the door handle. She yanked on it, but the door was locked.

"Amanda…"

She made a small sound, incoherent except for that damn fear.

Josh didn't know what the hell to do. Never in his blighted life had he dealt with a hysterical woman—hysterical because she didn't want to be with him!

Luckily, her seat belt restrained her so he didn't have to chase her through the parking lot.

Josh kept his tone calm and soothing. "What are you doing? I can take you back to your car if you don't want to have dinner after all. You don't have to walk." He sounded like an ass and hated himself. But she listened. "It's just that… I'm exhausted after two emergency calls on one shift. I want to relax, not sit in a public place."

That sounded plausible to him. Pleased with his excuse—entirely made up—he waited.

Amanda paused, facing the window, her shoulders hunched. In a small voice, she said, "I don't see why we need to go to your place."

"We don't." Minutes ago, he'd have tried insisting, now he just wanted her to relax again. "Hell, we can eat here if you want. Or in the parking lot."

She looked at him over her shoulder. "You're really that tired?"

Enormous relief washed over him. "Yeah." He smiled. "You should have seen me in the shower."

Her eyes widened and he laughed. "Get those lecherous thoughts out of your mind, woman. I meant because I was so tired, I sat on a chair to shower. All of us did."

She shifted around, interested, calmer. The line moved at the same time, and Josh drove forward.

"Why?" she asked.

"I told you, exhaustion. We keep these old wooden chairs in the shower for such occasions." She looked fascinated, and he found himself breaking one of his rules. "After a fire, it's often like that. The adrenaline fades and you're left weary down to the bone, filthy with grime and soot."

His heart jumped when he felt Amanda touch his arm.

"I'm sorry."

He practically held his breath. Women touched him all the time, damn it, and in more interesting places than his elbow. But her touch…it meant something. And he liked it. "For what?"

"For acting so foolish. It's just that sometimes…"

Josh reached for her hand, laced his fingers with hers. When she didn't pull away, he felt as if the sun had just come out and shone on his miserable head. "Sometimes you get afraid? You remember something and you find yourself just reacting?"

She stared at their entwined hands. "Josh, I want to be honest with you, okay?"

He waited.

She transferred his hand to both of hers. "I meant what I said." Her gaze was direct, unflinching. "I know lots of women adore you. I even understand why. But I really, truly, am not interested. I don't want you to understand me, I don't need your friendship or your affection. Of course I have...issues. Everyone does. But I like my life the way it is and I have no intention of changing a single thing." Her gaze implored his understanding. "All I need, all I want, is for you to agree to pose for the calendar."

Josh rested back in his seat and studied her. Whatever plagued her, he wouldn't find out about it tonight. Tactics that usually had women laughing and flirting back only fell flat with her. He needed a new plan, and he needed it now.

He made a sudden decision. "I'll do the pose."

She released him to clasp her hands together in excitement. Her face lit up. "You will?"

It was his turn at the drive-thru and he gave her a long look before pulling up to the order window. Despite everything she'd just said, he ordered enough for two.

After the food was handed to them and safely stored on the floorboards, Josh clarified. "I'll do the calendar, but I won't stop wanting you. And I won't stop trying to change your mind about wanting me."

He heard her gasp, but damn it, she couldn't expect him to just walk away. Not now.

As he eased back into traffic, he stared out the windshield into the endless black night. "It's your decision, Amanda. If you have me in the calendar, then you'll have to deal with my courtship."

"Courtship, ha!"

Josh hid his smile. At least now she wasn't squashed up against the opposite door, doing her best to put a mile between them. She was facing him, talking to him, and he chose to see that as progress. "Make up your mind, okay? You can either walk away now and use one of the other guys to fill up the calendar, or you can learn to deal with me. And understand, sweetheart, I would never force you, and I'd never hurt you." He took the turn off the main drag to the quieter, emptier street leading toward his place.

"But I am determined," he finished saying, "to have my own way."

Pigheaded lout.

Amanda stewed, unsure what to say next. Not only had she made a complete and total fool of herself, behaving like a spooked child, but she hadn't accomplished a thing with her honest, up-front admission to him. If anything, she was in deeper now that she'd spilled her heart.

True, Josh had listened. She'd felt his undivided attention. But then he'd disregarded everything she'd said.

She'd been truthful and so had he and now they were at an impasse. Amanda eyed him in the dark confines of the car and knew what she'd have to do.

Still, she gave it one more try. "It won't do you any good, you know."

"What? To chase after you? Hey, just call me an optimist." He smiled, looking so handsome and teasing. "Besides, I'm thinking you might be worth the trouble."

"I'm not."

"No?" He sounded amused. "How come?"

"Because you'll only be wasting your time."

"You think you're that boring, do you?"

Tension tightened her fingers on the strap of her purse and made her neck ache. "Josh, I don't date and I don't do…anything else."

He turned speculative as he asked, "Anything else like kiss or fondle or make love?"

Closing her eyes only made her more aware of him beside her, a large hard man who exuded energy and heat. He threatened the foundation of her existence. Everything she'd worked so hard for, including emotional peace, had to be kept in the forefront of her mind. She could not let him distract her from her convictions.

She forced herself to look at him. "I can't imagine you'd be content to just share a chicken dinner with me every now and again."

His big hand patted her knee, startling her. "It's a start."

"It would also be the finish."

He retreated physically, but not verbally. "Again I have to ask, Amanda—how come?"

With no streetlights on the narrower road, the night was black and all she could see of Josh was a faint outline and the glitter of his eyes.

"That's none of your business." The fragrant smell of fried chicken teased her nostrils and Amanda's stomach rumbled. She was hungry, stressed and still hopeful. "Tonight we can iron out the details and tomorrow I'll bring a release form by the station. I'll leave it with the watchman. If you'd get it back to me right away, I'd appreciate it. We're really pressed for time—behind schedule actually."

"Because of me?" He turned down a cul-de-sac with duplex housing.

"I always try to do what's best for the project. I know you'll help sales, so yes, I held things up hoping you'd change your mind."

"Hoping you could change my mind."

"Yes. Everything's gone to the printers already, except the cover and the November photo, because those are what I'd like you to do. Once that's taken care of we can finish printing the first set of calendars and have them bound. They'll be ready for sale by early November, and we can cash in on some of the Christmas purchases."

Josh pulled into the driveway of a modern duplex home. He parked his car in an open garage spot, and with a remote, closed the garage door. "I'm to the left," he said, explaining which of the homes connected by the spacious two-car garage was his. He turned the headlights off and killed the engine, then turned to face Amanda.

Being in that closed garage made Amanda feel even more confined. Flustered, she started to open her car door, but Josh's long fingers closed around her upper arm. Panic, as fresh as it had been earlier, churned inside her.

What Josh didn't know, what he couldn't understand, was that her panic wasn't inspired by physical fear, but rather emotional. Her body didn't mind his touch at all, but her heart, her head, knew the danger in allowing him any familiarity at all. Seven years ago she had made a promise to herself, sworn to make reparations in the only way left to her, and she didn't want anything or anyone to sway her from that course.

She fought off the drowning emotions, drawing one breath, then two. She'd long ago learned that they came from memories and overwhelming guilt—she'd also learned to control them by isolating herself.

Josh wouldn't let her do that.

He caressed her arm. Through her outer coat, her suit coat and her blouse, his touch was still disturbing. Amanda could detect the seductive strength in his hand, the leashed tenderness that had likely lured so many women.

Just as it lured her.

"Even this upsets you, doesn't it?"

The overhead garage light, which had come on when he activated the door remote, now flickered off. A blanket of inky darkness fell that was both a comfort for what it concealed, and a threat for what it unleashed. Her voice shook when she said, "I'd prefer you quit touching me, yes."

She held her breath waiting for his reaction to that statement, but all he said was, "Sit tight while I get the light."

He left his car door open as he went to the door leading into the house from the garage. Light spilled out of the car and across the concrete floor, showing a tidy display of tools. It also showed a heavy ax, hung against a pegboard. For one brief moment Amanda imagined Josh swinging that ax, ventilating a burning house before the heat and smoke overtook him. She gasped with the image, hurt and fearful.

The sudden bright light nearly blinded her. She glanced up to see that Josh had unlocked the door and reached inside for a wall switch. Now that she could see her way, Amanda opened her own door and climbed out. She took a single step and then Josh was there beside her—the consummate gentleman, the pushy contender, she wasn't sure which.

He reached into the car for the bucket of chicken and the bag of side dishes, then maintained his hold on her elbow as he led her inside.

They walked directly into an informal dining room. Josh plopped the food onto a thick cream-colored enamel table edged in shiny brass and surrounded by cream leather chairs. He reached for her coat and she had little choice but to slip it off. He put it over the back of a chair and while she removed her gloves, he shrugged out of his leather jacket.

All the while he watched her, leaving her unnerved and uncertain.

To escape his probing gaze, she looked around his home. The sparse dining room opened into a modern stainless steel kitchen and to the right of the kitchen was an archway leading into a living room. She could just see the edge of a beige leather couch with brass-and-glass end tables topped with colorful deco lamps. A short flight of carpeted stairs went up, likely to bedrooms, and a flight went down, maybe to a den.

He wasn't much for decorating, she noted. Most of the tabletops were barren; there were no photos or knickknacks about. Everything looked clean and utilitarian—perfect for a bachelor. She turned back to Josh with a smile. "Your home is lovely."

Hands on his hips, he asked, "So what's it to be? You wanna eat first and then talk, or talk first?"

"Eat."

The corner of his mouth quirked at her quick answer. "Is that decision inspired by cowardice or hunger?"

It was a little of both, but she said, "I'm just starving."

Josh smiled. "C'mon. You can help me grab a few things in the kitchen." He strode to the refrigerator, peered inside and asked, "What do you want to drink? Wine, cola, milk, juice…?"

"A cola would be great."

Still bent into the refrigerator, he glanced at her and said, "I suppose you want it in a glass over ice?"

"Well…yes."

He grinned and straightened, pulling out a couple of cans. "Plates are in that cabinet if you want to grab a couple. Tableware is in the drawer below it."

Josh snagged two glasses and held them under the refrigerator's icemaker. Over the sound of clinking ice cubes he asked, "So what do you do, Amanda? Besides chase firefighters around and organize this charity-type stuff, I mean."

Amanda had to go on tiptoe to reach the shelf of plates. In

her home, she stored only the most seldom used items so high, but she supposed for a man of Josh's height, it wasn't an issue.

She began saying, "I'm a buyer for one of the mall's clothing stores—" when the telephone rang. She and Josh both looked toward the wall unit. Neither of them moved. "Aren't you going to answer it?"

He shook his head. "The machine will pick it up."

He no sooner said that than the answering machine beeped and a woman began to speak.

"Josh." A wealth of disappointment rang in that utterly feminine voice. *"I was really hoping you'd be home. I miss you, baby, and you know exactly what I mean. After last week, well, let's just say I'm anxious to try that again!"*

A giggle, ripe with suggestion, made Amanda blink.

"I need an encore, Josh, and I'm not taking no for an answer. So whatever time you get in, I don't care how late, give me a ring. I'll be here—waiting." The woman said goodbye with a string of kissing noises and then the phone disconnected.

Amanda, feeling almost like an eavesdropper, looked at Josh.

He said, "So you're a buyer? Does that mean you get to help pick out which fashions will be most popular?"

Astounded that he intended to ignore the call, Amanda said, "Well...um..." Her mind was still back there on that *"I need an encore."* What had he done to the woman?

"I can see you being a buyer," Josh continued. "You always look really put together, so it makes sense I guess. Let's go eat. I'm starved."

Like a zombie, Amanda walked back into the dining room. Josh took the plates from her hand, held out her seat for her, and then left the room saying, "I'll be right back."

She sat there trying to gather her wits, then shook her head to clear it. She didn't care about Josh Marshall's sexual exploits! The man was such a rogue, there was no telling what the woman referred to, but no doubt it would be shocking.

With that tantalizing thought, her heart thumped hard, making her catch her breath. What type of shocking things did he indulge in?

A few seconds later a thrumming musical beat began to filter into the room from ceiling speakers. Josh reappeared just as a male singer started crooning. "You like Tom Petty?"

Since her brain was muddled, still pondering that phone call and the intimated sexuality, and she almost never listened to music anyway, Amanda merely nodded.

"Great."

Josh sauntered back to the table and began loading both plates with corn on the cob, stiff mashed potatoes and biscuits. When he reached for the chicken, Amanda said, "A breast please."

Josh glanced up, winked, and pulled out two crispy fried chicken breasts. "See, we're already finding things we have in common."

Amanda opened a paper napkin into her lap. "You think so?" After that phone call, she had serious doubts. While she avoided sexual conduct, Josh apparently embraced it.

"Absolutely." He saluted her with his glass of cola before taking a long drink. "Drinks, music and we both love breasts."

Amanda choked—and then amazingly enough, she laughed. Josh was so outrageous, it was impossible not to be entertained by him. He said and did things she'd never before imagined, much less experienced.

At the sound of her hilarity, Josh looked very pleased with himself. He sat down across from her, propped his head on a fist, and smiled. "I like your laugh," he said in a low, rough timbre.

Amanda struggled to collect herself. These spontaneous losses of decorum were not acceptable. She just couldn't seem to help herself with him. "Thank you."

"It's sexy."

Knowing she blushed, Amanda rolled her eyes. "It is not."

"Yeah," he said, searching her eyes and disconcerting her, "it is."

Refusing to be flattered, she scoffed, then shook her fork at him. "A woman can't believe anything from a man on the make."

Josh looked startled for only a moment, then he threw back his head and roared with laughter. Trying not to smile with him, Amanda ducked her head and primly, precisely broke her biscuit in half.

That only made him laugh more.

His lack of propriety was contagious, she decided, making *her* say outrageous things now. She shook her head but inside, she felt more lighthearted than she had in years.

She watched him continue to chuckle, pausing to wipe his eyes every so often and then bursting into new fits of mirth. And he kept looking at her, his expression tender and hot and happy.

No one had ever looked at her with quite that combination of feelings. Seven years ago, she'd been too young to inspire any real or complicated depth of emotion from males.

Since then, she hadn't been interested.

Finally, he dropped back into his seat, his laughter having subsided into occasional snickers. He rested his clasped hands on his hard abdomen and gave her a fond smile. "You're something else, lady, you know that?"

Something else, but *what?* She wasn't sure she wanted to

know. Instead, she said, "We need you to pose for the shoot as soon as possible."

He nodded, but said, "Have lunch with me tomorrow."

With a forkful of potatoes halfway to her mouth, Amanda wavered. Did the man ever give the right answer, an answer she could anticipate? Likely not.

She put her fork down and leaned toward him. "But...we're eating now! Or rather, *I'm* eating. *You*," she accused, "are just sitting there watching me."

"I like looking at you," he said, as if it explained everything.

Amanda sat back, mimicking his pose. "Well *I* would like for you to give me some answers."

"Shoot."

That took her by surprise. She hadn't expected his ready agreement, which was probably why he gave it. "Okay." She bent a wary look on him, but his smiling expression didn't change. "When are you free to meet with the photographer?"

"My schedule rotates. I'm off tomorrow, then not again until Saturday. I regularly work ten-hour days, and this week it's eight to six, so I'm really not up to photographers on a work day."

Tomorrow would be a Tuesday, less busy than a Saturday, but... "I'm not sure the photographer can do it tomorrow."

"No problem. I want to see the poses first anyway, to see what I'm getting into. I warn you, I'm not going to do anything dumb."

Amanda rushed to reassure him. "We want the men to look appealing and sexy, not dumb. You don't have to worry about that."

He looked far from reassured. "I want to see the poses."

"I don't...how?"

"Meet me tomorrow for lunch," he repeated, "and we can

look over the photos you've already taken. It'll give me an idea what type of pose I want."

"The pose isn't up to you."

"Yeah," he said, "it is." He stared at her, implacable.

Amanda wanted to throw a chicken bone at him. "You're just doing this to force me to have lunch."

He neither denied nor confirmed that. "We can meet at Marcos. Are you familiar with it?"

"Yes." It was a nice family-type restaurant in the center of town, accessible from just about anywhere.

"How about noon. Does that work for you?"

"No, it does not. My lunch break is at eleven."

"Eleven's fine. I'll be there. Or would you rather I pick you up from work?"

Throwing a bone became a real possibility. "No," she groused between her teeth, "I'll meet you."

"Great. Don't be late, okay?" After all that, Josh sat forward and dug into his food.

He knew how to eat, she'd give him that. In the time it took her to eat a biscuit and about a third of her piece of chicken, he'd downed no less than two legs, a breast and a thigh, along with the remaining biscuits and potatoes and two ears of corn.

Amanda shook her head in wonder. "Do you always eat so much?"

"Lusting after you has given me an appetite."

Her mouth opened, though she wasn't sure what she'd say, and the phone rang again.

Dropping back in her seat, Amanda waited with a "here we go again" feeling of dread.

"Josh? Are you there, sweetie? No? Well damn. I've been thinking about you, about last week and how fantastic you were, and now I've gotten myself all worked up. I miss you, Josh. Let's get together okay?"

And then, just in case Josh hadn't understood that blatant insinuation, she added, *"I need you. And I promise you won't be disappointed. Bye-bye."*

Amanda rubbed her forehead.

Josh said, "You want me to see if I've got anything for dessert? There's probably some ice cream in the freezer, or maybe a couple of cookies."

Cookies? He hungered for snacks while women everywhere hungered for him. Without looking up she said, "No. Thank you."

"Coffee then?"

Her throat felt tight, her stomach was in knots. Josh was a rogue—carefree and fun loving—everything she knew she'd never be, everything she'd learned early on *not* to be.

Did he have women begging for his favors all the time? Apparently, or he wouldn't be able to so easily ignore them. She sighed. "I think I need to be heading home, Josh."

He managed a credible look of hurt. "You mean after I bought and served dinner, you're not going to help clean up the mess?"

Even mired in melancholy, she smiled. "Yes, all right." Josh sat there and watched while she made quick work of sticking the two plates, two glasses and silverware into the dishwasher. Everything else went into the trash can in his garage. It took her all of two minutes, tops. "There. All done."

"I was really wanting some coffee."

His expression was that of a hopeful child, and she almost ruffled his fair hair. The man was too appealing for his own good, and he knew it.

She lifted her coat to slip it on. "We'll probably pass a place on the way back to my car that'll sell you a cup."

He stood, his movements so deliberate and precise she found

herself automatically stepping back. She caught herself and stopped, bracing for his approach.

"Josh," she warned, watching him edge around the table and come closer and closer.

"Amanda." He stopped directly in front of her, making her tip her head back to see him. His stance was loose, relaxed, but his green eyes seemed warmed from within, giving away the intensity of his thoughts. A shadowing of beard stubble on his face lent the illusion of danger.

Ha! He *was* dangerous, with or without beard shadow, and Amanda knew it. So did her heart and her head—and her body.

Catching the lapels of her coat, he asked in a rough whisper, "If I kiss you, just a teeny tiny kiss, would you faint on me?"

He was so close she could smell his cologne again, mixing with the sexier earthy smell of man. Her stomach flip-flopped. "Uh…" She nodded dumbly. "It's probable."

He bent closer. "Let's see."

At the last second, Amanda remembered that this was a game to him. He'd set out to get her in his bed as retaliation for the way she'd pestered him about the calendar. Kissing her now would only be the first step in his campaign to have sex with her.

It would be pleasurable, she had no doubts on that, but still meaningless. Never could she let that happen.

She ducked away.

Josh caught her arm and pulled her back. "Okay, I won't kiss you. But don't run from me, all right?"

She looked pointedly at his hand on her upper arm. "I can hardly run with you restraining me." She raised an eyebrow, waiting.

He had the grace to look sheepish. His hand opened wide and he held his arms out to his sides. "Sorry."

Amanda stepped aside to pull on her gloves. Her heart still raced from his nearness, from the close call. *What if she had let him kiss her?* No!

"We're not ending the night like this."

That sounded so ominous, his tone disgruntled, that she whirled around to see him, half expecting him to pounce.

Josh cursed. "Damn it, I didn't mean… Don't look at me like that. I much prefer your laughter." He ran a hand through his hair, putting it on end. "I just don't want you going home upset. I want you to understand."

"Understand what? That you intend to…to…have your way with me, no matter what it takes and no matter what I think of it?"

His eyes glittered, one side of his mouth curled. A second later he chuckled. "Have my way with you?" He laughed again and when she scowled, he said, "Okay, okay, don't get all riled. Truth is, I want you to have your way with me. I promise not to resist too much."

"You're impossible."

"Not so." His smile epitomized masculine charm. "Hell, most women think I'm easy."

"And do they call here around the clock?" Amanda snapped her mouth shut. She wanted to choke herself, to bite off her unruly tongue, to somehow call the words back. She'd sounded petulant. She'd almost sounded… jealous. Damn.

Hoping to retreat, she held up her hands. "Never mind. I don't want to know."

"Oh, but I want to tell you." He wore a taunting smile,

which perfectly matched his mussed hair and the sinful twinkle in his beautiful green eyes.

"Take me home, Josh."

"Spoilsport." His sigh was exaggerated and profound. "All right." He pulled on his leather jacket, but she saw his satisfaction. The jerk.

Once they were on the road, Josh reached for her hand. She didn't have time to evade him. He squeezed her gloved fingers and said, "Tell me you at least enjoyed part of the evening."

She shouldn't. If she gave anything away, anything at all, he'd use it against her.

"Come on, Amanda. Stop being a coward. Admit it."

"If I'm a coward then you're a bully."

"Just meet me halfway. A little admission, that's all I want. For now."

"All right, yes." She made a feeble attempt to retrieve her hand, but he didn't let go and she wasn't about to make an issue of it. "I enjoyed myself. It was a novelty."

"A novelty? You calling me odd?" He didn't sound particularly insulted.

"No, I meant going out with a man at all, eating fast food, listening to music and…laughing."

"It's been a long time since you dated?"

Thinking the truth would make him understand her resolve, she said, "Seven years."

He almost ran the car off the road. "Seven years!"

"By choice, Josh."

He fell silent for a long time. "You'd have liked the kiss, too," he eventually predicted, "if you hadn't run scared."

She believed him. There were times when she craved everything he now offered. But she'd learned the hard way that sexual frivolity could mean disaster. And she already had one disaster to make up for.

"It wasn't fear, Lieutenant. It was self-preservation. I have no intention of becoming another conquest for you."

"Those women who called?" He waited, but she refused to reply. She could hear the smile in his tone when he said, "I don't consider them conquests. That's dumb. They're just women looking for a little fun, and I'm glad to oblige them. It's a good arrangement."

"A good arrangement?" she repeated.

He shrugged. "Yeah. Casual dates, Amanda, nothing more."

She looked at him in amazement. "Casual dates do not do unspeakable things!"

His face twisted as he tried hard not to laugh, but he lost the battle. *"Unspeakable things?"* he guffawed. "Is that what you thought? Were you imagining some type of perversions in that active little mind of yours? What? Tell me, Amanda. Did you think I dragged out the fire hose?" He kept laughing—at her expense.

"Shut up, Josh."

He couldn't. But he did lift her hand to his mouth to treat her knuckles to a tickling, chuckling kiss. "You are so funny. Unspeakable things." He shook his head. When they pulled up to a red light, Josh shifted toward her. "I can promise you this, Amanda honey, when I get you into my bed, you'll not consider anything we do perverted or unspeakable." His tone dropped. "You'll just enjoy yourself."

"And then I'll start calling your house begging for your favors? Don't hold your breath." She should have stopped there, but she heard herself ask, "How many women do you see anyway? A baker's dozen?"

"As of right now, only one."

Her heart plummeted. "Someone special?" Not that it should matter to her. It didn't matter to her. Her association with Josh Marshall was based strictly on the calendar. Once the photo shoot was finished she wouldn't see him again.

He pulled up next to her Beetle, put the car in Park, then tugged her just a little bit closer. Looking at her mouth, he said, "Yeah, she's special." He touched her cheek, drifting his fingers down to her chin, to the sensitive skin of her throat. "And very soon, she's going to tell me all her secrets."

THREE

IT HAD BEEN the slowest morning of his life. The minutes had ticked by, and after a night fraught with erotic dreams of Ms. Amanda Barker, Josh's temperament was on the surly side.

What was she hiding?

In between those smoldering dreams of naked bodies and wet mouths and soft moans, Josh had worried. He didn't like to worry, and generally didn't waste his time with it. But that was before he'd gotten involved with Amanda.

He'd already considered every unspeakable thing that could happen to a woman and every one of them made him madder than hell. Somehow she'd been hurt, and he hoped whoever had been to blame was still around so Josh could get a piece of him.

That is, if she ever fessed up.

Just the fact that he wanted to avenge her, that he wanted to protect her, was strange for him. As strange as the damn worrying.

Whenever he'd slept, she'd occupied his thoughts. When

he woke, he could think of nothing but her fear, her reservation. *Seven long years.* Incredible.

In the darkest part of the morning, when the chill air had kept him beneath the blankets staring at the ceiling, Josh had contemplated what he'd do if Amanda never softened toward him. What if she continued to refuse him, if she wouldn't let him help, if she went on in her isolated, cold lifestyle?

What if he never even got to kiss her?

No, he wouldn't think that way. She had softened already, and he'd build on that. Last night she'd even been enjoying herself, until…

He made a sound of disgust. It had been unfortunate, those two calls coming in when they did. Amanda had relaxed enough to chat with him, to even tease him some. Then the women had called.

He was cursed with bad timing.

The restaurant was mostly empty when Josh arrived ten minutes early. He peeked in, but since he didn't see Amanda yet, he decided to wait for her by the door. The day was cool, but not overly so and the sun shone brightly. It was a day full of promise—and he intended to take advantage of it.

He was deep in sensual thoughts when a soft female hand tickled the back of his neck. Josh whirled—and came face-to-face with Vicki, one of the women who'd called the night before. He started to scowl, but then she laughed and threw herself against him.

"Josh! I fell asleep waiting for you to call me back last night! What did you do, stay out all night?"

Josh said, "No, I—"

She kissed him, her soft mouth opening on his with determination. Josh held her back. "Vicki," he chided, "slow down." Her full-steam-ahead enthusiasm, which had first attracted him to her, now seemed a problem.

She leaned into him, pushing her full breasts into his chest, looking at him through her lashes. With one finger stroking his chin, she whispered huskily, "Come over tonight."

"I can't."

"I'll make it worth your while." Her smile made a number of promises, all of them heated.

Josh grinned. He truly loved women and the way they flirted and teased. "Sorry, babe, no can do."

Now she pouted. And Vicki's pouts were enough to bring a man to his knees. Luckily, Josh had become recently immune, thanks to Amanda.

"But why not?"

"Because as of yesterday—" he started to explain, and was interrupted from behind with a strident, *"Excuse me."*

Wiping the cringe off his face at that recognizable voice, Josh looked over his shoulder and sure enough, Amanda stood directly behind him, primly dressed in a soft gray business suit and matching cape, her arms stiff at her sides, her mouth set.

Despite Vicki's still tenacious hold on him, Josh smiled in pleasure at seeing her. "Amanda."

Her big brown eyes snapped with fury.

He tried to tactfully ease Vicki aside, but she held on like a limpet. "Well," Vicki said with a predatory smile, "this is awkward."

Amanda's gaze shifted to the other woman and she said, "Not at all. You're welcome to him."

To Josh's surprise, she didn't turn on her heel and leave. No, she shoved her way around him and went into the restaurant.

It took him a few seconds and then he started chuckling.

She was jealous! And not just a little jealous, but outright furious with it.

It was more than he'd dared hope for. The night before, he'd suspected, but her performance today left no doubts. He looked at Vicki and gave her a quick hard smooch on the lips.

"She's jealous," he said, still grinning like the village idiot.

Vicki peered at him askance. "I was…um, under the impression you didn't like jealous women."

"Amanda is special," he told her by way of an explanation.

"She is?"

"Yes." And then gently, "That's what I was just about to tell you. I'm officially out of commission. No more dating."

Her jaw loosened. "You're kidding."

"Sorry, no." It was all Josh could do to keep from laughing. Oh, some men might run from the sudden idea of getting pulled from the dating scene, but not him. Hell, he'd spent all his life playing around. He'd enjoyed himself and he was pretty sure the women he'd been with would say the same. He had no regrets. But now… Amanda affected him differently. She was different.

He thought of Mick and Zack, how they'd gotten involved recently. Mick had already married Delilah, and Zack and Wynonna had set a date. But before that, both men had fought the inevitable tooth and nail, to the point they'd almost messed things up.

Josh considered himself smarter than that. He'd been with enough women to know what he felt around Amanda was different and unique. As he'd told Vicki, special.

He wouldn't blow it. No way.

Vicki frowned at him, looking like someone had just goosed her. He gave her an apologetic shrug. "I'm sure you understand why you shouldn't call anymore, and why we can't be standing here in the walkway like this."

"No, actually I don't understand." She searched his face, then put the back of her hand to his forehead. "You're not acting like yourself, Josh. Are you okay?"

Josh set her aside. He almost rubbed his hands together, thinking of his plans. More to himself than Vicki, he said, "There's a good chance this might work out with Amanda. I don't want to blow it by fooling around. As you just witnessed, she doesn't like the idea of me with other women."

"And that matters to you? Her likes and dislikes?"

"Of course it does."

Josh decided he'd make a few calls that night, let the women he still saw know that he wasn't available anymore. He'd give Amanda all his considerable concentration. It'd have to be enough.

Having made up his mind, he nodded to Vicki. "I need to get inside. The longer she sits there, the more she'll stew and the longer she'll want to make me suffer."

Still wary of his sudden turnaround, Vicki said, "Well, okay. But if you change your mind…"

"I won't."

She shook her head. "Good luck then." She gave him another brief hug and left.

Good luck indeed, Josh thought, peeking into Marcos and seeing Amanda staring stonily toward him. Had she watched the whole exchange in the doorway, and seen that last farewell hug? Probably. She sat at a round table in the corner, and she didn't look happy.

Josh shoved his hands into his pockets and sauntered in. He almost whistled, but he thought that might be overdoing it.

When he reached the table, Amanda snapped open her menu, using it to hide behind.

Josh dropped into his seat. She was so adorable. And so damn vulnerable. And *so* incredibly hot. "I hope you're hungry, because I'm ravenous."

She harrumphed.

"Yeah," he said, trying to gauge her mood, "about that woman I was with outside…"

"Not my business."

Her words were brisk and cold and, damn it, he couldn't help himself. He liked it that she was piqued. He sat back in his seat, crossed his arms over his chest, and said, "I told her I was unavailable now."

Amanda slapped the menu down. "You did *what?*"

"I told her I was—"

"I heard that," she snapped impatiently. "Why would you tell her such an idiotic thing?"

Josh slid his foot over next to hers. The long tablecloths on the round tables hid their legs, and gave him the opportunity to play footsies. He rubbed his ankle against hers. Amanda's eyes rounded and she jumped, making him smile.

He was willing to bet Amanda had never played footsies under the table.

He was willing to bet there was a lot she hadn't done, *and thinking that would definitely give him a boner,* so he brought his mind back to more important issues. "I told you I was only seeing one woman right now."

She denied that with a hard shake of her head. "Not me."

"Yeah, you."

"Josh, no." The pulse in her throat fluttered and her hands flattened on the tabletop. "Once the calendar is complete, there'll be no reason for me to see you again."

He didn't like the sound of that at all. "Unacceptable."

She drew back like a verbal prizefighter, ready to go for the knockout—and luckily the waiter stepped forward. "What can I get you folks to drink?"

Amanda sputtered. Josh slid in smoothly with, "Coffee for me. Amanda?"

Her teeth clinked together. She glared at the hapless waiter, then muttered, "Ice water."

"*Only* ice water?" Josh questioned.

Without looking at him, she said again to the hovering waiter, enunciating sharply, *"Ice—water."*

"Yes, ma'am. I'll get your drinks right away."

Josh chuckled. "You terrorized that poor boy."

"I did not."

"Look at him."

She glanced toward the kitchen area where the waiter whispered to another while gesturing with his hands. Both young men glanced at her, then quickly dashed away, trying to look busy, when they saw they had her attention.

Amanda moaned. She propped her head up with her hands and said, "You're such a bad influence."

"Blaming me for your nasty temper?" He pretended a grave affront. "*Tsk, tsk.* Not fair, sweetheart. In case you haven't noticed, I'm in a cheerful mood."

Rather than comment on his mood, and why he was cheerful, she said, "I am *not* your sweetheart."

"Not yet anyway. But I'm working on it." It was a good thing they were in a public place, Josh thought. He had no doubt she'd just mentally bashed him real good.

"I never had a nasty temper before meeting up with you."

"I noticed." He said it kindly, with a measure of sympathy. "You kinda worked in one gear, didn't you? Bland."

"Controlled," she grumbled through her teeth. "Polite. Mannerly, considerate, respectful…"

Josh laughed. Riling her was so easy, he could hardly credit that he'd ever believed her prudish or bland. "Okay! I get the picture. So I bring out the beast in you, huh?"

"Unfortunately, yes." Her fingernails, today painted a rosy almost-red, tapped on the tabletop. "Actually, I thought about that last night."

"About me?" Now they were getting somewhere.

"This is not a reason to be hopeful, Josh. I thought about how horribly I'd behaved, how I'm going to have to work doubly hard to maintain an even keel around you."

The bottom dropped out of his stomach. She sounded so serious, so self-castigating. "I wish you wouldn't." And before she could go into another cold explanation, he added, "I thought about you a lot last night, too. About how nice it was to hear you laugh and see you being just a little bit devilish. Much nicer than when you're working so hard to be refined and unemotional."

"I have my reasons."

"I wish you'd share them with me."

"I doubt they'd make any difference to a man like you."

Now that was an insult he couldn't ignore. "A man like me, huh? Why don't you explain that."

A stony expression had entered her eyes. "I care about the calendar, about those less fortunate who'll benefit by the proceeds. I would think with you being a firefighter, you'd be especially empathetic also."

His face muscles felt too tight to allow him to speak, but he managed. "What makes you think I'm not? What gives you the right to judge me?"

A moment of uncertainly flashed over her features. "You wanted nothing to do with the calendar."

"I see. And your project is the only way to help? Money and time can't be donated directly? There aren't other projects going on?"

Just like that, she paled. Guilt, heavy and ugly, visibly weighed her down. "You do all those things?"

He'd said too much. God knew, he hadn't wanted to upset her, to bring on such a pained expression. He flattened his mouth in self-disgust, and reached for her hand.

In turn, she reached for a leather case by her seat and he was left grasping air. Josh retreated as she extracted a folder. In a small, apologetic voice, she said, "I brought the photos you requested."

"Amanda."

"You can look them over and see which ones you like."

He ignored the glossy eight-by-ten photographs. "You're right that my job makes me more sensitive to some issues, especially concerning burn victims."

Face averted, she rushed to say, "We don't need to talk about this."

"I've seen the reality of what a burn victim suffers, how his life is affected."

"Josh, please." She looked around the restaurant as if seeking help.

Josh frowned, and pressed her despite her upset. *He had to know.* "Why are you so concerned, baby? Explain it to me."

She exploded. Hands flat on the table, voice elevated enough to draw attention, she all but shouted, "I am *not* your baby! I will never be your damned baby!"

So much bottled emotion, so much she kept repressed. Josh tickled his fingertips up her wrist to her elbow. "I figure your jealousy is a good sign. At the very least I know you're not being honest when you say you're uninterested."

Her face frozen, she fanned out the pictures, slapping them into place one by one, and growled, "As you can see, the photos are done in bright, eye-catching colors with natural backdrops—"

"The way I see it, once you tell me what your hang-ups are, we can work on getting past them." *God, let him be able to get her past them.* He now had a few suspicions and consequently his stomach was in knots and it felt like his heart had cramped.

Gently, with loads of reassurance, he added, "I'm willing to be patient, by the way, if you need some time for that. It'll make me nuts, because I want you really bad, but I figure you're worth the wait."

One of the pictures tore in her hands. She stared at it, appalled. "Look what you made me do."

"You have other copies?"

She nodded. "Yes. And it's already been sent to the printer anyway. But..."

The waiter cautiously approached. "Um...I have your drinks and if you're ready to order..."

Josh scooped up the photos. Amanda looked a little numb and he soothed her by rubbing his thumb on the inside of her delicate wrist.

She jerked back. "I'll have the soup and a salad with lo-cal Italian dressing."

"Yes, ma'am." The waiter hastily scribbled down her order, anxious, no doubt, to escape once again. The tension at the table was thick enough to choke on.

He looked at Josh.

"A burger, loaded, double order of fries, and a chocolate

malt." He eyed Amanda. "You sure you don't want something more than soup?"

She appeared too dazed to answer, so Josh closed the menus and said quietly to the waiter, "That'll be it."

The waiter escaped with alacrity.

Josh sought her small feet out again and enclosed them in both of his, making sure she couldn't escape. Amanda looked up at him.

"It's okay you know."

"No." She shook her head and her eyes looked shiny with dazed confusion. "It's not okay."

"Why?" He reached for her hand and amazingly enough, she let him enfold her fingers in his own. She even gripped him tightly.

"You're making me muddled, Josh. I don't want to be muddled."

"Muddled is good. It means you're maybe just a little bit as affected by all this as me."

"All this?"

She looked skeptical again. "Sexual chemistry, instant attraction, whatever you want to call it."

Regaining some of her old self, she scoffed. "Do I really look that naïve, Josh, that stupid? Or have you forgotten you already told me what you want and why? A little retaliation, a little payback because I was too persistent in getting you involved with the calendar."

"That is what I wanted—at first."

"Oh, and now you've suddenly got more altruistic motives?"

"No, now I know you a little better and I've smelled you and laughed with you, and I want you. Just because you're sexy as hell and you turn me on and because in some strange skewed way, your laugh is almost more exciting than sex with other women."

Her face flamed. She almost choked, swallowed a large drink of her water, then said, "You *smelled* me?"

Covering his grin, Josh pressed his thumb to the racing pulse in her wrist and said, "The smell of your skin makes me hard. I want to get you naked and smell you all over, everywhere. I want to rub myself against you until our two scents mix."

She went mute.

Josh leaned across the table and lowered his voice to a barely-there whisper. "Do you know what you smell like, Amanda?"

She shook her head and stared at his mouth.

Damn, he thought, seeing her skin rosy with warmth, her eyes darkened. He wanted to kiss her, right here, right now.

He had a feeling she'd let him.

So what did he care if they were in a public place, if other patrons saw them? *He didn't.* They'd already seen them arguing, so now they'd just think they'd made up.

Besides, he ate at Marcos regularly with Mick and Zack. Most everyone there already knew him, so they'd understand.

Josh slowly moved closer to her, watching her lips part, seeing her tongue move behind her teeth, and…

"Hey, Josh." A hard thwack on his shoulder almost took him out of his chair.

Josh straightened with a wince. Mick and Zack stood there, smiling down at him.

"Go away."

Amanda gasped.

Josh shook his head at her. "Don't worry, they won't think I'm rude."

"Of course we will," Zack disagreed, and pulled a chair from another table to join them. "Hey, Ms. Barker. How are you doing?"

"Fine." Her voice squeaked and she cleared her throat. "How are you, Mr. Grange?"

Josh stared at one of his best friends. "You know Amanda?"

"Sure I do. We've spoken several times."

Amanda looked flushed. "I wanted Mr. Grange to pose for the calendar, too. I know he's a paramedic, but he does work for the fire department. With his excellent physique and good looks, he'd have been perfect."

Zack chuckled. "Don't you just love how she states all that without leering? Too bad it never worked out." He said that tongue in cheek, because Josh knew exactly how Zack would feel about posing in a beefcake photo. "I had all that over-time, remember?"

Josh remembered that he'd volunteered for a load of over-time just recently.

Mick, too, pulled up a chair, turning it around and sitting with his arms braced on the chair back. "Hi. I'm Mick Daw-son, a friend of theirs, too."

She nodded. "Hello." She looked Mick over with profes-sional interest. "Hmmm. I never saw you at the fire station. Are you a firefighter, a paramedic? Either way, we could have really used you on the calendar, too."

Josh rolled his eyes. "Amanda, please stop telling all my friends how sexy and gorgeous you think they are. It's em-barrassing."

Zack snickered. "For you maybe."

Amanda, red-faced with embarrassment, threw her spoon at him. It bounced off his chest. Josh caught it, grinned and handed it back to her.

"I'm with the police," Mick interjected, regaining Amanda's notice before a war broke out. "Undercover."

Amanda looked awed at that information. "Undercover!"

Josh spread his arms wide. "Gee, why don't you guys join us?"

His sarcasm was completely ignored. "Thanks," Zack said, then asked, "What's with the pics?"

Amanda cleared her throat yet again, though she kept sneaking peeks at Mick. Josh was used to that. Mick was so dark, an air of mystery just clung to him, attracting women for miles. Amazingly, Mick had been mostly oblivious to them all—until Delilah invaded his life. Then he'd fallen hard.

While peering at Mick, Amanda's blush intensified, but now her expression was clear of any sexual interest. If anything, she looked more remote than ever. "The lieutenant has finally agreed to pose for the calendar," she explained to Zack, "but he wanted to see some of the various shots first."

Mick snatched them out of Josh's hand and flipped through them. After he looked at each picture, he handed it across the table to Zack. Together they "hmmed" and "hummed" to the point of real irritation.

"They're all ridiculous," Josh grumbled, feeling a little ill at ease. "Firemen do not work without shirts or helmets. That's just plain stupid. Why aren't any of them in real uniform? Where's the turn-out gear? The steel-toed boots?"

Amanda made an impatient sound. "We wanted them to look sexy."

"Yeah, well no one cares how sexy they look when they're putting out a damn fire. There's no helmets, no Nomex hoods, and not a single S.C.B.A."

Zack shrugged. "The calendar isn't meant as a career description. It's just for fun."

"Fun? Did you see this one? The guy has his bunker coat on, but it's hanging open to show off his *shaved* chest." Josh grunted in disgust. "Wouldn't do him a damn lot of good that way would it?"

Zack turned to Amanda and excused Josh's surly mood by saying, "Being the lieutenant and all, he has to take his responsibility to the crew pretty serious."

"You know," Mick interjected, putting the remaining photos aside, "I've seen Josh at a fire when he's pulled on his bunker gear right over his underwear." In a lower, confiding voice, he added, "You know—*no* uniform."

"Yeah," Zack said, nodding. "He does do that a lot. And after he finishes with the call, he has a habit of jerking off his jacket and strutting around all dirty and bare-chested with his suspenders loose enough that you think his pants are going to fall right off." Zack leaned toward Amanda, who leaned away. "Josh has a hairy chest, not like the Romeo in the photo. I think he likes showing it off."

"I do not strut," Josh said. Since Amanda had already seen him in the locker room wearing nothing more than a towel, she was intimately aware of his hairy chest so he didn't comment on that. "And I take off my jacket when the job is done because it's usually hotter than Hades and we're roasting in our own sweat."

"The civilian females are always whispering about him. They—*ouch!*" Mick reached beneath the table to rub his ankle. "Damn it, that hurt."

Josh thought about kicking him again. "Shut the hell up, will you?"

"Why?" Zack asked. "She already knows your reputation. Any woman who's been around you ten minutes sees how it is, and she's been around you longer than that."

Almost on cue, three women at another table laughed conspicuously and when Josh looked up, he saw they were staring at him. One even gave a flirtatious, three-finger wave.

Amanda shoved back her chair and threw her napkin on the table. "I think I need to visit the ladies' room."

Josh, Mick and Zack all lurched to their feet with gentlemanly haste.

"You *think?*" Josh asked, seeing that she once again looked jealous. It gave him hope, that very human emotion meant she cared. "You don't know for sure?"

"Oh…be quiet." Spine military straight, she marched away, and the men reseated themselves.

Mick and Zack peered questioningly at Josh, who just grinned. "She'll be back," he said, "after she composes herself."

Mick whistled low. "Wow. She looked ready to bite your face off."

Zack said, "I've never seen her in a temper. Whenever she's been around the station, she's always been so…" He searched for a word and finally settled on, "Cool."

Josh shook his head. "That's just a front."

"It is?"

"Yeah. She's actually a very warm woman. And she doesn't like other women flirting with me."

"Is that what set her off?" Zack lifted a mocking brow. "Because I thought maybe it was the way you harangued her about the calendar. After all, it's her pet project, and you, my friend, just ran it into the ground."

Josh froze. His stomach cramped, even his brain cramped. For a man who professed to know women, he'd blown that one. He wanted to kick himself in the backside. *"Shit."*

Mick snickered.

As soon as Amanda presented herself again, he'd make it

up to her. He'd explain why he was sensitive on the subject, and maybe, just maybe, she'd confide a little about her own sensitivities.

He saw Zack nudge Mick in shared amusement, and he asked, "What are you two doing here anyway?"

Zack held out his hands in a placating gesture. "We came for lunch. We haven't gotten together in a month."

Mick shook his head. "Hard to believe we used to manage a regular get-together, what? At least once a week, right?"

"We were pathetic," Zack agreed.

Because Zack and Mick had seldom dated, they'd had plenty of time to meet at Marcos. Mick was a natural loner who trusted very few people, and Zack had a four-year-old daughter who normally took up all his time. Until they'd met the right women, they'd made meeting at Marcos for lunch a highlight of the week.

Josh, as a once confirmed free-wheeling lady's man, hadn't been bothered with any commitments other than ones he arranged himself, so he'd been able to adjust his schedule around theirs. Being with his buddies had been important to him—then.

Now he wished they'd disappear.

"What's Delilah doing?"

Mick rolled his eyes. "She's interviewing a bunch of prostitutes down on State Street."

"What?" As a writer, Delilah Piper-Dawson engaged in a lot of strange research, but usually Mick was at her side, protecting her whether she needed protection or not. At one point in time, Josh had entertained a secret infatuation for her. She was the type of woman who told it straight and charmed a man in the process. But then Mick had fallen in love with

her, and she adored Mick from first sight, so Josh had forced himself to think of her only in platonic terms.

"It's all right," Zack assured him. "Wynn went with her and besides, the women are reformed prostitutes Mick busted months ago. They're nice ladies—with a wealth of information to share."

At nearly six feet tall with strength far surpassing that of most females, Wynn Lane could serve as protection, Josh supposed. But she was still a woman, still very female in the most important ways—ways he sure as hell couldn't help but notice.

He thought his two friends about as lucky as men could get. "One of you asses should have gone along."

"They wouldn't let us," Zack replied.

Mick nodded in agreement. "They said the women wouldn't be as open with us around."

Josh shook his head in pity. "You're both whipped."

Zack slapped a hand to his heart and sighed. "Happily so, yeah."

Envy gripped him. Josh wanted to be that happy, damn it, and he wanted Amanda. After meeting Delilah and Wynn, he'd thought he wanted a woman like them—tall with mile-long legs, outgoing, ballsy and honest to a fault.

Instead, he'd gotten thrown for a loop by a tiny, prissed-up woman with well-hidden secrets and a definite lack of attraction for sex.

What the hell was taking her so long?

Here he was, worrying again, and that was enough to make any man crazed. He heard himself mutter, "She doesn't want anything to do with me."

Mick and Zack shared a look. "Who?"

"Of all the stupid questions! *Amanda.*" They looked as incredulous as he often felt, so Josh nodded. "It's true. I've had to coerce every single second out of her. If it wasn't for her damned project, she wouldn't be here with me now."

"She's not attracted to you?" Zack asked, forcing Josh to admit the awful truth again.

"No. And I don't like it."

"No man would."

At that moment, Amanda came rushing back to the table. Her animosity had been replaced with excitement. "I just got a call!" She waved her cell phone at Josh. "The photographer had a cancellation. We can do the shoot today."

Josh was so stunned he forgot to stand. "Today?"

Mick held her chair out for her, and Zack took her arm as he seated her.

Josh thought about clouting them both.

"Yes. At six." She dropped back in her seat, all smiles again. "That'll give me enough time to finish up at work, and you'll be able to go to the station to pick up your gear."

Still feeling slow, Josh asked, "My gear?"

"Of course. For ambiance. You and I can meet at the park at five-thirty, by the nature trails. That way we can get set up before the photographer arrives."

She seemed to have everything all figured out and simply assumed he'd go along with her. As if he didn't have a life, as if he were at her beck and call.

Which, at the moment, he was.

Disturbed by that reality, Josh almost lied and said he had other plans. But one look at the excitement on her face, and he knew he couldn't disappoint her.

"I have the perfect image in mind," she told him.

Josh looked at Mick and then at Zack. They both shrugged, unable to offer any help.

"The perfect image?" he asked.

She nodded. "I know exactly what I want."

Josh closed his eyes. He knew what she wanted, too, and it wasn't him, damn it. But he liked seeing her smile too much to *not* do it. And this way he'd get to spend more of the day with her.

He opened his eyes, accepting his fate and not all that displeased with it. He grinned. "All right. I'll do it."

"Thank you."

"There's a small catch."

FOUR

AMANDA CROSSED HER arms and stared stonily out the windshield. What kind of stupid "catch" was this? "I don't know why we couldn't bring both cars."

"Because if I'm going to do this," he explained, not the least bothered by her mood, "I at least want to get to spend time with you."

She wouldn't explain to him again. Sooner or later he'd give up. Intimacy was not in her future, whether she wished it or not. That part of her had been permanently frozen seven years ago, thanks to stupid mistakes and irresponsibility.

She said, "I like your friends."

"Mick and Zack?"

"Yes." She twisted toward him. "Tell me about their wives."

"Mick is the only one married so far. Zack has to work around his daughter and Wynn's nutty family." He glanced at her and smiled. "No easy feat that. If you ever met her family, you'd understand."

"He doesn't get along with them?"

"Sure he does. Everyone likes Zack. He's so easygoing and all. Well, he wasn't always easygoing around Wynn. In fact, she kicked his ass a few times."

Amanda said, "Right."

"No, she did. Wynn is a lot of woman." He wore a secret little sexy smile as he said that. "Almost six feet tall—with the longest most incredible legs you'll ever see. She's strong, and outgoing and athletic."

Admiration dripped from his tone, making Amanda want to grind her teeth.

"Zack got thrown to his back more than once. 'Course, letting a woman get you on your back isn't always a bad thing." He bobbed his eyebrows suggestively. "I personally think Zack knew exactly what he was doing all along."

Amanda couldn't conceive of a woman wrestling with a man. It seemed much too farfetched, like something out of a sideshow. "You sound very taken with her."

"Wynn? Yeah, sure. She's great. I suppose if Zack hadn't involved himself, I might have asked her out."

Amanda stiffened; he hadn't even bothered to deny it! "Does Zack know how you feel?"

"How I *felt,* and sure he did. I rubbed it in every chance I could, just to keep him on his toes." He smiled at her. "A little competition is good for a guy. Besides, Wynn never gave me a second look, except when she wanted to ask me questions about Zack."

Amanda didn't want to hear any more about the amazing amazon who Josh respected and liked so much. "What about Mr. Dawson? You said he's married."

"To Delilah Piper. You ever heard of her?"

She shook her head. "Should I have?"

"She's a popular mystery writer. A real sweetheart with a

twisted imagination, which I guess comes in handy when she's writing those awesome stories." He shuddered. "The stuff she does in the name of research is enough to make a man crazed."

Locking her teeth, Amanda ground out, "You sound rather partial to her, too."

"Yeah." He said that so softly, she wanted to thwack him. "I fancied myself in love with her for a while. But again, she set her sights on Mick and that was all she wrote."

"Do you make a habit of trying to seduce your friends' girlfriends?"

"Nope."

He didn't elaborate. Amanda stewed for a few minutes in silence until she realized why she was stewing. God, it was ridiculous for her to even entertain such ideas of envy. She'd learned the hard way that anything beyond casual acquaintance with a man was impossible.

Josh pulled into the entrance for the park and slowed the car. As he maneuvered the winding roads toward the walking trails, he reached for Amanda's hand.

"I used to think I wanted a woman like them. Just goes to show we never really know our own minds."

Amanda felt her heart flutter and called herself a fool. "What do you mean?"

He pulled up to a gravel lot and parked the car. Turning toward her, he said, "These days, there's only one woman plaguing my thoughts. And she's nothing like Wynn or Del."

Amanda drew her own comparisons. They sounded like wonderful women who led exciting, normal lives. They sounded like women who relished their sexuality and gave with all their hearts.

Her heart was encased in a layer of guilt, crushed under the burden of reparation.

She drew an unsteady breath. "Let's try to get set up before Jerry arrives."

"Jerry is the photographer?"

"Yes." Josh had picked her up at her home and together they'd gone to the station. One thing she'd insisted he bring along was his ax. He'd mumbled and grumbled and done as she asked.

She hadn't been quite so accommodating.

When he picked her up, he'd wanted to get out and look at her house, but she'd been waiting at the end of the long drive and hadn't invited him any farther. Because the trees on the property were thick, even when barren of leaves, and the driveway winding, he hadn't really seen anything at all. Her unusual little whimsical home was nobody's business but her own.

"Don't forget the ax," she reminded him when he left it behind on the floor of the back seat. He rasped something she couldn't hear, and she smiled. "Here, I'll take your pants. You can leave your bunker jacket and helmet behind for now." No way would she cover up his gorgeous face or magnificent body any more than absolutely necessary. "Bring your boots, though."

She walked away, not waiting to hear Josh's reaction to her directions. She peered up at the beautiful blue sky and hoped Jerry got there on time because the sun would soon be fading.

She found a spot on the ground with no grass and bent down, careful not to soil her suit. Josh reached her just as she finished rubbing the front and back and especially the knees of his once clean pants into the dirt.

He didn't ask, so she turned to look up at him and said, "They were too clean. We want you to look like you've been working."

"Firemen don't roll around in the dirt."

She hid a smile; he could be so prickly at times. "Believe me, I know exactly what it is firemen do."

Speculation darkened his green eyes. "Had firsthand experience have you?"

Rather than meet his gaze or answer his question, she stood and shook out the pants. They now looked well worn. "Here, put these on."

Allowing her the evasion, Josh looked around. There weren't many people in the park this time of year, certainly not so far back near the trails. He asked with sinful suggestiveness, "Over my jeans, or not?"

She knew he wanted her to gasp and blush, but she'd already made up her mind about the shot, so she said simply, "Not."

He cocked out his hip, bunched the heavy pants in one fist, and glared at her. "You want me to skin out my jeans right here?"

"There's no one watching. If you're shy, then you can step behind that large tree. But hurry. I want you ready when Jerry arrives." No way did she want to try to organize another session with Josh. More than anything, she needed to get away from him. He tempted her, when she knew from experience there was no point.

He didn't go behind a tree. No, not Josh Marshall. He stared her in the eye while he kicked off his shoes and unhooked his belt.

Now she blushed.

"No, don't run off," he taunted. "I'll need you to hold my jeans. That is, if you can refrain from grinding them into the dirt."

Amanda assumed a casual pose. "Fine. But hurry it up." She'd already seen him, she reminded herself. The shock of that first viewing still haunted her at night—so what was a little more haunting for such a worthy cause?

He shoved his jeans down to his ankles and stepped out of them. Luckily, the shirttails of his flannel covered everything of interest.

It had been dry lately, leaving the hard ground cold but thankfully not wet. His socks would have been soaked otherwise.

A car pulled into the lot. They both turned, but to Amanda's dismay, it wasn't Jerry.

Mick and Zack stepped out, identical expressions of hilarity on their faces when they spied Josh in his underwear. They laughed while trying to keep two women stuck in the car.

Amanda watched as one slender, almost fragile woman with incredible dark hair slipped out to stand beside Mick. She wore sloppy jeans, an unbuttoned corduroy coat over an enormous sweater, and a fat smile. She took one look at Josh and gave a loud appreciative wolf whistle—destroying the image of frail femininity.

On the driver's side of the car, Zack got shoved aside and a veritable giant of a woman emerged. She wore gray sweats, no coat and had the fuzziest hair Amanda had ever seen. Raising her long arms into the air, she applauded, then yelled, "Hey, don't let us stop you, Josh! Keep going."

Josh laughed. "This is all I'm taking off, you lecher."

Amanda felt as if she'd faded into the background. An easy camaraderie existed between the five people, a nearly palpable friendship that excluded her. She crossed her arms under her breasts and tried not to feel resentful.

These people deserved happiness. Unlike her, these people hadn't committed any terrible transgressions.

Still without pants, Josh nearly felled her when he threw

his muscled arm around her shoulders and urged her forward. "Wynn, Del, I want you to meet Amanda Barker. She's doing this crazy benefit calendar and I'm her newest victim."

The word *victim* echoed through Amanda's head with painful clarity. From somewhere deep inside, she dredged up a polite smile and met the two paragons who had nearly stolen Josh's heart. "Hello."

Del stepped forward and embraced her. "Hey, I'm Del, Mick's wife and a friend of Josh. Sorry if we're intruding, but Wynn and I finished our business and had the rest of the day free and Josh and Mick insisted on coming here to stick their noses in, so naturally we had to tag along, too."

She'd said all that without taking a breath and Amanda's brain whirled. "No, that is, I don't mind as long as Josh doesn't care."

Zack cuddled his big wife into his side. "Doesn't matter if he cares, we don't pay him any mind anyway."

With a beautiful smile, Wynn reached out her hand. "I'm Wynn, Zack's soon-to-be wife if we can ever get everything arranged."

"Where's Dani?" Josh asked.

Wynn said, "With my mother. They're doing some tie-dye. She'll have Dani looking like a hippie in no time."

Zack just laughed and explained, "Dani is my daughter, four years old going on forty. It took her all of about five minutes to get Wynn and her entire family wrapped around her little finger."

"And when he says little, he means little," Wynn added. "Dani is a tiny little thing. I feel like a giant around her."

Amanda wondered that the woman ever *didn't* feel like a giant. Not that her height mattered, because she was lovely even with that awful hair that kept dancing in the wind like dandelion fluff. The loose sweats couldn't quite hide all her curves—Wynn had a body like a model.

Amanda caught herself standing there stupidly with everyone looking at her, and she said, "Oh, I was just telling Josh how we'd do the shoot." She turned and shoved the soiled pants at him. "Here, you can put these on now." The man had absolutely no shame, lounging around without pants.

Grinning, Mick said, "It is kinda cool today to be out here in your drawers."

While Josh pulled on the pants, Amanda fetched his boots. She hated awkward silences and explained, "His is the last picture we need and we'll use it for the cover and other promo, too. I want a candid shot of him without a shirt, holding his ax, maybe with a small smile."

Wynn said, "Josh does have a very nice smile."

Josh blew a kiss toward her, then grunted when Amanda shoved the boots at his midsection, making him scramble to grab them. He looked at her and laughed—the jerk.

Realizing what she'd done, Amanda peered up at the women and caught them watching her with gleeful expectation, curiosity and consideration.

Thank God, Jerry arrived.

Amanda rushed to greet him and help him with his equipment while Josh donned the steel-toed boots. Normally, she knew, the boots were already in place at the bottom of the pants. The firefighters stepped into their pants and boots at the same time, making it easier and quicker to dress.

There was nothing "normal" about this particular day. "I'm so glad you're here, Jerry. I know you're not late or anything, but I was afraid we'd lose the light. And Josh is antsy. I don't know how much longer we have before he storms away. He's not always the most agreeable man about this stuff. Not at all like the other firefighters we've been working with."

Amanda realized she was babbling and snapped her mouth shut.

Jerry gave her a long look. "No worries. I take a lot of outdoor pictures in less light than this. Like most photographers—" he bobbed his bushy brows "—I have special cameras and lenses with me. It'll be fine."

She tried to busy herself by pulling a leather bag out of Jerry's car and he said, "Hey, hey, easy with that, okay? Just let me get it."

Flustered, Amanda moved out of his way.

Jerry was a large man, thick through the middle with a drooping mustache and balding head. Though he seldom rushed, he always looked flushed with exertion. Even now, he wore only a pullover without a jacket yet he appeared overheated.

Laden with equipment, Jerry turned and surveyed the collection of people. He frowned. "So who's our model today?"

They all pointed at Josh.

Jerry huffed and lumbered across the lawn. "Off with the shirt then." He dug into a bag and pulled out a small can of something. "For the photo, Ms. Barker wants it to appear as if you've just been on the job. Very macho stuff, you know."

Josh's jaw tightened, but he did tug off his shirt and threw it toward Mick, who caught it handily. He stood there in only the pants and boots. His suspenders hung at his side, and the waistband to the bunker pants was loose, curling outward to show his navel and a downy trail of hair on his abdomen.

Amanda forced her gaze upward, to safer, but no less tempting ground.

Gooseflesh had already arisen on his arms. The air had a

definite nip, but Amanda assured herself it would only take a few minutes to get the picture. Josh was a big man layered in muscle. He'd be fine.

"I've got some blackening here," Jerry announced. "We'll rub it all around on you, your chest, arms, neck, maybe even your gut, dirty you up a bit so you match those scruffy pants and then I'll spray you with baby oil to simulate sweat, and voilà, a hard workin' man."

Jerry carefully set all his equipment on a nearby picnic table then opened the jar. He started toward Josh and Josh said, "No damn way."

Jerry wavered. He looked at Amanda, one bushy brow elevated.

Amanda looked at Josh. He stood braced as if for combat, jaw jutting slightly forward, eyes narrowed, his arms loose but fisted at his sides, his feet braced apart, his stomach tight.

She stomped forward. Her high heels sank into the ground with the ferocity of her pique. "Josh," she hissed close to him, "you agreed."

Green eyes glittering, he said, "I never once agreed to have some guy smear black stuff on me."

"Only a little," Jerry explained, oblivious to the static tension in the air. "It won't take much."

Josh shook his head. "Hell no."

"I need you to look like you've been working," Amanda insisted.

He glared at Jerry while replying to her. "I've never in my life had a guy rub me down and I'll be damned if I'm going to start now."

Mick choked and Zack guffawed. Even Wynn and Delilah began chuckling.

Amanda wanted to shout at them all; their hilarity didn't

help the situation. Despite Jerry's assurances, she wanted to make use of the remaining light. She could just picture Josh with a halo of crimson sunshine behind him.

She wanted everyone else to see him as she saw him.

She was in far too deep and she knew it.

"Fine," she said, refusing to dwell on her growing admiration for Josh. "You can rub it on yourself."

He gave one hard shake of his head. "No way. I don't want my hands in that goo."

Wynn shouted, "Oh for pity's sake, *I'll* do it." She started forward, her long legs eating up the distance in record time.

Amanda whirled on her just as Zack snagged her by the seat of her pants. *"No,"* Amanda said.

"No," Zack said.

It was a contest who frowned more, Zack or Amanda. Left with few choices, Amanda snatched the jar from Jerry's hand and stuck her fingers into the greasy goo. No way would she let one of the paragons touch Josh's naked flesh, not now, not right here in front of her. The slick inky gunk went between her fingers and beneath her manicured nails. She wrinkled her nose in distaste.

Then she looked at Josh's magnificent chest.

"Hold still," she grumbled at him, seeing that he now looked triumphant.

"I won't move a muscle," Josh promised, and then he held his arms out to the sides, his muscles going all rigid and tight as he waited for her touch.

With a fortifying deep breath that did her no good at all, Amanda smoothed in the first dark smear, right across his pectoral muscle. Despite the late October weather and the lateness of the day, he felt warm. And hard. And...sexy.

God, she hadn't learned a thing. Every moral reparation that

she'd fought to gain over the past seven years had been obliterated by Josh Marshall. Now what was she supposed to do?

Josh watched Amanda, knowing he'd end up aroused but
not giving a damn. She looked adorable. With fierce concentration, she watched the movements of her hand on his body
as she smeared the blackening here and there. It wouldn't take
much imagination on his part to visualize her making love
with that same degree of intense focus.

He shivered.

Amanda glanced up and in a low, slightly raspy voice, she
asked, "Are you cold?"

He answered in kind, every bit as affected as she. "You're
touching me, sweetheart. I'm getting hotter by the second."

Her lips parted.

Jerry said, "Put a little on his abdomen, around all those
macho muscles. Highlight 'em a bit."

Amanda looked down at Josh's stomach and hesitated.

"Go ahead," Josh encouraged her, wanting her hands on
him even if they had a damned attentive audience. Mick and
Zack would give him hell the rest of the month, but he could
live with it.

She swallowed, and dipped her delicate hand back into the
can. Her fingers and the goo felt cool against his heated skin.
Hoping she wouldn't notice too much, Josh put his hands on
her shoulders in the guise of steadying her. Their foreheads
almost touched as they both watched the progress of her fingers caressing him.

Jerry made an impatient sound. "Hey, you two. If we're not
going to take pictures after all, then at least go get a room."

Mick and Zack howled with laughter—until the paragons
hushed them into reserved chuckles.

Amanda sprang back, appalled, mortified and without thinking. She wiped her hands clean on the skirt of her suit. Josh thought about breaking Jerry in half, but then Amanda wouldn't get her damn photo.

He caught her wrist and pulled her closer. "Ignore them."

"I'm...I'm done anyway." She tugged her wrist free and began tidying her hair, making sure no strands had escaped the elegant twist.

Used to be, Josh hated to see her fussing around. Wynn and Del seldom did the feminine fretting that seemed so much a part of Amanda.

But now that he understood Amanda better, he knew that she used the busy little movements to collect herself. His heart wrenched, seeing her look so lost, so alone.

Jerry appeared with a spray bottle and began misting him all over.

"Damn! *That's cold*."

Jerry paid him no mind. "Almost done," he said, and then, "Close your eyes." He gave Josh just enough time to comply before spraying the oil right in his face.

"There. You're dirty, sweaty, everything a *real man* should be."

The irony in Jerry's tone couldn't be missed, and Josh shared his sentiments on that one.

Amanda protested. "It's not about being a real man. I just want the illusion that he's been hard at work. I want to capture the..." she cast about for a word, and settled on, "*drama* of fighting a fire."

This time Josh didn't take exception. He had a few troubling ideas about Amanda's preoccupation with the benefit calendar and her reluctance to get involved sexually. He hoped like hell he was wrong, and tonight he intended to find out. Whether his suspicions proved true or not, he still wanted her. More so every damn day.

But until then, he would treat her with kid gloves. "Let's get this over with," he said.

Amanda rushed to hand him his heavy ax. "Prop this on your shoulder, and lean on the tree."

"Prop it… What? Like Paul Bunyon?" he teased.

"No, like Josh Marshall, firefighter extraordinaire."

He shook his head, but inside he was pleased with her description. He sauntered to the tree, propped the ax handle on his shoulder and lifted his brows. "Good enough?"

"No." She rushed up close to him again. "You need a sexy smile."

Everyone else stood a respectable distance away—Jerry adjusting his camera, Josh's friends huddled together by the car chuckling. Josh felt safe in touching her chin and saying, "I don't have anything to smile about right now."

"Bull. Your mind is probably crowded with thoughts of… physical things."

"My mind is crowded with thoughts of you."

She huffed. "Must you always be so difficult?"

"Yeah, because you're difficult." She drew up and he said quickly, "You know what would make me smile?"

"I'm afraid to ask."

Taking her by surprise, he leaned down and kissed her forehead. "Don't ever be afraid with me, okay?"

"I didn't mean… Okay, what? What does it take to make you smile?"

"Promise me a kiss."

Her eyes narrowed and her brows beetled. "You just took a kiss."

"Uh-uh. A real kiss. On the lips. Mouth open, a little tongue play…"

She started to turn away. Josh waited. She took half a step, crossed her arms around her middle, then propped her fists on her hips, then rubbed her temples. Such a telling reaction to such a small request!

Whirling back around to face him, Amanda asked in a low hiss, "Just what is it you hope to accomplish? I've told you I don't want to be involved."

"Even to a teenager," he explained gently, "one kiss doesn't equal involvement."

"But if I kiss you once…" Her voice tapered off like a fading echo.

"What?" Damn he wanted to touch her. He wished like hell that they were already alone. "You might want to kiss me again?"

Sounding tortured, she said, "Yes."

It felt like his knees got knocked out from under him. "Ah, babe…"

Jerry yelled, "Ready when you two are."

Josh touched the small gold hoop in her left ear. "Promise me, Amanda. Give me something sexy to think about, a reason to smile."

She closed her eyes, swallowed hard. "Okay."

The sexy little smile came of its own accord. So did the boner, but damn, he'd never in his life anticipated a kiss quite so much.

Luckily, the bunker pants were, by necessity, thick and insulated. It'd take an impressive man indeed to tent them.

Amanda looked at him, her eyes widened, and she quickly backed up. "There, Jerry! Take that shot."

Josh continued to watch her, their gazes locked and his

imagination in overdrive, while Amanda backed away and Jerry's camera clicked enthusiastically.

Amanda blushed, her brown eyes darkened, her lips parted. Josh took it all in, all the signs of beginning arousal, and wanted to groan. He knew his own face was flushed and his eyes hot, but it was so much like foreplay, sharing thoughts with her this way.

Amanda kept backing up until she was eventually pressed to a wide bare tree trunk. Her arms were crossed over her middle and her chest rose and fell with her breaths. Josh thought about taking her right there in the woods, with the cool air around them, his hands protecting her soft bottom from the rough bark, lifting her, grinding her forward...

But Amanda, with her prissy suits and polished appearance, likely wouldn't appreciate a romp in the dirt.

He'd have to be patient—not his strong suit.

"All done," Jerry called out. "I think I got some good ones. I don't know what you said to him, Ms. Barker, but..."

"Nothing! I didn't say anything to him!"

"Then he's one hell of an actor." Jerry, not one for small talk, saluted them both and headed back to his car.

Josh called out, "When will the prints be ready?"

"It's a rush job," Jerry answered. "I can pull them up on the computer tonight. Amanda can have the disk to look over tomorrow morning. Once she chooses which shots she wants I can have 'em ready in a day."

Amanda, still looking tongue-tied, pushed herself away from the tree and rushed after Jerry. Josh approached Mick and Zack.

Without preamble, he said to both men, "Take off, will you?"

Mick grinned. "You got plans?"

Del elbowed her husband. "Of course he does. Did you see the way they were looking at each other?"

Zack edged in. "What happened with that business of her not wanting you?"

Wynn pretended to reel. "My God! You mean there's a woman who doesn't want Josh?" She shook her head, making her frizzy hair bounce. "No. I refuse to believe it. All my illusions will be destroyed."

Zack pinched her behind, and she jumped.

Laughing under his breath, Josh said, "Yeah, a few actually." He gave Wynn and Del pointed looks, because they had indeed made their sincere disinterest well known. Then he explained, "I don't know what's going on, but I hope to find out. Only I can't find out a thing with the curious quartet hanging around, watching my every move."

Zack leaned around his wife to see Mick. "Does he mean us?"

Mick nodded slowly. "I think he might."

Del swatted her husband, then went on tiptoe to kiss Josh's cheek. "We'll drag them away. And good luck."

"Careful," Zack told his wife when she went to kiss Josh, too. "You'll get all greasy."

Wynn was tall enough that she could reach Josh's cheek without bracing on him anywhere. "You'll win her over with your charm," she assured him, all kidding put aside.

Josh remembered a day when Wynn hadn't noticed his charm, but evidently she considered her resistance superior to that of most women.

Half a second later Amanda was at his side, scowling, furious maybe. Her normally arched brows were lowered in a dark frown and her mouth looked pinched. "What's going on here? Why is everyone kissing you?"

"Just saying goodbye," Mick told her, and he and Del turned to get in the car.

Zack said, "I hope you got some good shots, Ms. Barker. Thanks for letting us observe." And he and Wynn also got into the car.

Amanda just stood there, looking self-conscious and be-mused. Together they watched the car back out and drive away, Jerry following close behind them.

Josh looked down at her, and said softly, "Alone at last."

She blinked several times, her nervousness so apparent that Josh wanted to just lift her and hold her and rock her in his arms. Instead, he caught her chin on the edge of his hand.

His heart thundered, surprising him with his over-the-top response. Amanda breathed hard, her hands fluttered, then settled on the waistband of the heavy pants, just over where his suspenders connected in the front.

He leaned down, touched his mouth to hers, heard her soft moan, and like a virgin on prom night, he lost it.

FIVE

AMANDA'S HANDS SLID over Josh's oiled shoulders, up to his neck where she caught him and held on tight. Josh forgot about her nice gray suit and matching cape, about her styled hair and her reservations.

All his senses were focused on the fact of her kissing him, her taste, her indescribable scent, the feeling of rightness having her small body inching closer and closer to his own.

He tunneled his fingers through her hair, dislodging pins and clips to cradle her skull, to keep her mouth under his so he could continue to kiss her. Her mouth was hot and sweet and her tongue shyly touched his own.

Her breasts, discreetly covered by bra and blouse, suit and cape, brushed his abdomen with the impact of a thunderclap. Josh tilted his pelvis into her, lifted her to her toes, crushed her close.

She was such a petite woman, all softness and sweetness and femininity. She took his breath away with the need to devour her, the urge to protect her.

She bit his bottom lip and her nails sank into his shoulders. Slowly, in small degrees, Josh lifted his mouth. "Baby, you burn me up."

Her beautiful brown eyes, heavy and unfocused, stared at his mouth. She licked the corner of her lips and whispered, "*Yes.*"

Josh groaned and kissed her again. He didn't know how long it had been for her, but he felt like he hadn't had sex in years and now he was at the boiling point. Even through the damn bunker pants, he was aware of Amanda's pelvis pressing into his swollen erection with blatant, yet probably unconscious, invitation.

Her cape was soft—and easily removed. Amanda didn't even seem to notice when it fluttered to the ground to land around their feet in a soft gray heap of material.

He slid his hand down her back, over her curvy hip to the bottom of her sweet cheek. He groaned low in his throat—damn, but she had a nice ass, firm and round.

He hadn't realized. Her suits did a lot of concealing, not that he minded. The last thing he wanted was every other guy ogling her butt. Or for that matter any part of her anatomy.

Edging his hand farther downward, he found the hem of her skirt and tugged it up enough to let his fingers drift over her nylon-covered thigh. Her breath hitched as he went higher and higher...when he reached the edge of a garter, he nearly collapsed.

"You little sneak," he murmured, his mouth still touching hers, but gently now. His fingertips encountered the warm, bare satiny flesh at the back of her thigh and he stroked her. "You came here today with sexy stockings, and you weren't even going to tell me."

Amanda went still, then she stumbled out of his arms so

quickly she tripped over the cape and landed on her rump. Josh tried to catch her, but he wasn't quick enough. She'd taken him totally by surprise and now she was sprawled at his feet, staring up at him in horror, her face utterly white.

She'd landed more on the cape than off it. She had one hand braced on a clump of dirt, the other pushing frantically at the hem of her skirt. Her knees were pressed together, her feet apart, giving her an adorably posed look, especially in the high heels and prim suit, her hair more down than up, her lipstick now gone.

Josh felt hornier than ever, and more confused.

He knelt down in front of her, elbows braced on his knees, his hands dangling, hoping to appear relaxed when he was so tense a touch could shatter him. "What is it, sweetheart?"

She scampered back, her heels kicking up the hard ground and her skirt rising a little more, showing a sexy stretch of slim smooth thigh and the edge of a lacy garter. Damn she had nice legs. Before she could go entirely out of his reach, Josh caught her left ankle.

"Hold up. I just want to know what's wrong."

She started to smooth her suit jacket with busy hands, realized it was now covered in the baby oil that coated his chest and she grimaced. "My suit is ruined."

"I'll buy you another one."

Her head flashed up so quickly, she startled him. "You will not!"

"I ruined it," he pointed out reasonably, still with his long fingers wrapped around her ankle.

"You did no such thing. It was…it was me and my behavior…"

"We kissed, Amanda. There was no behavior, at least not the way you're saying it, as if you killed someone."

Her eyes widened and she gasped. Just as quickly, she turned her head to stare toward the woods. "Josh, please, let me go."

"Hell, no. Not until you explain."

"You have to be cold!"

"Not even close." She looked disbelieving and he shook his head. "Nice try, but after the way you kissed me, you gotta know I'm burning up."

Amanda pulled herself together. It was a visible effort, and Josh watched in fascination—and remorse—as her cold shell fell into place. "I told you this wasn't what I wanted. But as you just said, you got your kiss. So now we're through."

Josh thought about his options, letting them run through his mind in rapid order, sorting and picking until he decided on the only course of action that just might get him what he wanted—her trust. And ultimately, her.

Maintaining his hold on her ankle, he levered himself over her, moving slowly to cover her, not letting her draw away.

"Josh!"

"Shh," he soothed. "I just want to talk and we can't say anything important when all you want to do is lock me out."

"We're in a public park!"

Raised on one elbow, she flattened a hand on his chest to ward him off. Josh released her ankle and caught her shoulders, then pressed her down to lie flat. "No one is around."

She turned her head so far to the side her nose touched the ground. "I don't want you to do this," she said in a voice gone thin and shrill.

"Oh? Is that why your pulse is racing?" He kissed the tiny telltale fluttering of excitement in her throat. "Besides, I'm not going to do anything to you. At least know that much, Amanda. I'd never force you."

She squeezed her eyes shut, and said, "I know it."

That was something, he supposed. Not much, but it'd have to do for now. "Amanda? Come on, look at me, honey." He knew she wouldn't so he cupped her head and brought her face around to his. "I want to ask you a few things, and I want you to know that no matter the answer, it won't make a difference about how I feel."

Her lips, swollen from his kisses, parted. "How do you feel?"

With a tiny smile he couldn't contain, Josh admitted, "Poleaxed. Dumbfounded. Smitten, bit, infatuated and so physically attracted I'm learning to live with a perpetual hard-on."

Her eyes grew round, her pupils dilated. "For me?"

Now he laughed out loud. He kissed the end of her nose and said, "Yeah, for you. And it isn't easy being here with you like this, on top of you, able to smell you—"

She scoffed. "There you go with the smell thing again."

He nuzzled his nose against her cheek and whispered in a voice gone husky, "I love how you smell."

Her lashes fluttered at the *L* word, and again she turned her head to the side.

"Amanda," he chided. "Don't hide from me."

She nodded, looked at him directly, and whispered, "Thank you."

"You're welcome." Josh wasn't at all sure what she thanked him for, and at the moment, he didn't care. He prepared himself and blurted, "Were you burned?"

Her whole body stiffened and jerked. The word, *"No,"* exploded from her and she began to struggle. "I wasn't," she said, still fighting. *"I wasn't."*

"Amanda, I swear it doesn't matter to me!" Josh easily subdued her, catching her wrists and pinning them beside her head. His own throat felt tight, making it hard to speak, even harder to breathe. Her legs shifted under his but he was so much bigger, she had no way to dislodge him. "It doesn't matter, honey. If you have scars…"

"No!" She shook her head hard, ruining her hair and bumping his chin. "I was never burned. You don't understand…"

She practically sobbed out those words and Josh, his heart breaking but needing to know, said, "Then explain it to me. Make me understand."

She stopped fighting him to press against him. He was so stunned he released her arms and she flung them around his neck, squeezing him so tight he felt it in his heart, in his soul. Her hot, frantic breaths pelted his throat and the wetness of her tears touched his shoulder.

He squeezed his own eyes shut. "Amanda?"

"I wasn't burned," she swore with raw guilt, her voice shuddering, her body shaking. "I wasn't even in the fire."

The fire. Discovering he was right, that there had in fact been a fire, gave Josh no satisfaction. Instead, it made his skin crawl and his stomach cramp with thoughts of what she might have gone through. He knew firsthand the damage a blaze could cause, both physically and emotionally.

At least Amanda claimed she hadn't been in the fire, not that it would matter to him now if she had been burned. He'd meant what he said. But then what *had* happened?

Josh knew he had to go slowly. Cradling Amanda close, keeping her tucked protectively to his chest, he sat up. He brought her into his lap and just held her.

Someone she loved had been burned? Another man? Questions raced through his mind, but he didn't dare push her. She was already at the end of her rope, and he knew how she'd feel once she regained control. She'd blame him, and he'd have to start over from scratch.

Josh nuzzled her cheek, seeking forgiveness, because despite what he'd just told himself, he needed to know.

Hoping to help soothe her, he coasted his hands up and down her narrow back and kept on kissing her, her temple, her hair, her ear. He didn't care where, so long as he got to kiss her.

Minutes slipped by and neither of them broke the quiet. The sun sank down behind the bare, gnarled treetops, leaving the park shadowed and cold. A breeze rustled the dry grasses and brush, chilling his naked upper body.

Sounding sleepy, Amanda rubbed her fingers over his chest and muttered, "You're all slippery."

He smiled. That wasn't at all what he'd expected to hear from her after her emotional display and the lengthy silence.

She lifted her face and he saw her cheek was shiny with tears and baby oil. Around her right eye the blackening made her look wounded, bruised. A thin smear decorated her chin, the fine line of her delicate jaw, the edge of her nose.

It seemed the rightest thing in the world to lean down and kiss her mouth.

She kissed him back, letting the touch of their mouths linger, long and soft and caring.

"I'm sorry," she said on a sigh, snuggling close again, unmindful of the mess their embrace had already caused to her appearance. "I don't usually carry on like a deranged woman."

"Not deranged," Josh corrected. "Upset. We all get upset sometimes. It's nothing to apologize for."

Amanda nodded and then started to rise. His arms tightened. "Hey," he asked gently, "where do you think you're going?"

"Just to get your shirt. I don't want you to catch a cold and it's getting nippy."

True. Chills roughened Josh's skin and made him shiver. Still, he didn't want to move. With Amanda in his lap, he felt more content than he had in weeks. But because he'd been forward enough for her to bring sexual assault charges against him, he helped her to stand.

She tottered for a moment, her legs unsteady as she looked around to locate his discarded clothes on the picnic table. Her steps methodical, a bit too slow, Amanda fetched the jeans and his T-shirt and flannel.

Josh rose, too, brushing off his backside and wishing he could read her mind. With most women, his confidence was iron strong, but Amanda was an enigma and he never knew for sure where he stood with her.

He watched her lift his flannel to her nose and inhale for just a second, before crushing it close and strolling back to him.

"Here," she said, acting as if nothing had happened, as if she hadn't just lost control in front of him.

As if she hadn't kissed him to the point of no return—and then backed down.

Josh accepted the clothes and yanked his shirt on over his head. It stuck to him, thanks to the oil and blackening. As a fireman, he'd had many occasions where soot had coated his body, even getting beneath his gloves to cake under his nails. By comparison, a little oil could be ignored.

He shrugged the flannel on while Amanda watched, her expression distant, impossible to read.

"If you don't mind," Josh said, "I'll change pants, too. These aren't exactly the best to drive in."

"All right." She bent to get her cape. Dried leaves and twigs stuck to the material so she shook it out, then gave him her back.

Josh noticed a run in one of her stockings, dirt on her dressy high-heeled shoes, blackening and oil streaks on her once-impeccable clothing.

He felt like a marauder, like a ravisher of innocents. But damn it, he didn't know how to deal with her. It was like floundering in the dark. He had to push her, or give up on her, and giving her up wasn't an option.

Her back still to him, Amanda put her fingers to her hair and discovered how he'd wrecked it with his impatient hands. Personally, Josh thought she looked sexy as hell rumpled—even with the grease streaks on her face—but he knew she wouldn't agree.

He watched Amanda as she fussed with her hair for a few moments, then her head dropped forward when she realized there was no way to repair it, not out in the park near the woods with only the diminishing sunset and a tugging breeze to help her.

One by one, she began removing pins, and with each silky light-brown lock that fell over her shoulders, Josh's heart punched hard. He skinned out of his bunker gear and steel-toed boots, and tugged on his jeans, awkwardly hopping on first one foot then the other while keeping his attention on Amanda. He stepped into his shoes, slipped his thick leather belt through the loops and bundled up the rest of his gear.

By that time, Amanda's long hair was free and she combed her fingers through it, trying to bring some order to the tumbled mass. Her movements were innocently seductive and sexual. Unable to stand the physical and emotional distance between them, Josh approached her.

He clasped her shoulders. "Amanda, are you ready to talk now?"

She reached back and patted his hand in a distracted, al-most avuncular way. "Why don't we talk in the car?" Even as she asked that, the wind picked up, tossing her hair so that the silky strands brushed his chin and throat.

He shuddered with raw need.

Amanda shivered with cold.

The park was dark now, cast in long eerie shadows. Josh hadn't realized how quickly the sun would set once it began its decline. But with the tall trees surrounding them, little of the fading light could penetrate.

He didn't want to leave, but then he was aroused and equally concerned. With the odd combination of emotions, he knew he wasn't thinking straight.

"You're cold," he said, giving himself a reason to stroke her, to rub his hands up and down her arms under the guise of warming her. What he really wanted to do with her and to her would no doubt make her hotter than hell. It was certainly making him hot just thinking about it. But for now, he had to content himself with a little arm rubbing.

Amanda patted his hand again, then turned to face him. "I just think it's best if we get on our way."

Her eyes looked luminous in the dark, her skin pale.

"You're not afraid of me?"

She shook her head. "No."

"You're going to talk to me, to help me understand?"

"Yes. I'll try."

Josh searched her face, trying to read the truth there, but Amanda always did a good job of closing down on him whenever she wanted to. He tucked his extra clothes under his arm and hefted the ax. "Let's go."

Once they were in the car she said, "I still need you to sign the release."

"Sure." He started the car, flipped on the headlights, and drove out. "As soon as I approve the pictures you'll be using."

Her sound of impatience turned into a laugh. "You are so impossible, Josh Marshall. What am I going to do with you?"

Love me. The wayward thought scared the hell out of him, making his hands tighten on the wheel, his heart pound, his stomach roil and his brain stutter. He'd never before wanted a woman to really care.

His throat burned with the need to curse, to rage at the fickle hand of fate that had shown him a woman he wanted more than any other, only to keep her out of reach because she didn't feel the same.

After so many women had admired him, women who were attracted to him, some of them a little in love with him, he was deathly afraid he'd gone and stupidly fallen for Amanda.

"Talk to me," he said. "That's what you can do."

"All right." She seemed very small and still in the car beside him. Her tone was hesitant, but she continued. "First, the reason I don't want to get involved with you is that there's no point. Beyond what we just did, things can't progress."

Having no idea what she was trying to say, he asked only, "Why not?"

"I'm not...capable of it."

He swung his head toward her, then forced himself to watch the road. *Not capable, not capable, not capable...*

"I'm a little slow here, babe. Can you explain that?"

"Quit calling me babe and I might try."

He shook his head. Damn, she could make him nuts. "Go ahead."

"I'm twenty-four years old, Josh."

"So? I figured you to be somewhere around there. I'm twenty-seven."

"I've never been intimate with a man. I'm still a...a virgin."

His heart lurched. Before his sluggish brain could assimilate that confession and make sense of it, she continued.

"That's not by choice. I tried a few times, but..."

Her voice turned cold, remote. It was as if she'd gone on automatic pilot, telling him things he'd insisted on hearing, but not allowing them to hurt her again.

Josh blindly reached for her hand. It didn't matter whether or not she needed the touch, because *he* needed it.

"Sometimes stuff happens in our lives and it affects us. When I was younger I did some really horrible things."

"Just a second here, okay?" He tried to keep his tone re-assuring. "Are we talking physical reasons why you can't, or emotional reasons?"

She laughed. "I've got all the same parts as any other woman, they just don't work right. And the doctors call it mental, not emotional."

"I don't give a rat's ass what they call it."

She squeezed his fingers. "It's all right. I've accepted my life."

"Well good for you, but I'm not accepting it." He'd be damned before he'd accept this as anything other than an emotional setback. "And you're only giving me bits and pieces of stuff here. Amanda, I *care* about you."

Her next words were choked. "I'm sorry. I wish you didn't. I don't want to hurt anyone ever again. Not for the rest of my life." She dug in her purse for a tissue and blew her nose. After a shuddering breath that ripped out his heart, she said, "All I want to do now is try to make up for things in the only way I can."

"The calendar?" he asked.

"Yes. And other projects, other ways to help those who've been hurt or killed. Some things, well, there's no way to make up for them. They happen and you have to live with the consequences."

It was a good thing, to Josh's way of thinking, that her home wasn't far from the park. Otherwise, he'd have pulled over on the side of the road. But he reached her driveway and rather than stop at the end as he was sure she'd prefer, he drove right up to the front walkway.

Then he sat there in stunned disbelief as his headlights landed on the front and side of her home. Would Amanda just keep knocking him off balance?

"Is this a schoolhouse?" he asked.

"It used to be, yes."

The tiny rectangular building of aged red brick had two arched windows on each outer wall and an arched double front door of thick planked wood. The steep roof had slate shingles and a small chimney protruded off the backside. It looked like a fairy cottage, set in the middle of towering trees and scraggly lawn with dead ivy climbing up the brick here and there, waving out like a lady's hair caught in the breeze.

Other than the driveway that ended at the side of the house where he could see her Beetle parked under a shelter, and a short path to the front door, there was no relief from those tall oaks and elms and evergreens. No neighbors, no traffic, no real lawn to speak of, no...nothing.

She'd isolated herself so thoroughly that Josh wanted to get out and howl at the moon.

He wanted to take her back to his place where it was noisy and busy with life.

He wanted to keep her.

Amanda opened her car door and stepped out. Josh followed, fearful that she'd skip away from him and he'd never get his answers. No way in hell could he sleep tonight with only half the story, and her hanging confession about virginity.

Looking at her over the hood of the Firebird, he said, "Ask me in."

She tipped her head back and looked up at the treetops, swaying against a dark gray sky. "I suppose I might as well," she said with little enthusiasm. "We can finish this, and you can sign the release and it'll be done."

So saying, she found her key in her purse and walked on a short cobblestone path to the front door. Josh listened to the hollow echoing of her high heels on the rounded stone.

Finish it? Ha! Not by a long shot.

Tonight, to his way of thinking, was just the beginning.

Amanda watched as Josh stepped into her quaint little eclectic home. She flipped on a wall switch, which lit a tiny side-table candle lamp. While he stood in the doorframe, she went on through the minuscule family room and into the kitchen to turn on the brighter fluorescent overhead lights. Whenever she needed light to work by, she used the two-seat kitchenette table. Even now, it was filled with photos and contracts for the calendar.

Her home was barely big enough for one, and with Josh inside, it was most definitely crowded. Especially when he closed the door. He looked around with a sense of wonder, then said the most unexpected thing.

"I thought you were rich."

After all the emotional upheaval, Amanda burst out laughing. She peered at Josh, saw his look of chagrin, and laughed some more.

His expression changed and he stalked toward her. "I do love it when you laugh." She stalled, realization of their situation sinking in, and he said, "I also thought you'd be immaculate."

Shrugging, Amanda looked around at the clutter. "No time. I work a regular forty-hour week like most people, then put in another twenty hours or more a week on projects. My place is never really dirty, but yes, it's usually messy."

Dishes filled the small sink and an overloaded laundry hamper sat on the floor. Amanda shrugged again. She did what she could, when she could. If Josh didn't like it, he shouldn't have invited himself in.

"I wasn't complaining," he said. "It just surprised me. Will you show me the rest of your place?"

Amanda gathered herself. She'd explain things to him, but there was no reason for more hysterics, no reason for an excess of the pitiful, useless tears and dramatics fit for the stage.

What had happened to her was the least tragic thing that had occurred that awful night. She wouldn't allow herself to pretend otherwise.

"There's not much to show, only the four rooms. You've already seen two of them, the family room and kitchen."

"No television," he noted.

"It's in my bedroom, along with a stereo, through here." The house measured a mere fifty feet by thirty feet. The front double doors were centered on the overall width of the house, which put them into the far left of the family room. An open archway, draped with gauzy swag curtains in lieu of a door, showed her bedroom. The curtains weren't adequate for privacy, but since she lived alone, it had never mattered.

Straight ahead of the family room was the kitchen. The two rooms seemed to meld together, with only the side of the refrigerator and the location of her tiny table to serve as a divider.

The kitchen was just large enough for a stacking washer and

dryer, a parlor table, an apartment-size stove and her refrigerator. The cabinets were almost nonexistent, but open shelving and one pantry offered her all the storage space she needed.

At the back of the house, opposite the kitchen, was the minuscule bathroom that opened both into her bedroom and into the kitchen.

A bare toilet, a pedestal sink and a claw-foot tub filled the room with elegant simplicity. Other than the creamy ceramic tile in the bathroom, the whole house had original rich wood flooring.

Josh peeked into each room. Her bedroom had a full-size cherry bed and one nightstand that held an alarm clock, phone and lamp. A large ornate armoire held her clothes and a TV-VCR combination. Her modest stereo sat on the floor beside it.

One narrow dim closet was situated next to the door for the bathroom. It wasn't deep enough to accommodate hangers, so she had installed shelves and stored her shoes and slacks and sweaters there.

The tall, wide windows and cathedral ceilings made the house look larger than it was. The absence of doors gave it a fresh openness, while natural wood furniture and earth tone materials brought everything together.

"I like it," Josh said, and she could see that he did. His eyes practically glowed when he stared at her old-fashioned bathtub. "How old is this place?"

"An engraved stone plaque, embedded above the front door, says it was erected in 1905. I had to do some work to it before I could live here. Some of the windowpanes were busted out and the roof leaked. The floors all had to be sanded and repaired."

Hands on his hips, Josh looked around again and shook his head. "A schoolhouse."

"A hunter had converted it into a cottage years ago. He's the one who put in modern plumbing and electricity. When he passed away, his kids just sort of forgot about it for a long, long time. I'm glad they finally decided to sell because I love it."

"Lots of charm," Josh agreed. "You know, you need a school bell."

"I have one. It's in the back, next to the well."

"A bona fide well?"

"Yes." She smiled at his enthusiasm over that bit of whimsy. "It even works, though I can't bring myself to drink anything out of it. I guess I'm too used to tap water."

They still stood in her bedroom, and Amanda began to feel a little uncomfortable. "Should I make some coffee? Not that I think this will take long, but…" She headed out of the room, assuming Josh would follow.

Of course, he didn't. "I'd rather talk."

"Fine." She clasped her hands together. "Let's at least sit down."

Josh nodded and followed her into the family room. She had only enough room for one bookshelf, a loveseat with end tables and lamps and a rocking chair. Josh tugged her down into the loveseat, and then kept hold of her hand.

"So you're a virgin?" he asked in that bald, shocking way of his. "That's not a crime, you know. Especially these days."

Many times in her life, Amanda had forced herself to face her accusers, to face the truth while trying to apologize, to make amends even when she knew that to be impossible.

She could force herself to face Josh, and to tell him the whole story. "I told you it's not a moral choice. I tried, several times, but I'm frigid."

He lifted his free hand to stroke her hair, and ended up removing a piece of a twig. He smiled at it while saying, "You didn't seem frigid to me. Just the opposite."

Her reaction to Josh had surprised her, too, but she wouldn't be fooled. Too many times she had thought herself whole—perhaps forgiven—only to be disappointed again.

Shaking her head, Amanda said, "I want what you want, that's not the problem. But you saw what happened. I can only go so far and then I start remembering and then I…I just can't."

"What?" Josh cupped her chin and brought her face around to his. "What do you remember?"

"Josh…are you sure you want to hear this?" She felt she had to give him one last chance to leave without causing an unpleasant scene. It'd be easier for both of them. "You could just let it go," she suggested, "just sign the release and leave."

"I'm not going anywhere, so quit stalling. And quit acting like whatever you have to tell me will horrify me and send me racing out the door. That won't happen, Amanda."

He twisted further in his seat to hold her shoulders and give her a gentle shake. "When I said I cared about you, I meant it. I don't go around saying that to every woman I want to have sex with."

She laughed. He was so outrageously honest about his intentions.

Josh wasn't amused. "When I said scars wouldn't matter, I meant that, too. It doesn't make any difference to me if the scars are on your body or in your heart. They're still a part of you, and so I want to know. All of it."

Well she'd tried. If it took the full truth to make him understand, then she'd give him the full truth. Amanda looked him in the eyes and said, "When I was seventeen, I killed a man."

LORI FOSTER

Josh froze, his expression arrested, disbelieving.

Better to get it all over with quickly, she thought. "I also wounded two others. They're the ones who wear the awful scars, not me. God knows it would have been so much better, and certainly more just, if it had been me. But that's not how it worked out."

"Amanda..."

She shook her head. "There are so many people who will never forgive me, but that's okay, because I won't ever forgive myself."

SIX

JOSH SHOCKED THE breath right out of her when he yanked her into his arms. He felt so solid, so strong and brave and heroic. He was everything she could never be.

It seemed criminal for her to be with him, but Amanda couldn't stop herself from knotting her hands in his T-shirt and clinging to him.

He sat back and again lifted her into his lap. In a voice gone hoarse with emotion, he said, "Tell me what happened."

That he bothered to ask for details amazed Amanda. A few men had, men she'd tried and failed to be intimate with in college, and when she'd first moved here. But macabre fascination and selfish intent had motivated their queries, because they wanted to know why they were being rejected. Not one of them had asked out of genuine caring.

She *felt* Josh's caring. She felt it in the way he held her, in the steady drone of his heartbeat against her cheek, in the way his large hands moved up and down her spine, offering her comfort. It settled over her like a warm blanket, almost tangible.

Tears pricked her eyes, but she staved them off. She'd cried enough, and besides, she didn't deserve to sit around whining.

Amanda rubbed her cheek against him, breathing in his masculine scent. "You were right—I did come from money. Dad not only has his own company and more stock in other companies than I can remember, but he inherited a fortune from his family. My mother's family isn't quite as well off, but they're definitely upper-crust. Whenever they weren't around, there was a housekeeper or tutor or someone to keep tabs on me and my sister."

"You said you were seventeen? That's a little old to have a baby-sitter, isn't it?"

"I thought so. But my parents were determined that my sister and I would never embarrass them. So many of their friends had kids who had gotten into trouble, unwanted pregnancies, drugs, bad grades. I don't blame them for being extra cautious. Being influential puts you in the limelight, so we had be exemplary in every way."

"Sounds rough."

She started to lift her head, but he pressed her back down and kissed her temple. She subsided. "Don't get me wrong, my parents loved me."

"*Loved* you? As in past tense?"

She didn't want to delve too deeply into the broken ties with her family. It hurt too much. "Things have been…strained since that awful night. I embarrassed them. I caused a huge scandal that still hasn't died down, even though it happened seven years ago. We keep in touch, but I doubt we'll ever be close again."

"Tell me what happened."

Deciding to just get it over with, she said, "One night I slipped out of my house to meet with my boyfriend. We were going to have sex in the woods behind my house. Can you believe that? A very risqué, exciting rendezvous. I felt totally wicked and very grown-up." She lowered her head and laughed though she'd never remember that night with anything but horror. "Looking back, I realize how immature and ridiculous I was."

"You were young," Josh said without censure, "and most seventeen-year-olds are ready to start experimenting, to start pushing for independence. You sound pretty average to me."

If she had ever been average, Amanda thought, she'd been changed that awful night. "He showed up at midnight. I crawled out my second-story bedroom window and shimmied down a tree, and away we went." She absently plucked at a wrinkle in her skirt, not seeing anything, not wanting to see. "While I was gone, making out in the dirt on a borrowed blanket, our house caught on fire. An electrical short or something they eventually decided. Everyone got out of the house by the time the fire trucks arrived, only…"

The muscles in Josh's arms bunched. He was a firefighter, so she knew he could easily picture the scenario. "Only when no one found you, they all thought you were still inside?"

"Yes." She swallowed hard, but the lump of regret remained. "My parents were hysterical. My mother collapsed on the lawn with my sister, both of them screaming. My father tried to get back inside when he couldn't find me. He punched two firefighters who tried to hold him back, but he finally gave up when three of them went inside instead."

Remorse clawed through her, as fresh and painful as the day it had happened. "My bedroom was in the middle of the upstairs floor. While they were searching for me, going on my parents' assurances that I had to be in there, the floor caved in. One man…" An invisible fist squeezed her throat, choking her. God, she hated reliving that awful night.

Josh waited, not saying a word, just stroking her.

"Even in the woods, I heard the sirens. They seemed to be right on top of us and I was afraid they'd wake my family and they'd know what I did, that I'd sneaked out. So I came home."

Shuddering, rubbing at her eyes so she could see, Amanda said, "The fireman fell into the downstairs and got trapped. He was unconscious and the smoke was so thick, they almost couldn't find him. By the time they got him out he was badly burned."

She gave up trying to wipe away the tears and just dropped her hands into her lap. "He only lived three days. Three days of wavering in and out of consciousness, constantly in pain."

Josh still didn't say anything, but there was such a ringing in her head she wouldn't have heard him anyway. She tried to breathe but couldn't. She tried to relax, to be unemotional, but she couldn't do that either. "The other two men are badly scarred, their arms, and their hands."

Pushing herself away from Josh's embrace, she rocked forward and covered her face, ashamed and embarrassed and sick at heart. "They hated me of course. Not that I blame them. And that man's widow…"

She felt Josh touch her shoulder and she lurched to her feet, then paced to the window. She couldn't talk anymore, but there wasn't much else to say. She stared blindly out at the blackness of her yard, and the blackness of her life.

Then Josh was behind her, drawing her into his warmth, wrapping those incredibly strong arms around her so she had no choice but to give him his way.

"Hush now," he said.

Amanda felt her mascara run, knew she needed to blow her nose. "It was on the news," she said, the words coming on their own. "My parents screaming, the firefighters working so hard, dirty and beat but not giving up. They had videos of my mother in her nightgown, curlers in her hair, my sister bawling. And my father, such a stately, dignified man…acting almost insane, fighting the firemen."

"Trying to get to the daughter he loves. That's typical, Amanda."

"They showed the videos of me, too, just standing there, not hurt, not even in the house. My hair was wrecked, a tangled mess, and my blouse was buttoned wrong. There were weeds on my clothes and…everyone knew. They knew where I'd been and what I'd been doing and my parents were just devastated." She squeezed herself tight, but it didn't help. "It wasn't only on the local news, it was on every station everywhere."

Josh turned her.

She couldn't look at him yet so she pushed away and went to the table for a tissue, blowing her nose loudly and then hiccuping. When she did finally look at Josh, she saw his pity, his sad eyes, and she wanted to die.

"My dad took me to the hospital to see the two men who survived." The things she'd seen that night would live with her forever. There were still nights when she couldn't sleep, when she'd close her eyes and relive every frightening, too real moment. "It was so awful. Firemen pacing, wives crying, and they all looked at me like I'd done it on purpose."

"No," Josh said quietly. "I can't believe that."

Memories bombarded her, and she said, "You're right." Amanda recalled an incredible incident. "One of the firemen who'd gone inside for me, Marcus Lindsey, told me he had a daughter my age. He told me kids made mistakes and that he didn't blame me, so he didn't want me blaming myself. He told me I was too pretty to keep crying."

A new wash of tears came with that admission. Marcus Lindsey was an unbelievable man, a hero, like most firefighters. He'd deserved so much better than what had happened because of her.

Josh touched her hair. "And he's right. We know the risks inherent in our jobs. Lindsey did what he's supposed to do."

"He spent weeks in the hospital, and he'll carry the scars for the rest of his life. He's not a fireman anymore. Neither of the survivors are." She blinked and more tears rolled down her cheeks.

Josh plucked another tissue and wiped her face. He was so gentle and tender it amazed Amanda. "What happened was a freak accident," he murmured, "not a deliberate act, definitely not something to keep beating yourself up for."

Amanda couldn't believe his reaction. "How would you feel? If you'd done what I did, if you'd slipped off against your parents' instruction to fool around in the woods and someone had *died* because of it, how would you feel?"

"There's no way I can answer that, honey, because it didn't happen to me." He tucked her hair behind her ear, rubbed her temple with his thumb. "But I can tell you that I've made mistakes, in my job and in my social life. Everybody has— it's one of the side effects of being human. All we can do is try not to make the same mistakes again, to forgive ourselves, and to make amends."

"I'm trying to make amends."

"No, you're driving yourself into the ground with guilt. It's not at all the same thing."

Confusion swamped her. He sounded so reasonable, when there was nothing reasonable about what had happened.

"Tell you what," Josh said. "Why don't you go take a warm shower? Your clothes are dirty and torn and your makeup is everywhere it's not supposed to be."

"Oh." She started to touch her face, but he caught her hands and kissed her forehead.

"You look like a very adorable urchin, so don't worry about it. But I know you'll be more comfortable if you shower and change. While you do that I'll go ahead and make some coffee. Are you hungry? I could maybe rustle you up a sandwich."

Amanda pushed her hair out of her face and looked around her small house in consternation. She'd bared her soul, then prepared for the worst. But not only wasn't Josh disgusted, he offered to fix her food.

He could muddle her so easily. "You plan to make yourself at home in my kitchen?"

"Yes."

Truth was, Amanda didn't want him to leave. She felt spent, wasted right down to the bone, and she didn't want to be alone. He wasn't blaming her, wasn't appalled or shocked or disapproving. He'd listened and offered comfort.

It was so much more than she usually got, so much more than she thought she deserved.

She was selfish enough to want him to stay.

And realistic enough to know it wouldn't make a difference in the long run.

"All right, but no food. I'm not hungry."

Josh gave her a long look. "Can you manage on your own?"

"To shower?" She frowned. "Of course I can."

"Spoilsport."

Amanda stared. Now he wanted to tease her?

Smiling, Josh bent and kissed her softly on the mouth. "I'll be in the kitchen waiting."

Amanda watched Josh stroll from the room, a tall powerful man who had invaded her heart and then her home. Despite what she'd just confessed, he appeared to have no intention of withdrawing.

Amazing. From the start, Josh had seen the worst from her. She'd been first badgering and defensive to gain his involvement in the calendar, then hysterical and tearful while giving him her truths. He knew all her worst qualities and her darkest secret, yet he didn't leave.

From deep, deep in her heart, something warm and happy and unfamiliar stirred.

It scared her spitless, because what would happen when he realized their relationship would never be an intimate one? Would he remain her friend? Somehow, she doubted it. Josh was a very physical, a very sexual man.

That meant that she had to take advantage of every single second she'd have with him.

Amanda hurried to get through with her shower.

Josh waited until he heard the pipes rumble from her shower, then he punched the wall, hurting his knuckles but relieving some of his anger. Luckily, the old schoolhouse was solid so all he hurt was himself.

He couldn't remember ever being so enraged, to the point he'd have gladly horsewhipped a few people, starting with himself. Everything that had happened since first meeting her now had fresh meaning. And it hurt.

He wanted to pass backward in time and save a young lady from a life-altering mistake.

He wanted to redo about a hundred moments with her, times when he'd been too forward, too pushy. Times when he'd made it clear he wanted sex, when actually he wanted so much more.

He wanted to tell Amanda that it would be all right. But he just didn't know.

Thinking of what she'd likely gone through, what he knew she'd felt judging by the expression on her face during the re-telling made him ill.

Josh believed Amanda's father loved her, based on what she'd said. He'd seen many people fight to try to save their loved ones, willingly putting themselves at risk. But her father never should have taken her to visit the injured men in the hospital.

He'd probably thought to teach her a valuable lesson, or perhaps he'd gone strictly out of goodwill, wanting to offer thanks as well as his apologies for what had occurred. But putting Amanda through such an ordeal, making her deal with the accusations wrought from grief, had caused her so much harm.

People in mourning, people afraid and worried, were emotionally fragile, not given to clear thinking. Of course family members and friends had at first blamed Amanda—they'd needed a way to vent and she'd been far too handy.

Her father should have protected her from that, not exposed her to it.

While standing in the middle of her kitchen, struggling to deal with his turbulent thoughts, Josh heard the faint tinkle of bells. He paused, lifting his head and listening. The sound came again, louder with the whistling of the wind and he went to the window to look out.

Nothing but blackness could be seen, and a fresh worry invaded his already overwrought mind. Amanda was too alone here, too vulnerable. She literally lived in isolation with no one nearby if she needed help.

Josh searched for a light switch and finally located one by the sink.

A floodlight illuminated the backyard and an incredible display of wind chimes, large and small, brass and wood, colorful and dull. With each breeze, they rang out in soft musical notes.

He also noted the birdhouses and feeders, dozens of them everywhere, on poles and in the trees.

With his head lowered and his eyes misty, Josh flipped the light back off and leaned on the sink. Damn, he'd never known a woman like Amanda Barker. She was all starch and hard determination one minute, and so soft and needy the next.

The shower turned off, jarring Josh out of his ruminations. He rushed through the coffee preparations, noting the fact that her coffeemaker only made three cups, proof positive that she never entertained guests.

Rummaging through her refrigerator, he found cheese and lettuce and mayonnaise. He remembered how little she ate and made two sandwiches, one and a half for himself, a half for Amanda. He'd just finished putting pickle slices on a plate and cutting the sandwiches when she appeared.

Josh looked up, and smiled. Amanda's face was still ravaged—her eyes were puffy, her nose pink, her lips swollen and her cheeks blotchy. But the oil and blackening was gone, as was her makeup. She'd tied her hair onto the top of her head, but she'd been hasty with it and long tendrils hung down her nape, around her ears.

Though she was bundled up in a white chenille robe, Josh could see her pale yellow thermal pajamas beneath and the thick white socks on her feet.

Her hands clutched the lapels of the robe and she said, "I told you I wasn't hungry."

Josh lied smoothly, without an ounce of guilt. "But I am,

and I hate to eat alone. Even you ought to be able to choke down half a cheese sandwich."

While she stood there hovering just out of his reach, Josh cleared her table. He neatly stacked a small mountain of papers and photographs and transferred them to the washer, the only uncluttered surface available.

Evidence of her continued efforts was everywhere; the papers he'd just moved, contracts, old calendars, fundraising schedules and event planners.

"Can I ask you a few things, Amanda?"

She braced herself as if expecting an inquisition on the fires of hell. "Yes, of course."

Her guilt was so extreme, he knew she wouldn't give it up easily. She'd been living with it for seven years and it was now a part of her. "If you're not interested in getting cozy with a guy, why do you dress so sexy?"

Even without makeup, her big brown eyes looked lovely, soft with long lashes that shadowed her cheeks when she blinked.

"I don't. I wear business suits."

Business suits that in no way looked businesslike. They had nipped waists and above the knee thigh-hugging skirts. And those sexy shoes she wore...

Josh had his own theories, but he wondered if Amanda realized the connection that she'd made.

The night of the fire, by her own account, she'd been caught disheveled, her activities apparent from her rumpled appearance. Now she was always dressed impeccably, polished from her hair to her high heels. With every tidy suit she donned, she made a statement. But she also emphasized that she was a woman.

"Your suits are sexier than a lot of miniskirts." Josh wasn't a psychologist, but it seemed obvious to him. "You also wear stockings and high heels."

She pulled out a chair to sit, and then picked up a pickle slice, avoiding his gaze. "No one knows that I wear stockings."

Josh drew his chair around next to her. "I do."

She glanced at him and away. "You wouldn't have if things hadn't gotten out of hand."

"Okay, let's look at this another way. *You* know what you're wearing. So why do you?"

She chewed and swallowed before answering. Her cheeks colored. "Sometimes," she whispered, measuring her words, "I don't feel much like a woman. I suppose it's my way of… balancing things. For me, not for anyone else."

Josh's heart pounded. She was trusting him, sharing with him. "You make yourself feel more feminine because you're a virgin?"

She shook her head. "No. Because I'm frigid."

He wasn't at all convinced of that, but he'd argue it with her later. "I guess it makes sense. But I gotta tell you, I can't imagine a sexier or more feminine woman than you. With or without experience."

As more color rushed to her face, Amanda stared hard at another pickle slice and then picked it up.

Josh smiled. He had her confused and that was nice for a change. Maybe he'd eventually get her so confused she'd forget her ridiculous guilt.

"What about this house?" he asked. "If your parents are rich, why the tiny home? And why a Volkswagen? I pegged you as more of a Mercedes gal."

She lifted the bread on her half of a sandwich, looked beneath critically, then replaced it. Since she'd only had mayonnaise in her refrigerator, no mustard, he didn't know what she'd expected to find.

"I love this house, so don't go insulting it. I'm just me and I don't need much room. And my car runs great. When other cars won't start in the cold, she always kicks over and gets me where I'm going."

"That's not what I'm asking and you know it."

"I know." She sighed. "Truth is, I live in a small house and drive an economical car because that's all I can afford. I only have what I earn, and it's not that much. But," she added, giving him a look, "I'd have bought this house regardless. I do love it, and now, after being here for a while, I can't imagine living anywhere else."

"What about your family?"

"You mean what about the family coffers?" She shrugged. "My father and I had a major falling out. Since we weren't close emotionally, I couldn't use him financially. I decided to make it on my own."

"What did your father have to say about that?"

"He was naturally furious that I refused his money, doubly so when I took out student loans to finish paying for my college tuition. He didn't think I'd make it, but I've proven him wrong. I have to keep an inexpensive car and house to do it, but I'm totally independent and I like it that way."

Josh watched her bite into her sandwich and waited until she'd swallowed to ask, "What caused the falling out?"

She waved a negligent hand, but her big sad eyes darkened again. "What I did, the fire and the damage—"

His back stiffened, his muscles tightened. "He blamed you?"

"Oh, no, never that. But he's never understood how I feel, either."

"You didn't cause the fire, Amanda."

"No, but I sure caused a lot of the damage. As my mother used to say, a house can be quickly rebuilt, but a damaged reputation is impossible to repair."

Disgust filled him. Josh was thinking rather insulting things about the mother until Amanda clarified, "My mother said that in regard to herself—she'd been seen on camera, in her robe and her curlers."

"She was worried about her appearance in the middle of the house burning down?"

"My mother wouldn't normally be caught dead without her makeup. She was mortified. My whole family was. And it was my fault." Amanda peered up at him. "What she said was true, at least when applied to me."

Josh frowned. "Your reputation is that of a beautiful, giving woman who works hard at helping others."

"To some. To those who don't know it all."

"To anyone with any sense."

Amanda stared over his shoulder. "All of us had our lives, our backgrounds thrown out there to be scrutinized. Everyone knew the girl who'd been screwing around in the woods while a man died trying to rescue her, and they knew my family, my sister who was younger than me, the mother and father who had raised such an irresponsible child."

"Amanda, damn it…"

"That's what the papers called me, 'irresponsible.' All things considered, it's not such a horrible insult." She picked at the crust on her sandwich, pulling it apart. "Things quieted down when I first went away to college. Problem was, though, after about a year and a half, I got another boyfriend. Big mistake, that."

"Every college kid dates, Amanda." He could already guess what had happened, and it made him want to shout.

"I shouldn't have. I should have learned."

"Bullshit. You were getting on with your life. That's what we're supposed to do."

"Sometimes," she agreed without much conviction. "But not that time. I thought I liked this guy a lot. He was popular and fun and outgoing. When he wanted to make love to me, I couldn't. It literally turned my stomach to go beyond kissing."

Josh remembered how she'd clung to him, how hot and open she had been. He refused to believe that what had happened with a boy in college would hold true with him. She'd been young then, and college boys weren't known for technique or patience.

"I broke things off with him," Amanda explained, "and he got offended. I guess I wounded his male vanity by not getting...aroused by him. He told everyone I was a cold bitch and a tease, and the next thing I knew, someone remembered my name and the whole story was there again."

Hands curled into fists, Josh said, "I gather he spread it around to salve his own ego?"

"Yes. My father was outraged. He wanted me to press charges against him. Sexual harassment, if you can believe that, and slander even though what the guy said was true. I refused, and that's when I took over all my financial obligations."

Josh felt tense enough to explode, but he held it together for Amanda. "Has it been retold since then?"

"No. Well, not until I just told you." She put her sandwich back down and folded her hands on the table. "When I got my job at the mall, right out of college, I met another nice guy. He wasn't like the first. He wasn't overly popular or loud. He was the new manager, shy and studious, eight years older than me. We dated for six months and he was so patient, I really hoped... But I just couldn't."

Talking about it, thinking about her with other men, especially men who had upset her, made him nuts. But there were things he had to know, things he had to ask about if he ever hoped to make headway with her. "Were you sexually attracted to him?"

She looked perplexed by his question. "I liked him."

"It's not the same thing."

"I *wanted* to make love with him."

"Because you wanted him, or because you wanted to prove something to yourself?"

Amanda shoved back her chair so fast it nearly fell over. Josh was on her before she'd taken two steps. He curled his hands around her upper arms and held her still. She was so skittish, forever running from him. "Tell me, honey. Did you want him like you want me?"

"I don't remember. That was two years ago."

"Amanda." He cupped her face and stroked her cheeks with his thumbs. The feel of her soft, warm skin tantalized him. "Don't lie to me, honey."

Her chin lifted. "All right, then no. I didn't want him like I want you. But it doesn't matter."

"I think it does."

"Then you'd be wrong. I can't ever enjoy that part of being a woman. I'm not meant to enjoy it."

Because she didn't deserve it? Josh wanted to shake her. "That's idiotic, Amanda, and you know it."

"I tried after that, Josh. I tried a couple of times. But no matter what, it never worked out. I could only go so far and then I'd hate it."

"Hate it how?"

"All of it, in every way. I hated being touched, looked at. I hated being kissed. It always made me remember…"

He quickly interrupted. "I'm touching you now and you like it. And you didn't mind my kisses at all."

She glared at him and then thumped his chest. "Stop it! You're seeing what you want to see. Odds are if we try this, you'll just be disappointed, too." She thumped him again, then tangled her hand in his shirt and held on tight as she whispered, "Just as I'm always disappointed."

"Like hell." Josh drew her up, kissed her long and hard and held her close. She struggled for just a second or two, and then she clung to him.

Panting, Josh said against her mouth, "Here's what we'll do, Amanda. We'll go really slow. Excruciatingly slow. If at any point you start to feel bad, in any way, you're going to tell me and I swear I'll stop. I won't rush you and never, ever, will I be disappointed. No matter what."

Amanda stared up at him, her gaze filled with hope and excitement—and that damned guilt. Josh had no more doubts. In that single moment of time, he knew he loved her. He also knew he wouldn't tell her yet. She'd get spooked all over again and he didn't want to risk that.

"Can I stay another hour?" he asked, his voice so low and rough he didn't recognize himself.

Amanda nodded and at the same time, asked, "Why?"

"Because I want to kiss you silly." He held her face and put small damp pecks on her chin, her forehead, her ear and the corner of her mouth. He licked her ear and whispered, "I want to lie down in your bed with you and hold you close and feel all of you against me like I did at the park, and I want to kiss you for an hour. And when I leave, I want you to lie awake at least another hour, missing me and wanting me." He looked into her beautiful brown eyes and added, "The way I'll be wanting you and missing you."

Her lips trembled—with nervousness or excitement or fear, he wasn't sure. "It won't do any good…"

"Just kissing. That's all I want."

She ducked her head, smiling, and said, "Liar."

God he loved her. Josh hugged her close and laughed. "Yeah, that was a lie. An *enormous* lie. I want you all the time, right now especially. What I meant is that for tonight, for maybe a week, all we'll do is kiss."

"*A week?* But why?"

"Because I want you to get used to me. I want you to know that you can enjoy the kissing because it won't go any further so there's nothing to be afraid of. I want you to learn to trust me, and to trust yourself again."

"Ah." Her dark eyes shone with blatant doubt. "And when the week's over and nothing has changed? Just how long do you think this super-human patience of yours is going to last?"

"As long as it takes." Josh smiled at her surprise. "Get used to it, Amanda. I'm not going anywhere, so we've got forever."

Amanda's eyes widened and she pushed back from him. Josh wanted to curse. He hadn't meant to say that, hadn't meant to rush her again. Just because he now thought in terms of a lifelong commitment didn't mean the same applied to her. It wasn't that long ago that she had denied even being attracted to him.

But then she drew a deep breath—for courage he thought—and went on tiptoe to put her arms around his neck. She said, "Yes, all right."

"You're willing to try?"

Looking like she faced the gallows, she said, "If you are, then I'd be a fool to say no."

Slightly insulted, Josh asked, "You're willing because you

want to test yourself again, or because you actually want me, *me,* not just any guy."

She smiled. "With you around," Amanda told him, "there are no other guys."

Josh picked her up and headed for the bedroom.

SEVEN

AN HOUR LATER, Amanda felt smothered in a cocoon of sensuality. Her heartbeat raced, her skin tingled, her womb ached and pulled and her breasts…her breasts were so sensitive she couldn't bear it.

But Josh only kissed her.

It was wonderful because she didn't have to worry about freezing up, about not being able to perform. She knew how to kiss, and enjoyed it.

But at the same time, it was frustrating because no matter how excited she got, no matter how much she might want him to touch her a little more, he wouldn't break his word. They'd kiss and that would be all, so she tried to relax and enjoy him.

Relaxing, she found, was out of the question.

"Josh," she gasped, as his lips tugged at her earlobe and his hand opened on her belly. Inside her robe. Stroking.

Normally that would have made her nervous, but not tonight. Not with Josh.

"Yeah, baby?"

Mmmmm. The way he said that, she no longer objected to the endearment. "When you said kiss—ah!" His tongue licked into her ear, making her tremble and shattering her thoughts. She stiffened, and he retreated.

"When I said kiss?" Josh trailed damp love bites down her neck to her shoulder, into the hollow of her collarbones.

With an effort, Amanda gathered her wits. "I thought you just meant kiss. You know, on the mouth."

"I love your mouth," he murmured, then feasted on her lips for a good three minutes until she felt nearly mindless again.

He untied the belt to her robe and opened the material wide.

Amanda opened her eyes and watched him curiously.

"I want this out of my way." Josh stared down at her with heated eyes and a smile of promise. "I adore your jammies."

Forcing her head up, Amanda surveyed her body. Her thermal pajamas were warm and soft, a pale yellow trimmed with white daisies on the neck and the cuffs of her sleeves and pants. Josh hadn't asked her to strip. No, instead he'd complimented her very silly sedate nightwear.

It embarrassed her a little, until Josh sat up and jerked off his T-shirt, throwing it off the foot of the bed.

"I want to feel your hands on me," he explained. "Is that okay? You're all right?"

Amanda stared at his hard chest, now smeared a little with the blackening that hadn't yet rubbed off. His shoulders glistened from the residue of baby oil, and muscles bunched and flexed as he waited for her answer.

"Yes, all right."

Josh groaned. "Touch me anyway you want to, anywhere you want to." He lowered himself back to her, once again taking her mouth.

Amanda knew about kissing, but this wasn't just kissing. This was full body contact, hot breath and a soft tongue and so thrilling she'd never expected it. Every man she'd ever known would have been frantic by now, pushing her for more, trying to convince her with arguments and unwanted touches.

But not Josh. He had large hands and they roamed everywhere, up her arms, over her shoulders, sometimes cupping her face tenderly, sometimes stroking her thighs suggestively. Everything he did was geared toward her pleasure, at her level of comfort.

He seemed to know what she felt before she could understand it. If she stiffened even the tiniest bit, he changed direction. If she gasped in wonder, he intensified his efforts.

She loved it when he touched her belly. He touched it a lot. But he stayed away from any place that might push them beyond the kissing stage, and the result was that she felt on fire.

"Josh, please…"

"Please what? Tell me what you want."

Daringly, she tasted the skin on his neck. He was salty and hot and she wanted more. "I don't know." She glided her hands over his bare skin, rasping his small nipples, tangling her fingers in his chest hair. He felt so hot, so hard. "I'm afraid to say."

He made a low sound of carnal delight at the feel of her tongue on his neck, her hands exploring his flesh. "Afraid the good feelings will go away?"

"Yes." Guilt nudged at her, memories trying to invade, but above it all was the smell and feel and taste of Josh. She'd probably regret it later, but for now she wanted to be a normal woman, not one filled with fears and reservations. It was what Josh deserved, even if she didn't.

She opened her mouth and sucked on the hot skin of his

throat while her fingers pressed into the hard tensed muscles of his shoulders. He tasted *so* good.

Josh dropped his head to rest beside hers on the pillow. "Ah...*damn*."

"Josh?"

"I think we need to stop," he rasped.

She'd disappointed him! She'd been selfish, taking what she wanted while knowing he wouldn't be satisfied. "I...I'm sorry."

Josh leaned up on one elbow to see her face. His expression was hard and tensed with arousal, his eyes glittering. "For what?"

For everything. Amanda bit her lip, then said, "If you want to try..."

"I want more than a quick screw, sweetheart." He smiled and nipped at her bottom lip, stealing it from her worrying teeth, laughing softly when she gasped.

"I want you," he said, "naked and hot, and I want you laughing and I want you crying. I want you now and tomorrow. None of that has anything to do with having sex right now, but it has everything to do with how you'll feel about me forever."

Her heart stumbled. He'd said it again, used that *"forever"* word twice now, as if they had a future together.

His eyes were smiling and happy, not disappointed. But dark color slashed his cheekbones and she could feel the heat radiating off him, making his skin damp.

He offered her so much; he offered her forever.

Amanda couldn't stop touching him, coasting her hands over his hard muscles and long bones. He was big and macho and very sexy. He was a lot of man, and he claimed to want her forever.

In her heart, she knew forever was impossible. But he was here now, and she was just selfish enough to want a small part of him, for now.

"Will you come over again tomorrow?"

A smile curled his mouth and lit his eyes. "Yeah, I'll be here. But I have a long shift. I work till six. How about I bring dinner?"

"How about I cook dinner?" she countered.

"And after you feed me," he teased, rubbing his palm over her belly, "we can neck some more?"

She touched his jaw where beard shadow rasped her fingertips. "I hope so."

"We'll watch a movie, too. I like the idea of lounging here in your bed, making out and just getting familiar. It sounds real cozy."

Amanda looked up at the ceiling and laughed, a little amazed, a lot confused. "I can't imagine any man saying what you just said. Men want to have sex, not just get cozy."

"Some men, maybe. Not me. Not with you."

Every guy Amanda had ever dated had worked hard toward getting her into bed, and when he accepted that wouldn't happen, he'd walked. Men wanted no part of a dysfunctional woman, a woman who couldn't offer sexual satisfaction. To most guys, that disqualified her as a real woman.

To Amanda, they were right.

Josh apparently disagreed.

"You're making me crazy," she said.

"That's the whole idea." He gave her another hard smooch, then pushed himself off the bed. "I want you crazy enough that you can forget everything but me."

She didn't tell him, but she was already halfway there. And she didn't know if that was good—or bad.

★ ★ ★

Josh was so proud of Amanda. She stood at a podium and directed people to various tables and displays. Her idea of a charity reception to launch sales of the calendar was brilliant, even if he did feel like an idiot strutting around without a shirt, being ogled by females of all ages.

Amanda had insisted all the guys dress in work gear, sans shirts. Of course, they'd all complied, strutting around with their bunker pants slung low, chests bare, their steel-toed boots clunking on the floor as they moved. But she'd also insisted that Josh carry his ax, which was something Amanda found sexy—not that he understood why.

The fun part was that every time a woman got too close to him, Amanda showed up like a fussy White Knight, ready to defend and protect. Josh chuckled to himself, amused by her, and so damn in love he felt ready to burst.

He was also so sexually frustrated he didn't know how much more he could take. Night after night, he'd gone to see Amanda and every time their intimacy grew, though they'd held to the rule of mere kisses. Still, kissing Amanda was wonderful, because her reactions were wonderful. She literally wallowed in her newfound sexual freedom.

And just yesterday, after nearly a full week of pleasurable torture, he'd held her breast in his hand and felt her nipple pressing into his palm. The moment had been so sweet, and he'd felt so triumphant, he'd nearly come in his pants.

Amanda hadn't objected to his familiarity, and in fact her eyes had gone smoky, her breath choppy, her skin warm. She'd arched into him and given a sexy little moan that drove him nuts.

But Josh had forced himself to go no further. It had nearly killed him, but he'd kept control. More than anything, he wanted her to want him—without restrictions, without any bad memories haunting her. When he finally got inside her, he wanted her to be aware only of the pleasure and the heat and the tantalizing friction as they moved together....

Josh groaned. Much more of that fantasy and he'd be making a spectacle of himself. He stared down at his lap and silently ordered his male parts to behave. He'd been giving that damned order since first starting this strange seduction. His body was about to go into full rebellion.

A swat on the butt, followed by a squeeze, made Josh jump. He turned around, and came face-to-face with Vicki. He hadn't seen her since that day outside Marcos, when he'd told her that his free-wheeling days were over.

"Hey, stud," she teased, then went on tiptoe to give him a kiss. Her mouth was soft and warm, and it moved him not even a tiny bit.

Josh said, "Uh," and looked around to see if Amanda had witnessed the byplay. Luckily, she was busy schmoozing a local society matron who would likely grace her with a sizeable donation.

Watching her, Josh appreciated the pretty picture Amanda made today. She'd worn a trim-fitting peach-colored skirt that sported a jaunty little matching jacket and made her skin look velvety. The hem of the skirt landed well above her knees and showed the sexy length of her calves and part of her thighs. Josh knew damn good and well she had a garter and silk stockings on underneath, and knowing it made him sweat.

Pearl studs decorated her delicate ears and a triple-strand pearl collar circled her throat. Her rich hair was swept up with a studded comb.

She looked...edible, Josh decided. Especially since she wore very high, high heels and he could too easily imagine her without the dress, standing there looking delectable in nothing more than her soft skin, nylons, heels and pearls.

Vicki stroked his bare chest, letting her fingertip stroke a nipple. "Yoo-hoo, Josh?"

He jerked around, feeling mauled, like fresh meat. He wanted a shirt, damn it.

He wanted Amanda.

"Sorry." He stepped out of reach. "What did you say?"

Her smile was slow and wicked. "Look at you, all warmed up. I recognize that hot expression in your eyes."

That expression was for Amanda, not that Vicki would ever believe it when she stood so close and was acting so suggestive.

"Glad to see me?" she asked. "Things with Ms. Snooty not working out?"

Josh frowned. "She's not snooty."

"No? She comes across that way."

"She's...timid."

"Yeah, right."

Josh rolled his eyes. "Okay, so she's not timid. What are you doing here, Vicki?"

"I'm giving my fair share, of course. I ordered two dozen of the calendars—one for myself, and the rest for female relatives. They'll be thrilled."

"Thanks." Josh felt like a dolt, but what else could he say?

"Thanks? That's it?"

He sighed. "What do you want, Vicki?" She opened her mouth and with a grin, Josh waggled his finger at her, knowing exactly what she'd say. "Other than me."

Vicki laughed. "You know me too well." She touched his chest again so Josh caught her wrist and held it. He felt exposed enough bare-chested in a room full of people dressed in casual evening wear, without having a woman play with him.

Looking up at him through her lashes, Vicki said, "We had some good times together, didn't we?"

Because he knew women, Josh saw the vulnerability in Vicki's eyes. She needed to be reassured, so he did just that. He kissed her knuckles and said, "We had a terrific time. I always enjoyed your company, hon, you know that."

"But?"

Gently, because he hated to hurt anyone, Josh reiterated, "But it's over. I really am a one-woman man, now. That hasn't changed."

Vicki looked beyond him and winced. "Well, your one woman looks ready to string you up by your toes. I suppose I should get out of the line of fire."

Josh turned and sure enough, Amanda was fuming. He smiled and gave her a wave, still holding on to Vicki with his other hand, though Vicki did her best to edge away from him. Amanda huffed and turned her back on him.

Finally releasing her, he said to Vicki, "I should mingle."

She just shook her head and gave her farewells. He knew Vicki considered his actions strange, but he couldn't help being flattered every time Amanda showed her jealousy. He was used to women who were openly admiring, women who said what they thought and felt—especially about him.

He had to work hard to get any kind of commitment from Amanda—except when she saw him with another woman.

Mick wandered up next, his suit coat open, his hands shoved in his pants pockets. "Doing a little flaunting tonight, huh?"

Josh made a face. "Amanda's idea. All the guys from the calendar are shirtless, but I swear, some of them are enjoying it more than others."

"Others meaning you?"

"I can think of things I'd rather be doing."

Mick glanced around the crowded room. "Not having any fun here, huh?" It was in his nature to be forever on the lookout. Being cautious was partly his nature, partly his job.

Josh felt like an idiot, but he wouldn't tell Mick that. It wasn't that he was ashamed of his body, but it seemed ridiculous to make such a big deal of it. "I'll survive."

"Since you appear to be the theme of this bash, you better."

Everywhere Josh looked, there hung poster-size pictures of himself as Mr. November. Women would see the pictures, then either seek him out with their eyes and start twittering, or rush to buy the calendar. It was humiliating. "If it'll help make money for the charity, then what do I care?"

Mick looked over the buffet table filled with hors d'oeuvres donated by a local caterer. He chose a cracker piled with pinkish cheese, then eyed it closely. "It's for a great cause," he agreed. "I'd think you'd be enjoying yourself with all this attention."

"Would you?"

Mick snorted. "Okay, this is a little overdoing it. But the thing is, it seems you've given up completely on having fun."

Josh frowned at Mick as he held the cracker eye level and scrutinized it. "Meaning?"

"Meaning you just sent a little 'fun' packing."

Confused for the moment, Josh asked, "Vicki?"

"Yeah, Vicki. I remember her as one of your favorites. Any reason you've decided to become celibate?"

"Ha!" Josh crossed his arms over his bare chest and smirked. "Not in this lifetime."

"Oh?" Mick popped the whole cracker in his mouth and made appreciative noises. "Not bad."

"Just what the hell are you getting at, Mick?" Both Mick and Zack knew he was involved with Amanda. Hell, he'd been with her every available moment. He was here now, dressed in bunker pants and steel-toed boots, toting that damn ax she seemed so fond of, just for her. That should explain it all right there.

Mick searched the table for another cracker. Josh thought about hitting him in the head. "Damn it, Mick…"

"Zack is a little worried about you."

That set him back. "The hell you say!"

"Yeah, seems you've been…distracted." Mick glanced at him, then gave his attention back to the cracker. He sniffed at the cheese and made a face. Glancing around, hoping no one would notice, he set it back on the table.

"Distracted how? And if you pick up another bite to eat," Josh warned, "I'll take the ax handle to you."

Mick grinned and held up his empty hands. "Distracted at work. Zack says it's dangerous for you not to give your full attention to the job. We both figured you were just antsy over things with Amanda, but I gotta admit you have me confused. You two seem tight, but here you are, all jittery. And if you're not tight with Amanda, then why did you turn Vicki away?"

Josh sat the ax against the wall and rubbed his face. "Things are…difficult. Different. That's all. Amanda is…" He shook his head, unwilling to betray Amanda's trust, but wishing he had someone to talk to.

"She's what? Not falling at your feet?"

"Of course she wouldn't do that! She's…"

Mick raised a brow and waited.

"Oh hell, I love her, all right?" The words left his mouth and then he grinned. "I really do. I'm crazy about her."

Mick looked as if that was the last thing he'd expected to hear. It rattled him so much that he picked up the smelly cheese and ate it without thinking, then choked and had to grab for a drink.

Wheezing, he said, "You're in love?"

"Yeah."

"With *Amanda?*"

Eyes narrowed, Josh asked, "Any reason you're saying it like that?"

"No! I mean, she's terrific. Pretty, smart, sexy. It's just that she doesn't…" Mick struggled, then shrugged "…seem your type."

"She's unique."

Mick downed the rest of his drink in one gulp. "God, that cheese was nasty."

Laughing, Josh said, "That's good old American cheese and Swiss down there on the end, with the fruit."

"Thanks." Mick picked up a plate and moved in that direction. Josh followed. "So, uh, does Amanda feel the same way?"

"What is this, Mick? Are you my Father Confessor? Did Zack send you here to pick my brain and make sure I wasn't screwing up my life? Are you supposed to advise me and set me on the straight and narrow?"

"Yeah, something like that." Mick popped a grape into his mouth and smiled. "Now that's good."

His mood quickly turning black, Josh said, "Just let me go get my ax and then I'll…"

Mick caught his arm, laughing. "Don't bludgeon me. I swear, this was all Zack's idea. He'd have been here himself if Dani hadn't gotten sick. Wynn told him to come, but you know how Zack is, a real mother hen when his little girl isn't well."

"Yeah, I know how he is." Josh knew a buildup of sexual frustration had made him a little less than reasonable. He hoped Amanda told him how she felt soon, because he didn't know if he could take too much more.

"So is it true?" Mick asked. "Have you been distracted at work? And don't growl at me! With all the grief you gave us, you're due for some back."

Josh subsided at the truth of those words. He had harassed Mick and Zack plenty when they were trying to figure out the whole love thing.

Of course, Josh had it figured out. It was Amanda who seemed unsure. But damned if he'd tell Mick that.

"We're concerned," Mick continued. "Rightfully so, too. Hell, even Wynn and Del told me you were acting different. Not that I pay much attention to your moods, but now that I am, I see what they mean. And Zack sees you at work. He said everyone was razzing a probie, sending him outside repeatedly to find a hose winder—which I gather doesn't exist—and you never said a word."

All probationary firefighters caught hell on their first week at the station. As a lieutenant, Josh usually did his best to run interference, but true enough, he'd been distracted all week thinking about Amanda. He'd barely noticed the antics going on during his shift.

"Zack also says you've been slower on the drills."

He'd strangle Zack when next he saw him. "I know those drills by heart."

"Yeah, but that's not the point and you know it. So tell me, what's up?"

"It's private."

Mick gave him an incredulous look. "That never stopped you from butting into my business!"

"I know, but this isn't just my business. It's Amanda's business, too. She has some things to work out, and until she does, we're not...that is, I haven't..."

Aghast, Mick said, "Damn. You *are* celibate."

"It's temporary."

At the look on Josh's face, Mick sputtered and quickly snatched up a napkin. "Oh, this is priceless," he said, shaking his head while continuing to chuckle.

Through his teeth, Josh said, "It's not a big deal, damn it. I know what I'm doing."

"Hey, I'm not the one who thinks sexual variety keeps you young. That's your mantra, not mine."

Josh reached for his own drink. It was that or Mick's throat. "You always were a particular bastard."

"And you never were, not where women are concerned. But now you're hooked and she's making you work for it instead of throwing herself at you." Mick grinned. "This is great. I love it."

"Shut the hell up, will you?" Josh saw nothing amusing in the situation. Of course, if it had been Mick or Zack, he might have seen the humor.

"Damn, you're testy. Okay, okay!" Mick held up his hands when Josh started to reach for him. "Don't start foaming at the mouth. I wanted to get serious for a second, anyway."

His tone made Josh uneasy. "What? More unsolicited advice?"

Mick gave him that dark-eyed look he used to bring criminals low. "I didn't think *you* knew any other kind."

Remembering the hell he'd put Mick through when Mick had fallen in love with Delilah, Josh had to agree. He'd handed out advice—and aggravation—left and right.

"You need to be more careful at work," Mick said. "I know women troubles can rattle any guy, but if there's a fire, you have to be thinking with the right head, and I'm not talking about the one you let make most of your decisions."

Josh bristled. "You saying I can't control myself sexually?" Ha! What a joke. If only Mick knew, he'd be applauding his iron control.

"I'm saying I don't want to see you get hurt."

"I'm damn good at my job." Feeling defensive, Josh squared off and waited for Mick to dare disagree.

Mick didn't give him the satisfaction.

"I'm not questioning that," he said, "just your frame of mind. Being lovesick is all well and good—hell, I personally think you're past due. But don't let your mind wander when your life is at stake, okay? That's all I'm saying."

Josh started to agree, when suddenly he felt a familiar tension. He was so attuned to Amanda, so aware of her on every level, he instinctively felt her presence.

He turned, already knowing she stood behind him.

Hands clasped together and her cheeks pale, Amanda stared up at him. She looked equal parts furious and mortified.

Covering his uneasiness at being caught while discussing her, Josh pulled himself together and reached for her. She felt rigid under his palms, but she didn't fight him when he tugged her to her tiptoes and kissed her lips. "Hey, sweetheart. Finally got a break, huh? It's about time. I was feeling sorely neglected."

She said, "Yes of course. You've only got every woman here following you around, trying to get your attention."

Josh said, "You noticed," and he grinned.

Amanda stared beyond him at Mick, who looked as uncomfortable as a dark, enigmatic undercover cop could look.

Mick drummed up a sad excuse for a casual smile and said, "Hello, Amanda. It's nice seeing you again."

"Mr. Dawson. Thanks for coming."

"Mick, please." Mick glanced at Josh, probably looking for assistance though Josh had none to offer. There were still times when he couldn't figure Amanda out at all, when her moods were a total mystery to him.

This was one of those times.

Mick forged on manfully. "Your reception here is a hit. The, uh, crackers are great."

Josh snickered at that and took pity on Mick. "Go mingle. Go buy a calendar. Just go."

"Delilah already bought several. But mingling sounds nice."

"Coward."

Mick saluted him and wandered off.

Turning back to Amanda, Josh said, "It amazes me how such a small woman can make grown men quake in their boots."

She sniffed. "That's utter nonsense, and you know it. You certainly aren't quaking."

Josh lifted his brows. Acrimony? That told him something, like she was pissed. More jealousy, maybe? Somehow, he didn't think so. "Do you have any idea how badly I want to kiss you?"

Her gaze skipped away from his and her shoulders stiffened. "I wanted to talk to you about that."

"About kissing me? You been having the same naughty thoughts as me?"

"I… No! That's not what I meant at all." She frowned, chewed her lower lip, and then said, "I think we should calm things down a little."

Damn, she had overheard. Josh pretended he didn't understand. "Now why would you want to do that? Especially when last night was so nice?"

Nice, what an understatement. They'd lain together on Amanda's bed after watching a science-fiction movie and they'd kissed for an hour. Josh, feeling as randy and naughty as a teenager in the back seat of his dad's Chevy, had nonetheless enjoyed holding her close. He'd relished the way she'd gradually relaxed with him, and he'd enjoyed listening to her talk about her work and the stupid calendar and her plans for shade-loving flowers in the spring.

Hell, he just loved listening to her—because he loved her.

Amanda shook her head. "I saw you with that woman."

"Vicki?" He squeezed her shoulders, unconsciously caressing her, hoping to ease her just a bit. "She's an old girlfriend. I already explained things to her."

Stepping away from him, Amanda avoided his direct gaze. "Perhaps you were hasty with that," she said.

Josh crowded close to her back, refusing to let her put a physical or emotional distance between them. He'd worked too hard for the headway he'd gained to just give it up. "Mick already has me edgy. Don't piss me off more by suggesting I go to another woman, okay?"

Her head dropped forward as she tidied the tablecloth on the buffet table and sorted the silverware. Whenever Amanda got nervous, her hands got busy. "This isn't right, Josh. None of it is."

He kissed the ultrasoft skin beneath her ear. "Mmmm. Feels right to me."

"It's not fair."

"Yeah? To who?"

"To you." She whirled around and flattened both hands on his bare chest. She started to speak, then noticed the attention she drew to them. Plenty of women who'd been watching Josh all along now stared openly. "I'm making a spectacle of us both."

He didn't mind, but apparently, she did. "So let's find someplace to be alone."

"There's no place here. Besides, I can't just sneak off. I'm trying to successfully drum up interest in the calendar. Too many people donated too many things for me to simply…"

"Take time with me?" He knew that shot wasn't fair, but still couldn't stop himself from saying it. "Yeah, that'd be a waste, wouldn't it?"

Her eyes widened. "Josh! That isn't at all what I meant."

He ran a hand through his hair, regretting his hasty words, feeling his frustration rise. But damn it, she was trying to pull away. "I know it. I'm sorry."

"Don't apologize, either. It's just…" She looked around. "You're right. We should talk. Let's go into the office in the back." She lifted her wrist and Josh saw a coiled band with several keys on it. "I can get us in."

The idea of a private talk no longer appealed. Josh had a terrible suspicion that she wanted to dump him. The damn calendar was done, and God knew the thing was a hit. Local groceries, bookstores and gift shops had agreed to sell them. Orders were coming in faster than they could be filled. The hall she'd gotten donated for the night was now crowded with interested parties, and the firemen who'd posed were considered local celebrities.

Amanda had no more use for him.

Josh marched behind her, cautiously holding the damn ax away from other people, feeling more ridiculous by the moment. He'd let her draw him in, let her use him…

The lock on the door clicked open and she stepped inside.

Josh pushed in behind her and before she could find a light, he turned her and pressed her against the door.

He'd always been a breast man, and now, with Amanda's plump breasts pressed to his bare chest, he felt all his repressed lust boil over.

"Josh!"

He kissed her. He kissed her with a week's worth of frustration and with the fear that she'd reject him now. He kissed her the way he'd been wanting to for a long time. He dropped the ax with a clatter and caught her rounded behind with one hand, urging her closer. With the other hand, he sought her breast, squeezing and cuddling, searching for and finding her nipple, wanting to groan when it puckered tight. He stroked her, then caught her straining nipple between his fingertips and plucked, rolled.

Filled with explosive urgency, he ate at her mouth, devouring her.

Until he felt her frantic hands trying to push him away.

EIGHT

"JOSH, PLEASE!" AMANDA could barely catch her breath under the impact of that intense kiss and the experienced touch of his hands. She'd been thinking about him all day, stewing each and every time she saw another woman get close to him. She shouldn't care. The whole point of the reception was to share Josh's appeal so more calendars would be purchased.

All the men had shown up shirtless, as she'd directed. One by one, they'd stepped up to the podium with her to be introduced. Amanda had given their names, told what month they could be found, and then they'd removed their outer coats to reveal their hard muscled chests and shoulders. The women had "oohed" and "aahed" as each upper body was bared.

None of them had affected Amanda at all. She'd done her self-assigned job, seeing the men as a means to an end, a way to build up the donation to the burn center, a way to repay her debt.

They were a gorgeous lot, and Amanda was proud of each of them, but she barely noticed them as men.

Until Josh. As she'd suspected, he got the lion's share of attention. When he'd slipped off his jacket, looking chagrined and put out with the whole affair, the women had roared their approval.

All night long, she'd had to watch while the women ogled him and wanted to touch him and competed for his time and attention. His old girlfriend had been especially brazen, but Amanda wasn't surprised. No woman would want to give up on Josh easily, and knowing that, knowing what each woman thought while looking at him, drove Amanda crazy.

He drove her crazy.

She'd barely had a chance to talk to him, but now that they were alone, Josh seemed intent on kissing her senseless.

Amanda pressed his shoulders again and suddenly he cursed and pulled away from her, then cursed again when he stumbled into a chair and sent it skidding onto its side.

With shaking hands, Amanda hastily searched the wall for the switch. Bright fluorescent light shone down on Josh's naked back and shoulders, which he had turned toward her. He stood over the fallen chair, the ax on the floor beside it. His tawny head was down, his large hands curled into fists at his sides.

Her chest hurt just looking at him—and then she remembered what she wanted to talk to him about.

Because of her, Josh was no longer being as cautious at work as he should be. He was thinking of her, of being forced into celibacy, when he should have been concentrating on the job. That would never do. His job was dangerous enough without her adding to it.

She knew what she had to do.

"If you want," Amanda said, her voice sounding hollow in the silent enclosed room, "we can have sex tonight."

Josh snapped his head around. His green eyes blazed with some emotion she didn't recognize. "What the hell did you say?"

Amanda swallowed hard and took a step back. He didn't look particularly pleased by her offer. After the way he'd just been kissing her, after the way he'd kissed her and touched her all week, she'd thought...

"I heard what Mick said," she admitted, hoping he would understand. "I don't want you to get hurt." His narrowed gaze searched hers and she added with a whisper, "If you did, it would kill me."

He took two long strides toward her, then wrapped his long fingers around her upper arms, lifting her. "Why? Why would you care, Amanda?"

Her feet left the floor. She grabbed his biceps, holding on in the awkward position. This wasn't at all what she'd expected. Why couldn't he ever once do as she anticipated? She'd thought...what? That he'd be happy? Anxious?

Her thoughts were in a jumble, but she did her best to explain. "I've hurt enough people. You've been too good, too helpful... Josh, you're a *hero*." Surely he knew that, accepted it. "We need you. Everyone needs you."

For the briefest moment, his hands tightened almost to the point of pain. There was such a look of raw emotion in his green eyes, she flinched away.

Abruptly he set her on her feet and took two steps back. He seemed remote, even angry, when he said, "Why do you want to sleep with me, Amanda? Or should I ask if you *do* want to sleep with me? You made the offer, but then, that doesn't tell me much."

She licked her dry lips and tried to order her thoughts. It wasn't easy with him standing there half-naked, looking so sexy while glaring at her. "We've been fooling around all week."

"Not me." His jaw hardened. "I was dead serious."

"Oh." Her brain seemed a wasteland, not a clear thought to be found. "I mean, with all the kissing and the touching we've been doing, I assumed... In fact, you've told me!" Her head cleared and she crossed her arms defiantly. "You said you wanted to have sex with me!"

"No, I told you I wanted to make love. There's a difference." He shrugged one massive, hard muscled shoulder. "But either way, so what?"

This whole situation got more difficult by the moment. Had he changed his mind about wanting her? Amanda didn't think so, especially given that hot kiss just a minute before. He'd so taken her by surprise, her knees had nearly buckled.

So why had she thought to make the suggestion? Oh yeah, his well-being. "You've been distracted at work," she pointed out, "and not thinking clearly, and Mick seemed to think it's because you're..."

"Not getting any?"

He made it sound so crude. Well, she wouldn't let him bully her or embarrass her. She met his gaze head-on and raised her chin. "Yes."

Josh laughed. He looked at her and then he laughed some more. But it didn't sound like a happy laugh. Just the opposite. "I guess that answers my question, doesn't it? You didn't offer to sleep with me because you want me, not because everything we've done has gotten to you as much as it has to me."

It had, but he didn't give her a chance to explain that. Everything he'd done, every moment with Josh, had been wonderful. Sometimes she couldn't sleep for wanting him. Her need for him increased every day, with every sight of him, every touch, every kiss, until now it was a constant ache. She dreamed of having him inside her, and it was always so good… and then she'd wake up and feel embarrassed and guilty as she remembered that awful night long ago.

But still she wanted him. Her emotions were so conflicted these days, she didn't know what to think or feel. She only knew that Josh was important to her and she couldn't tolerate the thought of anything happening to him.

He bent for the ax, straightened, and looked at her with an expression of emptiness. "I'm not interested in screwing a martyr."

Amanda reeled backward, bumping into the door, then had to move quickly when Josh reached for the handle.

On his way out, he said, "Thanks, but no thanks," and he left the door standing open behind him. His stomping footsteps were drowned out by the noise of the crowd in the outer room.

For a minute, Amanda just stood there, her body and mind thankfully numb so that she barely felt the quaking of her legs, the riotous pounding of her heart, the constriction of her lungs. Her eyes burned with hurt and humiliation.

That *"thanks but no thanks"* had sounded pretty final. But then what had she expected? That he'd wait around forever for her to change? For her to get over her silly phobias and be a real woman? No other man had; no other man would.

She was still standing there, unable to assimilate anything except her sense of loss, when Josh reappeared. He stomped in, cursing under his breath, his face tense.

He took one look at her, groaned and stepped into the room, slamming the door behind him. He propped the ax against the wall and turned the lock.

Amanda stared stupidly at the doorknob.

"Come here." Josh said it gently and reached for her at the same time.

"But…"

"God, I'm sorry." Then he was holding her close to his bare warm chest and rocking her a little and it felt so good, Amanda got angry.

She pushed back and asked with a good dose of suspicion, "What does this mean? Just what are you doing, Josh?"

He smiled and opened his big hand on the small of her back, urging her close again until her belly was against his pelvis and her breasts flattened against his hard abdomen. "Hell if I know," he groaned, and propped his chin on top of her head.

Amanda could feel the solid thumping of his heartbeat vibrating throughout his big body, and the warmth radiating off his skin. She also heard the smile in his tone.

"It's not funny!" Her nose got squashed into his sternum and she inadvertently breathed his scent.

"No," he agreed in a gravelly tone, "it's really not."

"Then why do you sound so amused?"

"Are you kidding?" He kissed the top of her head. "If it was Mick or Zack floundering around like a fish out of water, I'd be laughing my ass off."

Furious and cold one minute, teasing and tender the next. And they said women were fickle. Amanda shook her head and strained away to see him. "I don't understand you."

"I know. Most of the time I don't understand myself." He made that sound like a grave confession. "But damn it, Amanda, I am not going to give up on you."

She frowned. "I didn't ask you to." Then she muttered, "Though I probably should. This whole thing—"

"What *thing*?"

"Us. Me. It's bad enough that you're having to woo me

as if I'm a Victorian maiden, instead of a modern mature woman, but…"

Once again annoyed, he asked through his teeth, "But what?"

If he wanted the whole truth, she'd give it to him. "But now, instead of using your…assets to garner more sales for the calendar, I'm warning women away from you."

Josh straightened and his brows shot up. "You are?"

"Yes, I am. Half the women out there are single and, of course, they just have to ask me about you. As if I'm supposed to help set you up or something! If I'd been thinking straight, if I'd been doing what I should be doing, I'd have encouraged them to buy another calendar and get you to sign it, sort of as a way to break the ice."

He crossed his arms over his chest and scrutinized her with great curiosity. "So what'd you do instead?"

Amanda couldn't quite look at him. "I told them you were taken," she murmured.

"Come again?"

Amanda knew good and well that he'd heard her, he just wanted to make her say it again. Well fine. She glared at him and almost shouted, *"I told them you were taken."*

"Ah." Josh flexed his jaw, whether because she'd irritated him or because he was trying to hide a smile. She wasn't sure. "Why, Amanda?"

"Because I didn't want you to get involved with any of them."

"Yet you made me that ridiculous, unemotional offer."

Angry, remorseful and now insulting. She'd about had enough of his mood swings. She reached out and smoothed her hand over his broad chest. Her fingers found a soft curl there in the middle of his pectoral muscles where the hair was thickest. She smiled up at him, and yanked hard.

"Ow, damn it!" Josh lurched, yowled again when she didn't release him, then caught her wrist and held her hand still. "That hurt!"

"Did it ever occur to you," she asked, retaining her hold on his chest hair in a threatening manner, "that I'm not sure how to go about offering? I've never had much practice. Every other guy I've been close to has been the one pressing me, so I never had to offer!"

Now Josh frowned. "I haven't pressed you because I want you to want me. What I don't want is you making some damn offer like a sacrifice. Like you'd be doing me a favor."

Sacrifice. So, that's what he thought? And it had insulted his macho pride?

Her eyes narrowed again. "It'd be nice if you explained all this to me instead of being insulting and mean."

Josh softened. He worked her fingers loose and carried her hand up to his neck, safely away from his chest. "I was mean?" he asked apologetically.

"Yes." Amanda put her other arm around his neck and laced her fingers together at his nape. His dark blond hair felt cool and silky on her knuckles. "I didn't know what to think. You're a very confusing, complex man."

Josh chuckled, then squeezed her close. "That's the pot calling the kettle black, sweetheart." She started to object and he kissed her, a softer, gentler kiss this time. "And here I used to think I knew women."

"You do." Boy, did he ever. Josh knew how to look at her, how to touch her just the right way to make her hot and needy. He also had an uncanny ability to read her mind on occasion. It unnerved her.

"Not you," he denied. "You're a mystery, Amanda, always keeping me guessing. I never know what's going through that head of yours."

"I love kissing you," she said. "That's what's going through my head right now."

His eyes darkened, turning a rich forest green. With her gaze snared in his, Josh very slowly brought his hand up over her waist to her ribs, then higher, just below her left breast. Her heart galloped—in anticipation and excitement.

"You liked me touching you, too, didn't you?" he asked.

Breath catching, Amanda murmured, "Yes."

He leaned down, his mouth touched hers, and his hot palm slid up and over her until he held her breast securely. His long fingers were gentle, molding over her, weighing her, caressing. Against her mouth, he said, "I've always loved breasts."

A laugh caught Amanda by surprise, even as she closed her eyes to absorb more of his touch. "As I understand it," she breathed, "most men do."

"Some of us like them more than others." And he growled, "Damn, you have great breasts."

It was the most absurd conversation she ever could have imagined. Josh touched her nipple, rubbing the very sensitive tip, and her voice broke as she said, "Thank you."

"It's not just your incredible rack that turns me on, though."

Amanda couldn't keep up with his verbal nonsense, not while he was deliberately arousing her. She dropped her head onto his chest and groaned.

"No," he said, still enticing her. His fingers closed on her nipple in a soft pinch, and even through her blouse and bra, it was enough to make her muscles brace, her breath catch. "Talking to you, hearing you laugh, smelling you, hell even thinking of you gets me hard."

Her hold on his neck was now a necessity. Without it, she might have slid to the floor in a puddle.

"I want to touch you between your legs, okay?"

Her eyes snapped open and everything inside her clenched and curled against a wave of heat. They were at a reception, hidden away in an empty office with over a hundred people only a few yards away. "Josh…"

"Shhh. Tell me if you like this."

He pressed his hand to her belly, then pushed lower until his fingertips just touched her in a barely there caress. His palm was on her lower belly, his fingers together, not moving. There was only that fleeting press, nothing more. Her wool skirt felt nonexistent. Her body rocked with her heartbeat.

He didn't move any further.

Panting, held in suspense, Amanda rasped, "Josh?"

His mouth touched her temple. "Everything okay?"

His voice was low and rough and added to her urgency. She bobbed her head, anxious to reassure him. "Yes. Fine."

"Good." He kissed her ear. "How about this?"

"Ohmigod." Amanda squeezed her eyes shut as his big hand pushed lower, dipping down between her thighs, stroking, seeking through the layers of material to find just the right spot. She felt hot on the outside, wet on the inside.

"Is that good?"

"*Yes.*" Better than good. Astounding, really.

Other than her aborted attempt at sexual satisfaction the night of the fire, she'd never felt so aroused. And even then, it wasn't the same. She'd been just seventeen, more excited about doing the forbidden and feeling grown-up than about the boy she'd been with.

Those thoughts were morbid and Amanda did her best to

block them from her mind. She wanted to concentrate on Josh,
not the past. Yet, the past was there, forever a part of her...

"Imagine how it would be," Josh whispered, interrupt-
ing her disturbing retrospection, "with nothing between my
hand and your body. My fingers are rough from the work
I do, but I'd be really careful, Amanda. A woman is so soft
here, so tender."

Her body jerked in reaction to those words.

Josh made a sound of pleasure. "I bet you're silky wet right
now, aren't you? I'd love to feel my fingers inside you. Or my
tongue slipping over you. Or my—"

A fine tension began to build inside her. Her nails sank into
his shoulders and she arched against him with a raw groan.

Josh moved against her protectively. He still toyed with her
nipple, continued to put warm damp kisses on her face, her
ear, her neck while saying such tantalizing, provoking, *stimu-
lating* things to her.

And his hand... Josh's hand was between her legs making
her feel incredible things.

"Yeah, that's it," he encouraged, stroking her, pushing her.

A loud rapping rattled the door, making them lurch apart.
Amanda barely stifled a small yelp. Josh cursed.

"Josh?" called a familiar, hushed voice. "Are you in there?"

Josh froze, his body taut and hot, his nostrils flared. "I'll
kill him."

"Ohmigod," Amanda whispered, then covered her mouth
with shaking hands. She was in charge of this project, responsible for its success. And instead of supervising things,
she was hidden away, being pawed. Just the way she'd been
seven years ago...

She drew up on that awful thought. No, Josh made it all
different. He made it all...special, not ugly.

"I swear," Josh muttered, rubbing his hands up and down Amanda's back as if to soothe her, "I'm going to—"

"You have my profuse apologies," Mick said through the door, "but there's at least a dozen people out here looking for Amanda and they'll be checking back here in another two minutes."

"Damn it." Josh held her away from him, his gaze searching, concerned. Frustration vibrated through him, shone in his eyes and in the set of his mouth. "Amanda, are you okay?"

Okay? She felt weak with mortification and shaky with arousal—and on the verge of discovering something truly wonderful. "Yes."

"Don't look like that, Amanda," he snapped, misinterpreting her expression of wonder. "What we did—"

"Josh, I can hear you," Mick called, "every damn word. I'll leave if you'll just tell me what to tell everyone else?"

Without looking away from her, Josh shouted, "Give me a minute!"

Regretfully, Mick said, "That's about all you've got before the posse is sent out."

With a heated curse, Josh told Amanda, "Don't move," and turned away to open the door. In a nasty tone that more than gave away his frustration, as well as what they'd been doing, if it hadn't already been painfully apparent, he barked, "What the hell is it?"

Mick answered in a rush. "A whole group of secretaries and assistants from the office complex down the street just showed up, but all the calendars Amanda had out are sold. Some women already left because the calendars were gone, but the secretaries are a little tougher. They're eyeing the ones other women have bought and gotten signed, especially if anyone is holding more than one. You know a bunch of people bought more than one so they could give them away as gifts. Anyway, I'm afraid you're about to have a riot on your hands if you don't get more calendars out here and fast."

Struggling past an amalgam of rioting sensations, Amanda stepped around Josh and forced herself to face Mick. "I'll be right there," she assured him. "If you could let everyone know I'm getting more calendars right now…?"

Mick looked her over, then quickly averted his eyes. Was it that obvious? Amanda wondered. Could Mick tell so easily that she'd been fooling around with Josh at the most inappropriate time? That rather than tending to her obligations and pushing sales of the calendar to earn more money for the burn center, she'd been getting groped instead?

Wonderfully groped, Amanda corrected herself. Almost groped to the point of oblivion.

Her face flushed.

Evidently, her situation was very obvious, because Mick rubbed a hand over his jaw and stared at the ceiling. "Yeah, sure," he said, sounding ill at ease. "I'll tell them. That ought to buy you a few minutes at least, as long as they know more calendars are on the way."

"Thank you."

"I could, ah, fetch them for you," Mick offered to the ceiling, "if you want to tell me where they're at?"

Amanda wondered if she had a big red *G* on her forehead for "groped." The way Mick acted, she wouldn't be at all surprised. "Thank you, but I need to get back anyway."

Mick glanced at Josh, and Amanda saw their shared man-to-man look. Mick's expression said, "I tried," and Josh returned a silent "thanks for the effort."

"All right." Mick headed off, saying over his shoulder, "I'll go appease the mob. Just don't be too long."

The second he was gone, Josh closed the door and turned to stare down at Amanda with his fists propped on his lean hips. "Don't you dare start feeling embarrassed," he ordered.

She all but sputtered a laugh. "Josh, *anyone* would be embarrassed right now! Mick knew exactly what we were doing."

"So?" Josh shrugged, the picture of unconcern. "Now he knows we're human. Big deal. He's not exactly a choirboy himself."

Amanda wasn't about to discuss all this with Josh now, not with people waiting for her. Besides, she was embarrassed, but she wasn't exactly ashamed. And not for one single second did she fool herself into thinking *she'd* have called a halt to what they were doing. If it hadn't been for Mick's interruption, they might have ended up being caught in a much more compromising position.

That thought brought another, and Amanda wondered just what position Josh might have initiated. No doubt, he knew dozens of positions appropriate to making love in an empty office.

"What?" Josh asked. A crooked smile tilted one side of his mouth as he leaned closer. His eyes warmed. "What naughty things are you thinking, Ms. Barker?"

Amanda bit her lip, chagrined once again that he could so easily read her. But she was too curious not to ask. "How would we have...you know. In here?"

Josh froze, then groaned and ran his hand through his hair, leaving the dark blond locks on end. "You're killing me." He pretended his knees were weak and slumped against the wall. "That's a loaded question, honey, guaranteed to give a guy a boner. That is, if I didn't already have one, which I do."

Amanda's eyes widened, but she managed not to look. She

ended up with a dazed, goggle-eyed stare, but she kept her attention fixed firmly on his face.

Josh laughed and reached for her. "Tell you what. Tonight, when we finish this damn reception, I'll show you."

Her heart lodged in her throat at that promise. "Yes, all right."

Amanda smiled at him, then edged toward the door. If she didn't leave now the damn posse might find her accosting Josh. Seeing him look so disheveled, she paused and reached for her hair with a sudden concern. Would everyone know what she'd been doing? Or was Mick just more intuitive because he knew Josh and his sexual propensities? "Do I look okay?"

Josh touched her cheek with an unsteady hand. "Babe, no woman could look better."

Amanda was still high on that compliment when she slipped from the room and hurried down the back hallway to the rear door. She assumed Josh would present himself out front shortly, and would buy her enough time to restock the calendars.

The frigid wind cut right through her suit jacket and blouse when she stepped into the lot where her car was parked. Silvery light from streetlamps lent an eerie glow to the cold dark night and reflected off the falling sleet, which now covered her car and was turning the lot into a slick treacherous sheet of ice.

The driver's door was frozen shut and Amanda had to work to get it open. She looked around and saw ice hanging heavily from every phone wire and tree branch. The crackling of sleet peppering the pavement mingled with the sound of the howling wind.

It was a miserable night.

Her hands and nose felt numb and her knees were knocking together by the time Amanda headed back in. She wished she'd had enough sense to grab her coat, but she'd been daydreaming about Josh and that carnal promise of his instead. Shivering uncontrollably, arms laden with boxes, she struggled with the heavy back door.

A second later the door flew open and she almost toppled over. *Josh.*

"What the hell are you doing out there alone?" he demanded.

Her uncontrollable shriek of surprise echoed up and down the hallway. Josh relieved her of the cumbersome boxes and Amanda thanked him by punching him in the shoulder. "You scared me half to death," she accused, once she'd caught her breath.

"You need scaring." He caught her arms and hugged her close, sharing some of his warmth. Amanda noticed he was now wearing a shirt and coat.

Through chattering teeth, she said, "I had to get more calendars. You already knew that."

His scowl darkened. "I thought you had them somewhere in the building, not outside. You should have sent me, or let Mick go when he offered."

Her face was still pressed against him. He felt warm and smelled delicious and she said without thinking, "I needed to cool down anyway."

His hands, which had been coasting up and down her back, paused. Then he squeezed her and groaned. "I must be cursed."

Amanda tilted back to see him and got an awful premonition. "Josh, what's wrong?"

"I have to go into work."

Her heart sank. *"Now?"*

"Unfortunately, yeah." He began rubbing her again, in

apology, in regret. "One of the supervisors has the flu. He's heading home, so I need to finish out his shift."

Amanda wanted to cry. Her body still buzzed with need, every part of her felt too sensitive, too…ready. She said, "Damn."

Josh smiled. "I know. Believe me, if I had any other choice, I'd grab it."

Her next thought was whether or not he'd come over after he'd finished the shift. She knew she'd gladly wait up. She finally felt ready to take the big step. Tonight could be the night. Sure, she'd had a few ill moments, thinking of that long-ago fire and what had resulted from her irresponsibility, but she still wanted Josh. Fiercely.

As usual, Josh read her mind. "I won't be off till sometime in the morning. Probably around three." Then he cupped her face and tipped it up and kissed her. His tongue moved softly, deeply into her mouth until her shivers were all gone and she felt feverish. "Think about me tonight," he murmured against her mouth, "and tomorrow I swear I'll make the wait worth your while."

With those provocative words, Josh turned and stalked out through the door she'd just entered. Amanda was left with only the churning of lust.

Lust, and something so much more.

NINE

JOSH STARED THROUGH the thick, angry black smoke and gave a silent curse. Long before they'd arrived on the scene, they'd smelled the acrid scent and he'd known, he'd just *known,* this particular fire was going to be a bitch.

His muscles hurt, his head pounded and he was so hot it felt like his skin was roasted beneath his turnout coat. His gear, including the S.C.B.A., or air-pack, seemed to weigh more than the usual fifty pounds, thanks to his exhaustion.

They'd first gone in without hoses, intent only on rescue. They'd accomplished that much while neighbors all shouted at once, pointing, telling them about the shy quiet single lady still inside on the upper floor. The woman, who Josh had carried out himself, was now in the back of the ambulance being tended. She was a skinny little thing, in her late thirties, disoriented, probably suffering some smoke inhalation and shock, but she'd live.

Given the frigid temperatures and general nastiness of the

frozen night, it was one of the worst fires Josh had ever encountered.

They worked their asses off with little success.

The fire spread too quickly, feeding off piles of old newspaper and accumulated junk, licking across dry rotted carpet and up the blistered walls. The howling wind seemed to spur it on, rushing in through shattered windows.

Josh's flashlight flickered over a faded floral couch, now turning orange in flames, then over a pile of books, what looked like an antique desk, a rickety footstool. The place was cluttered, proving the small female being treated outside was a pack rat. Josh searched through the house, seeing objects take shape, forming in the dark as he approached them.

He felt his way through the blackness, checking carefully, watching for a hand, the reflection of pale flesh, anything that might prove to be human.

The narrow flashlight beam bounced off a moving object and Josh crawled closer, then heard a cat's warning yowl. Twin green eyes glowered at him from beneath a small round table tucked into a corner. The cat looked panicked, ready to attack.

Josh's thick gloves provided some protection when he snagged the fat animal and hauled it protectively close to his body. The smell of singed fur burned his nostrils and he crooned in sympathy.

His croon turned to yell a second later as sharp claws managed to connect with his flesh. Josh was barely able to maintain his tight hold on the feline.

Three loud blasts of the rig horn penetrated the crackle and hiss of the surrounding fire.

"Let's go," Josh said, and signaled the retreat. Three blasts of the horn meant the house was compromised. It was get out now, or maybe not get out at all. Everyone began exiting, Josh a little awkwardly given he had a furious cat tucked into his side.

The second he stepped into the snow-covered yard, the fresh cold air hit him like a welcome slap. Josh flipped up his visor and removed his air mask. There were reporters everywhere, mingling with the noisy neighbors. A flashbulb temporarily blinded him and enraged the cat. It lurched out his arms and shot up a nearby tree in a blur of breakneck speed. Perched on an ice-covered branch, out of harm's way, it took to yowling again.

Josh heard his name called and turned. More pictures were taken, but he didn't even have the chance to get annoyed. The woman they'd pulled from her bed hung on the arm of one of the firefighters. She was now wrapped warmly in someone's coat and a blanket, her thin legs shoved into heavy boots to protect her feet from the cold. Her hair stood on end, and she stumbled toward Josh, her eyes wide and unseeing, her face utterly white in the glow of the moon and the reflecting flames.

"My baby!" she screamed, nearly beside herself. "You have to get my baby!" And she lurched toward the house, falling to her knees in the snow, sobbing, trying to crawl.

Josh went rigid. He looked back at the house, glowing red from within. His heart struck his ribs, his muscles clenched. *Goddamnit, no!*

"Please," the woman moaned, "oh please," and she fought against the restraining hands, as vicious in her upset as the poor cat had been.

Josh locked his jaw, trying to think in the two seconds he didn't really have. His senior tailboard firefighter, fists clenched, shoulders hunched, said, "I'll go."

Josh felt sick. This was the type of decision he didn't like to make. "You're volunteering for a blind, left-hand search in a totally involved fire?"

The firefighter nodded grimly. "Damn right."

Josh understood. He'd already decided to go back in himself.

Then, almost like a gentle stroke, he remembered Amanda. Men had thought she was inside, when she wasn't. During the trauma of a fire, it was difficult as hell to be rational, but that was his job, and now Amanda had helped him.

The probability seeped into him, easing past the exhaustion and fear and the rush of adrenaline, beyond his instinct to charge back inside to save a child, regardless of the odds. It helped him to think above the roar of the fire, the consuming heat, the shouting of all the neighbors, the local media and the wailing of the panicked woman.

A *single* woman. Living all *alone,* the neighbors had said. In her late thirties...

Josh took three long strides to the frightened woman, dropped to his knees so he could hold her shoulders. "Where's the baby?" he asked, and got nothing but hysterical sobs in reply.

He caught her thin, ravaged face in his dirty gloved hands and made her meet his probing gaze. "Where," Josh demanded, "is the baby?"

She blinked tear-swollen eyes, sniffed, then covered her face. Her voice quavered and rose as she wailed, "Upstairs. I think he's still upstairs!"

I think. Josh drew an unsteady breath, silently praying. "Give me a description."

Wiping her eyes on the edge of the blanket, she nodded. "He's fat, mostly black with a white tip on his tail." She shuddered. "Oh please, please find him for me."

Josh collapsed. All the strength left his body and he slumped onto his ass with a great sigh of relief.

"The cat," he said, and smiled. Without giving it another thought he caught the woman and pulled her into him, hugging her close. "I got your cat, miss. He's fine, I promise. Look there in the tree." Josh, still supporting her, turned her with his body and pointed. "See him? He's plenty peeved, and howling to raise the moon, but he's not hurt."

With a cry, the woman stumbled away from Josh and ran awkwardly in the too-big boots and long coat. Two men, concerned because she was so frail, raced behind her. Josh laughed out loud, then scrubbed his hands over his face. "Oh, God."

"You okay?" Another firefighter, a friend, put a hand on Josh's shoulder.

"Hell yeah." Josh looked up at the starless sky, felt the prickling of frozen rain on his face, the bite of a cutting wind. "Hell yeah," he said with more energy. "I'm great."

It was another two hours before they'd finished raking the charred insides of the house out to the sidewalk. It all had to be broken apart and hosed down. Normally that was the hardest part for Josh, seeing someone's life reduced to a black heap on the curb. Furniture, clothing, memories, all gone.

But this time what he saw was the woman sitting in the back of the ambulance, dirty and disheveled, wearing someone else's clothes—and cuddling her "baby" wrapped in a thick warm blanket.

Josh was amazed to see her smiling, occasionally singing, and even from where he swung his ax several yards away, he could have sworn he heard that big cat purring in bliss.

Tears stung his eyes, not that Josh gave a damn. If anyone noticed, he'd blame it on the smoke. But in that moment, he made up his mind. When they finished, he wouldn't go home to get some much-needed sleep as he'd intended. He'd go to Amanda, where he belonged. He'd tell her how much he loved her, how much he needed her, and it would have to be enough.

He'd make it be enough—for both of them.

Amanda jerked her front door open the minute she heard the rumbling of the approaching car. Josh! She'd watched the unfolding details of the fire on the news, fretting, sick at heart, wanting and needing to be with him. At first she just hoped he'd come to her when his shift was over. Then she'd decided if he didn't, she would go to him.

Snow and ice crunched beneath her slippers as she ran through the twilight morning to greet him, unmindful of the cold frosting her breath, the wind howling through her robe.

Josh turned off his car lights, and Amanda noticed the sheer exhaustion that seemed to weigh him down as he sat a moment behind the wheel.

Then he saw her.

Quickly stepping out of the car, Josh said, "Hey," and he caught her as she launched herself against him. "What is it, babe?"

He was warm and hard and alive, so big and so strong. Amanda wanted to touch him all over, to absorb him and his strength and his goodness. She needed to know that he was all right, that the fire hadn't touched him.

Her arms locked around his neck and she squeezed him when he hauled her off her feet, out of the snow. She couldn't speak at first, but then he must have decided that was okay. He lifted her into his arms, cradled her to his chest and stalked to her front door with a type of leashed urgency.

Once inside he kicked her front door closed and went

straight to the bedroom and the bed, stretching out with her. Amanda just held on, aware of the tension in his muscles, in his mood. He trembled, his face buried in her neck, his breath coming too fast. His thick arms were steel bands, circling her, getting her as close as possible.

Her throat felt tight and she tried to soothe him. "Josh."

Had something happened to him? Just the thought made her frantic, but she kept her tone calm and easy for him. Smoothing her hand through his thick, still damp hair, she said, "Please, tell me you're all right."

He nuzzled into her. "Yeah." His voice was thick with emotion. Rolling to his back and pulling her into his side, he said, "You heard about the fire?"

"It was on the news." They didn't look at each other. Amanda pushed his coat open so she could touch *him,* not leather. He wore an untucked flannel over a soft thermal shirt and he felt warm and hard and—she wanted him naked.

The thought came out of nowhere, but it was true. She wanted to assure herself that he wasn't hurt in any way.

Josh groaned. "I'm sorry. I didn't even think of that."

Amanda went to work on the buttons of his shirt, almost popping them in her haste. "You're not supposed to think of me. Not on the job, not when it's dangerous."

Josh started to protest and she sat up to work his coat off him. He obliged her, twisting his arms free, then giving a raw chuckle when she did the same with his flannel. Amanda tossed them both to the floor. She eyed his thermal shirt, caught the hem and tugged it upward.

"What are you doing, baby?" Josh asked, even as he rose up to help her get it off.

"Undressing you." The second the shirt was free, she saw the red, welted scratches on his neck. Her breath caught. "Oh,

God. Are you all right?" She bent closer, touching his hot skin carefully.

Josh smoothed the backs of his knuckles over her cheek. "Yeah, I'm fine. I got that tangling with a fat cat who didn't have the sense to know I was his savior."

Amanda melted. He was the finest man she knew, and right now, he needed her.

She put several gentle kisses on his injured neck and then turned, straddling his legs with her back to him. His boots were lace-up and took her a minute, but she got them free and tossed them into the pile on the floor.

Josh's hands moved up and down her back. While her touch was agitated, his was more so. "When I'm naked," he asked, "will you get naked, too?"

"Yes."

He went still, then suddenly he was as busy as she, yanking at her robe, distracting her from her efforts as he tended his own. Amanda had to leave the bed to remove his jeans. Josh stood to help her. They bumped heads when they both bent at the waist to push the denim down his long muscled legs. Josh kicked free and reached for her, wanting to remove her nightgown.

Amanda didn't give him a chance. She pushed him onto the bed and stretched out over his tall, naked body. She kissed him, holding his face and feasting on his hot mouth, his throat, then down to his smooth shoulders and broad chest. He was alive, unharmed, and for now, he was hers.

The night had been endless and horrifying. She hadn't slept. Instead, she'd sat in bed watching television while waiting for the occasional update on the fire. Knowing Josh was good at his job, that he was well trained, hadn't helped. She just kept remembering how a man had died for her in just such a fire....

The memories had a different effect this time. Rather than filling her with shame that caused her to withdraw emotionally and physically, they spurred her on. They made her want to grab everything she could, every special moment so that not a single second of her life was wasted.

Josh risked himself every day on his job. He never knew when he'd be called upon to fight a fire, never knew which fire might be his last. He was a hero in the truest sense of the word, and he wanted her.

For that, she was very grateful.

Amanda licked at his hot smooth flesh, biting and sucking, hungry for him in a way she had never experienced, not even seven years ago. She wanted to give him pleasure. She wanted him alive with it.

Josh groaned and put his arms out to his sides, making himself a willing sacrifice.

"I was so scared," Amanda said between kisses and touches and deep breaths that filled her with Josh. It still wasn't enough. She didn't know if she'd ever have enough of him.

His abdomen contracted sharply when she put her mouth there, taking a gentle love bite of a sharply defined muscle. He settled one big hand in her hair, caressing, encouraging. "I was, too," he rasped. "I didn't want to go home alone." He paused to groan, then added, "I want to spend the day with you, Amanda."

"Yes." Amanda could smell him, fresh from a recent shower, but still with the lingering scent of smoke clinging to him. She saw traces of soot under his nails, and remembered him telling her how hard it was to remove, even though he wore gloves.

The hair on his chest, narrowing to a silky line down his abdomen, was brown rather than dark blond. But the hair at his groin was darker still, and thick. Amanda looked at him in fascination and awe and barely suppressed excitement.

His erection rose thick and long, a drop of fluid at the head, proving that he was excited, too.

With her heart pounding, Amanda touched him, exploring the hot, velvet-soft skin over tensile steel. She saw him flex with pleasure. Aware of his accelerated breaths, the intent way he watched her, she wrapped her hand around him in a firm hold. Gently, cautiously, she stroked up his length and back.

Josh's body strained from the mattress—and abruptly dropped when she bent and pressed a kiss just above where her fingers held him. It was a light kiss, tentative, but his wild response and guttural groan lured her. She licked up and over the tip, tasting his salty essence.

A sound of pleasure and pain exploded from his chest. His entire big body quivered. While her mouth moved over him, she cupped his testicles in her other hand, cradling him.

"Damn," he said, twisting on the sheets, "I like that, sweetheart."

"Me, too." She breathed in the strong musk scent of his sex, feeling swollen with emotion. It was nearly painful, feeling this way about a man.

"Take me into your mouth," he whispered urgently, "as much of me as you can."

Aroused by the carnal command, Amanda parted her lips wide and drew him in. Both his hands settled in her hair, tangling there, pressing her closer.

"Suck," he growled, arching his hips at the same time.

Amanda squirmed around for a better position to do as he needed her to. It was wonderful, tasting him like this, making him lose control, knowing he enjoyed her efforts. Long before she was ready to quit, Josh pulled away from her. His movements were clumsy, rough and fast and she found herself on her back on the bed, Josh between her thighs, in a matter of seconds.

He stared down at her, heaving, his face hard and dark and his eyes glittering. Not giving her a chance to speak, he took her mouth in a demanding, tongue-thrusting kiss.

His long fingers were between her legs, petting her, quickly parting her. She could feel her own slippery wetness, heard his low murmur of satisfaction. Her heartbeat thundered in her ears, a riot of emotions clamored for attention.

"I need you *now*," he panted into her mouth. Against her sensitive flesh, she felt the broad head of his penis, and then his penetration, unrelenting, forceful, going deeper and deeper.

She gasped, and he kissed her fiercely again, swallowing the sound of surprise and wonder.

Amanda twisted as he filled her, a little uncomfortable, a lot turned-on. She'd never had a man inside her and she found it to be an amazing thing, given the man was Josh.

He didn't allow her time to absorb the new sensations. No sooner was he all the way inside her than he began thrusting, sliding all the way out and then driving in deep again, harder and faster with each stroke.

With a groan, he pushed to his knees, forced her thighs wider apart and levered himself on one arm. Using his free hand he touched her everywhere, her breasts, her belly, down between her legs where he circled her, feeling himself as he pounded into her, feeling her stretched taut around him, holding him so tightly.

Amanda felt a scream of intense sensation building. She lifted her legs and locked them around Josh's waist—and he was a goner.

He cursed, long and rough and lurid and then he gripped her close, so close she couldn't draw a breath. His face pressed hard into her shoulder and he said, *"Amanda,"* on a broken whisper.

She knew he was coming, could feel the spasms of his erection inside her, the jerking of his taut muscles, the stillness of his thoughts in that suspended moment. His broad back grew damp, heat rising off him in waves. His buttocks were tight, his thighs rigid. It went on and on and Amanda just held him, so pleased, so awed, until he dropped heavily against her, breathing hard, his heartbeat rocking them both.

Long minutes passed and Amanda relished his limp body cradled against her own. Finally, Josh lifted his head. His movements were slow and sluggish. He looked at Amanda, smiled tenderly, then shook his head. "I'm an ass," he said, his eyes twinkling lazily.

Startled, Amanda frowned. "No you're not. You're wonderful."

He smiled again, then stretched and moved to his back with an earthy groan. "Oh, hell." He put his forearm over his eyes. "That didn't go at all as I meant it to."

Amanda touched his sweaty chest. She couldn't *not* touch him.

"I should be horsewhipped," he complained.

"No, you should sleep here with me." She loved the feel of him, the sleek skin, now damp from exertion, over hard planes and hollows. He was so impressive in every way. "Stay all day, and then tonight again. Let me take care of you, Josh. I don't have to go into work and I assume you won't either now."

"I'm off for the next forty-eight hours." He lifted his arm and looked at her with heavy, sated eyes. "C'mere," he murmured, pulling her onto his chest, "let me show you 'wonderful.'"

It was almost six in the morning and they'd both been up all night. Amanda had spent the night worrying and waiting, but Josh had worked hard. She knew he had to be exhausted, going on lost reserve, but instead of sleeping, he kissed her forehead and asked, "Are you okay?"

"I'm astounded," she told him, and rubbed her cheek against his shoulder. "I'm also a little…messy."

"Mmm." Josh stroked his hand down her back, over her bottom, and between her legs. "Messy with me. And with you."

The things he did, the things he said never failed to shock Amanda. She was engorged, her flesh still tingling, and his rough fingertips rasped over her, gently exploring. She caught her breath and he pushed slightly inside her. The careful prod of his finger only served to exacerbate already sensitized nerve endings.

"I didn't use anything," Josh whispered, and began kissing her ear, her neck. He didn't sound apologetic so much as matter-of-fact.

Amanda couldn't assimilate the repercussions, not while his fingers were there, making her crazy.

"I still don't want to use anything," he told her, but rather than explain why, he pushed his middle finger deep inside her, making her gasp and stiffen.

Amanda nodded. She didn't want him to use anything, not if he didn't want to.

Her quick agreement drove him to action. "Spread your thighs wide around me."

She did, and felt him catch her knees to draw them up so she literally sat astride him, but with her cheek still to his chest. It was an awkward position, forcing her behind up.

"Hmm," Josh growled in satisfaction. "Now I can get to you better."

And he did. Feeling open and vulnerable, Amanda curled her fingers on his shoulders and held on. All the tension began building again, quicker this time, making her vision blur, her skin burn. She squeezed her eyes shut.

"Stiffen your arms so I can get to your nipples."

Amanda moaned. She wasn't sure she could move.

"Amanda," he scolded in a rough throaty purr. "Trust me, honey. Rise up. You'll like this."

Swallowing hard, she forced her arms straight.

With heated eyes, Josh surveyed her breasts. "Beautiful. Damn, honey, let me taste you." So saying, he lifted his head and closed his mouth around her nipple to suckle.

A tearing moan escaped her. She was already so aroused, but now his mouth drew at her breast and his finger moved gently in and out of her, easily because her lust and his climax had made her very slick. She trembled. "Josh…"

He seemed to have all the patience in the world now that he'd come. He licked a path to her other nipple and put that breast through the same sensual torment.

Amanda hovered over him, her belly drawing tight, her nipples aching, her vulva hot and pulsing. Josh released her breast with a last leisurely lick and looked up at her. "You're close," he said with a tender smile. "I can feel you contracting. Almost there."

Amanda couldn't answer him. She bit her lip and concentrated on breathing.

"Do you want to come, sweetheart?"

She nodded.

"Tell me how this feels." He pulled his wet fingers from her and found her clitoris, gently stroking.

Amanda tipped back her head, moaning, so close…

Using his free hand, Josh positioned his erection against her and slowly pressed upward. He sank in to the hilt on the first stroke. "Let's sit you up," he said.

Amanda was too mindless with newfound carnality to do anything, so Josh gently guided her. The new position left her filled, impossibly stretched, and it was wonderful.

Josh bent his knees to support her back, cupped her left breast firmly in his hand, and started the rhythm that she knew would make her wild.

"You're so damn beautiful," he whispered, looking at her belly as it pulled tight, at her breasts as they bounced. She flushed, her muscles tensing and she did her best to stifle a scream.

Locking his intent gaze with hers, Josh licked his middle finger, wetting it, then reached down to toy with her turgid clitoris again.

The scream broke free.

Amanda reached back, clutching his thighs for support as her body shook and bowed with her first orgasm. Josh was so high inside her, filling her up, encouraging her, she felt shattered.

It was her turn to drop onto Josh, and she did so just as he cupped her hips, held her to him tightly, and gave into his second release with a rumbling groan.

Their hot sweaty skin felt fused, their heartbeats mingling. In slurred tones, Josh mumbled, "Sleep."

Mindless, Amanda reached out with a limp hand, snagged the corner of the sheet and pulled it up and over their bodies. Just as Josh began to breathe evenly in sleep, she felt him slip from her body. Smiling, she realized she was really messy now, but she didn't care. She closed her eyes on a sigh, and fell asleep.

TEN

JOSH WOKE WITH a groan and without even thinking, he reached for Amanda. He found an empty bed.

His head fuzzy from lingering exhaustion, he looked toward the bedside clock. It wasn't even noon yet, but it felt like he'd been out cold for two days. His body was lethargic, his brain sated for the first time in weeks.

And he smiled, knowing why he was sated, remembering Amanda's scream as she'd climaxed, how her sexy brown eyes had gone all soft and vague in her pleasure. She'd been a virgin, so snug and warm his brain had almost shut down. She was all his—he'd given her her first climax.

At that thought Josh frowned and jerked upright. His head spun, but he ignored it. *Her first time.* God, he hadn't been gentle and coaxing and understanding. He hadn't eased her into lovemaking.

He hadn't even insured her pleasure that first time.

He'd been a pig, concerned only with his own pleasure.

He'd coerced her into giving him a blow job! He'd been wild, like a crazy man, pushing her and…

Naked, Josh threw his legs over the side of the bed and cupped his head in his hands. For weeks he'd been planning to make Amanda limp with pleasure while utilizing iron control over his own urges. She was emotionally fragile where sex was concerned, and more than a little wary about commitment.

He'd hoped to woo her with sex, to show her how beautiful it could be between them. *Ha!* He remembered the way she'd taken him in her mouth, the way he'd instructed her, and he squeezed his eyes shut. What they'd done had been raw and uncontrolled and just remembering made his blood boil.

He pushed to his feet, going over in his mind all the things he'd say to her, how he'd explain and try to make it right.

A quick trip to the bathroom was top of the list. He recalled Amanda saying she was messy, and what had he done? He should have bathed her, cherished her. He should have used his mouth to bring her to orgasm. It was one of the most intimate methods of making love, and it was something he especially enjoyed. But he hadn't tasted Amanda, hadn't shared that with her.

Instead, he'd had her ride him, and he'd been so deep… Josh groaned. At least that second time she'd gotten her own orgasm.

Josh washed up, splashing his face with cold water to clear away the cobwebs. Though he now smelled more like sex than smoke, he still felt coated in soot. God knew he'd scrubbed long enough under the shower before coming to Amanda early that morning. He hadn't wanted any reminders of the fire for fear it would trigger her memories.

Last night he'd needed her more than he'd needed air.

He needed her still.

Josh located his jeans, now neatly folded over the foot of the bed, and he stepped into them. He didn't bother with the zipper or the snap and despite the chill of the air, he never gave his shirt a second thought. The moment he entered the small living room, his eyes were drawn to her.

She sat at the tiny kitchen table, the morning paper open before her and a blank, almost shocked look on her face.

Damn, damn, damn. Josh strode to Amanda and pulled her from the chair. He'd tell her he loved her and she'd just have to accept it. Sex was great, damn it, not something to shy away from, not something to mentally link to a bad memory. Sex between them was so incredible he didn't know how he'd survived.

So what that he'd shown her the more carnal side to sex, rather than the gentle beauty of it? He was a man, and he didn't see a thing wrong with enjoying a woman's body in every way possible.

Those thoughts had him shaking.

"Amanda…" he started, but she looked at him and there were tears in her big brown eyes that stopped his heart. She glanced away at the paper, opened to an article about the fire. Accompanying the text was a large color picture of him, carrying that ungrateful cat. He was backlit by the fire, and the photo looked more staged than anything.

Josh released her to pinch the bridge of his nose. His head pounded. "Sweetheart…"

With shaking fingers, Amanda touched his mouth. "I have to tell you something."

He felt sick. "Me first." He drew a bracing breath. "I love you."

Her eyes opened wide in shock. Her mouth moved, but nothing came out.

"I love you, damn it!"

She blinked at his raised voice and stepped away from him. Even rumpled from a night of debauchery, wearing only a robe, Amanda managed to look elegant. Her hair had been brushed and her nails were pink and he wanted her again. Right now. He eyed the cluttered kitchen table. Probably not sturdy enough, he decided. He shook his head.

"Amanda," he warned, about ready to lose his cool, "you better say something and fast."

She nodded, and gestured at the paper without looking at it. "I saw that and realized I should use it to help promote the calendar. You're a remarkable hero and the whole town knows it by now. It's…great publicity."

Josh locked his thighs. The hell she would. The hell he'd let her! Last night had been—

"But I knew I couldn't."

His anger died a rapid death.

She turned her face up to him, appearing dazed again. "I don't want to share you anymore. That damn reception was hard enough, having all those women fawn over you and knowing what they were thinking because I was thinking it, too."

His tension eased. Cautiously he asked, "What were you thinking?"

"How much I wanted you. How sexy you are, how heroic and wonderful and—"

"I'm just me, babe." And he reiterated, "And I love you."

She swallowed. "I need to start getting things set up for the next calendar."

"The *next* calendar." Her verbal leaps made his head spin. Two more seconds and he was carrying her back to bed for more of that primal mating that made *him* feel a whole hell of a lot better.

"I'd like to make it a yearly event. All kinds of possibilities occurred to me, only…" Amanda bit her lip, then forged on. "Only I can't stand the thought of sharing you."

Josh smiled and explained, "You don't have to share me."

She put a hand to her forehead and looked away. "I don't own you."

"Marry me." He made the offer with a racing heart and a lot of uncertainty. "That's close enough isn't it?"

Amanda whipped around to face him, dropped into her seat, and watched him with the same fascination she might have given a snake. "You want to marry me?"

Josh went to his knees in front of her. He really had to make her understand. "I've known a lot of women—"

She put her hands over her ears, and he pulled them away. Amanda was such a jealous little thing—and he loved it.

"I've had a lot of fun, Amanda," he explained. "But no one has ever made me feel like you do." He carried her hand to his chest, held it there over his heart. "I *love* you. I want to make babies with you and plant gardens and go on family vacations and all that." Josh frowned with sincerity. "I want us to grow old together. And I damn well want you to tell me you love me, too."

She started to speak, but he wasn't ready for her to yet. He had a few more points to make. "Amanda, you do love me, you know. Last night you were incredible. I'm sorry I lost my head there, but you're just too much—"

"I'm just me!"

"—and once you touched me, well, baby, I went a little nuts." Josh shrugged. "There's nothing wrong with us having great sex. I'd meant to be really gentle and romantic, but it didn't work out that way. I'd been thinking about you all night and I guess I was half-cocked before I got here."

Amanda choked at his wording, and then sputtered, "I told you, you shouldn't think about me when you're working!"

"You," Josh told her, "are never far from my mind." He pulled her from the chair and into his lap on the floor. Any space between them was too damn much. "Besides, thinking about you is what saved the day."

Josh explained about the cat and how her experience made him stop and think. "If it hadn't been for loving you, I'd have followed my gut instinct and gone back in that house last night, looking for an infant. Then who knows what might have happened to me."

"No!" Amanda curled around him, desperate and sweet, protective even though he outweighed her by over a hundred pounds.

Cradling her head to his chest, Josh said, "What happened to you was awful, sweetheart, but it's in the past and I'm here now. *I love you.*"

"I love you, too."

Josh froze. He grabbed her shoulders and tried to lever her away so he could see her face, but she clung like a stubborn vine. "Amanda!"

He felt her smile against his throat. "That's what I was going to tell you. Last night, you needed me. Not just a body, not just any woman. You came to me and I knew you needed *me.*"

"Hell, yes I need you! Isn't that what I've been saying?"

"You didn't have to work at getting me into bed because I'd already decided I wanted you there. Everything was different because you're different and how I feel about you is different."

His chest expanded, with love and a dozen other elusive emotions. "You love me?"

"Yes. So how can making love with you be anything but wonderful?"

Josh squeezed her until she squeaked. "You little sneak! I've been in agony here, trying to figure you out, trying to decide how to get you to say 'I do,' and all along you knew you loved me."

"You wouldn't let me tell you."

"You only wanted to talk about another damn calendar."

Now she pushed back to see him, and she grinned. "I will."

He frowned suspiciously. "You will what?"

"I will marry you."

"Oh." Josh wanted to shout, to jump up on the table and dance, to drag Amanda to the bedroom and strip her naked. He just nodded. "Good. What a relief."

"And I will do another calendar—"

He groaned and started to topple to the floor.

Amanda laughed and pulled him upright "—but you won't be in it."

"Thank God."

"I want new blood," she said, making him scowl with his own share of budding jealousy. "This is turning out even bigger than I'd first planned. The amount of money we made last night was astronomical. I have all kinds of ideas for letting women in on choosing the models for next year. This time we'll include the paramedics, and maybe we'll even be able to talk Mick into…"

Josh pulled Amanda down to the floor as he reclined, arranging her on top of him.

"Josh! What are you doing?"

"I want you to make love to me again."

"Oh." She relaxed.

"And I want you to quit talking about other men. I don't like it."

"I am doing the calendar." She levered herself up, digging her pointy elbows into his chest to scowl at him, just in case he didn't hear the seriousness in her tone. "I'm good at it and I enjoy doing my share to help."

Josh slanted her a look. "You aren't doing it for retribution? This isn't your idea of donning a hair shirt?"

"I'll always feel horrible over what happened that night, Josh. There's no way that'll ever change."

"I'll always love you," Josh whispered. "There's no way that will ever change."

Amanda smiled, bent and kissed him sweetly. "No," she said, "I'm not mentally flogging myself. Not anymore. I just want to help a worthy cause. I've seen now how much the money helps."

"Okay. I'll help too—just not by posing ever again." Josh caressed her behind. "Can we live here?"

Amanda had just started to stretch out over him again, but drew herself back up. "What?"

"After we're married," he explained. "I'm thinking we could do a large addition, something that would work well with the existing structure and the grounds. We'll need room for babies and all my stuff, a bigger kitchen and another bathroom."

Amanda laid down on him and hugged him tight. "Yes, I'd love that. Living here with you would be perfect."

He held her hips against his growing erection. "You wanna have a baby right away?"

She laughed, leaned up to look at him, then laughed some more. Her body shook atop his and Josh had to smile. Her laughter was such a turn-on, he started inching up the hem of her robe to get to her luscious behind.

"My parents won't believe this."

"Hmmm?"

"That after everything, I've fallen crazy nuts in love...with a firefighter."

EPILOGUE

"MICK, YOU HAVE to move your hand so I know which guy to vote for."

"I'll cast the vote for you. Hand me your card."

Amanda laughed as she watched Mick and Zack doing their best to keep their wives from viewing the strutting men on stage. They'd paid big money in the name of charity to get front row tables for the event, but now they were turning into prudes. Amanda had every faith that Del and Wynn could hold their own.

Josh was backstage with the men, directing them on when to showcase their assets, while constantly heckling and provoking the young men. He enjoyed his role as assistant and supervisor much more than being a model.

Amanda couldn't imagine being happier. She was now the president of the Firefighter's Calendar yearly production, and as he'd promised, Josh freely gave his help. He was, as she'd accepted from the first, a most remarkable man. And he was all hers.

They'd married two months ago. Their wedding was a huge elaborate celebration and Wynn and Del had teased her mercilessly about her fancy lace and pearl dress, her long train, her veil. But when they'd appeared in their own lacy, feminine gowns, as part of the procession, Mick and Zack had nearly fallen over. Their eyes had glazed and their shoulders tensed and Josh laughed out loud at them.

Amanda learned that the men didn't see their wives dressed up very often, and apparently, seeing them thus was a huge turn-on. She'd heard Wynn whisper to Del that dressing up more often might not be such a bad idea. They'd both turned to Amanda, and said she'd have to give them some tips. Amanda really liked them both and valued their friendship.

Her parents had attended the wedding, along with her sister, and of course, they all loved Josh. He charmed them easily, all the while holding Amanda close.

To Amanda's surprise her father had gotten teary eyed when he hugged her. They'd had regular, friendlier contact since.

Josh stepped up behind Amanda and put his large hot hands on her belly. "You feeling okay?"

She leaned her head back on his shoulder. "I feel fabulous."

"No sickness?"

Amanda laughed. "Josh, I just found out I'm pregnant two days ago!"

He kissed her temple. "I'm going to take such good care of you."

"Mmmm."

"Mick tells me pregnant ladies are always horny."

Amanda sputtered a laugh. Del was in the family way too, but then, Amanda doubted that had anything to do with her heightened sexuality. As far as she'd been able to tell, both

Wynn and Del were always willing to indulge in a little physical love-play with their husbands.

Now that she'd been with Josh, Amanda totally understood that sentiment. All he had to do was look at her and her knees went weak. She felt weak now, and they were in the middle of a special program!

With that thought, Amanda gave her attention back to the stage.

"If I'd have put you up there," Amanda said, eyeing the young firefighter now flexing his muscles and grinning at the feminine catcalls, "we'd have made a fortune."

"You'll make a fortune anyway and you know it. Besides, my wife is territorial. She hates having me ogled by other women, and I love her too much to upset her."

Amanda turned into his arms and hugged him fiercely. The past, for her, was just that. In the past. All the hurt, all the guilt, were now faded memories, buried beneath the incredible love she shared with an incredible man.

He was a hero. He was *her* hero. And working together on the calendar benefit, they'd make a big difference to a lot of people. She couldn't ask for anything more.

★ ★ ★ ★ ★